Praise for *Kingdom of Women*

Kingdom of Women is a brilliant, moving novel that delves deep into questions of revenge and compassion, justice and mercy. Can we build a just society based on acts of violence? Rosalie Morales Kearns writes with a deftness and warmth towards her characters. This is a novel full of inventiveness—a must read.

—Rene Denfeld, author of
The Enchanted and *The Child Finder*

A raw, fierce, and provocatively sexy and smart take on women rising up in armed conflict against male violence. This is a war story with magical touches that never forgets the tragedies—and pleasures, whether they be carnal desire or the "holiness of running water"—that no human can escape.

—Katherine Vaz, author of
*Fado & Other Stories, Our Lady of the Artichokes
& Other Portuguese-American Stories*, and
The Love Life of an Assistant Animator

The conflicts that have given rise to the world of Erda are all too familiar: the corrosiveness of patriarchy in personal lives and political regimes.... Not a fixed vision, rather Erda is a utopia in formation struggling to keep reimagining a future.

—Frances Bartkowski, author of
Feminist Utopias and
co-editor of *Feminist Theory: A Reader*

KINGDOM
OF WOMEN

Also by Rosalie Morales Kearns

Virgins and Tricksters
The Female Complaint: Tales of Unruly Women (editor)

KINGDOM OF WOMEN

Rosalie Morales Kearns

Jaded Ibis Press

Kearns, Rosalie Morales
Kingdom of Women / Rosalie Morales Kearns
1. Women priests—Fiction. 2. Catholic Church—clergy—Fiction.
3. Mysticism—Fiction.

Published by Jaded Ibis Press.
http://www.jadedibispress.com

JADED IBIS PRESS

All the women who were standing there, a great crowd, answered Jeremiah: "Since we gave up offering incense to the Queen of Heaven and pouring libations in her honor, we have been destitute and have perished by the sword and by famine."

—Book of Jeremiah

I have come with a sword.

—Jesus, in Gospel of Matthew

Contents

Part Three   *199*

MAKE STRAIGHT THE PATHS

Remember all men would be tyrants if they could.

—Abigail Adams, 1776

Fran's Bar was a world unto itself. The patrons—working people and people-with-not-so-much-work, and a few college students—liked to complain about its seediness. The floor was so sticky, they said, it kept you upright when you were falling-down drunk. There were so many mice and cockroaches, they said, Fran hired them to work in the kitchen.

But the beer was cheap and the customers got into fewer fights than at your average New Falls dive. They were more than a little afraid of the owner, all ninety pounds of her, a sixty-year-old with stringy, faded blonde hair who stood watch behind the bar all night, drinking cup after cup of hot tea and smoking unfiltered cigarettes nonstop. No one had ever seen Fran touch alcohol. Or food, for that matter.

Ciara Neal, bleary eyed at the bar, was vaguely aware that her friends had left. In fact, all the customers were gone except her, and still Fran didn't call closing time.

What a waste of an evening. She hated feeling gauzy-brained. The beer hadn't done a damn thing to improve her mood, and her friends seemed to lack all sympathy for her complaints. She should have stayed home and worked on her seminar paper.

Fran, meanwhile, hovered nearby, clearing off glasses and muttering. Something about a priest. Then a word that managed to penetrate Ciara's brain fog.

"Did you say 'vigilantes'?"

"Drink this."

Fran slammed down a coffee mug in front of her. It didn't smell like coffee. Didn't taste like any tea Ciara knew of. Presumably it was the same stuff that Fran swilled down every night. If she had to guess, she'd have said it was brewed from tobacco leaves.

"I've been listening to you mouth off all night," Fran said, "louder and louder with each beer you put away. And here's what I have to say to you: quit your whining. How many people even have the chance to go to college?"

"You don't understand—"

"I got the picture clear enough. Some teacher's turned on you 'cause you won't sleep with him. College ain't so different from the rest of the world."

Ciara drank some more of the foul-smelling tea. The hot fumes did seem to be clearing away the gauze.

"I've finished college," Ciara said. "I'm in graduate school now. I'm getting a Ph.D. and this professor could ruin everything for me. He's a big name, he throws his weight around. He says he'll stop me from getting any more fellowship money. Even if I could afford grad school after that, he'll blacklist me from getting jobs when I finish."

"And now you're telling your friends and the rest of the bar and who knows who else, that you're going to kill the wretched man if it's the last thing you do."

Ciara picked at a forgotten bowl of bar nuts.

"I filed a complaint. It went nowhere. My word against his."

"So the next step is what, a bullet in his brain?"

"What's the alternative, walk away quietly while he ruins my life and fucks over anyone who won't put out for him? Don't tell me forgive and forget. I'm so fucking tired of hearing that."

Fran studied the girl. She had a head of auburn hair that reminded Fran of her nieces back in Ireland. Even the personalities were similar. The same blazing anger and beauty, equal parts.

"Here's the next thing I'm going to tell you," Fran said. "But for god's sake don't go blabbing about it every time you get some beer sloshing through your bloodstream. There are people—women—who feel the same way you do, who'll help you free of charge and no strings attached.

There's women like that in every town. They're all around you, if you know where to look."

"They'll help me—how?"

"Rock through a window. Slash his tires. Shatter his kneecaps."

"Do they go any further than that?"

"You don't want to go that far."

"Yes I do."

"Don't argue with me, girl. Killing's not a light matter."

"I want this man to suffer. I'm not going to stop wanting that. I want to hit him back, hard, and move on with my life."

Fran suddenly felt tired. It took endless work to keep this bar from subsiding into a pile of beer-soaked lumber. But it was her place, all her own.

There had been a time when she was young, and not so watchful as she was now. Men had seemed larger then. Louder. They seemed to have no limits unless the limits were slammed down on their heads like two-by-fours.

"Can you give me their names?" Ciara said.

"Before I do, there's someone you should talk to first. A priest."

"That's the last person I need. What's he going to do, pray for me?"

"She. Not he. And you haven't met anyone like this."

3

Part One

It was in my 43rd year ... that a voice from heaven
addressed me: O fragile child of earth,
ash of ashes, dust of dust, express and write
that which you see and hear.

—Hildegard of Bingen, 12th century

CHAPTER 1

ADVENT

These heretical women—how audacious they are!
They are bold enough to teach, to preach.
They may even baptize people!

—Tertullian, 3rd century

For those with ears to hear, voices of long-dead monks still lingered at St. Anthony of Padua's Monastery in rural Connecticut. The voices resonated off stone walkways, gathered like mist under the church portico, thrummed in the weathered plank walls of the barn and workshops. The monks had been there for over a hundred and sixty years, when ancestors of the now-venerable oaks and maples had been saplings, when the grape arbors and cherry and pear trees had been newly planted. They tended vegetable garden and fruit orchard, cleared underbrush from the forested hills, kept the wide lawns neatly mown. They laid down flagstone paths, repaired church pews, scaled roofs to replace tiles and fix gutters. For visitors they built picnic tables and a playground lined with mulberry and crabapple trees.

Through all that work and all those decades they had chanted and sung, hummed and whispered, together, in mostly perfect unison, Matins and Vespers, Te Deums and Ave Marias.

Then their numbers thinned. The few remaining monks grew old and died. The garden was choked with weeds, the orchard spectral and overgrown. People called the place picturesque when they really meant dilapidated.

But the brotherhood persisted on the other side of that bright dividing line, and the monks were still there, humming and watching, when the archdiocese of Hartford bought the place, and when the two priests arrived to transform it into a retreat house: curmudgeonly Peter Byrne and his idealistic young colleague Marc Cvetko.

Then came the renovations: workshops turned into guesthouses, barn into meeting rooms.

Last year a new one had shown up: a *woman* priest, of all the daft, new-fangled things this new century had wrought. The monk-spirits were inclined to be disapproving, but they couldn't help pitying her, knowing the bloody beginnings of her priestly career. And she looked so fragile: sharp elbows and jutting shoulder blades, fever-bright eyes. You would have thought she was recovering from an illness if not for that exuberant dark hair, that reckless smile.

On this autumn afternoon they watched Averil Parnell stride to the playground, drawn by the high, clear laughter that had reached her all the way to the Refectory. Two children were there, a little girl on a swing and an older boy who sat on the carousel reading. .

The girl looked to be about four. Averil chose a swing a few seats away, straightened her legs out and lowered her back. On the upswing, with her feet pointing to the sky, her hair grazed the ground. "See, I'm a broom," she said.

Some of the sterner monks frowned. So undignified.

The little girl tried it herself. "I'm a broom too."

They could hear the boy behind them: "I don't know if you should be doing that, Ginnie."

The two of them, woman and girl, picked up speed, bodies tilting backward on the upswing, forward on the downswing. Averil closed her eyes, concentrated on the headlong rushing sensation and that moment at the top of the arc where she was that much closer to the sun, buoyed up by light and air.

Like an echo to the boy's anxious treble came another voice, the booming baritone of her colleague Peter Byrne: "Averil. There's someone who needs to speak to you."

As she dragged her swing to a stop, Peter noted the playground dust in her hair, the dark eyes looking at him with no trace of embarrassment. How she could have been a pastor of her own parish for all those years was a mystery.

The girl who was with him started speaking before Averil was even close enough to shake hands.

"This conversation is just a formality," Ciara said. "I've already made up my mind. I want him dead, the son of a bitch."

"There are *children* present." Peter tried to hiss, but the words sounded more like a low roar. The monks respected Peter for that voice of his.

Barrel-chested, angry men had lungs like a set of bellows. He would have made an impressive addition to their choir.

Averil, alarmed by Peter's beet-red face, pictured heat and pressure building up inside him like a red dwarf star until some kind of explosion resulted. Whatever stars did, implode, explode. Topple from the heavens.

"Let's go somewhere and talk," she told the young woman.

Peter later thought of Ciara's visit as the beginning of what he called The Onslaught. Some people had known all along that Averil was here at St. Anthony's now: Her former parishioners at St. Margaret's, none too happy at her departure. Her off-beat friends from exotic religions: Wicca, Santeria, United Church of Christ. Later, others found out too. People who suddenly became regulars at Mass at St. Anthony's. People who had never darkened the door of any church prior to that.

But before all that, before The Onslaught, was the first one. The girl with the red hair, was how Peter thought of her, failing to do justice to either Ciara's age, her hair's magnificent burnt-gold color, or her majestic anger.

~

Ciara had never given much thought to religion, hadn't known what to expect from this meeting with the woman priest. She'd pictured an office like a therapist's, coffee in styrofoam cups. Instead they sat on the grass near a picnic area. An enormous gray tabby cat showed up and the priest introduced the animal as if it had been invited to observe.

Both the priest and the cat were gazing over at the church, more focused on that, it seemed, than on what Ciara was saying about the harasser, about Fran and her mysterious hints.

"I suppose I had an easier time in college," Averil said finally. Or, she reflected, maybe she'd been oblivious. Living with Asher had been like being in a cocoon.

"It must be an urban legend," Ciara said. "Groups of vigilante women. If they really existed, it would be all over the newspapers."

She waited for a response. Averil said nothing.

"Well, this is an awkward moment," Ciara said. "You don't want to lie, I suppose, being a priest and all, but you don't want to tell me what you know, either."

"When I finished seminary," Averil said, "they had an ordination ceremony for the Roman Catholic Church's first women priests. There were twenty-three of us."

9

"Damn. I didn't realize that was you. I'm sorry."

The Cathedral Massacre. Ciara was a child at the time but had learned about it later. One man with a semi-automatic weapon and a venomous hatred of women. Averil Parnell was the only survivor.

"What happened to the motherfucker? Pardon my language."

"People finally reached him, wrestled the gun away. There were some shots fired in the scuffle and the man was killed."

"You couldn't even get revenge."

In the silence Averil heard the unspoken questions: What do you do with the anger? And the young woman's more immediate, more pressing concern: What should I do with it?

She consulted the authorities, conveniently located in her head: Leander Jameson's *On Pastoral Counseling*; the Vatican's third edition of *Reconciliation*. Our Lord tells us to forgive. Pray for strength. Cultivate forbearance. "When in doubt: ten Hail Marys," old Father Saavedra used to tell them in seminary.

"Anger doesn't just disappear," Averil said. "It bubbles along, it surfaces in different ways. You try not to feel it every waking minute. You learn to live with it."

The authorities, duly consulted, shook their heads.

Right after her ordination, before the years at St. Margaret's, Averil had been assigned to a quiet parish out in the countryside, nominally to assist the pastor, but actually they wanted her to pick up where her dissertation left off, start the brilliant career in academe they all assumed she would have.

Women she'd never seen before had showed up, made offers. Fuck him, they said, and the horse he rode in on. Of course the bastard was dead, but there were others who could be made to pay. The gun dealer who sold him the weapon. The judge who paroled him after he'd beaten a woman bloody. Hell, anyone who'd ever given him a kind word instead of grinding him into the dirt where he belonged.

Averil wanted no part of it, barely understood what they were talking about.

They returned a few times. What about justice? they said. Isn't that what your god is all about?

I don't know what my god is all about, Averil said.

Mostly she worked in the rectory garden. People made complaints about the scarecrow she'd put up. Too realistic, they'd said. The way he's hanging there—it looks like a real man she's tied up to that crosspost.

"Learn to live with it?" Ciara said. "That's your answer?"

Averil stroked the grass beneath her hands, closed her eyes and felt the breeze on her face. *As for man, his days are as grass.* She had heard that phrase as a child, recognized its biblical cadence but not its meaning, pictured sunny warm days in the backyard. Only later did she wonder about the other possibilities. Days as grass—meant to be cut short? Meant to wilt? Meant to keep coming back?

"You could hang him in effigy," Averil said. "Then again, in a few weeks it'll be Halloween, a good time for bonfires."

"*What?*"

"Symbolic revenge. I know people who would help set it up."

"That won't do a damn thing."

"Try it," Averil said. "For my sake. Before you go back to Fran."

~

The monk-spirits fretted over Averil Parnell. Her undignified behavior and general unkemptness they could overlook. More worrisome was her procrastination. Not perhaps a Deadly Sin, but certainly a moral failing.

In her life before the priesthood she'd been a scholar, a historian of medieval Christianity and a rising star in the field. They felt—and Averil did too—that she should get back to her scholarly writing. She was forty-two years old, well past time to produce another book on the medieval women writers she'd specialized in before.

But if she were working on it, the monks saw no evidence. Piled on her desk were the books she'd bought this month at library sales. A how-to on perennial borders for vegetable gardens, a biography of Aung San Suu Kyi, well-worn copies of first-year college textbooks: *Earth's Formation* and *Physics for Idiots.*

She had been the pastor of St. Margaret's for ten years—reason enough, she used to console herself, for not returning to her scholarship. Now she had no excuse.

The few remnants of her old collection were gathering dust on her bookcase. Worn hardcovers from graduate school, in Latin, Old French, Middle Dutch: Mechthild's *Flowing Light of the Godhead*; Marguerite Porete's *Mirror of Simple Souls*, and of course the writings of Hadewijch, the topic of her dissertation. Three translations of the Bible, four of the Gnostic Gospels. A new edition of the Catechism, gift from a parishioner who'd assumed Averil's copy must have been worn threadbare.

She opened the Catechism at random. "Pray for the living and the dead," the last item in the list of Spiritual Works of Mercy. "Pray *to* the dead," would have been Averil's version if someone had let her correct it.

11

"Any advice?" she asked the framed picture of Jesus by the bookcase. "Wise as doves, right? Harmless as serpents?"

The monks smirked.

An old habit of hers: tweak biblical phrases and see if anyone noticed. Catechism students, Bible study participants, the random St. Margaret's parishioner at coffee hour after Mass. A blank stare the typical reaction. Even Jesus's smile seemed sad.

She pulled out the next book, *WomanSpirit Rising*. A brochure slipped out, its pages stiff and brittle with age.

Come to Erda, read the brochure, in faded organic ink. *Here, prairie vistas meet big sky. Here, breezes from glacial lakes stir the leaves in the oaks and the cottonwoods.* Averil could feel how hard that long-ago writer must have worked on her prose.

The Republic of Erda, that feminist utopian experiment in what was formerly North Dakota, could not have been an easy sell. She imagined the woman, sweating over her keyboard on a sweltering August day, or maybe it was November and she was looking out her window at a blizzard, shivering a bit because no window in the entire country was ever properly weather-proofed.

All paths lead to me, read the back panel, above a photo of a tallgrass prairie.

Not yet, Averil thought. She'd been invited to Erda to give talks, and always had to cancel. Snowstorms in May, tornados in September, that kind of thing.

For a moment she felt tempted to run off. Cottonwoods, glacial lakes. Peace.

Focus, woman, the monks urged.

Averil gripped her pen and notebook. A scholar needed to narrow down a topic. Identify a research question. She would decide on something. Now.

She closed her eyes. Nothing.

"I had a fine mind once," she said out loud to the empty room.

The words had flowed easily all through the child-prodigy years, a high school diploma at age sixteen, graduating college at nineteen. Sailing through her graduate work in history, when the momentous decision was made to accept women to the priesthood. Earning an M.Div. while finishing a Ph.D. and hardly breaking a sweat.

Then came the massacre. The words skittered off into dark corners, crouched down and dug in and refused to come out.

All the words she'd had, they'd done her no good. Her fine mind was no match for blood-soaked horror.

Jesus could not have been clearer: Turn the other cheek. For all you could argue about who he really was, what he thought he was, you couldn't get around the basic message. Forgive, forgive, and then forgive some more.

Women in the confessional, whispering even in the privacy of the small cushioned booth, memories of being wronged, angry thoughts of revenge, and Averil had said forgive.

When they whispered that the revenge had been taken, she gave them absolution.

God is love. Love is forgiveness.

She thought about Ciara, and about the long-gone scarecrow.

She had torn that scarecrow down, dragged it into the church one evening when the elderly pastor was away, pronounced anathema on the cathedral killer and his straw stand-in. A brand-new priest taking on a power technically reserved for the pope.

"In the name of God the All-powerful, Father, Son, and Holy Ghost," she had said, using for once the patriarchal language, "in the name of the Blessed Peter, Prince of the Apostles, and of all the saints, in virtue of the power which has been given me of binding and loosing in Heaven and on earth . . . "

She held a lit candle in each hand, raised them over her head as she stood at the altar. Besides not being the pope, she was not surrounded by the requisite eleven other priests, all chanting in unison. Nor was she following the correct wording. Gone was any mention of the possibility of reconciliation, should the sinner repent.

"I deprive you and all your abettors of the Communion of the Body and Blood of Our Lord, I separate you from the society of all Christians, I exclude you from our Holy Mother the Church in Heaven and on earth, I declare you excommunicated and anathematized and I judge you condemned to eternal torment."

She raised her arms and dropped them. The candles clattered onto the altar and went out.

"You are damned, you are damned, you are damned."

She had never told anyone about this private ceremony. Had never asked forgiveness. Had never considered that she needed forgiveness.

Now, in the peaceful darkness of her rooms at St. Anthony's, sins suffered and sins inflicted reverberated off each other, a hall of mirrors.

She looked at the empty page as if looking down a long corridor into the past. Not only the murders of her companions, but so many murders before that. A long, vast history of men killing women.

People sometimes asked Averil, obliquely, about the massacre and its effects on her. "How *are* you?" they would say. "Really, how are you *doing*?" and she knew what they were asking.

She wanted to tell them about the Black Death, the plague that carried off a third of medieval Europe's population. The survivors reacted with extremes of behavior.

It's a punishment from God, some claimed. They fasted, gave away their earthly possessions. They flogged themselves, earning the title Flagellants: holy fools with whips and blood-seeping scars.

On the opposite side were those who drank heavily, gorged themselves on food and sex. We're doomed anyway, they said, why not enjoy ourselves at the end? Maybe they too believed that the plague was sent by God, or maybe in private they decided there was no God, and this senseless destruction was the proof of it.

Sometimes roving bands of penitents met up on the road with wandering revelers. Averil liked to imagine the scene. One group heading east, the other west, they mingled as they crossed paths and forgot for a moment who they were, which group they belonged to. Ashen-faced penitents took swigs from flasks, boisterous carousers whipped themselves with nettles.

Years after the massacre, when well-meaning acquaintances asked her how she felt, how she survived, Averil wanted to tell them about those encounters during the plague years. She was still there, she wanted to tell them, still on that road.

~

Somewhere along I-80, the interstate that wound its way across the country, Catherine Beck realized she had been driving for hours. It was time to stop to eat.

Until a week ago she had been Captain Catherine Beck, U.S. Marines, but now there was a *(retired)* after the title, despite the disapproval from on high, the stern lectures about cutting short a promising career: You're young. You're up for promotion. What are you going to *do* with yourself?

Nothing could rattle her calm, not the seedy diner with its greasy windows and tasteless meat loaf, nor the equally seedy convenience store across the street, where she sensed the usual unwanted male attention as soon as she pushed through the door.

The clerk behind the counter, a boy in the spindly throes of adolescence, looked at her in shock and then quickly looked away, embarrassed to be so obvious.

Not so the man by the newspaper rack. This man, or someone exactly like him, would have been disturbingly familiar to most women: hair, skin, clothing in varying shades of dingy gray, pouchy skin beneath bloodshot eyes, reeking of stale beer and sweat and giving every passing female a mocking grimace that was supposed to convey lust.

There was an endless supply of these old lechers, distributed one apiece to convenience stores and downtown street corners across the country. Every woman, by virtue of being female and making it to puberty and beyond, has seen this slack-jawed troll examining her body, approving or finding fault, as if ordinary public space had been transformed into a beauty pageant, with him as judge.

Catherine had seen some women reduced to helpless rage at times like this. At the very least, the target of the nauseating scrutiny would shift awkwardly, adjust her clothing as if trying to hold on to her dignity, ignoring the sudden painful bout of self-consciousness.

Catherine didn't take it personally.

So many things in life weren't worth getting angry at. A pebble falling into a lake, a barely perceptible ripple, and then it disappears.

She turned to face the man, letting her jacket fall open to reveal her shoulder holster. You might be good for target practice, old man, she thought, but that's it.

Confused, he left the store muttering.

The cashier had seen everything. His eyes looked glazed, vacillating between fascination and fear. The kid would probably develop a lifelong fetish for blonde women with guns. She winked at him and watched a shiver travel down his body.

Captain Beck (now ret.) tried to be average. She kept her ash-blonde hair medium length, wore jeans and plain t-shirts. No makeup to accentuate cheekbones or make eyes seem larger and more deepset. No jewelry to draw attention to graceful hands or neck.

A tall, lean-muscled woman with eyes gray as mist, narrowed as if studying a stranger in harsh sunlight. She reminded people of a gunslinger in an old western movie, but that wasn't an accurate analogy. In her lack of theatricality, her indifference to the presence of any spectator, one would have to move to the animal kingdom to find an adequate comparison. An alpha wolf, perhaps, still as a sphinx but ready to spring as soon as prey announced itself through the movement of branch, the whisper of breath.

15

Unaware of her own beauty, as if needle-sharp sight and hearing, as if speed and grace and lethal incisors were the gift and burden of every living being.

In the refrigerator section Catherine picked out a bottle of apple juice. She could hear a man in the next aisle, speaking with barely controlled rage. "I *told* you I don't like this fucking decaf Coke." Even before she heard the whispered apology, she knew he was talking to a woman.

A jab to the solar plexus, she thought idly, would leave him doubled over, struggling to breathe. But she didn't want to draw attention to herself, didn't want people to connect a face, a car, a town.

Maybe iced tea instead of juice. So many choices.

She'd had to decide on where to live, for one thing. She'd settled on New Falls, large enough that a newcomer wouldn't be noticed, small enough for reasonable rents. Not far from major airports and train lines.

She'd toyed with the idea of leaving the country altogether, going to Erda, the republic of women. But she needed to be closer to her missions. And her missions hardly took her to places like that.

"How are you going to adjust?" General Chou had asked her when he found out she was leaving.

"There's more to life than the Marines, sir. I have things I want to do while I'm still young. Drive across the country, for one thing. Maybe go to law school."

"Pursue other interests" was her standard line when questioned. You could go far, people said, you're only thirty, you could rise to the top. Why give that up?

Other interests.

"It won't be easy," the general warned. "You're used to giving orders, being in charge. That uniform, those insignia, give you instant respect."

She had almost smiled. As if all these years she hadn't noticed the effect of the insignia on her shoulders.

She saw the couple when she turned the corner into the snacks aisle. The woman cringed, eyes downcast. The man continued to fume.

"Why should I even stay with a cow like you? I could get anyone I want."

Catherine stood close to him and plucked a bag of popcorn from the shelf.

"*I'd* slit your throat as soon as look at you," she said calmly.

The man stared at her, speechless. She paid for her groceries and left.

CHAPTER 2

DEA IN ADJUTORIUM

If you cannot be perfect, do what you can.

—Didache (Christian gospel,
1st century)

The monks of St. Anthony's sometimes wondered whether Averil was lonely in their old Refectory building. Everything else was located at the Chapter House: the priests' kitchen and sitting room, Peter's office, bedrooms for the two men. Averil, on the other hand, had been given a suite of rooms on the Refectory's second floor, where the monks' sleeping quarters had been. The only time the building wasn't resoundingly empty was when the retreat house hosted a reception on the first floor, in their former dining hall.

Averil would have put their minds at rest, had she known. She had never had so much space before, so much privacy: a bedroom with an adjoining office, large, unbarred windows, excellent reading lamps, ample bookcases. Even a comfortable armchair.

From her window in her office she could see the north end of the church, and beyond it a walking path leading toward the woods. Her view from the grimy, barred windows of St. Margaret's parish house had included dilapidated apartment buildings, a pawn shop, a diner, a check-cashing place. Further down the block, past the parish soup kitchen, were a used book store, a small dingy storefront offering chakra alignment, and a gambling establishment with the innocuous name Eighth Street Supper Club.

Of course God let the sun shine even on the urban decay that was downtown New Falls, Connecticut. Let the rain fall on respectable bodega owner and shifty-eyed drug dealer alike, hardworking garbage truck driver and exhausted drunk, graffitied rectory walls and shiny hubcaps of a slumlord's Mercedes.

Her parishioners hadn't wanted her to leave. Even a year later they were still angry that the archbishop had ignored their protests. You have to pick your battles, Averil told them.

She was a loyal soldier, going where the officers told her to go.

The soldier metaphor was not as inappropriate as some might think. The Church had always had its martial language. The Communion of Saints—admittedly a friendly enough term, redolent of shared meals and camaraderie—referred to the tripartite arrangement of the universal Catholic Church. Three parts, like the Trinity. As in Heaven, so on earth. Living people constituted the bracingly confrontational-sounding Church Militant. Then you had the dead, in two categories. The saintly ones in Heaven, members of the Church Triumphant. And then the vast masses of the ordinary, sent to Purgatory to get their sins wrung out of them: the Church Expectant.

The monks, hovering, knew the arrangement was more complicated than that. Here they were, clearly dead, clearly not in Heaven, but where was Purgatory? They were still waiting for their appointment with an administrator to get the matter cleared up.

Meanwhile, it was time to sing Vespers. They filed out of Averil's office, down the hall toward the Night Stairs into the East Transept.

As it was in the beginning, they sang, *is now and ever shall be.*

Averil lit a candle and moved into her bedroom for Night Prayer.

In Averil's private, abbreviated version, she often left out the problematic names for God altogether: Lord, Father. The prayers became simple imperative statements: Come to my assistance. Make haste to help me. Glory be to everyone, always. So be it. Alleluia.

She sat cross-legged on her bed, running her fingers across her rosary beads during the examination of conscience. The rosary, a gift from a parishioner, had rose quartz beads interspersed with silver decade markers in the form of what she assumed were roses. Averil preferred peonies herself. They were messier, more generous with their fragrance. Thornless.

She opened her breviary. The psalm for that night, Tuesday in Ordinary Time, was 143 ("The enemy pursues my soul; he has crushed my life to the ground"), then the reading, a few lines from the First Letter of Peter ("Your opponent the devil is prowling like a lion"). All that fear and anxiety, just before sleeping.

She put aside the book. She knew the rest by heart: the responsory, the Canticle, the concluding prayer. The blessing, condensed into Averil's private shorthand: "A restful night, a peaceful death."

She blew out the candle and lay down. This was how she always recited the very last part, the Antiphon of the Blessed Virgin, which, unlike any priest for hundreds of miles around, she prayed in Latin: Ave, Regina caelorum, ave, Domina angelorum. The same words used by women eight hundred years ago. Daughters praying to the Mother.

She thought of Asher's favorite question: Why do you believe? Through their final year in college, through graduate school, through her years in seminary, he would ask it as if someday Averil would assure him she had outgrown the outlandish habit.

"You don't need your dusty books," he would say. "This world is beautiful and mysterious enough. Why not be content in the here and now?"

His slow, sleepy voice gave people the impression that his thoughts were coming slowly. He would take in a breath as if he were about to speak, but stop, as if thinking some more. He paused between sentences, sometimes between one word and the next. At any second, it seemed, the thought would run out of steam or he would lapse into sleep.

"There must be a pleasure center... in the brain," he said, "that gets stimulated by the sensation of religious belief. And then once you feel that pleasure you want to go on feeling it." He felt her skull as if checking for bumps. "Or else it's just brain damage."

Why seek ye the dead among the living?

Averil sat up and squinted into the darkness.

Another biblical twist. The real wording was "living among the dead." Gospel of Luke. Angel speaking to the three Marys at the empty tomb.

Dead among the living. As far as she knew, Asher Rothenburg wasn't dead. He had merely disappeared from her life in his quiet but methodical way.

She lay back down and finished the praise song to the Blessed Mother. Salve, radix, salve, porta, ex qua mundo lux est orta.

The root, the gateway. Light of the world.

~

Everything was ready for the bonfire. Ciara had bought a man's suit, shirt, and tie at Goodwill for a few dollars, had stuffed it with rags and leaves.

The women had set up the dry wood and kindling, arranged neatly in a pile, waiting only for the effigy to be thrown on top, the match to be struck.

"A drumming circle," Averil Parnell had said vaguely in answer to Ciara's question about the group. Ciara had expected women with flowing hair, dangly earrings and gauzy skirts, who led chants and talked about energy and chakras and home altars to the goddess. But the women who waited patiently, smoking cigarettes or checking on their sand buckets and fire extinguishers, seemed to represent a whole range. Some looked as if they'd lived in the rugged outdoors for years, others looked like suburban moms with practical haircuts and overcrowded schedules: kids' soccer games, parent-teacher meetings.

Ciara gripped the professor's effigy under the armpits and heaved it onto the piled wood. The women were all paying attention now, standing silently with arms folded. One of them handed Ciara a box of matches.

She couldn't do it.

Now that she was actually there, about to burn a body—no, a body-shaped *thing*, but still—there was something too gruesome about it. Something too helpless about the inert form lying there.

"God damn it."

She dragged the effigy down again, tore open the clothing and picked it apart till it was reduced to a shapeless pile of stuffing.

"Now?" someone said quietly.

"No, … uh, it's … "

Ciara kicked at the pile to disperse it more. She mumbled something about fire hazards.

Later she would ask Averil again who the group was, what these women did, and would receive more vague answers: "Some people like building fires." And "Ritual takes all kinds of forms."

The women helped Ciara gather up the effigy's rag-and-leaf viscera into a garbage bag, walked her back to her car, waved silently as she drove away. Each of them had been down that road, revenge in some form or other, symbolic or real. They knew its dubious satisfactions, and would neither celebrate nor condemn it.

~

For millennia Europeans believed in four basic substances, the humors, that circulated throughout the body and determined one's basic personality. The scheme had a certain neatness to it, four being seen as a solid, well-ordered number: four corners to a square, seasons to a year, directions to a compass. Creation itself could be reduced to the four basic elements: earth, air, fire, water. Clearly, God liked to arrange things in fours.

Those ancient observers would have quickly recognized the introspective Averil Parnell as melancholic, gentle Marc Cvetko as phlegmatic, and Peter Byrne, he of the loud voice and extra-large clothing size, as choleric.

One could surmise this, for example, from Peter Byrne's reddening face and skyrocketing blood pressure when he opened a letter from the archbishop's office one snowy January day. The inquiry was phrased as politely as possible: "keep us apprised," "allay our concerns for her well-being," and so forth, but he recognized the request for what it was: Spy on Averil. Report back to us.

He pondered the reason for the sudden interest. She had been at St. Anthony's a year and a half. It was several months since the angry girl had showed up spouting death threats, and as far as Peter knew, Averil had talked her out of it. More people were starting to attend Mass, but that couldn't possibly be a cause for worry at the archdiocese.

He started to compose an answer in his head.

After careful scrutiny I can report that the Subject engages in the following suspicious activities: Takes long walks. Travels to libraries and used book stores. Reads.

He debated whether "Does miscellaneous chores" should be broken down further: Plants vegetable garden. Pulls weeds. Picks mulberries. Scrubs stovetop.

It had been Averil who revived the monks' long-dormant garden. And though no one had asked her to, she helped Marc with the preparation for retreat groups, went with him to fold sheets and towels, vacuum and dust the guest rooms, set out bread and fruit in the mornings, get sandwiches ready for the lunches. No one could say she was lazy.

Of course he could have composed an entire other list under the heading Irritating Activities: Stares into space. Gives incomprehensible sermons. Quotes the Bible using the entirely un-Catholic King James version ("I like the poetry").

He didn't know what he'd expected when she first arrived. Certainly both he and Marc had seen photographs of Averil Parnell over the years: a semi-celebrity since before she was ordained, a member of that first, doomed class of female Catholic seminarians. He hadn't quite expected a skinny, witchy-haired little person with shabby clothing and the haughty expression of exiled royalty.

Then there was the glitch with the praying.

Peter, Marc, and Averil had tried to do Morning Prayers together, and she kept veering from the words in the breviary. Turned out she'd changed a lot of words to "gender-inclusive language"—whited out the original terms in her copy of the Divine Office and wrote in other things: "Source" for "Lord," "Divine Parent" or "Mother-Source" for "Father," and so on, God help us all.

So, to add to the list: Can't do a synchronized prayer with normal people. Needs to take more pride in her appearance (e.g., stand up straighter, iron shirts properly, comb hair at least once a day).

Is, in general, faintly ridiculous.

He threw the archbishop's letter in the trash. Then he fished it out, smoothed its wrinkles as best he could.

The monk-spirits jostled Peter with their elbows, kept pace with him in their swishing robes as he left the Chapter House and strode toward the Refectory and up the stairs to Averil's office. He was impervious to their presence, of course. They were used to that. The woman priest, they weren't so sure about. Her attention always seemed divided, like she was straining to hear something just beyond range.

Peter and the monks looked at the book Averil put down on her desk as they entered: *Einstein Made Simple.*

"Did you know," Averil said, "that space and time are really one thing, spacetime, and that it curves and buckles like a fabric?"

Peter had no intention of trying to picture that image. "The reason I—"

"You have to wonder, though, whether it's really true. It seems almost like a semantic trick: take two words that are different, even opposite, and put them together and say they're the same thing. Like bodysoul. Warpeace."

She was pleased with herself for understanding Einstein, at least slightly. She planned to work slowly toward the later stuff: quantum physics, string theory, dark energy.

"There's so much we don't know," she said. "Can you imagine a parallel universe where the Church didn't ordain women priests?"

There would have been no Cathedral Massacre. The parallel Averil would have gone on with her trajectory, whatever that would have been. Theologian/gadfly, most likely.

Since she didn't seem likely to ask why he was there, Peter handed her the letter.

She read it carefully, her expression unchanging.

"I've no intention of spying for them," he said, "in case you're wondering."

Good old Peter. She was becoming fond of him, gruff and blunt as he was. He grumbled about the people who'd been showing up more and more through the fall and winter, called them "the hordes" when he was feeling irritable, or her "fan club" when in a calmer mood, but he was more than happy to accept their donations to the retreat center. Peter was a pragmatist, as rock-solid as his name.

"The muckety-mucks don't like me," Averil said. "I guess you've been wondering why."

You don't have to tell me, Peter could have answered. *It's none of my business.* It was something she'd never talked about, and he hadn't wanted to ask.

"I think I'll have a seat," he said.

"Actually, why they don't like me would be too long a story. I'll concentrate on why they transferred me from St. Margaret's."

"I've already guessed it wasn't child abuse," he said.

"I was afraid that would be your conclusion. Thanks for the vote of confidence."

"You're also not the type to embezzle funds."

"I don't think I would know how. It was—"

"—those organized crime connections?"

"I don't have *connections*. Good lord, is that what people are saying? I was fund-raising—"

"Interesting as that story sounds," Peter said, "can we get back to the original point?"

"*You're* the one who keeps interrupting. I seem to recall you telling poor Marc that curiosity is a sin."

"I've also heard it's a sin to start telling a juicy story and then stop."

～

It had begun almost three years ago. She hadn't known what he was after, when the FBI agent first showed up at St. Margaret's and demanded a meeting. He made vague statements about hate groups and terrorists, the threat they posed to national security. He mentioned Averil's duty to help her country in its "hour of need."

He took out his notebook. "What do you know about this activity?"

"Terrorists? Nothing at all."

He looked at her with distaste. "Let's start over. You must understand how dangerous these women are."

23

"Now you've lost me."

What the agent didn't say was that the FBI had in fact suspected Averil herself of being involved. A twelve-month surveillance revealed nothing, but at the very least, they reasoned, she knew others' secrets. She was well known, practically a folk hero for feminist extremists. Surely some of them confided in her.

"What I'm asking about," the agent went on, "is a matter of the highest confidentiality. You could be charged with violating the National Secrets Act if you discuss it with anyone."

Averil didn't like his tone, but now she was genuinely curious.

He was looking for women who were organizing against men, forming vigilante groups, "conspiring to destabilize our whole society and its democratic fabric."

Through the haze of clichés and unintentionally mixed metaphors, Averil discerned that he was talking about women who took action against men who had attacked them, or who had attacked other women.

"That sounds like a matter of individual anger," she said. "Personal revenge. Not that it's condoned, but why do you call it terrorism?"

"I'm not here for a theoretical discussion. We need to know what your parishioners tell you."

"In the confessional? Not a chance."

"You don't have to name names. We want a sense of whether it's happening here. You only need to answer yes or no, has anyone confessed this sort of activity to you?"

"I can't answer that. The church has its own rules about confidentiality."

There were other visits, from different agents. There were vague threats of arrest.

She knew *something*, of course, which she revealed neither to the agents at the time nor to Peter Byrne now, during the retelling. Ever since that visit from the unknown women after the massacre, and from what she learned later in the confessional, she knew there were women who took things into their own hands.

But organized, permanent groups, much less a network—these were things no one mentioned to her. Maybe they thought it was better that way.

The archbishop's office contacted Averil by letter, ordering her to cooperate with law enforcement officials on this vital (unspecified) matter.

She wrote back, saying the archbishop's office must be mistaken.

For years, official Church policy had allowed for the seal of confession to be broken only in the case of a confessed child abuser. But after the pedophilia scandal had died down, Pope Hadrian VII repealed the exception. Priest-penitent confidentiality, he declared, was absolute.

Averil was called into a meeting with the archbishop himself, who explained politely that the Church needed to be a force for stability in society, that it was on the side of law and order, that it had its reputation to protect and didn't need to be associated with terrorism. When Averil, expressionless, continued her stubborn silence, the archbishop asked the secretary and assistant to leave the room, then told her he would do everything short of defrocking her: she would lose her parish, she would be farmed out to unofficial retirement, she would say no masses, hear no confessions. It would be as if she weren't a priest at all.

"You're facing the end of your career," he said. "After what you went through to be ordained. And for what? For the sake of protecting a few man-hating lunatics?"

She left his office without a word.

When three FBI agents arrived for the final meeting, they thought Averil looked pensive, perhaps conciliatory.

She was thinking about the last few years, the dissolution of so many peaceful, mainstream community groups that helped women fleeing domestic abuse or advocated for survivors of rape, offering shelter, funds, legal help. Some of the organizations had existed for decades, and then from one day to the next, it seemed, they were torn apart by internal feuding or sudden accusations of fraud or mismanagement.

Averil still retained traces of the brilliant student she had been, drawing together disparate bits of information, arranging them into a stunningly complicated pattern.

"You've set up a whole secret counterinsurgency campaign," she said, "against a nationwide network that may not even exist. And if it doesn't, your repressive tactics will bring it into being."

The agent in charge stood up irritably.

"Are you going to cooperate?"

Averil looked mildly surprised. "Of course not."

"Why do you want to be ruined over this?"

Later they would remember the expression in her dark eyes as inscrutable, but during the moment, each agent had felt as if Averil were looking into his core, without animosity and without judgment, clearly seeing his hypocrisy and cowardice.

It made them hate her.

~

Averil and Peter were silent for several minutes after she finished telling the story.

"You know," he said finally, "when you first came here, I was told through informal channels that the archbishop's 'strong preference' was for you to have no role at St. Anthony's, no counseling duties, no administration work, not even saying Mass."

"You never told me."

"He has no authority to make that kind of unilateral order. All he could do was put pressure on me and hope I was spineless enough to go along with it."

"I've always said, Peter, you're nothing if not … spiny."

Peter made a vague, snorting sound in response. His version of a grudging laugh.

"And of course," he said, "you won't actively abet vigilantes."

He could see her mind navigating through the necessary mental reservations: the definition of *abet*, the definition of *vigilante*. They had both gone to Catholic school; they knew how to pick their way across rhetorical minefields.

"I discourage aggression," she said. "Always."

How do you define *discourage*? he could have asked. Or *aggression*?

It was the best she would do.

"You were a fool to defy the federal authorities," he said. "They could have arrested you."

"I doubt it. That would have exposed the existence of whatever it is they're trying to keep secret."

"They could have held you indefinitely, without charge, without access to an attorney. You're nothing to them. You're a tiny ant in a world full of angry stomping creatures."

"I like ants," Averil said.

~

She remembered the day the archbishop's letter arrived, decreeing her banishment ("reassignment") from St. Margaret's. They would give her a few months to wrap things up and help her successor, when they found him—and of course it would be a *him*, female priests being hard to find and no doubt suspect because of Averil's precedent.

She had worked late at the soup kitchen the day she received the official letter. Close to midnight she stepped outside for a few moments. No garden-scented breezes made their way to downtown New Falls at night, but still she sensed the movement, the ease of spring, and breathe it in, let it carry her along.

That was when she saw the man walk past her.

It was not at the intellectual level or even a conscious level that noted the insolent body language of the young and healthy. She did not stop to wonder what message that bottle-blond hair color was supposed to suggest, or the suppleness of the leather that hugged his pectorals. If she had, she may have concluded, correctly, that the effortless beauty of this young specimen was nothing more complicated than the age-old mating call of all gaudily feathered males: *Notice me.*

She watched him as he walked up the block to the Eighth Street Supper Club.

She followed. The doorman let her in, and she stood quietly near the entrance, watching. A security guard quickly approached. Right behind him was Vladimir Melendez, white teeth and gray silk suit agleam.

"Reverend, I'm disappointed—"

"I'm not here to gamble," she said quickly.

She used to visit, years ago, a pleasant and unassuming guest well liked by the staff, but she went on a winning streak that no one seemed able to explain. In return for her agreeing to stay away, the owners of the gambling club made generous yearly donations to St. Margaret's soup kitchen.

"Can we just say I'm enjoying the scenery?"

Melendez turned and followed her line of sight, saw a young white man with a bleached blond crewcut and a leather vest over blue jeans. A bit young for the lady priest, he thought, and more than a bit trashy. But it was Melendez's job to make sure the nights at the club went smoothly, and he was too much the professional to comment on the patrons' taste in clothing and sex, no matter how dubious. As long as they emptied their wallets and left quietly, and kept coming back.

"Right," he said. "I'll leave you to it, then."

If all the priest wanted tonight was eye candy, that was fine with him.

Who can tell the human heart, was perhaps the lesson one might take that evening from the pragmatic crime bosses of downtown New Falls.

Catholic priests, of course, had human hearts, and bodies, despite their vow to pretend otherwise. Considering that Averil Parnell had lived "in sin" with a man right up to the morning of the massacre, it was remarkable that she had been mostly celibate as a priest. The falling-aways had been neatly compartmentalized and never involved a parishioner. Her list of indiscretions amounted to all of two liaisons, in moments of flayed

᷃neliness, both occurring near anniversaries of the massacre. Something never spoken of or even thought about later, any lingering tenderness or gratitude strictly locked away.

That night at the club was a moment's distraction, with no intent to act on it or embarrass the man with her attention. A pleasant half hour at the edge of a crowded room, watching him strut about and show his perfect jawline and lean profile to their best advantages. She allowed the feeling of sexual stimulation to pulse through her without struggling against it.

Afterward she went back to the soup kitchen. She knew she wouldn't be able to sleep. She was scouring pots when a tall, elderly Black man walked in. She had never seen him before.

"You're a good person," he said in a strong accent that she couldn't identify. "Misguided, but I believe in freedom of religion." He handed her a prayer card. "This is your orisha," he said. "Babalu-Ayé. I thought you should know."

The card depicted Saint Lazarus as a rag-draped emaciated Black man on crutches. *Pray to the holy beggar Lazarus for healing*, the caption instructed.

CHAPTER 3

ANNUNCIATION

Whoever dances belongs to the whole.

—Round Dance of the Cross
(Gnostic gospel, 2nd century)

W hen she was finally well enough to start driving again, Grazyna
Sienkiewicz steered her taxi clear of certain streets at certain
times. She constantly scanned her surroundings. Made sure she wasn't
alone on a street, or in a quiet neighborhood near an alley, where an
otherwise respectable-looking man could drag her out of her cab and no
one the wiser. When she wasn't driving one of her regulars she looked for
female passengers, or couples or families. She took the medications the
doctor prescribed. She tried not to dwell on it.

The woman she picked up this afternoon wore a belted gray trench
coat that seemed much too light for the sleety March weather, and only
a silk scarf draped round her head, but she didn't seem cold. Her perfect
posture, while other pedestrians hunched over in vain attempts to conserve
body heat, reminded Grazyna of the indomitable schoolteacher-nuns of
her childhood in Poland. Slouching, for them, was a moral failing.

"Where to?" Grazyna said, already signaling to pull out into traffic.

"Here will be fine. You can start the meter."

In her rearview mirror Grazyna stole a glance at the passenger, who
had taken off her scarf and tinted glasses. Pale blonde hair, silvery eyes
looking at her intently. Grazyna wondered if she was a movie star or
something, to hide her appearance so carefully.

"I know what happened to you," the stranger said.

Before Grazyna had a chance to respond, the stranger reached forward
over the seat and held up a photograph.

"O matko!"

"Does that mean 'son of a bitch' where you come from?"

Grazyna felt nauseated. "It's a face I never wanted to see again."

The stranger withdrew the photo.

"Are you police?" Grazyna said.

"I go after criminals in my own way."

"But you know who he is?"

He was richer than God, the stranger told her. More money than the treasury of some entire countries. There were rumors about what he'd done, the women he'd raped. One case made it as far as a courtroom before it was dismissed for lack of evidence. The others, the prosecutors always refused to pursue. Most of the time, all the woman could do was describe his appearance, and the police never brought in anyone for her to identify.

Grazyna slumped in her seat, stared out the windshield into the icy gray afternoon. She should have guessed. He wasn't nervous, didn't look over his shoulder. He knew how easy it was going to be for him to get away with it.

"Tell me his name," she said.

She heard the stranger's level voice behind her, neither surprised nor eager, merely curious. "So you can take revenge into your own hands?"

"Whose hands does it belong in?"

Later Grazyna would think of the stranger as the ice queen. In her memory she couldn't separate those pale eyes, that wintery calmness, from the sleet and mist that enveloped the cab, cutting them off from the outside world.

"I have friends," Grazyna said. "Other cabbies, men from my country. You tell us where to find him and they rough him up, show him a lesson."

"What's the worst he'll suffer? A broken jaw, maybe. Meanwhile your friends will end up in jail and that's the end of it."

The stranger leaned forward again, holding the photograph in front of Grazyna.

"You're sure this is the one? I need to know."

She didn't want to look at him, but she couldn't tear her eyes away from that smug, confident face.

She hesitated. So much depended on her answer. The stranger was like a spring, waiting to be set in motion.

"What would you do to him if you could?" the stranger said. "If you knew you'd get away with it?"

She was so close that Grazyna could feel her breath against her ear.

"You could put an end to it. You could know that you were the last woman to suffer because of him. I'll take care of it for you. It'll do you way more good than those anti-anxiety pills."

Again Grazyna was reminded of the teacher-nuns. The sisterhood this woman was in, they too had a moral code, but in their universe hesitation was a weakness, forgiveness a moral failure.

Weeks later she read about the man's death in the newspaper. The investigation was going nowhere.

As far as Grazyna could tell, he was a big shot in international banking and was just starting to enter politics. At the peak of his career, people said. Richer than God indeed.

She pictured him walking along the dark street, unsuspecting—he was a master of the universe, he was safe everywhere—and the ice queen materializing behind him, her breath rippling along his skin while she held the knife against his neck.

~

If Catherine had believed in a god, perhaps she would have found comfort in the idea of an afterlife, the possibility of some arrangement by which each rapist, each woman-killer would be punished not only for what he had done to his victims, but also for the collateral damage he inflicted on every woman. The unease each woman lived with, the background static formed by the knowledge that she too could become a victim at any time.

But for Catherine religion was merely a pastiche of poetic phrases, perhaps heard at a baptism or other event that required her presence at a church and some semblance of polite attention. *The poor in spirit*, things like that. *Love your neighbor.*

One line in particular stayed with her: *For surely justice and mercy will follow me all the days of my life.*

Justice and mercy, lovely words, conjuring a god who practiced them and created people in its image. Pretty to think so.

~

"Mighty are the fallen" is what came to John Honig's mind when he entered St. Anthony's Church.

That couldn't be it. Where in the fucking Bible would they say mighty are the fallen? Trained by Dominican friars and here he was thinking in snippets of Bible-speak pidgin.

31

A few other people were in the church: a middle-aged woman in a back pew, an old man kneeling at the altar. That was all right. He would ignore them and they would disappear. He would be alone with the beleaguered stained-glass saints, the larger-than-life Jesus in the process of being crucified, a succession of smaller Jesuses making their dreary way through the Stations of the Cross, to end up being crucified yet again.

"You only die once" was a line he liked to say on dates. It fucked with a woman's mind when he said things like that—she'd try and figure it out, chase after it as if it were some key to his personality.

You sure as hell couldn't use that line on Jesus.

The place had an interesting feel. Older than the twentieth-century rash of cinderblock hell boxes. Here the architect knew what he was doing.

He would enjoy working on the restoration project.

The fat grumpy priest in charge of the place had been at a loss for words when John showed up and made the offer. Finally he started rumbling something about largesse, about gratitude, blah blah. But there was something cautious about the man, as if he suspected John's motives.

It was win-win, John pointed out. The place needed the restoration, John had the money to fund it, and it counted toward the internship he needed for his architecture degree. Besides, there was his larger project he would work on after architectural school. This would be a perfect learning experience.

He made no mention, of course, of the other motive behind it.

Funny how things worked out.

Now he studied the light streaming through the Rose Window above the doors.

Lo how the mighty have fallen. That was it, the line he'd been trying to think of.

At the same moment, he sensed someone standing behind him and turned around. The woman priest.

"I understand you're here to start a preservation project," she said. She didn't look pleased.

It had been two years since he'd seen her that first time, back in New Falls. Of course she hadn't noticed him then. She was too focused on something—someone—else.

"Father Byrne was called away," she said. "He's asked me to show you around. As you can see, this is St. Anthony of Padua Church." She pointed left. "The building over that way is the Chapter House. The monastery archives are in the basement if you want them for your research. I've made sure everything is unlocked." She turned to go.

"Wait a minute," he said. "What if I have questions?"

"I'm sure I wouldn't be able to answer them," she said as she walked away.

Arrogant little bitch.

He could respect that.

~

Averil washed the supper dishes and wiped off the table. It had been a light dinner. Since Peter was still not home, she and Marc had shared a can of minestrone and some buttered toast.

She heard scratching at the kitchen door and opened it to let in Mehitabel, then sat down with a cup of tea to enjoy the quiet of the kitchen in the spring twilight.

The man she'd seen that morning in the church—she'd forgotten his name but kept thinking about him all day. Instead of struggling against her initial reaction of instant dislike, she had groped for reasons to justify it. The insinuating voice. The smile that didn't reach to his eyes. The sense that he was laughing at her.

In the midst of life we are in death. In the few moments she'd spent with the strange man, this line had come to her as clearly as if a choir of monks were chanting a Requiem Mass right behind her.

She had pondered the meaning of the phrase before, as she tended to do with so many of the poetic, abstruse lines scattered through scripture and liturgy and prayer book. To "be in death" could mean we humans were on our way to death, we were mortal and on a path with one unavoidable end point. Not very comforting.

Then sometimes she thought the line related to reincarnation, that in the midst of one incarnation we were living with the results of all those other lives and deaths, memories like echoes, poorly understood, piling onto each other so their cumulative effect was a constant background noise.

But now that she was struggling her way through her physics books, she was starting to think in terms of atoms and molecules, particles and waves.

To "be in death" in the midst of life might mean that whether we were alive or dead, we were merely a different reconfiguration of the same atoms. Same deck, reshuffled.

Or in the midst of this life we're living in other, parallel universes.

Mehitabel wandered the kitchen, sniffing in corners and trying to pry open cabinet doors.

"Why can't we just be alive," Averil said to her, "when we're in the midst of life?"

Peter Byrne lumbered in before the cat was inclined to answer. He put the kettle on the stove and took out a clean mug and saucer.

"Long day, Peter?"

"Meetings. My favorite activity." He sat down heavily as if the effort had exhausted him.

"Marc and I filled your shoes as best we could."

Peter nodded. "Honig. You showed him around?"

Averil decided to treat that as a rhetorical question. "What's he doing, anyway?" she said.

"One of the many things I've been busy with—in case you haven't realized—is getting this place declared a historic landmark. Now we're eligible for grants for restoration and preservation. The landmark status attracts private donors too. This man Honig is getting a degree at the architecture school, says he wants to fund the restoration himself."

"What's in it for him?"

"Nothing's in it for him. He's not like you and me, Reverend, he's got more money. A lot more. Try and be nice to him."

~

To go to the Renaissance Faire was to immerse yourself in a mélange of fake everything: the armor was cardboard, the history confused. Vendors and paid actors mouthed garbled Shakespearean English: "Hark, mistress, thy credit card has come to ill." Even the visitors got into the act. "Where art the restrooms?"

Still, it was a pleasant June day and it was an excuse for Catherine Beck to be outdoors.

"I'm the mayor of this fair town," bellowed a man in a leather vest as he handed out programs.

"Did women *have* a Renaissance?" Catherine asked him.

Someone less attractive would have brought out the bully in him: "feminazi" or "humorless bitch" would have leapt to mind, but while he stood gaping, scouring his brain for a period-appropriate flirtatious remark that didn't include the word "wench," Catherine walked away.

She passed a live chess game getting set up, a woman yelling through a megaphone for the pawns to pay attention. A leper begged for alms (proceeds to go to the homeless shelter) among the crowd gathered at the outdoor theatre.

She stopped at a booth selling daggers and knives that seemed more nouveau Pagan than Renaissance-era Europe. The seller, a man in a blue linen tunic and leather leggings, was lecturing a customer on the minute differences between boxwood and applewood knife handles for Samhain services.

Catherine looked at the intricately carved, jewel-studded daggers.

"Too pretty to use," she said dismissively.

"They're for ceremonial purposes," the man said in the same voice of bored superiority he had used on the previous customer. He didn't even look at her.

Catherine could imagine this jerk playing multiuser knight errant games, or making elaborate symbols in the air with his hands and imagining himself a wizard.

She picked up a particularly overdecorated blade and thrust it, point down, into the wooden table near his ring-studded hand.

"What's the use of a knife that doesn't cut?"

He looked at her then. Watched the way the dagger's topaz and ruby cabochons reflected light onto her face. Afterwards he tried to capture that effect. He included her in the Tarot card set he was painting. Queen of Swords, of course.

Catherine, bored, headed off to look for the jousting.

~

Averil, also at the Faire, stopped at a booth marked WISEWOMAN/PSYCHICK READER, where a woman sat at a shawl-fringed table with a Tarot deck. Next to her was a hand-printed sign: PROCEEDS TO PAGAN CHARITIES.

The woman grinned at the sight of Averil's clerical collar, but made no comment on it. "Ask a question," she said. "We'll see what the cards answer."

"What's the next new thing in my life?"

"Okay. Cut the deck three times. Pick the top card."

"The Eight of Swords," Averil said. "That looks ominous. The caption is 'Disillusion.'"

"The card usually stands for a person, a man."

"I'm going to meet a knight on a gray horse, with a bloodied sword?"

The woman laughed. "The cards aren't that literal. Turn over the next one, it'll give us more information."

Averil picked the next card. "Prince of Cups."

"Reversed. Definitely a man. A difficult one, from the looks of it."

~

To say that Catherine Beck made a habit of people-watching would be to grossly understate the seriousness of her project. She researched civilian behavior with the thoroughness she had once devoted to ballistics testing in battlefield conditions and reviewing military tactics in fierce, closed-door debates.

She read the works of psychologists, kinesiologists, sociologists. She researched anatomy and physiology, martial arts, weapons of all kinds. Libraries and bookstores had long since surrendered to government surveillance of their customers' lending and purchases, so Catherine had to take precautions. She read the books and articles in the library without checking them out; she went to used book stores and paid in cash. Most of all she relied on her own personal observations.

Settings varied: the gym, the riverfront park, the gas station. She watched people when they were off guard, doing something so routine that they were on autopilot: dragging the trash to the curb, buying a newspaper. Or when they were doing something the opposite of routine, such as gathering to watch a live chess game.

Averil, on her way toward the Foode Courte, paused a few moments to watch also, just as two of the pawns got into a loud argument with the opposing side's bishop.

"Those aren't the rules!" the bishop kept saying. "You can't change the rules of chess at will!"

Averil, grinning, had to resist the temptation to join in the argument.

That was where Catherine saw her. It took a moment, but she recalled where they'd met before. A month ago, perhaps, outside the Y building. Catherine was just leaving after a workout, and this woman, wearing black and a clerical collar, was at a table collecting signatures for some cause or other. Protesting deportations, as Catherine recalled.

"You're just handing the government a convenient list of names to keep under surveillance," Catherine had told the woman, who smiled and said, "They've known about me for a long time."

She wouldn't have caught Catherine's attention at all that day at the Faire, except for the fact that someone else was watching her.

He stood along another edge of the game, a man in his twenties, lounging against a tree. Anyone else would have thought he was there waiting for someone and glancing idly at the chess pieces. Catherine, however, could read the tension in the elaborately bored pose. He was keeping something—someone—in his line of sight.

She edged around the audience until she was positioned directly opposite the man, his body angled one way and his face turned another, so intent on seeming not to look at anyone behind his tinted lenses.

In later years when Catherine remembered that moment, the three of them triangulated that way, she wished she had killed him then. How different things would have been.

~

At the Foode Courte Averil bought a bowl of garlicky lentil pottage and was mopping it up with chunks of buttered bread when a man approached and sat down next to her. He was part of the swirl, part of the music and the pleasantly confusing crowd noise. She could tell he was young and handsome. People turned to look at him as they passed.

After a moment she realized she'd seen him a couple of months ago, in the church. He was going to fund a restoration project.

"You'll have to remind me of your name," she said.

"John. Like the Evangelist."

"And John of the Cross. John of God. John the Almsgiver."

"John the Beloved."

She could always tell the people who were curious about meeting a woman priest. Some were disturbed by her, others pleased. This one looked like he was seeing a sideshow freak, amused and repelled at the same time.

"What should I call you—Father Averil?"

"Sure," she said. It was carnival time, after all. "Why the hell not?"

"You should have a booth here, as a representative of the Inquisition. Charge money to tie people to a rack. Sentence them to death in a mock trial."

"Nostalgia's not what it used to be," she said.

He seemed to laugh at this, but he made almost no sound. She could tell he was laughing only by his brilliant smile.

"You and I have something in common," he said.

"Which is?"

"You sleep in a monastic cell. No comforts, just a narrow bed, a chair. I live in a hotel. My room looks like that too. Only without the crucifix."

"Maybe you should get one," she said.

~

Only afterwards, when she wandered around trying to find the Booke Stalle she'd seen earlier, did it occur to her that this man had bothered to imagine what her bedroom looked like—her monastic cell, he'd called it.

Someone handed her a cup of cherry-pomegranate juice, telling her it was melted rubies. Maybe it was.

She started down a path that soon curved into a wooded area, away from the squabbling chess pieces and other crowd noise. She came across a troupe moving in the opposite direction. Men and women, emaciated and grim, flailed themselves with knotted leather cords and looked convincingly as if they were entranced. Amazingly realistic.

"Not to be picky," Averil said, "but the whole penitent thing is more Middle Ages than Renaissance."

"Mistress Abbess," a gaunt man answered, "you spend too much time in the scriptorium."

"Fair enough," Averil said, and saluted as she passed.

"Godspeed," he called out after her.

Godspeed. Godspell.

God's Spiel.

Ahead of her came the telltale mandolin and woodwind sounds of the Faire's wandering troubadours, and Averil braced herself for the usual ahistoric merrymaking. Instead she found a clearing with a cordoned-off workshop area, and no trace of a musical instrument. A pale woman with dark hair and long, thin fingers sat alone at a loom. The tapestry taking shape before her depicted a woman against a luminous teal background and a tree in the same color scheme as the woman—light shades of cream and gold.

"Beautiful," Averil said.

The tapestry weaver gave her a stern look under glowering eyebrows.

"Quiet, please. I'm an artist."

"Right," Averil said meekly. She sat on a bench.

After one last glare at Averil, the weaver became absorbed again in her silk-thread world. Averil became absorbed in the movements of those graceful fingers.

Another woman sat down next to Averil, looking vaguely familiar. Pale eyes, sun-dappled light hair. She could have stepped out of the tapestry herself.

"None of my business," the stranger said casually, "but there's a man following you."

Averil wanted to tell her to speak more quietly. She looked nervously at the weaver, but the fierce concentration on the tapestry continued undisturbed.

"He's in his twenties. Dark hair."

"Carrying a sword, no doubt," Averil said in a whisper. "On a gray horse."

The woman looked at her but didn't answer.

"Didn't I see you earlier?" Averil said. "At the joust maybe? No wait, you were a knight in the human chess game."

"Must have been someone who looks like me."

Averil felt as if she'd been drinking that awful-smelling "English ale" they were peddling.

"Aren't you worried?" the stranger said.

"It's probably someone curious about me," she said. "It happens sometimes. But I appreciate that you noticed."

The woman nodded, and they both turned to watch the progress of the tapestry. The next time Averil looked around, the stranger was gone.

"Come! This way!" a man called, beckoning her further along the path.

Averil stood up and followed him.

"Where are we going?" she said after a few minutes. The man was in such a hurry he was far ahead of her by then.

"All aboard! Ship of Fools, departing immediately."

They rounded a curve. Again a clearing, perhaps the same one where the tapestry woman had been. This time, women in ribbon-threaded satin bodices and velvet skirts turned one way, then another, hand on hips, while a line of men across from them stepped forward. The first man held out his hand to Averil and bowed.

They danced, as solemn and focused as if a band had been playing. Averil found herself following without effort, arm raise, dip, turn, step ahead, step back. They broke into arm-linked couples, formed lines again, separated, joined. Now swaying, now skipping, now turning in stately circles. Stars wheeling, electrons dancing, particle and wave. Merry meet and merry part.

CHAPTER 4

NATIVITY

Since you are my twin and my truest companion,
examine yourself, and learn who you are.

—Jesus, in Gospel of Thomas, 1st century

C atherine unfolded the newspaper and scanned the front page as she
started her breakfast.

A dozen dead, the top headline informed her.

There had been an explosion in Cleveland. A small building used
for anger-management classes, mandated by the courts for men who beat
their wives to a pulp but somehow had been deemed uncriminal.

The building was completely demolished.

Catherine looked out the window as she sipped her coffee. Another
beautiful June day. There was a 5K run for charity that was a big deal in
this town, and she had agreed to go watch it with a friend. She'd been
glad to find out she knew someone who had been here for years, knew
everyone.

The article ended with the usual disclaimer: "While early reports
assumed the presence of an explosive device, authorities now insist that
the cause was a gas leak."

It wasn't difficult for Catherine to find Gretchen Lehning in the
crowds milling around the starting line. She was wearing a flower-print
shirtwaist dress, high heels, and carrying a baby.

"Jeez, Gretchen," she said as they moved out of earshot of the crowd.
"You didn't steal it, did you?"

"You should get one," Gretchen said. She had the softest, highest-
pitched voice Catherine had ever heard. "They're great cover."

They watched the runners organize themselves. The mayor or
someone was making a speech.

"Been busy?" Catherine said.

"Fuckers won't have problems with anger anymore."

Catherine nodded as if Gretchen had made a statement about the weather.

Then she noticed another familiar face. Seated at a table, giving out water bottles to runners, was the woman Catherine had seen collecting signatures, the one who'd wandered around the Renaissance Faire yesterday, oblivious to the man stalking her.

Gretchen, noticing the direction of her stare, told her the woman's name.

"In the Department?"

"No. But she's a friend. We've tried to recruit her for more, god knows—ha, what a pun!"

The baby leaned over and patted Catherine on the cheek.

"We could use your help on my end," Gretchen said.

"Explosives? Not my thing. I'll stick with bullets."

"Or knives, from what I've heard," Gretchen said. She shifted the baby to her other hip and gave Catherine's arm a friendly squeeze. "PTA meeting tonight, seven o'clock. There's a bake sale!" She breezed away as if going to greet another friend.

Catherine lingered, looking around casually as if expecting to see other acquaintances. Events like these, in the open air, were convenient for a chance to talk, to gather in one of the few ways that hadn't been criminalized, didn't draw suspicion.

Bake sales. People in the Department had a macabre sense of humor.

~

"I remember you," Averil said. The woman who had come out of the tapestry the artist was weaving. And now she was real, with a real name, Catherine Beck.

Catherine gestured at the brochures for the retreat house. "St. Anthony's," she said. "You're Catholic."

Averil had seen the process before. People would estimate her age, calculate how long she must have been a priest. Then the name, the face, the history of the Cathedral Massacre clicked into place like abacus beads. After that came the awkward part: the embarrassment, the pity, the politely stifled curiosity.

Not so for Catherine. She put the pieces together in a moment, her face never losing its granite calm, but her eyes glowed with something like respect. Perhaps approval.

41

"When we met before," Catherine said, "I saw that clerical collar and assumed Unitarian Universalist, or Lutheran, maybe. Something more ... "

"Sensible?" Averil prompted.

"I was going to say Protestant."

"Have a seat. You can help me give away sports drinks."

Catherine drew up a folding chair and sat down.

"No offense," Catherine said, "but I never had much use for religion."

"Yes."

Yes what? Catherine thought. Yes, you knew? Yes, you can spot them? Yes, there *is* no use for religion?

"The way I see it," Catherine said, "life is chemistry. The forming of bonds, the breaking of bonds, between atoms, between molecules. That's what keeps life going, from plankton to primates."

"That's very beautiful," Averil said.

"Not that there isn't some beauty in religion. Some poetic stuff, anyway. Like that line about justice and mercy, following you your whole life."

Averil looked at her with something like pity in her large, dark eyes.

"I'm afraid it's 'goodness and mercy,'" she said. "Not 'justice and mercy.' The Twenty-Third Psalm. In the King James translation. Surely goodness and mercy shall follow me all the days of my life, and I will dwell in the house of the Lord forever."

"No justice?" Catherine said.

"Not in that Psalm, anyway."

So all these years she'd gotten it wrong. "I'll be damned," she said.

"Probably not."

~

Averil, preparing for the Night Prayer that evening, was struck by a memory: Asher's dorm room when he and Averil were undergraduates. An evening soon after they'd met. They sat talking until they were exhausted, and lay down in his bed side by side, fully dressed. She woke up to a room bathed in early-morning light, a moment of perfect clarity. Asher was lying next to her in the narrow bed, but she didn't feel crowded. For the first time she thought that being in a relationship might not be so bad, with a man like this. He didn't intrude on her solitude, in fact he seemed to be sharing it with her. She hadn't had sex with him, at that point. But they had slept together, truly together.

Years later as a seminarian she'd declared, "Nothing will stop me from being a priest."

And Mercedes Ortiz, always gentle and tactful, had asked, "Does your … Does the young man understand that?"

They had separate bedrooms in every apartment they lived in. An acknowledgment, Averil thought, that he understood they weren't in a couple, not really.

She was a scholar, immersed in the life of the mind. She would come home from graduate seminars in theology, her soul strafed by the hateful things the wise ones, the saints, the princes of the Church said about women: "weak and frivolous," "defective males," "devil's gateway." Asher would greet her at the door and she would back him up against the wall, kissing him hungrily, the antidote to the poison.

"I've never made him any promises," she answered Mercedes.

She had been so arrogant. No man was closer to her heart, yet she'd had less compassion for him than for a total stranger.

Gone. Gone. Long gone.

She held another man close to her heart now, sweet Brother Jesus. But sometimes he talked to her with a slow, sleepy voice and she felt a longing of the body as strong as the soul's desire.

The memories eased into other images, from which Averil half-awoke hours later. She had been with two other women outdoors somewhere, speaking-chanting. As she sat up now in the armchair she could still hear their voices, her own and the two others: "A restful night, a peaceful death." Then one of them said, "When shall we three meet again?" and she woke up completely, amused to think of Shakespeare's three Weird Sisters reciting the Night Prayer.

She had to hold her watch up to the window to look at it by moonlight. Three a.m. The witches' midnight.

A coven was what they'd called themselves sometimes, Averil's sister-seminarians. But Averil had come up with another metaphor.

They had been discussing their research projects for a seminar on Feminist Theology and Ecumenical Outreach. One woman was researching the pre-Islamic spirituality of Africa; another one, the pre-Columbian spirituality of Central America; another, the pre-patriarchal spirituality of Northern Europe.

She had made them laugh, comparing them to Arthurian knights as they sat around the seminar table at Mount St. Mary's. Companions of the Oval Table, she called them.

"It's true," she said. "We're on a quest, the search for the ancestresses. We'll inspire a new Grail myth."

"Averil," said Olive Ruonovaara, "the priesthood is never going to be the same after you," and Elizabeth O'Hare corrected her:

"*Catholicism* is never going to be the same."

Mercedes Ortiz smiled at Averil and pressed her hand. "You know, we have to be careful about the changes we introduce, especially in doctrine. Our presence here is revolutionary in itself. If we go in trying to change things right from the start, it gives them cause to say we never did belong, that we've mutated from Roman Catholics into something else."

"Not mutated," Averil had said. "Evolved is a better word. We represent what's best about this Church. The rest of you are too modest to say that. Modesty isn't one of my virtues."

All the things those women would have accomplished if they had lived. Averil was flattened by the thought.

The dead seminarians had rallied around her in those first excruciating years. Without knowing it, Averil felt them in countless ways. In the hands of her women parishioners, who tried to spruce her up when she first arrived at St. Margaret's. One of them would make her sit still long enough to corral her wayward hair and brush it till it shone, plaiting it back into a long elegant French braid while another one trimmed and buffed her ragged nails. Her normal unkemptness would reassert itself soon enough, but the parishioners were undaunted. They liked challenges.

The sister-seminarians whispered in Averil's ear the idea for the soup kitchen. They made a newspaper fall open to an article about a local philanthropist, who soon became the parish's first major donor. It was on their prompting that Averil first went to the gambling club down the street, and they were there to choose roulette numbers, arrange blackjack cards just so.

They heaved her out of bed in the mornings despite her paralyzing grief. When she was slumped exhausted over her desk in the evenings they were there to jostle her elbow: *Too much to do! You must go on!*

At last they handed her over to the monks of St. Anthony's, who caressed her with cool breezes and whispered, *Rest you now, daughter. Rest.*

~

FBI Agent Stephanie Hernández-Caribe was working late. She could think more clearly when the office was quiet, when she could look out her tenth-floor window and see the lights of Washington D.C. traffic far below, soundless and graceful from this distance.

It had taken a year. An entire year at the ridiculously named Research Division on Designated Activities to come up with a few slight traces of what they were looking for.

Things had been much easier before the Internet had been dismantled. Then they could easily trace emails, texts, social media messages. Now they had to rely on old-fashioned surveillance: recording devices planted at people's homes and offices, intercepted mail, operatives eavesdropping at coffeehouses. So much more labor intensive.

But now she had something.

It could turn out to be nothing. It was so small and tenuous. Her subordinates had missed it. Another reason for Steph to look over the transcripts herself, which everyone else said was obsessive.

A strange throwaway comment in a memo from the director of a women's center to a social worker: *Could be D.O.T. thing eventually.*

A scribbled note from a community organizer with a quick reference to *DoT.*

A phone conversation from a therapist who specialized in rape survivors. She was talking to a friend (yet to be identified), who said at one point, according to the transcript: "Be careful what you say." "Why?" the therapist said, "who's going to connect the dots?" The transcriber had written "[laughter]" at this point.

Stephanie had gone back to the recording itself. "Who's going to connect the dots?" she heard, followed by laughter from the speaker and groans from the listener, the way people do when they're making a pun.

It could be nothing, of course. It probably was nothing.

Stephanie doodled on a piece of paper. *D.O.T.* The *O* was probably "of." *D* for daughters? *Daughters of____,* she wrote. Thor? Or what else could the *D* stand for, division, perhaps. Detachment. *Department of Transgression,* she wrote. Clever. Or what if *O* stood for something else? *D____ Over Time?* *D____ Outstanding T____?*

One of their surveillance targets was a woman Steph simply thought of as The Prof. She taught philosophy at a small college in Oregon and had written a few books on feminist theory. The Prof was not one of those who had mentioned D.O.T. What made her interesting, or at least amusing to Steph, was that she seemed to know her mail was being intercepted, though her friends laughed at her when she told them her suspicions.

She actually started mailing notes to the FBI directly. *Dear FBI agent,* one note read, *Why hasn't wife beating ever been classified as domestic terrorism?*

Another time she'd written: *Men simply do not live in fear/expectation of random violence by women.*

phanie had decided to write back, using her own name. It couldn't establish a conversation. The next note was addressed to Stephanie J.

Dear Agent Hernández-Caribe, Why is it that the FBI never hits the right targets? You disrupt ordinary organizations that aren't doing anything violent.

Interesting. A tacit admission that someone *was* engaged in violence. They're out there, Step thought. She'd always said she had hunting-dog instincts. She loved a chase. As long as the target was real.

This afternoon's mail had included another envelope from The Prof. It contained a photocopy of a printed document, plus a handwritten note:

Here's a short story you should read. "Wolfland," by Tanith Lee. A bit gothic for my taste, as I prefer realism. But it makes an interesting point.

Stephanie made herself a cup of coffee, the fifth of the day. Now that it was after hours, she decided to listen to some music. She flipped through her selections, picked out a Corelli piece. She began to read.

The story was in the form of a fairy tale, though written only a few decades ago. A woman in a castle, married to a man who ended up being a violent brute. She put up with him until it became clear that he planned to rape their daughter. Things got weird, but as far as Steph could tell, the woman joined the wolves that roamed around the castle, became a wolf herself somehow, and the next thing anyone knew, the violent husband was found dead with his throat torn out. By wolves.

Steph kept waiting for the scene where the wife turns back into a human woman. It never came.

The music had ended without her noticing it. Her coffee was cold.

At the bottom of the last photocopied page, The Prof had added a handwritten postscript to the story. *Dear Agent H-C: Here's something to remember. The biggest lie of patriarchy is to convince us women that we aren't violent.*

No, Steph wanted to argue. That's not what the story is trying to say. We might have to turn into something we're not, to protect ourselves. It doesn't mean we're that way by our nature.

Keep focused, she reminded herself. She had a job to do. Look for patterns. People communicating. Colluding. That was all she needed to think about.

In bed that night, that fertile time between wakefulness and sleep, Steph wondered what she would do if she ever did see concrete evidence of a network. The option of standing aside, saying nothing, presented itself to her for the first time, when she was too drowsy to be shocked and outraged at herself for the thought.

~

Averil, at the garden shed, gathered tools for transplanting flowers. She had a whole flat of pansies, donated by a parishioner who'd bought too many for his own use.

It was still morning, but the heat and humidity were already stifling. Averil wiped the sweat off her face with her sleeve and was tempted to feel irritated.

When she was a girl the nuns used to scold them for complaining about such things. "Offer it up to God," they said, which had only annoyed her more. Feeling hot and uncomfortable wasn't a *thing*, she reasoned, so how could you offer it, and besides, why would God want it?

If someone had explained back then the distinction between God's essence and God's manifestations, it would have made perfect sense to her, but ordinary Christians never discussed it, seemed to have no idea that this is what some of their most famous theologians had described—not only Christian thinkers, but also Hindu, Buddhist, Jewish, and Islamic philosophers. There is an Ultimate Reality that we can never truly understand, and then there are its manifestations in our lives: abstractions like wisdom or goodness, or people—deities, avatars.

It was a useful distinction, a preventative against smugness. Kept you from thinking that you knew what God "wanted." It would have kept presidents from saying God *wanted* them to make war on another country, or pastors from saying that God *wanted* marriage to be a certain way and no other.

There were ordinary people who understood this, even without the aid of learned authors. Averil remembered reading studies of elderly Afro-Cubans, explaining to white anthropologists the concept of a being beyond anyone's understanding, who was behind all this but couldn't be consulted, didn't want offerings. You had to go to the gods/orishas/santos with your gifts and your requests. The name varied—Olorun, Oloddumare, many others. Some said he was an old African man who'd made the universe and now was retired, interested only in plowing his fields. Averil imagined approaching him: "Aren't I spiritually advanced, sir, aren't I impressive, offering up to you my discomfort rather than feeling irritated by the heat?" And the old man saying, "Don't bother me" as he bent to adjust his plow.

It put things in perspective. You ignored the discomfort because that was the mature, self-disciplined thing to do, not because it pleased some large person in the sky.

And anyway, the heat was a welcome distraction. In a few more weeks it would be fifteen years since the Cathedral Massacre. She was determined not to think about it till then.

The pansies were purple-black toward the center, cream-colored at the edges. The purple held her attention. These were not your usual pansies, playful and flighty. These ones were stern. They held secrets.

Crouching barefoot in the empty flowerbed, she coaxed each plant out of its container, arranged and re-arranged before she started to dig holes for them.

A flock of birds rushed overhead with a sound like delicate pieces of glass all set to clinking. The force of their passage so close above her made Averil instinctively hunch her shoulders and lower her head. Surrounded by sound and wind.

The ancients said birds held divine power. Textbooks showed charts: hollow bones, aerodynamic feather configuration. No mention of clinking glass, or power.

The birds flew off and she heard John Honig's voice behind her.

"What's the concept?" he said. "Those flowers, the way you're planting them in the middle of nothing. They're not forming a border, or any other pattern. What's the concept?"

"No concept. It's a clump. Flowers like to grow in clumps. Or else in drifts. That's a clump that trails off to the right and to the left."

He sat down in the grass as if she had invited him to.

"Also," he said, "they're not native to the region or authentic for the monastery's restoration. If I were in charge of landscaping I'd get rid of every tacky hybrid like these."

Innocent flowers. He would uproot them for having the wrong pedigree.

She pictured his family: people who argued over wine vintages, bought art for its investment value, traveled to only the right vacation spots.

"So, Father, aren't you supposed to tell me to consider the flowers of the field, how they do not spin or reap or any other damn useful thing?"

"And what lesson are you supposed to gain from that?"

"That beauty is reason enough."

She looked down at her plants to keep from smiling at his vanity. Some people do anything, say anything, for attention, she reminded herself. She should try to feel compassion for him.

"You're familiar with scripture," she said.

"Catholic school from kindergarten through college. Dominican brothers."

"They taught you well."

"'Trained' is a better word, Father. The problem is, you wear that priest's collar everywhere, even when you're working in the dirt. I see it and I have an irresistible urge to make a confession."

"If you're sincerely interested in the Sacrament of Reconciliation, I can tell you Father Marc is much better at it than I am."

"I don't think so."

She didn't like this man. She didn't like his insinuating voice, didn't like the sexual overtones he managed to add to completely ordinary situations. Irresistible urge indeed.

An insect landed on her hand, a delicate winged creature the color of spring leaves. She had bought a field guide to insects once and was disappointed to learn that there were far too many species to even document, let alone include a representative sample of in a field guide. So much we didn't know.

"Swat it before it stings you," John said.

"Insects have a right to be here too."

"What, they're as good as humans?"

"They're shiny and they can fly. Can you say the same about yourself?"

She was close enough to him to hear the intake and quick rippling release of breath that was his version of a laugh.

And then he was gone. Looked at his watch, flashed a smile, and she was alone with the flowers and dirt and insects.

She lay on the grass. One moment she was under a maple sapling, looking up at the sky through the branches. The next moment she was lying on a raft, floating head-first down a river. Her *dead* body, on a raft. She distinctly felt the movement of the current, saw the branches overhead leaning over her as her body sailed past. The tips of her hair trailed in the water. Drops of river water misted her face.

She sat up. Lawn, maple, bright sunlight on pansies. Not a river in sight.

She convinced herself she'd fallen asleep for a few moments. Or else she was getting heatstroke.

~

"I thought we were going to your place."

"This *is* my place."

"It's a hotel."

49

John Honig swiped his room card and reached inside for the light switch. "I live here." He resisted the urge to say more. Why were the pretty ones always stupid?

She'd been pleasantly drunk when he picked her up at the bar. Or rather, she picked him up. As they usually did.

He ushered her in to the room. "After you."

The girl giggled uncertainly as she looked around. Maybe the rum and cokes were wearing off.

"I didn't know people *lived* in hotels," she said. "I see the way you're dressed, I saw your car. If you can afford all that, you can afford to buy a house or something."

"Right." He pulled her up against him and kissed her. The only way to shut her up.

After they fucked he tossed her clothes at her. "I need to get to work early," he said.

She sat up. "Jeez. You're one inhospitable bastard."

Good. A multisyllabic word.

"As you can see, I only have a single bed." God help him if he ever had to wake up next to another person.

The woman priest had asked him that, last week at the Renaissance Faire: why do you live in a hotel? And it had seemed natural to answer her, answer with complete honesty: "I don't want to deal with fucking people."

He'd watched her reaction. He liked to watch people, especially when they were uncomfortable.

But the priest only laughed.

~

Averil lit a candle and settled in to her armchair with her rosary, felt the rose quartz beads smooth and cool against her fingertips.

The Joyful Mysteries.

She finished the first decade, the Annunciation, and opened her eyes. It was different when she had others to say the rosary with, the prayer circles at St. Margaret's that met at the church or visited the homes of anyone who asked them, their chant rising and falling, blending together, pulling Averil out of herself and into a stream of voices.

On her desk sat a reproduction of one of the Willendorf goddess figures, she of the earth-colored skin and unflappable expression. Wide shoulders and bountiful breasts, sitting comfortably on huge haunches. At

St. Margaret's her image was at the altar along with the more conventional depictions of Mary. Here at St. Anthony's she was nowhere to be seen.

Joyful mystery. Mysterious joy. She is a woman. She is naked. She is old.

Averil moved through the next mysteries. The Visitation. The Nativity. Jesus as a child being presented at the Temple, and the prophet Anna ("of the tribe of Asher") singing his praises.

People never talked about Anna. Averil couldn't recall hearing a single sermon on her when she was growing up. A mysterious old woman who lived in the Temple and made prophesies. Can't have young girls hearing about that kind of role model.

She was nodding off in her chair when the singing finally got through to her in her half-sleep.

Singing.

She sat up and listened. A choir of monks, somewhere in the building.

The Refectory was supposed to be empty. Her rooms were the only ones occupied on the second floor, and the first floor was used only for the occasional banquet.

But they used to live here, the monks. Slept in these very rooms, ate together in the dining hall below.

The singing grew louder, as if the monks were moving down the corridor toward her door.

Jesus was among the monks, singing in a sweet baritone. She smiled. It was fitting; she'd always called him Brother Jesus. He had a sense of humor.

The next morning she assumed it was a dream, even though she was lying in front of the door when she woke up.

CHAPTER 5

PECCATA
MUNDI

It is no more harm for you to kill a man
who is trying to kill you, than it is for you
to take a drink of water when thirsty.

—David Walker, 1829

Some reporters hated covering crime. Give them corrupt politicians or
greedy plutocrats any day, environmental devastation, even nuclear
gamesmanship. Crime, they felt—or rather, the criminal justice system—
was so much uglier.

Kerry Muñoz was one such reporter. Her normal beat was community
affairs. You attend meetings, you translate bureaucratese into brief news
articles, you let ordinary people know precisely how the policy wonks
want to screw them over this time. And then when they stage a protest
march, you cover that too. Simple.

But crime? No rhyme or reason to sentencing patterns. Like this
creep, Bret Trevor, rich young white man. He'd killed a nineteen-year-
old girl he was having sex with—and got five to fifteen years.

Now he was being released after eight years, and no one was supposed
to know about it.

This should have been the kind of news she read about, not reported
herself. But the tip came to her, from an acquaintance with ties to the parole
board. Now she would have to figure out where the hell Ossining was,
anyway.

Trevor had done it by accident, he claimed, a reflex motion when
the girl hurt him by squeezing his testicles too hard. The victim's diary
was read out in court, every detail of her sex life presented as if somehow

to prove she was worthy of being murdered. Why ruin this promising young man's life, prosecutors asked, for an accident? The message: she was a slut, killing her was no big deal. Trevor showed no remorse. He was videotaped at a party pantomiming the murder and laughing about it. Five to fifteen years.

No doubt his father's contacts had a nice management job waiting for him.

Kerry waited for him too, alone, at the prison entrance. She would get a couple of quotes, snap a photo, and never again agree to cover a crime story.

Then again, maybe she would find him chastened, aged. She might see something human in his eyes from having suffered.

She started to ask a question. The sound of her accent, third-generation Brooklyn-Puerto Rican, unleashed all the arrogance and contempt Trevor had shown at his trial.

"Why don't you learn to speak English?"

I'm fluent in three languages, *pendejo*, she wanted to say. And I know how to squeeze balls too.

Trevor and the two prison guards had turned to look at her, so Kerry was the only one facing the car as it flashed past. She was also the only one who didn't fall flat when the gun was fired. She crouched down, but kept her head up. Only later did she have time to wonder whether this was reporter's instincts or sheer stupidity. Fortunately the woman at the wheel had perfect, deadly aim.

"I guess I'm in shock, officer, I can't remember anything."

"The make of the car? Anything at all about the driver?"

"I'm sorry, it's all a blur."

She remembered everything about that face, and saw it many times in years to come, when it became world famous.

~

The church doors at St. Anthony's were open as if somebody had wanted to air it out. No one was inside. Catherine Beck lingered near the doors, looked at the statues and stained glass, went so far as to stand near the back pew. People said they could feel a different energy in a church. In her enhanced state of perception, she reasoned, this would be the time to feel it.

She could have driven on to New Falls, found a church there. It was only another twenty minutes. But the woman priest lived here, did whatever it was that Catholic priests did. Cast spells, for all she knew.

53

She told herself she felt nothing and ignored the subsequent sense of relief at that fact. She also ignored faint images that came into her mind at that moment, shreds of a dream perhaps. A fugitive, seeking sanctuary in a church. An old woman with an herb garden telling Catherine to put her bloody hands into the upturned soil.

She walked out and sensed in the breeze something biting and sweet, followed it around behind one of the monastery buildings to where the woman priest knelt barefoot in a garden plot, in a black tank top and black canvas work pants, with a bushel basket beside her.

She seemed not at all startled when she straightened up and saw Catherine standing there.

"Would you like some help with that?" Catherine said.

"I won't say no. It does get to my lower back after a while, all this squatting."

Averil went to the toolshed and came back with a pair of garden gloves and some small tools.

"What is it we're doing?" Catherine said.

"Pulling weeds. Too bad we can't eat them, we always have a bumper crop."

Catherine easily developed a rhythm of loosening the soil at the root of the weed, then pulling and throwing it in the basket.

When they took a break they sat by the potato plants and shared Averil's water bottle.

"You should put your hands in the soil," Averil said. "It'll ground you." Despite Catherine's outward calm, Averil could feel her jangling nerves, the energy shooting out of her. "Come on, I'll do it too."

To Catherine it was New Age-y and vaguely embarrassing even though no one else was around, and weirdly similar to the dream image she had just recalled, but she followed Averil's lead and dug her hands into the loose garden soil in front of them.

If her comrades could see her. *Grounded?* they would sneer. *Like a sulky teenager? Like a lightning rod?*

The soil, moist and warm in her hands, felt so good she had to stop and close her eyes to concentrate on it. She did feel different somehow.

"Feels good, doesn't it?" Averil said. "It's why I garden in my bare feet." She looked around at the work left to be done that morning. She pointed toward a roll of galvanized steel chickenwire. "I'll put that up later," she said. "Once the green beans start germinating."

"Does it work? The fencing isn't high, and it doesn't seem strong."

"Good enough for the rabbits. It's kind of endearing, to watch them. They get to the fence and sniff at it for a minute. They look puzzled. Then they hop away. They don't jump over it or dig under it. They don't stay there and rage at it. Such gentle creatures. So reasonable. Imagine if humans were like that."

Catherine felt that some kind of response was expected. She thought about humans, about rabbits. "It's true they don't seem to have much of an agenda."

Averil smiled. "That's exactly it. They're themselves, with no ulterior motive. Sometimes I think I should reward them, you know? Maybe leave a patch of garden unfenced. What do you think?"

"They manage to feed themselves pretty well, even without access to your garden."

"Two different things," Averil said. "What they need, and what we can give them."

Catherine was beginning to lose the thread of Averil's thoughts.

"People aren't like rabbits," she said.

"Or like deer," Averil said. "I would also be glad if we were like deer."

~

It wasn't rocket science, John Honig had to remind himself. The textbooks were piled next to his double espresso. Contemporary design, both the book and the subject matter, could be summed up in two words: stupid and ugly. Then there was Postmodernism and Architecture, a required course that forced students to read Derrida and Foucault so that later, when their buildings were built, they could make gnomic pronouncements about deconstructing space or some such shit, and the art critics would take them seriously. He was learning more in his Engineering Materials course than anything he'd ever taken in the School of Architecture. Tensile strength of stone and wood, even glass. Useful things.

His thesis project proposal was due. He opened the cover sheet on his laptop. The instructions called for a one-sentence description of the project. Then a one-paragraph description. Then one page, etc. Torture unfurling outward.

Designing a church using medieval design principles and building methods. He would never admit to his father that he was doing something so unprofitable. He dodged Randolph Honig's questions and in their infrequent conversations talked only business. Tax loopholes, trust stipulations. As soon as John finished architecture school, Randolph

Honig was ready to transfer millions of dollars in startup funds for John's own architectural firm. "You'll have no excuse to fail," Randolph had said, and John had made a feeble attempt to disguise his hatred.

He moved down the proposal form. Next they wanted a brief phrase describing the general "effect" or "look."

Nothing sleek, he wanted to write. Nothing made of brushed fucking steel like every zombie in his class was enamored of.

Starkness, he typed. That's what people didn't understand about churches from the early Middle Ages. They heard "medieval" and thought of the later, overdecorated cathedrals. But even there, beneath it all was starkness. People were afraid. Hell was a real possibility.

Erotic and spiritual at the same time, he wrote.

There needed to be wrought iron. There needed to be leather.

Two women, talking animatedly, sat down at the table next to him. John looked away but could see them in the reflection of his screen. Brunette and redhead. Late twenties.

"Marriage—what can I tell you?" the brunette was saying. "There's pros and cons."

"Right," said the redhead.

They stared at each other in silence and then burst out laughing.

"Well," the brunette said, "that takes care of the pros."

"That's what I tried to tell her, Iris. You should have a talk with her."

A waiter brought two enormous ice cream sundaes. The redhead glanced over at John, and he could see her eyes get larger and then quickly look away. Iris turned to see what had gotten her friend's attention. After she looked at him she seemed to get angry.

"It's simple," she said to the redhead. "Tell her it's a losing proposition. And the more he looks like a catch, the worse he probably is."

John grinned at her and she turned away. The ones who acted like they resented him were the ones who wanted him most.

The women continued their discussion over what turned out to be a multi-course dessert marathon. Every time the waiter came near, they ordered more: cookies, brownies, iced cappuccino with whipped cream.

John could have told them that the question of marriage was a simple one, if you'd gone to an all-boys' high school run by Dominican friars. In eleventh grade the religion teacher was Brother Gerrit. "According to our syllabus," he'd announced one day, "today's topic is Christian marriage. No doubt some of you expect to find at least one woman who's desperate enough to marry you." He moved around the room as he spoke, coming to a stop near John's desk and glaring at him, like all his predecessors in grade school and high school. John never could decide whether it was his wealth or his looks that excited their envy—among other things. "Extreme beauty is a curse," Brother Thomas had told him in the second grade. "Remember that, boy." Almost all of them gave him variations on that line.

Brother Gerrit had looked at John and said sourly, "Saint Paul tells us, 'It is better to marry than to burn.' And since I would never presume to improve on Saint Paul, we'll move on to the next topic."

Better to marry than to burn. Burn how, John had wanted to know. Burn in hell? Burn with unconsummated lust? But when he fucked, he felt he was on fire, so he burned then too. Great thing about the Bible. You could interpret it any damn way you wanted.

The brunette was getting more worked up as they talked. "At the bottom of every marriage contract," she said, "there should be a note in large print: From the time you sign this document till you sign the divorce papers, your husband has the legal right to rape you. You might get the police to arrest him if he punches your lights out or breaks some bones, but once he sticks his cock in you, that's none of their business. And honey, if you get sick of it all, whip out a knife and chop it off—*thwack*—they'll put *you* on trial."

John laughed. The women watched him as he called the waiter over and paid his bill. He probably should have written his phone number on a napkin and handed it to the brunette. He knew she wanted him. Let her burn.

~

In his hotel room he took a shower and put on clean clothes. He turned on the TV, then turned it back off. The sound of human voices was unbearably inane.

He thought back to that girl in college. A smart-alecky bitch with bad posture and no fashion sense. Way beneath him in terms of looks. Why he'd ended up fucking her in the first place he could no longer remember.

It had started with her.

He hadn't planned it, not the first time. He had been in his dorm room, and the girl was lying next to him naked, drifting off to sleep. He wanted to fuck her again but she said no, she was too sleepy. She turned on her side away from him. He pushed her onto her stomach and went in her. She started complaining right away.

"You're ripping me apart. You'll cause permanent damage. Pull out. Please."

He was so aroused no power on earth could have made him stop. He stroked her hair. "Relax," he said. "It won't hurt so much if you relax."

"You son of a bitch," she kept saying. "You bastard."

Not that he didn't like consensual sex anymore. The girl did too. She resented him, hated him maybe, but she wanted him so badly she kept coming around. Most of what John remembered from that second semester at college was their evenings of verbal sparring and fucking. She was viciously witty, and he was her favorite target. He respected that.

It never occurred to him to think of it as rape, though each time he did it she had clearly refused him and he pinned her down and penetrated her against her will.

He thought about the two women in the café today. The brunette was clearly interested. He would run into her again. They could have a nice conversation about rape.

Choices for the afternoon. Stay home and write the damn thesis proposal. Go to the bars. Go to St. Anthony's and badger the woman priest.

He stood up, looked at himself in the mirror. Black cotton jeans, black linen shirt. All he needed was a white collar.

He smiled at his reflection. The priest.

~

Averil, at her desk, doodled in her notebook in search of ideas for a sermon. She picked up a book on string theory, wondered if she could weave Jesus into it somehow.

She closed her eyes in an effort to picture multiple dimensions. Instead she saw an image, clear as a memory. A covered walkway, stone arches as far as she can see, leaded glass windows along one side. A cloister.

The memory is not only visual but engages all her senses. She feels the grit of stone floors beneath her sandals, smells the cool dampness of an early spring day.

Her abdomen throbs with menstrual cramping. Her breasts are heavy and aching. Like backstabbing gossip unfurling itself in her head come thoughts of the curse of Eve, the disgusting bodies of women, weak creatures.

Male voices whisper these slanders. Averil argues with them in her head as she walks down the corridor: *And yet you die just as we do. Dust to dust.*

~

John Honig tried not to look people in the eye. Especially women. When women looked him in the eye they tried to stake a claim on him, as if they had some right to his attention or they thought they could trap him with their clinginess and their need. He wore variable-tint glasses that got dark in the sunlight but never became quite clear indoors. "Take off your glasses," they would plead, or worse: "Look at me."

The corridor leading to the priest's rooms was so dark he had taken off his glasses and forgotten to put them on again. Before she could register surprise and irritation at his presence, there was a moment when she looked into his eyes with no protective barrier between them. He tried to forget it as soon as it happened.

"Don't you knock?" she said.

"If you wanted privacy you'd keep your door closed." He sat in the chair by her desk, surveyed the clutter. Paperwork everywhere, little statues, books, what looked like a deck of oversized playing cards. "What's that?" he said, pointing at a heavy terra cotta figurine.

"Not what. Who. Our Lady."

"An obese naked woman?"

"She has a thousand faces."

God, this woman was bizarre. You never knew what she would say next.

"Then isn't it sacrilegious, Father, to use her as a paperweight?"

"I like her to be in the thick of things. Was there a particular reason for this visit?"

"I thought I'd take a look at where the famous Reverend Parnell does her work."

"Famous is an exaggeration."

"No it's not. You're famous. I'm rich. If we were one person we'd be ecstatically happy. 'The two shall become one'—is that how it goes? I hardly pay attention to that shit. Not that either of us has spoken a wedding vow. How does that work for you? I mean, if you were a nun you'd be a bride of Christ, right? And then male priests would be married to the Holy Mother Church. Kind of incestuous, don't you think, Father? A man married to his mother?"

The priest's face was unreadable. John thought he detected a hint of a smirk, but only a hint, as if he weren't interesting enough to merit something as strong as irritation.

She hadn't been so indifferent the first time he saw her, two years ago, at the gambling club in New Falls. She'd been focusing her dark-laser stare at some fizz-brained man-whore flexing his delts in her direction.

The security guard had told John who she was, and he sat at the bar and watched her and played idly with the idea of fucking a priest.

What a fucking rush. Forbidden. Dirty. His mother was dead and he had no sisters. A woman priest was the next best thing.

He had gone home and played with the idea some more, and the idea turned into a fantasy, and then another, and finally he had such a violent orgasm that he thought he'd hurt himself.

He had still liked the idea the next morning, even after the fine glow of single-malt scotch had subsided.

And in an old monastery, to make things more perfect.

Now the priest leaned forward and squinted into his face. "What color are your eyes?"

This was going to be easier than he thought. "Hazel," he said.

"No they're not. They're the color of swamp water, tinged with algae. I've never seen anything quite like it."

He could feel himself getting erect. He nodded toward the other door. "That leads where? Your bedroom?"

"Why?"

He smiled. He knew the effect of his smile on women. "Aren't you going to show me, Father?"

"No."

His erection was getting more insistent. He could have pinned her down beneath him in a second. But there was a possibility she might be real. And anyway he saw the arousal in her eyes before she looked away and made her face go blank.

That would be enough for now. Let her think about it awhile. Play with it.

~

Catherine Beck turned on the news and muted the sound. She was on her exercise mat, stretching for her run. Achilles tendons, calves, quadriceps. Some pushups to get the upper body warmed up. A summer storm was threatening. She'd need to get out there quickly before it started.

She glanced up at the silent TV screen, saw the most recent crime-related headline: a girl abducted at age eleven, discovered alive after eighteen years. Isn't that great news, all the commentators gushed, glossing over the fact that a man had been raping her repeatedly over that whole time, keeping her prisoner in a backyard shed.

The story did have its own happy ending, Catherine knew: the bastard was sure to be murdered as soon as he got to prison. There were enough inmates, your basic drug dealers, your basic convenience-store hold-up men, who were all too happy to dispatch baby-rapists.

She pressed the Off button and headed out of her apartment, leaving the television to vibrate resentfully with the force of all its unwatched violence: the latest woman to turn up in a shallow grave after being dragged off by a stranger; the latest murder-suicide by an enraged ex-husband; the latest alert on the latest vanished little girl, her smiling face plastered everywhere.

Catherine ran down neighborhood streets, her face flecked with a raindrop or two from the gun-metal gray sky, her fair hair whipping behind her. An arrow directed at a target, always running toward, never away.

~

Averil could have sworn the church was empty. It felt empty. She had left a book here, a collection of Hadewijch's writings she had used as part of her sermon the previous week. She moved quietly up the side aisle, retrieved the book from the lectern, and was heading back when she saw him. Sitting near the aisle, smiling, arms stretched out along the back of the pew as if watching an entertainment instead of being in a house of God.

It had been a week since she'd seen him. She had vaguely been hoping that he would be away the rest of the summer.

"Do you know how glass is made, Father?" John Honig said, nodding toward the stained glass window nearest him. The Fourth Station of the Cross. Jesus meeting his mother.

She said nothing.

"Silica," he went on. "Do you know what that is? It's in sand, Father, and quartz. The most plentiful element on the surface of the planet. Common as dirt. And look at what it makes."

She couldn't help looking at the window, the reds of Jesus's cloak, the golds of his and Mary's halos merging. Sand, the same thing you find in a sandbox, a beach. Now become hard and luminous.

"And then you think about who would have made that glass, Father. For that window. Some idiot in a glass factory, some ordinary schmuck who went home every day and slapped his wife around and drank beer till he passed out in front of the TV. Long gone now, and look what that asshole left behind. Something real. You can put your hands on it, see it. It lasts. Can you say that about the work you do?"

Averil knew he was trying to bait her, get her on the defensive.

"I don't owe you an accounting of my life," she said.

"That's what God said to Job, isn't it, Father? Job complains about all the shit that's happened to him, and God shows up and says 'Who the fuck do you think you are?' I never thought that was a satisfactory answer."

Where wast thou when I laid the foundations of the earth?

Who laid the corner stone thereof; when the morning stars sang together, and all the sons of God shouted for joy?

It was annoying how right he was. Averil had had those same thoughts herself.

He stood up, moved close.

"Father," he said, "I want you to hear my confession."

He couldn't be serious. Please God, he had to be joking.

"I don't have time," she said.

"I'm a lapsed Catholic, Father. Aren't you priests always looking for people like me? To reconvert us?"

How handsome he was, this unlikeable man. The beauty and the unpleasantness were inextricable.

You're a priest, Averil, she told herself. You have duties.

Maybe he was sincere. Maybe she was projecting.

"Fine. The reconciliation office is down these stairs."

"No, I want it in the confessional booth. The old-fashioned way."

She went into her side of the booth and closed the heavy red curtains behind her. She tried to imagine cool breezes on her face. Still, her hands shook when she slid open the grate. She felt his presence on the other side. Something lying in wait, smiling.

"Will I go to hell," he said, "if I have sex with a priest? There's this one, Father, but she's so skinny, if I fucked her I'd break her in half."

She walked out of the confessional.

There had to be a special category of punishment for tormenting a priest.

Worse was knowing that the leering, whispery voice, the dead-quiet laugh were going to seep into her brain.

Even worse: she had been at a loss for words, couldn't even give him a lecture about taking the sacraments seriously.

Worst of all: the feeling that she had failed in her responsibility. Leaving the confession unfinished. An actor walking off stage mid-scene.

The kitchen was a refuge, the ordinariness a blessing: Peter and Marc moving from stove to table, sounds of forks and knives pulled from drawer, water poured into glasses, lids clanked on pots. Afterwards dishes to wash, then coffee in the sitting room, easy conversation and companionable tiredness after a long day. Peter was folding up his newspaper as he always did when he was about to go upstairs to bed, but Averil didn't want it to end, didn't want to be alone with her thoughts and the memory of the claustrophobic confessional, the mocking voice.

When she asked whether they could say the rosary together, Peter felt as embarrassed as if she'd asked for a hug, but he couldn't very well say no, not with Marc looking so eager and Averil looking so weirdly desperate. Sleep could wait.

~

Averil closed her eyes and listened to the voices of her fellow priests. They were the antidote, these good men, to John Honig and his disturbing games.

They reached the point where the words lost their meaning and ran together—blessedartthouamongwomen—and the only thing she was aware of was the triple current of their voices, Peter's deep-chested baritone and Marc's earnest tenor and her own voice, familiar as her heartbeat. That was the purpose of the rosary: the repetition, the joined voices, put you in an altered state, open to a feeling of deep devotion washing over you, or perhaps an image of the Mother God saying, *All shall be well, all shall be very, very well*, as She'd told Dame Julian of Norwich.

Peter's words softened into a consistent low rumble, until finally his chin rested on his chest, and the rumble became unmistakably a snore.

He had never had much patience for the rosary.

"I think this is my cue to leave," Averil told Marc. She tried not to sound disappointed.

"I'll put him to bed."

Back in her office she sat crosslegged in the armchair and closed her eyes again, breathed in, out, in. She would continue where their threefold voices had left off.

The rosary beads in her hands start to glow. They seem to multiply. As she runs them through her fingers she can't get to the end of the loop.

She hears the rustle of cloth, sweep of the Holy Mother's cloak, and suddenly the beads have broken loose from the rosary, are tumbling onto the floor and turning into dark red roses.

Averil lies on the petals, thick as a mattress, and no thorns.

She hears the voices of the monks in the choir, coming upstairs, now moving along her corridor. She is lying in the dark, listening to them approach. Someone is near her, she can sense the closeness of his body even though she can't see him, then his hard lean hands are circling her.

"You're so thin," he scolds as he touches her ribcage. "Like a starving person." His hand is moving along her leg, insinuating itself below the hem of her rough woolen robe.

She tensed, opened her eyes to the quiet empty room.

She must have been dreaming. But she didn't feel like she had been asleep.

~

John lay in bed, thinking about the priest and then about that girl in college. That final time.

She had made one of her usual blazing put-downs—what a talent she had—and John had laughed and said, "You little bitch, I'm going to fuck you till you bleed." For once she saw it coming ahead of time and tried to get away. He grabbed her and pushed her to the floor, but it was hard to keep her pinned down and pull her jeans off at the same time. She was struggling violently to get an arm or a leg free so she could start punching or kicking. That's what made him angry, the resistance. But his anger made him cold and calm, not frenzied.

He gripped her by the shoulders and shook her.

"This is going to happen," he said. "Don't fight me or I'll make it hurt even worse."

With a last swift movement he yanked down her jeans and underwear. He was lying on top of her, weight balanced on one arm while with the other hand he unzipped his jeans.

Lying in his bed now, remembering it, stroking his erection, he imagined confessing it to the priest.

"I clamped her wrists together, Father," he would say. "Pulled her arms over her head. I rammed my cock into her as hard as I could. But she wouldn't give me the satisfaction of seeing her cry."

He remembered her clenching her teeth, turning her face to the side.

"Tough little bitch, wouldn't you say, Father? I've never had such a satisfying fuck in my life."

His hand gripped harder, moved faster. As his semen spurted out he had a fleeting image of Averil in a forest that turned into a church, light streaming through green stained glass, colonnades like trees.

CHAPTER 6

BAPTISM

I think back on what I have lost,
I recall with great pain that for which I was destined,
and my heart shatters.

—St. Umiltá of Faenza, 13th century

Averil started her vigil the evening before the anniversary. She had eaten lightly that day: plums, blueberries, a peach, a sprouted green salad. Fifteen years.

She got things ready for meditation. Lit the candle on the nightstand, propped pillows against the headboard of her bed. Random memories floated to mind. The apartment she and Asher had lived in, the green-and-white-checked plastic tablecloth over a table that wobbled when they set their elbows on it. Asher studying in his bed, surrounded by texts and notebooks. How he smiled at her when she walked in.

She never referred to him as her boyfriend, or thought of herself as being in a couple the way normal people were, people who had no vocation for the priesthood. At the seminary they gossiped about her, she knew, but the only one who ever approached her was Monsignor Riggio, who was eighty-three and had seen more of life than the rest of them put together, he always told them. He was the ethics professor.

"A word of advice, Averil, for when you join the priesthood. If you're going to have a lover, be discreet about it. And for God's sake don't make it a Jew."

Forbidden fruit. Poisonous, or possibly sacred.

Blessed are the hungry.

She opened her eyes to a dark room. The candle had gone out.

Are you a priest of God? a voice says. A deep frowning voice. A patriarch's voice.

I am a priest of Jesus and Mary, Averil says.

I was there, she says emphatically. Defiantly.

I was there when the morning stars sang together. I shouted for joy.

~

The day before the ordination ceremony, she had told Asher she would attend the vigil at the cathedral, then go back to their apartment to spend the night with him, rather than stay overnight in her book-filled dorm room at the seminary.

He wanted her to promise, but she was evasive. "I don't know how late it'll run," she said. "Anyway we'll see each other tomorrow."

As if what would happen in the intervening time would make no difference to their lives.

But the vigil did run late. No one had wanted to leave the gathering, that last time the sister-seminarians would be together as a group before they became priests and went their separate ways.

Averil was so tired by the time she left that she gave no thought to her choice to go to her dorm. She remembered only when she woke up on that humid July morning, bathed in sweat and guilt in her narrow dormitory bed.

But her problems were larger than sweat and guilt and nervousness. She'd left her ordination vestments at the apartment.

It was only a ten-minute walk. Conveniently, she would have no time to make apologies, explanations. She would rush in, grab the surplice and cassock, and leave. And then some hours later she would walk back in, a Roman Catholic priest.

The apartment was empty.

No furniture in the living room, no food or pots and pans in the kitchen. Nothing in Asher's bedroom. She hurried to her own room. Everything was gone: her books, her clothing. Her ordination vestments.

She rushed from one closet to another and then started the search all over again. No matter how many times she looked, every closet was empty. She staggered to the kitchen and leaned against a wall, trying not to hyperventilate.

A note was attached by magnet to the refrigerator door.

I am not a sin. Please believe that I wish you nothing but the best. Asher.

She rushed back to campus. Luckily the ordination was taking place there at Mount St. Mary's, where she knew the cathedral and its complicated layout of basement meeting rooms, storage areas, and stairwells that led up

66

to various entrances into the church. She could hear the opening music play as she went through a parody of her search in the apartment, opening basement closets and rifling through the contents. Finally she found a cassock and surplice. They were the right length but were obviously made for a much heavier person. The cassock flapped around as she sprinted down the corridor in search of the stairs that would take her closest to where she was supposed to be at that moment in the church.

What a disgrace. An event of world-historic proportions, a new era in the Church. And she was going to be late.

It wasn't so much that Averil didn't hear the gunshots as that she didn't understand what they were—just more turmoil to add to the rat-a-tat of her own heart and her footsteps galloping up the stairs. She burst through the stairwell door and into incomprehensible chaos, the sound of shots now mingled with the screams of witnesses and the groans of dying seminarians. Averil slipped on blood and skidded to a stop before she dropped to her knees beside Elizabeth O'Hare's body. She crawled from one woman to another, looked into dead eyes as if to demand an explanation, as if by figuring out what was going on she could make it stop, make everything go back to what it was.

She had no sense of the passage of time. Later she remembered trying mouth-to-mouth resuscitation on a woman who was obviously dead of gunshot wounds. She remembered the horrified shock of all those lives draining away around her, all that devotion and brilliance and profundity. She expected to be riddled with bullets at any moment, and she ceased to care. She wasn't meant to survive whatever was happening.

Then people were lifting her body, blood-slicked as a newborn.

This one's alive!

They tore at her clothes, felt for bullet wounds. *Where does it hurt? Can you see me? Can you say something?*

It was only at the hospital that doctors discovered she had no injuries at all.

It was only at the hospital that she started screaming.

The nurses, wiping off the blood and wringing the cloths in a basin, stopped what they were doing, fearful of some damage they hadn't detected. A chemical burn, perhaps, or abrasions.

"Does this hurt you?"

"It's all that's left. Of them. Keep it, keep it."

The blood of martyrs, sacred beyond telling. It had spattered onto her, mingling on her skin. To see it stripped away from her was the last unbearable loss.

From being a scholar of medieval Christianity Averil skipped slid skated right over into being medieval herself. She grabbed the basin of bloody water and started to drink it. That was when the doctors decided to sedate her.

~

There had been twenty-three women seminarians in all: the twelve from Mount St. Mary's, seven from St. Joseph's, and four from Sacred Heart. They had decided to be ordained together, and the news cameras that had gathered to record the ordination of the world's first female Roman Catholic priests instead filmed their bloody, terrifying deaths.

Averil's own ordination was postponed for months. Some were surprised that she went through with it after the massacre, but for her it was either ordination or suicide.

During seminary she had imagined the elation she would feel at the laying on of hands, the reading of the long line of priestly succession that was—finally—touching women officially. She would feel the ancient link and know that all along it had had tributaries: women of the Spirit, women who ministered, who saw visions. Finally they would all be acknowledged.

And she had daydreamed about the triumph she would feel when, newly ordained, the women stood at the altar and lifted up the Eucharist, saying *This is my body* and making it so.

Instead, when she faced the congregation as the only female Roman Catholic priest in the world, she was a shivering, plucked bird, the one ragged survivor of a magnificent flock. She had no sense, flayed by trauma as she was, of the presence of twenty-two spirits crowded round, gripping her hands and wrists so that all of them held the Host aloft.

Years later, when she finally could manage to look at the media coverage of her ordination, she gasped at the deep lines of exhaustion and grief on her face that day. She was twenty-eight and looked like an old woman.

And so Averil Parnell started her priesthood. No companions, no lover. Solitary and celibate.

~

She thought of Asher constantly in the early years after her ordination. She caught herself looking for him in airports, in crowded train stations. Surely he was there somewhere. She was entitled to him.

The dreams started later. Desperate searches, then she would find him at last, after traveling far, enduring every hardship. He would be smiling, he had always known she would come. In one dream she found him in her parents' old neighborhood, in the house next to theirs, and she had cursed herself for not figuring it out earlier, of course he would be there, where else would he be?

But then she would reach for him and the dream would end.

In retrospect she knew Asher had hoped all along she would give up her ambition of becoming a priest. She must have suspected it even then, on some level. Neither one could express this deepest secret: his hope, her unwavering resolve.

The throne of Peter should have been the throne of Peter and Mary. Mary the Disciple, Mary the Beloved of Jesus, Mary the Witness to the Resurrection. She was entitled to it.

Her confessor had told her that if she prayed for relief, she would be spared the erotic dreams, the memories, the painful longing. She could never bring herself to make that prayer.

~

Some years on the anniversary, the weather provided a small measure of relief, rain or cloud cover, cooling wind. This time, the fifteenth year, there would be no such mercy. As Averil awoke she was already sweating. Not a hint of a breeze came through the open windows. Exactly the same weather as it had been then.

The monks of St. Anthony's watched in disapproval as she sat up in bed, feeling weak and feverish.

They were becoming impatient. To put things bluntly, Averil had failed to gain perspective on the tragedy, even after all this time. One must, after all, reconcile oneself with reality. Despair was a sin against the Holy Spirit.

Get up, child, they said briskly. *Busy yourself.*

Averil stumbled out into her office, looked at the paperwork on her desk, and decided she needed rote activity.

Outside she passed Marc on the way to the garden.

"Don't talk to me," she said.

Up one row and down the next, she pulled weeds from around the tomatoes, the corn, the basil. Ragweed, pigweed, dandelion, wild carrot, some plucked easily and others clinging by long taproots that she had to dig around.

There had been some shade in the early morning; now the garden was in full sun. Averil tried to wipe the sweat from her eyes and only succeeded in rubbing dirt into them. Next row was green beans, the only crop ready for picking. She didn't want to think. She wanted to be aware only of her legs aching from prolonged squatting, her skin itchy and sweating, her whole body longing for water.

The monks, appeased, evaporated away, and in their absence Averil's dour mood took a sharp turn into guilt.

Trained in pastoral counseling, Averil well knew the concepts of survivor's guilt, post-traumatic stress. The knowledge did nothing to quench the nagging thoughts, which formed a rhythm with her actions. Pick green beans. Put them in the basket. Move along the row. Pick more. Put them in the basket.

What a disappointment you are. The others should have survived. You are not worthy.

She crouched lower to get at the green beans near the bottom of the bushes, but as she tried to back out and straighten up, a branch got caught in her hair. The struggle to free herself enraged her. She tore the branch off the bush and then felt devastated at the senseless killing of the plant. With the garden shears she hacked away a chunk of hair and twig, threw the hair onto the ground and fell on top of it, weeping.

She may have slept. She felt calmer, at any rate. When she got to the kitchen with her baskets of green beans she was surprised to see that it was already three o'clock. Marc and Peter, understandably reluctant to interrupt the frenzied gardening, had left a pot of lentil soup on the stove.

She ate the soup cold while she planned the next phase: washing and cutting and canning the green beans. She would go and take a short nap first, thirty minutes maybe.

She woke up to cool darkness. The heat had broken. In the bathroom mirror she could see her face and hair streaked with dirt, her eyes staring out at her so fiercely they seemed to belong to someone else.

I'll be all right, she told herself. A shower, a little food. She needed to be gentle with herself.

Watching the flow of tepid shower water transfixed her. This was a gift, this water, this nighttime. The Mother always showed mercy.

She let herself into the Chapter House, made her way silently to the kitchen to slice bread and cheese. She reveled in the feeling of clean clothes against her skin, clean kitchen tiles against her bare feet.

It was almost eleven o'clock and she was wide awake. She headed for the church.

The sound of John Honig's voice made her flinch. Near the path, a dark shape distinct from the darkness around him.

There was a reason for his presence, she decided—a trial, a gift, maybe.

"I thought you were asleep, Father. There was no light on in your monastic cell."

"I was asleep," she said. "But I woke up." She answered him simply, without bantering or harshness. She was still feeling the gifts, the water, the mercy.

"I've never seen a barefoot priest before, Father. Why bother to put your collar on and your—priest's uniform, do you call it?—when you have nothing on your feet?"

She looked at her feet, surprised. Then thought longingly of the church. At this hour it was lit only by dim side lights, and of course the perpetual flame. There would be mercy there. Not the fires of hell. Mercy.

"I want to make love to you, Father," he said, "in your monastic cell with Jesus looking down at us from the cross. Or we can do it in the church. Don't you want to touch me, Father? We can do it in the church with Jesus looking down at us from every wall."

She took off her collar, and, after a moment, the small silver cross from around her neck. She stuffed them in her pocket and walked toward him slowly. Stopped when she was close enough to see his confident smile.

He nodded toward the Refectory. "Are we going inside, Father?"

"No," she said. "Over there." She pointed to the garden wall.

The moonlight illuminated his face against the gnarled mulberry branches. She put her hands on his shoulders.

"On your knees," she said.

He kept up an endless stream of talk. She heard bits of it, as if from a distance.

"The power of the priesthood isn't what it used to be." He held her hips against him and looked up at her. "In some other life you could have declared me a heretic and had me executed. Or would you have tortured me first, Father?"

To silence him she kissed him. She pushed him onto his back on the grass, felt her weariness dissolve as if his kisses, his strong hands, his hard young body were a battery to revive her.

~

I am a fool, Averil says.

The Fool has said in his heart.

71

Only fools rush in.

Fool for love.

They are large and ungainly, these fools, mumbling to themselves, their torn clothing flapping as they rush.

To the ship, they try to shout valiantly, but their words come out raucous and nonsensical as crow calls. To the Ship of Fools, moving as fast as their foolish, shambling gait can take them.

Averil journeys on that ship through dark blue-green water, toward a horizon where the sky is turning purple and the light has the golden quality of late autumn afternoon.

They arrive at the ends of the earth, where she sees an enormous oak door and knocks on it.

Who goes there?

A fool.

The door opens inward and she steps into a dim flagstone corridor, which leads her toward a dark, drafty little chapel. How familiar it feels.

A priest approaches as she enters the chapel. He has brown hair, not black, and his eyes are gray. The thought of his beauty, so clearly a sign of God's favor and yet so undeserved, torments Averil every night in her damp cell.

How unfair, she often reproaches the Lord in her prayers, how unfair to make me young, and him young, and let my thoughts stray from your unending praise.

"Tell me your sins, my love," the priest says.

Averil looks around to make sure no one else is near.

"You shouldn't speak to me like that," she says coldly. "I intend to be abbess someday. My behavior will always be above reproach."

"By that time, this monastery will be ruled by the bishop, and that will be me. The Holy Father doesn't approve of silly women having worldly ambitions and presuming to govern themselves."

"I have no worldly ambitions."

"Clearly you envy me my power."

She tries to move away without answering, but he puts a hand on her arm.

"Another thing," he says. "Pleasure is a gift from God." He laughs silently. "Think of that tonight in your lonely bed."

~

A vision.

It was stupid to pretend it was anything else—dream, daydream, hallucination, narcolepsy, side-effect of stroke.

It was a vision.

Averil had no wish to be a mystic. She had studied enough of them and tended to agree with the practical Teresa of Avila that the miracles and visions got in the way of the important work. But then, despite her formidable organizational skills, Teresa herself still had visions. She even levitated.

More unsettling than the sense that reality was shifting was the realization that she may have had visions before and hadn't recognized them. The eerie events at the Renaissance Faire, the Flagellants, the tapestry—had they really happened? And what did "happened" mean?

It would explain why people seemed to act as if Averil were confusing them. They may have been negotiating different realities, talking at cross-purposes. She may have been in the juice aisle of the grocery store while she thought she was standing in a field. She may have thought she was in a medieval monastery while actually riding the bus.

Visions had nothing to do with living a moral life. She needed to remember that.

CHAPTER 7

AGNUS DEAE

Love nothingness, and flee somethingness.

—Mechthild of Magdeburg, 13th century

What she tried not to think about kept crowding out all other thoughts.

She had slept with a man and was having some kind of hallucinatory experiences. A symptom of stress, no doubt. Caused by this man.

This man who was nothing. Shallow and arrogant and steeped in self-approval. He had no right to disrupt her life.

People say you're arrogant too, Averil.

It is what it is, she told herself. Then corrected herself. Past tense: It was what it was. A moment's weakness. Better not to think about it.

What she did think about, however, what she couldn't fail to notice was that St. Anthony's new patron seemed to visit more often that fall than would have been required for the planning phase of the restoration project, and that he managed to casually cross paths with Averil more often than the laws of chance would suggest and despite her best efforts to avoid him.

"Whatever happened," she said at the first of these encounters, "it won't happen again."

"'Whatever happened'? Can't you remember, Father? Should I describe it to you?"

Their stilted conversations, her obvious discomfort, were like foreplay to him. He would be primed for whatever woman he picked up later.

"You know what my dream is, Father?" he told her a few weeks later, when he'd finally found her alone in the church. "I'm going to build a medieval chapel. I'm doing the design for it now, for my architecture degree, but when I'm finished school I'll actually build it. Completely authentic materials, authentic methods."

She looked at him then. Intellectual curiosity for Averil was always impossible to resist.

"Why?" she said.

"Why not, Father? I'm rich, I can do whatever the hell I want. And it's not as crazy as it sounds. There's a guy out in California who found some ruined medieval chapel over in Europe and bought it, had it dismantled piece by piece and shipped to him. He's going to reassemble and restore it over here, completely renovate it so it looks like it did when it was first built."

"That plan will spend money, it won't make it. Rich people don't do anything that doesn't increase their wealth."

Amazing—the priest was practically quoting his father. You'd have thought Randolph Honig had gone into mourning, the way he'd carried on back when John decided not to finish his fucking MBA.

"You should approve of the plan, Father. Building a holy place. You could be the pastor if you want."

"That's not for you to decide."

"What's the holiest place you can think of, Father?"

She looked up into the gloom of the vaulted ceiling, as if some angel would swoop down and relieve her of her torment.

"A forest," she said.

That stopped him a moment. A church that looked like a forest. An image from that first night came to mind: looking up at her and past her, gnarled branches of the tree looming over them, and past the branches, the moon.

"You're not like other women, Father, do you know that?" She didn't give him wistful, longing looks, didn't don't touch him in that proprietary way women have. "Anyone looking at us would think we didn't have a relationship at all."

"We don't have a relationship," she said.

"That's not fair, Father. We're lovers. And I've confessed to you. You know me intimately. You should be nicer to me."

"We're not lovers."

"Actually we are, by any standard definition."

She stood to leave. "I have things to do."

"You can't leave me here with this erection, Father. That would be cruel."

"You have two good hands, don't you?"

~

At some point during the mission, as she always did, Catherine Beck reached a state of flow. Calm yet hyper-alert, prepared for every complication. Things took on the feel of being choreographed, as if the world became a vast game of chess, every piece moving simultaneously, and Catherine herself aware of each one, its placement at this moment and its every possible move and countermove.

When she was in this state she was completely alive. A force ran through her and she was only its instrument.

What that force was, she gave little thought to. Justice, perhaps she would have said if pressed. That was the only thing she did believe in—at least its possibility.

The delicious calmness lingered. Catherine tuned into one public radio station after another as she drove north, and again heard the news about the grandson of a famous politician found floating face-down in the marina near his home in Orlando.

Sometimes the announcer reminded listeners that the dead man, Robert Boyland Thorpe, had been acquitted last week of rape after a high-profile trial. Catherine recalled the news coverage during the court proceedings, photographs of the accused everywhere, a smug, good-looking white man. Too handsome to commit rape, one news commentator had gushed after the acquittal.

Not too handsome to die.

As she drove she listened to the same news cycle over and over, some items dropping out eventually, a few new ones added. A politician admitting to an affair and tearfully asking Jesus to forgive him. An infamous swindler sentenced to ninety-nine years in prison. Another major wave of layoffs in manufacturing plants. The announcers still mentioned the accused rapist found drowned, but eventually the story was demoted to one sentence, sure to be bumped from the news roster altogether by the next juicy celebrity bit.

But something happened to bring it back to the top of the breaking news.

"At this hour: A possible lead in the mysterious death of Robert Boyland Thorpe, nephew of Senator Boyland and member of the famous Boyland political dynasty. Police have now revealed that they've found graffiti at Thorpe's house reading *Death to Rapists*. We're speaking now to a member of the group that's claiming responsibility."

Catherine, genuinely curious, turned up the volume.

The graffiti, it turned out, rather than spraypainted for the dripping-blood effect, had been drawn in chalk on his driveway, as if college students were announcing a social event on campus.

"Just to be clear," the reporter said, "the name of your group is the same as the phrase you left at the Thorpe residence: Death to Rapists?"

"That's right," burbled a high-pitched female voice, chipper as a playground mom offering fruit slices to a toddler.

"Are you taking responsibility for this death?"

"Taking credit, you mean? I wish I could."

Catherine tried to imagine a visual to go with the voice. Sweater set in pastel colors, silk-gloss hair. Glassy-eyed smile.

So many disguises for rage out there. Some more decorous than others.

Soon enough, however, it was announced that the group members weren't suspects, and the news cycle churned on.

The newest headline was yet another "unexplained" explosion, this time at the Top Gun Association. It had been a year since those naval officers had run amok at a conference and went groping and pawing any woman they could find; some women had even been raped. There was not a single trial, civilian or military. After two formal investigations there was barely more than a slap on the wrist for a few individuals. Even that empty gesture produced howls of outrage at promising military careers cut short, the "warrior culture" being diluted with political correctness.

Now the Top Gun headquarters had been blown to bits, along with a few of its members. Officials were denying that there was any sabotage involved. Gas leaks, they claimed.

Catherine remembered the original coverage of the Top Gun conference rampage. The photograph on the front page of the *New York Times*, drunken men with fists raised triumphantly at the camera, mid-yell. One wore a t-shirt reading *Women Are Property*.

She drove all night and much of the next day, pulled over and slept at rest stops when she needed to. Just before reaching New Falls, she stopped at St. Anthony's.

She meant to ask Averil about the Top Gun bombing, whether you could invoke the just-war theory when you lit a stick of dynamite under a drunken rapist pig.

But she went through those monastery gates and she was in a different world.

Averil was in the garden, in her clerical-collared black clothing, getting progressively dustier as she knelt in the dirt and kept wiping her hands on her trousers.

"I'm turning the soil over," she explained. "Then we'll put a cover crop in. My father always called this 'putting the garden to sleep.'"

"Don't you have some kind of tilling machine to do that?"

"A rototiller, yes, there's a parishioner who lends us hers. I just wanted to work on some stubborn roots near the edges."

She set the shovel point-down into the soil and stepped on top of it with one foot to push it further in. Then she brought her other foot down on it too, hopping as if to magnify the weight of her hundred-pound body.

Catherine was tempted to take the shovel away from her. Instead she went to the tool shed and got another one for herself.

Averil seemed content to work quietly side by side. To get her to talk, Catherine had to ask questions, and gradually they moved from gardening to other topics—books, travel. Averil started telling her about being a grad student, traveling for her research, going to archives in Rotterdam and Hamburg, Lyon and Paris. She had tried to imagine the cities as they had been seven or eight hundred years ago, the way they had looked to the women whose words she was reading, women of whom Catherine had never heard: Hadewijch of Antwerp, Gertrude of Helfta, Mechthild of Magdeburg.

"I managed to solve a minor mystery," Averil said, and even as she said it she knew she was bragging. She would have stopped there, but Catherine was waiting for her to go on. She explained about Hadewijch's series of poems, the *Mengeldichten*. The later poems in the series had been attributed to someone else, anonymous until Averil had discovered her identity: a woman named Rikardis at the same beguinage, a disciple of the elderly Hadewijch.

The monk-spirits, always interested in the garden, had gathered nearby and were frowning in disappointment. All that potential—the languages, the book-learning, the ferocious intellect and devotion. Her illustrious career in the church had come to a halt before it properly had a chance to begin. She'd gone from brilliant young scholar to ordinary parish priest in a ghetto. And now here she was, clothes muddy, hair unkempt, hopping on a garden shovel like someone trying unsuccessfully to use a pogo stick.

"You don't often hear of a woman having disciples," Catherine said.

"That's true. It must be quite a burden."

The young male priest brought out slices of peach cobbler still warm from the oven and they sat at the picnic table, sweaty and pleasantly tired.

The question about the bombing never came up. The last thing Catherine wanted to think about was war.

~

"I'd like to tell you a story," Averil began. She watched the people in the pews as they relaxed, sat back. Everyone liked to hear stories.

This one was about Sun Bu-er, a renowned holy woman and poet who lived in China in the twelfth century.

Sun Bu-er's spiritual advisor told her that if a person wanted to reach enlightenment, they had to travel to the holy city of Loyang, and spend twelve years there, studying and meditating.

"But *you* can't go to Loyang," the man told her. "It's a thousand miles away, and how would you travel there? Bandits will see a beautiful woman alone on the road and try to rape you, and you'll kill yourself to avoid dishonor. What's the point in throwing your life away?"

Averil paused in her telling, risked a tangent to talk about beauty, what it must be like to be burdened by it—"Not that I would know," she joked, and the congregation laughed quietly.

Sun Bu-er knew her husband would never go with her to the holy city. He wasn't an evil man, he simply didn't take her seriously as a devotee of the Tao. As far as he was concerned, it was a great kindness even to let her study under his own renowned teacher. So Sun Bu-er went to the kitchen and heated up some cooking oil. She poured cold water onto it and let the hot oil spatter over her face.

"While Sun Bu-er healed from the wounds on her ruined face," Averil said, "she let her hair go uncombed until it was matted and filthy. She dressed in rags and acted as if she were insane, laughing one moment, crying the next. She ran away from her husband's mansion and began her thousand-mile journey, disguised as a mad beggarwoman."

Or maybe, thought Averil, it wasn't a disguise.

Sun Bu-er reached her destination and spent the next twelve years there, praying and meditating. Then she returned to her husband's estate.

Next came the part Averil loved best.

"Friend in the Tao," her husband said to her, "how greatly you must have suffered."

"Brother," answered Sun Bu-er, "it is impossible *not* to suffer in pursuit of the Tao."

79

Averil closed her eyes. Spacetime, or timespace, unfurled behind her eyelids, an undulating purple fabric that dissolved her into itself. She stood there with the two of them, the woman transformed into a master teacher, one of the Seven Immortals of Taoism, and the man who had tried to hold her back.

"Her husband," Averil said, "had the humility to learn from her. He left on a spiritual quest, and Sun Bu-er went her own way, too. They never saw each other again."

She knew that since this was a sermon, she should try to explain it somehow, attach a moral that made it relevant to people centuries later and of a different faith. Instead, she simply left them with the image of the holy woman, face scarred and pitted. Sun Bu-er, Rose of Lima, any woman who disfigured herself so she could slide out from under the expectations of her misogynist world.

"Interesting," Peter Byrne said after the service. "Maybe next time you might want to mention Jesus."

~

The autumn slid into the Advent season. With every month that elapsed, Averil receded further from the indiscretion of July. Now more than ever, the cold weather felt like a safe retreat, a refuge. It was easier now to avoid John Honig: she spent less time outdoors, and he was busy, she presumed, with his classes.

Except that he showed up at St. Anthony's pre-Christmas party. He even had the presumption to give her a Christmas present, a small, book-shaped package that now lay unopened on her desk. She kept glancing over at it as she got ready for Night Prayers. St. Augustine's conversion experience came to mind, how he heard children somewhere playing a game and singing, "Take it and read it," and had picked up the Bible and opened to a line that changed his life. She highly doubted that John Honig had given her anything life-changing, at least not in a positive way. Still she felt curious. She had to open it sometime, and it would be ungracious to simply never acknowledge it.

The gift was indeed a book, a hardcover by a respected scholar entitled *The Great Heresies: Historical Struggles to Define Catholic Doctrine*. A message from Honig on the inside cover page said that he looked forward to discussing it with her.

What made a heresy "great," she wondered—how many enthusiastic followers it had at its peak, or later, how cataclysmic the defeat, how many mowed down by forces of king or pope, how many interrogated with rack and thumbscrews, how many burned at the stake. And all sides, everyone, believing passionately in Jesus, some willing to kill and others to die for the man who preached pacifism.

Taking the book with her, Averil opened the door to her bedroom.

She steps into a small, circular stone-walled chamber, like a room in a tower but airy and well lit despite the lack of windows. Daylight filters in somehow. There is only enough room for a kneeler and a red glass candle stand. Gray sky is visible in an opening far above her. She is at the bottom of a well.

She kneels down and starts to whisper, "Hail Mary, full of grace."

Echoes start up, all around her, soft voices in different tones and languages:

Ave Maria

Wees gegroet Maria

vol van genade

The voices float around her, fill the chamber, all the accumulated prayers sent out over all the centuries, and she is comforted.

Ruega por nosotros pecadores,

ahora y en la hora de nuestra muerte

Then Jesus is there, dressed in the rough brown wool of a monk, reaching down to help her climb out.

"I want to see your mother," Averil says to him, watching her breath make steam vapors in the room, which is suddenly freezing.

Brother Jesus smiles and wraps his arms around her. He puts her to bed and stays there with her as she falls asleep, cuddled against his warm robes. She has not been enveloped this way since she was a small child in her mother's arms.

~

At his stepmother's funeral John Honig stood next to his father and looked appropriately serious. His father wasn't a bad-looking man. As usual, the dignity of a widower suited him well.

"The best wife a man could ask for," he heard Randolph Honig murmur to Lily's weeping parents.

He'd said that at the funeral for Kathleen, too, and probably at the funeral for John's mother as well. Nine was old enough to remember something like that, he thought. He probably hadn't been paying attention.

He didn't look like his father, never had. After his mother died, John sometimes felt tempted to carry a family photograph to prove that he did have some connection with Randolph Honig.

At fifteen, a sophomore in high school, he had a girlfriend who was a senior honors student. "Your family history is straight out of a gothic novel," she said. "See, your mother is Rebecca, and your father is Max de Winter, and there's that stunning portrait of her in your entrance hall. You look so much like her it's scary."

"Except my father didn't murder my mother."

The girl had narrowed her blue eyes to look mysterious and knowing. "Can you be sure?"

"I saw her die myself. Cancer."

That shut her up. She apologized for weeks. John learned how useful pity was for getting a girl to put out. Any old lie would work.

And it could have been true. Cancer was what they told him. But his mother had looked healthy to him, right up to the last day. And with a long-expected death you wouldn't think people would be rushing around the house stunned. Lowering their voices, exchanging meaningful looks whenever he was nearby.

Another problem with the girlfriend's theory was that the second Mrs. Honig wasn't a pale blonde nobody like the second Mrs. de Winter. Kathleen was a short, curvaceous redhead with a loud voice. She wasn't a natural redhead, a fact she had demonstrated to John when he was seventeen. Only a few months before her car accident.

The third wife fit the bill perfectly: colorless, neurotically shy. Not at all interested in sex with John either. He still wasn't sure what Lily died of, but he could be sure of a tasteful wedding celebration not too far in the future. His father seemed to think two years was a decent interval between burying one wife and marrying the next.

"You have called your daughter Lily from this life," the priest was saying. "Lead her safely home to heaven..."

He thought about what the priest, *his* priest, would say in this situation. Not that she noticed his comings and goings. Or asked anything about him. How would he even start? *I was at a funeral today, Father.* And then what? It was impossible to imagine platitudes coming out of her mouth. *My condolences. Were you close?* Impossible to imagine any sort of comfort from her, or even normal human contact—not that he wanted that, usually. Still, any other woman, after he'd fucked her, would sidle up to him and act all playful, try to make eye contact, look inside. Such sickening neediness. The priest didn't do any of that.

82

"May eternal light shine on her, O Lord, with all your saints forever, for you are rich in mercy. Give her eternal rest, O Lord, and may perpetual light shine on her forever, for you are rich in mercy."

A lot of redundancy there, John wanted to say. You already have the light being eternal, so of course it's going to shine on her forever.

And rich in mercy? The people who brought us eternal damnation. The Inquisition. The witch hunts.

He was starting to smile as he watched the foolish priest mumble his lines, but he sensed Randolph Honig turn his head to look at him and made the smile disappear just in time.

Like a prison-wall searchlight, his father's gaze raked across him and moved on.

John returned to his own thoughts.

He would tell her while they fucked. In the church—he still hadn't convinced her to try that. He would be on his back, lying on the altar, she stretching above him like the sky.

My mother is dead, he would say.

Yes, she would say.

Or: *We all have to die.*

Or: *There has never been a time when I did not exist.*

The coffin was lowered. People threw flowers into the grave. Roses and carnations and, of course, lilies.

"Merciful father," the priest said, "guide us on our pilgrim way to your kingdom."

Back at his hotel room John was going to watch some porn but stopped to watch the news headlines. They were still yammering on about the explosion that morning. The corporate headquarters of Con-Mart had been completely destroyed, a week after it had defeated a decade-long lawsuit for sex discrimination filed against it by its female employees.

"While early reports assumed the presence of an explosive device," the announcer said, "authorities now insist that the cause was a gas leak."

"Right," John said. "Those bitches were pissed off."

It was useful to watch the news from time to time. Gave him a little inkling about how ordinary people lived.

Not that he gave much of a damn.

An ordinary life, for John Honig, had always been something to be avoided. And yet he felt that in a parallel universe somewhere, that ordinary life was being lived by a parallel self. Sometimes whole scenes from that life would unspool in his imagination. The parallel John pulls into his driveway after work. The next-door neighbor shuts off his mower

83

to wave at John and call out, "Hey there! Been out of town?" Or he arrives at his office job, sets his briefcase on his desk, and the woman in the next cubicle pokes her head around the corner and says in a fake-hearty voice: "Where ya been? We missed you."

"A funeral," John would have to say, which was true, in this life and the parallel one, only in the parallel life there would be an awkward silence, after which the questioner would offer unfelt condolences.

"Oh, I'm sorry. A family member?"

"A stepmother."

"How sad. Was it sudden?"

"For her, maybe. Not for anyone who knows my father. Luckily he has the taste not to have his wives buried all in a row."

The conversation would deteriorate from there.

He thought it was a talent, to know that something was outrageous and then say it anyway. At school the Dominican brothers felt otherwise. "You've got a devil in you, boy," Brother Philip used to say.

If so, it was the finest part of him, that devil. The part that was most alive.

CHAPTER   8

VISITATION

I saw an immense precipice, with dark water underneath.
And the angel said to me, "Here you see the abyss."

—Elisabeth of Schönau, 12th century

The gray brooding afternoon darkens into snowfall. The monks of St.
Anthony's, in procession, cross the courtyard between the Chapter
House and the South Transept door.

Their chanting, mournful voices, tenor and baritone, are muted by
the cold, by time, by the snow starting to accumulate under their sandaled
feet. Averil watches as they shuffle past, heads down, oblivious to her,
absorbed in the music they make together, their certainty that God is
listening, pleased.

That certainty is what angers Averil, what propels her to go around to
the front door of the church and walk boldly toward the altar, head high.
She manages to make her shapeless black coat and scuffed snow boots
seem like the finest cardinal's vestments as she sweeps up the aisle and
stands defiant before the tabernacle.

She is a priest and they are not.

After two thousand years of the door shut in her face, it is she, not
these pious singing monks, who can forgive sins, cast out demons, call
down the blessing of heaven and the wrath of God. She is the one who
has received ordination, the laying on of hands by the bishop, who had in
turn been ordained, and so it had gone, priest by priest, an unbroken line
to the first bishop of Rome.

"Do you see all this?" she says to the monks. "This is mine. Stone
upon stone. It's been mine all along."

The monks look at their sister-daughter, all flyaway hair and exposed
nerve endings, fragile as an autumn leaf. They meditate upon the Deadly

Sin of pride, how it creates a fog in the mind, a sense that one is entitled to what one has and accountable to no one. Perhaps arrogance is the better term here, they speculate. Whatever it is, they can't begrudge her. She wraps it around her like a protective cloak. The only thing holding her together.

Averil hurried through the Night Prayer and went to bed early, too tired to extinguish the candle on her nightstand.

Hours later, a noise outside her office door made her open her eyes to a cold dark room. The candle had burned out.

John Honig stood at the threshold.

She hadn't seen him in months, since before the Christmas break, had allowed herself to hope that he had tired of whatever he was playing at. That maybe she could learn to stop thinking about that night in July.

She felt no alarm, just vague surprise that he could be so comfortable moving around at night, navigating through a strange building with no lights on.

"Didn't I lock the door downstairs?" she said.

"Good to see you too, Father. You always make me feel welcome."

In her half-awake state she remembered something about ghosts, or was it vampires? If you don't invite them in, they can't enter.

"I have something to show you," he said. "Come with me."

They were in the car only a few minutes. John had rented a small house just beyond the monastery grounds.

He didn't bother turning on the lights. From starlight and a gibbous moon through the uncurtained windows there was enough light to see by. She walked from room to room, window to window. She could see a metal table in the kitchen, piled with books and coffee mugs. What should have been the living room and dining room were empty.

A creek in back of the house was the border to the monastery's land, and there were trees on the other three sides. No other houses were within sight. Massive oaks and maples stood silently, bare and stark.

A bedroom, also with uncurtained windows, contained only a mattress on a wooden frame.

He was standing behind her, close.

"Did you miss me, Father?" he said.

"I don't even like you."

She sensed rather than heard his smile, felt it as his lips brushed against her neck, then up toward her jawline, down again toward her collarbone. His hands rested lightly at her waist.

She was already so aroused she could hardly stop her body from arching against him.

"I like to watch you say Mass, Father," he whispered. "You should feel how hard my cock gets when you consecrate the Host."

"You're disgusting."

Now his hands started moving.

"One of these days, Father, I want to fuck you when you're wearing those priestly robes. Holding a Communion wafer."

"That's never going to happen," she said as they pulled each other stumbling toward the bed.

Afterward she put on her clothes quickly and got up.

"I'm not coming back," she said.

"See you soon, Father."

She walked back the way they had driven. She left her parka unzipped so that by the time she got back to her room she was shivering violently.

She wanted to feel no comfort. She wanted to put this behind her and never do it again.

But of course she did it again. Two or three weeks would go by with no contact. Then he would phone, or show up at the monastery, and she would say no, and then she would wind up there in the dark, comfortless cottage.

She should have known it even then, after that first night in the cottage when she was back in her own bed trying to recite the Night Prayer. Her teeth were chattering so hard she couldn't form the words. Then she feels a hand grasp her arm as if telling her to stop.

A priest with steel-gray hair, in the rough woolen robes of the monastery.

She glares at him. That priest's collar—he is unworthy and they both know it.

Kneeling by her bed he holds up a chalice, inviting her lips to taste, to kiss.

"This is my blood," he says.

~

Catherine Beck hadn't known what she had expected to find in Erda when she finally visited during the spring. It was hard to stop thinking of it as North Dakota, though the secession was decades ago. People in the U.S., when they talked about Erda at all, used words like "matriarchy" and "hippie peace freaks" and "utopia," but "matriarchy" wasn't quite the right word, as many Erdans were happy to explain to a visiting stranger. They organized their society along matrilineal lines, meaning that women lived with their mothers and siblings, not fathers and husbands. As for the "peace freak" part, one Erdan had exclaimed, "Hippies are white people. You see many of them around?" She had to admit she didn't, but the people she did see, Black or Asian, Latina or Native or White, somehow had the look of flower children. Serene and tolerant. Not terribly well dressed. Slightly buzzed. A multiracial utopia that had left behind all the things that plagued the U.S.: crime against women, police brutality, racism, extremes of wealth and misery.

A perfect place, Catherine thought, to rent a second home, a place to run to. In case.

She met with the person who seemed to be the director of immigration and several other divisions. Selene Marisela, a young Black woman with a commanding presence, was clearly used to being in charge and obviously on her way up. Whatever "up" meant in a place as radically egalitarian as Erda.

Catherine told her that she wanted to do volunteer work. "I can teach all kinds of self-defense. Plus handgun safety, marksmanship."

Selene smiled. "We're always on the lookout for experts who can teach their skill," she said. "Carpenters, metalsmiths, glass-blowers. People who know how to raise poultry or weave cloth, or preserve garden vegetables. But pointing a gun at someone? Not sure how the average Erdan would react to that."

Catherine wasn't surprised. The country was like a huge Quaker meeting, or a mini-Canada.

"Not that things are perfect here," Selene said. "We do have things to worry about. Just the fact that we exist has always bothered—let's call them a certain segment of the U.S. population. And now that we have a Black woman as our president, they're really foaming at the mouth. And they're starting to organize."

"Angry white men with guns and grievances," Catherine said.

"Right. Nothing new there, but one group in particular seems to be making a lot of noise. Calls itself a militia. The Aryan Awakening or some such bullshit."

"Erda has a border patrol, doesn't it?"

"No."

"Has your government ever talked about forming an army?"

"Have you met our leadership?"

"Do you at least have a national guard?" Catherine said.

She seemed to think that if she asked the right question she would arrive at the answer she wanted, an answer that would reveal the existence of some group of armed, trained, organized Erdan citizens.

"Don't think I haven't brought it up with the Council of Elders," Selene said. "The whole country talks about it. You should hear the objections. If we form a standing military, it'll disrupt our karma. We'll be putting combative vibes out into the cosmos. We'll draw the energy of potential enemies."

The two women looked at each other in silence.

"What the fuck," Catherine said finally.

"Yeah, well, people feel like, we've got our paradise on earth, our looms and windmills and organic farms on our little postage stamp of land, and that's all we're going to care about."

"And if these white supremacists decide to cross your borders and start shooting?"

"Like you said. We're fucked."

"There's always mercenaries," Catherine said.

"Only if they're willing to work for free."

"You might be surprised."

~

The history of Erda is well-enough known. By the end of the twentieth century, North Dakota had been rapidly depopulating for decades.

Then came the old women.

They rumbled across the border in their RVs. They put down roots, pooled their resources, bought tracts of land. Slowly they won elective office across the state—county commissioners, state senators, mayors, even governor.

There was almost no functioning cash economy. People survived on bartering and subsistence farming. They grew weather-beaten, even the young ones.

When North Dakota seceded to form Erda and several Indigenous American nations, the U.S. scratched its collective head. But by then so many crises were occurring that Americans soon stopped paying attention.

People poured into Erda from all over. Whatever they had been in their old lives, white collar or blue, urban, suburban, high-tech, highly educated, somehow when they got to the great northern plains they all turned into flower children. Power suits one day, cotton dresses and sandals the next. They wove their own cloth, grew their own food, didn't mind babies crawling about underfoot at their co-op meetings. They worked on school budgets and land allocation, drew up plans for watermills and windmills. They lived in houses built from haybales and recycled wood as if they'd never heard of steel and reinforced concrete.

Occasionally some debate over Erda would arise in the U.S. Some thought there would have been no point in keeping the state anyway. Some thought the secession had been a joke all along. Others were sure that the new, tiny country of old women would eventually fall apart and be absorbed into the Union again. After all, the pundits snickered, those old gals aren't getting any younger.

They failed to understand that some women, even before getting old, thought a country run by old women would be the sanest place to live.

The pundits also forgot that the supply of old women, after all, constantly replenishes itself.

And they had never grasped the meaning of the new country's name, Erda. Erda the Goddess Mother. Erda the Earth Herself. The entire earth.

~

In the middle of her room is a table with a chess board set up on it. Sitting at it is an old man with calculating eyes and a gem-encrusted pope's miter on his head.

"You can go first," he says solemnly.

The exquisite quality of the Pope's chess pieces has Averil riveted: the knight, a living man in miniature, in white armor on a pale horse that whinnies and stomps, the bishop in robes of white silk, the rook constructed of tiny Italian marble blocks.

"Which one were you?" she says as a delaying tactic. Her own pieces huddle near her, refusing to step onto the board. It's hard to get a good look at them. "Gregory? Leo? Urban?"

"Clement," he murmurs.

"The one they called the Butcher of Cesena?" She tries to grasp a squirming bishop. "Or the one who wiped out the Knights Templar so King Philip wouldn't have to repay his debts to them? That took some master strategizing."

"Do you think *you* are any less corrupt?" he hisses.

Her chess pieces turn into dozens of tiny snakes that swarm across the board and writhe gracefully over the Vatican pieces.

Then they disappear and she is sitting alone.

~

She pushed past Honig when he opened the door, headed straight for the bedroom. She craved sexual release, spurred perhaps by the irritation she'd felt, a murderous old pope accusing her of immorality.

She sat down on the edge of the bed. John took off his shoes. His leisurely pace was one more annoyance. She wanted to pick a fight with him, slap him hard.

"Tell me about your ambitions, Father. Would you like to be a bishop? A cardinal?"

"No."

Starlight came through the windows and shone on the bare wooden floorboards. John lay on the bed fully clothed, as if it were the most natural thing to lie there and talk, rather than tearing each other's clothes off.

"Can we get to it?" she said.

"You'd love to be Pope, I bet."

"I've never said that."

He sat up and took off his shirt. "Sex is like confession, don't you think, Father?" he said. "What more intimate human contact could you have than listening to someone tell you their sins?"

"They're not the same. Confession isn't mutual. It's all one-way. I don't tell the penitent about my sins."

"What's so mutual about sex? I fuck, I don't get fucked."

Completely naked now, he went around to the other side of the bed, knelt down and began pulling off her clothing. He pushed her back onto the bed, ran his hands up and down her emaciated body. She looked like an ascetic starving in the wilderness.

"Are they going to canonize you, Father, now that you're a mystic?"

"What are you on about now?"

"It's what they're saying. Didn't you know? You see things. Things that aren't there."

In her panic she hardly heard what he said after that.

This was impossible. She hadn't mentioned the visions to anyone. Her mind raced through one incident after another, times when people around her exchanged looks with each other, then looked at her warily, or in hopeful awe. Once when she had been a guest preacher at a parish in Vermont, she'd asked about the old woman standing near the door, and got only odd looks in response. Or when she was visiting a dying man in the hospital and commented on the beautiful music coming from the radio. The patient had nodded in agreement, but his family members were silent, and when she was on her way out of the room she had seen that the radio was unplugged.

She was giving herself away without knowing it. She should not say anything. Ever.

"Word's spreading, Father. You're the newest sensation in the Church."

She felt sick with anxiety. This was the last thing she wanted. It would have been better if people thought she was mentally ill.

"Are they going to canonize you when you're dead, Father? 'Cause that's one hell of a rush, to think I'm fucking a saint."

CHAPTER 9

EPIPHANY

When we asked her what she had seen,
she said, "I would tell marvels if I dared."

—*The Life of Marie d'Oignies*, 1215

For the first time, Averil observed the anniversary of the Cathedral
Massacre with a few friends, in a brief ritual at sunset in the clearing
to the north of the playground. For the vigil in the church that night,
however, she wanted solitude.

At the altar she lit twenty-two taper candles and slipped a glass
hurricane lamp cover over each. Protecting the fragile, precious flames.

She sat in the front pew, she and the flames contemplating each other,
breathing together, in, out.

Gradually she became aware of the voices in the choir stall: the monk-
spirits, praying the Litany of the Saints, in Latin. They moved on to the
Requiem Aeternam.

Eternal rest grant unto them, O Lord, and let perpetual light shine upon them.
Maybe it was just as well. Better not to be alone.

The Lord will open to them the gate of paradise, chanted the monks, *and
they will return to that homeland where there is no death, but only lasting joy.*

Lasting joy. And for the survivor, lasting bitterness.

Sitting with eyes closed in front of the retinue of candles, Averil
smelled rather than heard the person approaching her. The smell of
battlefield dirt and saddle leather and blood, a warrior striding up the
aisle, glowing with triumph.

She turned. Catherine Beck, poised as ever, stood close enough to
notice that Averil smelled of sweat and torment.

"I wish I'd been there," Catherine said. "To kill the son of a bitch
before he ever had a chance to touch the trigger."

Averil saw that the monks had gathered near Catherine and were stirring uncomfortably. Dismayed at her anger, perhaps. Or her beauty.

She drew in her breath, surprised that she was still seeing them when another person was near. Catherine reacted too, perhaps to Averil's body language. She looked around, slipped her hand inside her jacket.

"Are we alone?" she said.

We're never alone, Averil wanted to say. But she needed to calm Catherine down before she drew a gun in a holy place.

"There's nothing to worry about," she said.

Catherine sat down next to her in the pew, looked at the candles arrayed in front of them. "There's another phrase from the Bible I remember," she said. "Something about 'people who hunger and thirst for justice.' Or have I misremembered that too?"

"You haven't misremembered," Averil said. "It's in there."

"And what does the Bible say about them?"

"That they're blessed. That they'll have their fill."

"Do you believe it?"

More like wishes, the Beatitudes had always seemed to Averil. Blessed are the meek, for they shall inherit the earth. All kinds of promises, to the peacemakers, to the merciful.

Catherine thought of her mission that day. Unexpectedly, this one had put up a fight, they'd grappled on the floor like a pair of energetic lovers. She was in too close contact to draw her gun and had to use her knife instead, and then act quickly to leap away, in the opposite direction of the blood flow.

And then she had come here.

"I want to tell you a story," Catherine said.

The story was about an ex-cop who was a wife-beater. When his wife left him he tracked her down and shot her five times. The case never went to trial. The police—his former colleagues—mishandled the evidence and bungled the investigation so badly that the prosecutor dropped the charges.

Now this man had been found dead, his throat slit, this very evening.

Catherine kept her voice quiet so as not to rouse the odd echoes she noticed in this church. "Who do you think would have killed this man?" she said.

"It could have been an ordinary street crime. Or maybe a relative of his wife."

"Maybe a stranger," Catherine said, "who wanted to see justice done."

"Someone with no personal connection to the crime? They would have to be on a crusade of some sort."

"You know there are 'crusades,' as you call them, going on out there. Some have probably confessed to you."

The monks, robes rustling, had moved back to the choir and were singing Vespers. Averil wondered if they were trying to drown out Catherine's voice.

"A man like that deserves to die," Catherine said. "He would be more use as compost for that vegetable garden of yours than he ever would alive." With the altered perception she always experienced after a mission, Catherine knew that Averil heard what she was truly saying. "What would you do," she went on, "if you met someone on that kind of crusade?"

Averil's dark eyes had lost the distracted, hapless look they often had. "Let's say that you were this person," she said. "Hypothetically."

"Let's say I am."

"I would tell you that this sounds like a killing in cold blood. If the man wasn't armed, he had no way to defend himself."

"Neither did the woman he murdered. Any man who assaults a woman has declared war on all women. That man wasn't a civilian, he was a combatant."

"But there are rules, even for the conduct of war. The Geneva Conventions—"

"—don't recognize that men are constantly waging war against women. What do I care about the Geneva Conventions? Women didn't make those rules. Women have never had a say in the rules."

"If you had carried out this kind of killing," Averil said, "I would worry about the effect on your soul."

"A soul does me no good," Catherine said, "if it gets in the way of justice."

She didn't want help, Averil saw, let alone forgiveness, or even understanding. This was no confession. It was a proclamation. She wanted to be known, plain and simple. Truly known by at least one other person in this life.

The monks, quiet now, looked at Averil and waited for her answer. She had no answer.

"When I was a teenager," Catherine said, "a week wouldn't go by without an article in the paper about the latest rape-murder. Always the same plot, you know. A parking lot in broad daylight. A man spots a woman he doesn't even know, who's never done a damn thing to him. He abducts her, rapes her. Murders her. Throws her naked body away like so much useless trash. And I used to think, I want to be there."

For the first time in her life, Averil saw the sister-seminarians, crowding round them and holding their candles high. She realized she had always felt their presence. All these years.

They were singing the Benedictus: *Salutem ex inimicis nostris, et de manu omnium, qui oderunt nos.*

May we be saved from our enemies, and from the hand of all who hate us.

"I want to be there when he first sets eyes on her," Catherine said. "When he raises his knife. When he positions himself to rape her. I want to grasp him by the hair and slit his throat open and watch him die slowly."

And thou, child, sang the sister-seminarians, *shalt be called the prophet of the Highest.*

Who do you mean, Averil wanted to say. Her or me?

~

Later Catherine thought of Averil's face, her delicate skin that seemed to glow with inner light, or maybe fever, and the fine lines at her eyes, along her forehead, like someone prematurely aged. She realized she wanted to touch that skin and felt bewildered by this longing. She'd been with women occasionally, but the encounters were playful, spur-of-the-moment.

This was different.

~

Averil walked in before John had time to get to the door.

"Don't talk to me," she said.

"Hello to you too, Father."

She stopped. "Why did I never notice this place doesn't have air conditioning?"

"Maybe you were distracted."

"I want your bathtub."

Summers were never good for Averil. She didn't do well in the heat, she missed the long meditative darkness of autumn and winter evenings, and of course at the height of the summer was the anniversary of the Cathedral Massacre. Usually by the time her birthday came along at the end of August, the worst of the summer heat was over, but this year the

96

temperature had hovered in the high 90s for days, with humidity that left her immobile. The most ordinary tasks, garden work, meal preparation, seemed impossible. She felt exhausted all the time, yet too uncomfortable to sleep.

John followed her into the bathroom, watched her fill the tub.

"Don't you want to know where I've been all summer?" he said.

"I'm sure it was someplace expensive."

"Now, Father, the Church says you're supposed to accept your lot in life and not resent your betters."

"I don't resent my betters. I resent the rich."

She peeled off her sweaty clothing and lowered herself into the cool water.

"Jeez, I didn't think it was possible for you to get skinnier. I can see your ribs."

"I can't eat in this weather." She closed her eyes, rested her head against the rim of the tub.

"What do you want me to do?" he said.

"I don't care what you do. I'm staying here."

He took off his clothes and knelt by the edge of the tub.

"I've been reading about heretics, Father," he said. "Some of them believed that when you're advanced enough, you understand that the concepts of good and evil have no meaning."

"You're saying *you're* spiritually advanced? Don't flatter yourself."

"Come on, Father, it's all a game. You must sense that."

"Nihilism isn't the same thing. Don't you get tired of not caring? That constant indifference must get boring."

"I'm bored all the time, Father."

"A side effect of privilege. I'm never bored."

"So if I weren't rich, I'd have a better attitude."

"Is that a question?" she said. "Here's another: If I close my eyes, will you disappear?"

He laughed. "Arrogant little bitch," he said, and he kissed her. Her hard, slippery little body relaxed into his arms, stayed relaxed even when he pushed her down until they were both underwater. When they broke the surface she pushed her hair back and calmly wiped the water out of her eyes.

"Weren't you afraid I would hold you under?" he said.

"You wouldn't have done it," she said. "You would have been left alone with that terrible ennui."

He hauled her out of the tub and fucked her on the cold wet tiled bathroom floor.

He would never be bored with her.

~

Selene Marisela loved everything about her life in Erda, especially the old rambling house she shared with three generations: her mother and aunt, her brothers, her daughter. Even the after-dinner cleanup had its own comfort value, the ritual of dishes washed and dried, leftovers put away, table wiped off while they waited for the coffee.

Selene took the basin of kitchen scraps outside for composting. She could still hear the others laughing at the table as she crossed the backyard.

The town plan of Reservoir called for half-acre plots of land arranged on arrow-straight residential streets, with narrow gravel lanes running parallel to the streets, forming a boundary between backyards. Selene was used to seeing neighbors walking down that back lane with dogs and strollers. This evening, she could have sworn the lane was empty as she stooped over the compost pile. Then she heard a woman's voice.

"We hear you need some help," the woman said pleasantly. Selene looked around at the mention of "we," but no one else was there. The mention of "help" was equally puzzling. She assumed her mother had asked some favor of a new neighbor.

There was nothing mysterious about her, Selene would reflect later on. A short, stocky white woman, with walking shorts and a sleeveless shirt as if the cooling night air were as comfortable as a sunny afternoon. Short graying hair, brown-framed glasses. She radiated practicality. Could have coached your kid's soccer team or managed the mayor's re-election campaign or drank you under the table at the block party.

"You must be new," Selene said.

"We are," the woman said.

Again with the "we."

"Help with the borders," the woman said, then smiled at Selene's confusion. "Not flower borders, dear. Erda's borders. You're having trouble with arrangements for a border guard. The solution is volunteers. We'll do it as part of our civic duty to our new country."

"We?"

"Just ordinary people."

Selene could hear the sounds from her own house and the others around her, clatter of pots and pans being put away in cabinets, whistle of kettles, voices calling to each other, audible through the windows that people had forgotten to close against the evening chill. The circumstances couldn't have been more ordinary. Perhaps that dulled her surprise, made it all seem normal. Of course a woman she had never seen would know about Erda's security issues, would know how to solve them.

"The answer to boys with guns," the woman said, "is girls with guns."

"You say you've recently arrived. It's our policy not to allow newcomers to bring weapons into the country."

The woman smiled. She reached for Selene's hand and gave it a firm shake.

"We'll talk more, later," she said, and was gone down the lane.

Ordinary people? More like a seismic force in history. But that was often how people were introduced to the D.O.T. They understood the significance only in retrospect.

~

The man at the entrance to the bar looked bored. "S & M night," he said. "No cover charge. But we reserve the right to turn away unsavory clientele."

"I'm horny," John said, "and I want a drink."

That got the man's attention. "I get off work at one," he said.

"I don't like men." Then again, he couldn't honestly say he *liked* women.

A man in black leather glided up to him. "You're obviously a top."

"Get out of my way," John said. He couldn't even threaten the guy, damn it. The faggot *wanted* to be hurt.

He didn't understand S & M games. Safe words. Role playing. Like the geeks who reenact historic battles but would never have the stomach for real warfare. These people were revolting.

As soon as he reached the bar a woman sidled up next to him. This wasn't unusual, except that she was taller than John and was dressed in an English riding outfit. Her straight silky hair, dyed maroon, fell to her shoulders.

"In case you were wondering what to have tonight," she said, "may I suggest the joys of two tops battling it out?"

"I don't play games. I just want to fuck."

"Oh. How boring."

He grabbed her wrist and gripped it, hard. "Why don't you find out for yourself?"

"How dare you touch me." She was angry and intrigued at the same time, ready to launch into haughty bitch role.

"No games," he said. "No rules. There is no word in the human vocabulary that's a safe word with me."

She pulled away. "Honey, you're not healthy."

The bar across the street was more promising. Just the usual straight, desperate people trying to act like they were having fun.

He sat at a small table against the wall and ordered a beer. It took about five minutes before a woman sat down across from him. Slow night.

This one had long, frizzy blonde hair, brown eyes. Big tits.

"Ever wear riding outfits?" he said.

"What?"

"Can I buy you a beer?"

Ditzy and mothering, from the looks of her. John tried to look introspective and mournful. "Look," he said, "I probably won't be good company tonight. I'm not really up to being amusing."

Worked perfectly. She was oozing concern in a second. "That's okay," she said. "I'm not good at bantering either. Why don't you tell me about yourself?"

Their beers came. He sighed and took a leisurely swallow. So many choices.

"My wife left me for another man," he said.

The story unfurled with no effort on his part. He and his wife—he named her Diane—had lived the perfect life. Got married, bought a house in the suburbs, had two kids, little boys. He knew he was taking a chance when he told her the boys' names were Origen and Tertullian, but by then he had her hooked and the names blew by her.

"What would you do, John," his father said to him sometimes, "if you didn't have money?"

One of Randolph Honig's ways of torturing him.

"You would be an ordinary man, work in some white-collar wasteland, maybe insurance. No, that requires too much dealing with the public. Interpersonal skills aren't your strong suit, are they? An analyst, maybe, a numbers cruncher. You'd show up at the office at nine, leave at six, drive a half hour or so to your suburban house, with your wife and kids waiting for you. You'd have dinner, talk about your day. Help the kids with their homework, watch a little TV, do a little extra paperwork, and then turn in. And get up and do the same thing the next day, and the next. For decades, until you retired."

The picture nauseated John.

When you had money you floated along on the surface of the world, safe, you never had to go down into the suffocating midst of things.

He ordered them more beers. "It's losing the trust," he said, "that's the hardest part. You don't know if you'll ever be able to trust again." He forced a sad smile.

Blondie leaned forward, offering more cleavage to his view.

"Did you hear about that case in Maryland?" she said in what she must have thought was a whisper. "A man caught his wife in bed with another man, and killed her with a sawed-off shotgun, shot her right in the chest. But the judge only sentenced him to like, less than two years in prison. He said what the husband did was understandable."

John wondered what happened to the wife's lover.

"My point is," blondie said, "you were in that same situation, but you took the high road. You walked away instead of trying to take revenge."

Right. Congratulations on not being a stone-cold murderer.

"What good would revenge do?" he said modestly—or rather, the character he was playing, the ordinary schmuck, said it modestly. "It wouldn't undo the past. And it would only hurt my kids."

Blondie was melting fast.

He wanted some sport that night, some chase and struggle. As soon as they got into his hotel room he slammed her against the wall and pulled up her skirt. But the little slut was already ravenous for him. She only giggled and said, "I was wondering when we'd get down to it."

Jesus. Women were so fucking twisted.

And to make everything worse, he pictured the priest. Here he was nailing one woman and thinking about another, damn her.

~

Catherine Beck also monitored the coverage of the gunned-down judge: the small articles in the national newspapers, brief segments on the television news. She was interested not so much in the details given, but in what was absent from the reports.

No mention was made of any note left at the scene.

A note that explained precisely why this man was killed.

The silence could mean two things. Either the original crime scene investigators were incompetent, or someone was covering it up.

~

When Averil read the newspaper she tried to stick to the coverage of politics and cultural events and avoid the articles about violent crimes. It did no good, she knew, to be drawn into the sad details and then torment herself wondering why murderers did what they did.

Still she read them. "Judge in Controversial Case Found Murdered" was the headline that caught her eye that day. The victim had been in the news a few weeks before, sparking protests for a lenient sentence he'd given out. He had presided over the trial of a man who killed his wife with a sawed-off shotgun after finding her with another man. The judge, calling the husband's actions "understandable," had sentenced the killer to eighteen months in jail.

Averil thought about the person this whole thing centered on: the murdered wife, whose killer was about to be freed since he had already served most of the time before his sentence. Those last moments, the pain, the fear. And the pain of her loved ones, outraged by the slap on the wrist given to her murderer.

The article quoted local authorities, speculating on a growing trend of victims' families taking the law into their own hands.

But something about it made Averil uneasy.

The judge had been killed in a manner so fitting, so ironically apt: a single shotgun blast to the chest. As if the killing had been carried out not by a grieving relative in the heat of the moment, but by a cool and sardonic intelligence, by justice itself.

CHAPTER 10

TEMPTATION

Sometimes also the evil spirit is the cause of sweetness.

—Hadewijch of Antwerp, 13th century

As Averil left John's cottage, she closed the door and leaned against it for a moment, letting her eyes adjust to the starlight.

Then she hears it.

The whispering. The gossip.

People are talking about her and she should have known all along. She feels as if her ears have been plugged up and her hearing is suddenly restored, the sounds roaring toward her from all directions.

It was inevitable, the gossip, after all this time—over a year, she realizes, since it started. What's more, surely the story was working its way up the chain of command, the monsignors, the archbishop.

She knows all this. And she knows she needs to stop. Simple as that.

The gossip continues to surround her, a cloud of sound, as she walks back to the monastery. It stops only when she goes into the church. Before the statue of Mary she reaches for the candle matches.

"When you're pope," John had said that night, "you should bring back indulgences, Father, and saints' relics." He talked incessantly, talked right through sex, even when he was gasping for breath, while they grappled and pushed each other down, wrestling as if each were on the verge of strangling the other.

"When they make you a saint," he said, "they'll put your little finger-bone in a gold reliquary encrusted with jewels."

Try as she did to ignore him, the idea of him thinking about her skeletal remains, at a moment like that, made her reach orgasm suddenly and painfully. He laughed at her for it.

He had kept talking afterward, and she had tried to tune him out. Had tried to imagine other sounds she would have liked to hear that moment. Baby turtles at the pond, plopping into the water at her approach. The cat Mehitabel sighing in her sleep. The clanking hammered-metal wind chimes near the garden.

"Strength, Mother," she whispers now as she lights a candle, and instead of the gossipy whispers she hears the votive flames hissing on their wicks in their glass holders, little voices praying.

~

The gossip didn't reach Peter Byrne directly, but he was reaching his own conclusions about Averil and John Honig.

He noticed their interactions. After Mass, or at other events. Averil was worse than formal and distant with Honig. She was outright unfriendly, made no effort to hide her rudeness. She treated total strangers better. A suspicion started to awaken in Peter, and one day it formed itself into a conscious thought.

They couldn't possibly. She couldn't be carrying something on with that man. He was young enough to be her son, almost, though he was handsome as the devil if you liked the looks of a spoiled young rich man who'd never had to work a day in his life.

Jesus Mary and Joseph. He sent a silent prayer, a plea, across the monastery complex. Come to your senses, woman. And for the love of everything, be discreet.

~

Catherine at that time was unaware of the gossip, but she sensed Averil's unease. She looked for opportunities to take her mind off whatever it was that was preoccupying her. She even suffered through an afternoon or two with her at a women's café called Demeter's Cup, a nest of gauzy curtains and overstuffed chairs, with folk singers strumming guitars, bulletin boards featuring notices of lectures on Minoan Crete or workshops on female creativity. Averil loved the place.

While they waited for their coffee, Averil reached for a Tarot deck on a low bookcase near their booth.

What little Catherine knew about Catholicism included vague ideas about saints, candles, rosary beads. For all she knew, Tarot was part of the whole deal.

"Pick a card," Averil said, and they both smiled at the way she sounded like an inept magician showing off a new trick.

Catherine pulled one out. Two of Swords.

"Tell me about it," Averil said. "Start with the most basic, the most obvious description of what you see."

"A woman," she said. If Averil wanted obvious, she would give her obvious.

"Yes."

"Blindfolded. The ocean behind her."

"Yes. What else?"

Catherine frowned at the card. She was trained to read people's facial expressions, body language. Shoe prints on muddy floors, dry ground, pavement. Cards had not been part of curriculum.

"In one hand a sword. In the other hand a sword."

Averil nodded at the poetry of it, thought of inscriptions to war goddesses, unearthed on cuneiform tablets.

~

Averil woke up disoriented. The room, familiar and strange. Starlight on a bare wooden floor, soft shadows. A sleeping man with his arm around her.

A summons of some kind.

It had pulled her out of a place she needed to get back to, a dream, a theory. She was explaining something, and now it seemed she had had this dream, these thoughts, before, in the border country between sleeping and waking.

Something about particles and strings. About dissolving and flowing together.

A new distraction now: the alarming realization that the man beside her was John Honig, they had fallen asleep after sex, his steady heartbeat reverberating through her own body as she dreamed-thought.

The dream, the theory. Electrons, the uncertainty principle. The vast empty spaces between. And step past it: vibrating strings. Past them, a step further. What the mystics had been talking about. God Matter Mater Mother Source.

She gripped her forehead. She must have moaned.

"What is it, Father?"

"*Be quiet.*" God forbid his inevitable prattle swept away the delicate imprints of the thoughts. Not the thoughts themselves—those had already dissolved.

The mystics were describing holographic theory, millennia before the physicists did. But how she had arrived at this conclusion—gone, lost.

~

The letter from the FBI arrived in November, printed on expensive stationery. Our tax dollars at work, was John Honig's first thought upon receiving it. His impulse was to throw the letter away. A recruiter wanted to talk to him, about considering "a career in service to your country."

He agreed to the interview, for its potential amusement value. He wasn't disappointed.

The recruiter was earnest and humorless. The Bureau, he said, needed educated, intelligent, fit young men. The country was in crisis.

"As you know," the man said, "it's not only Muslim terrorists anymore, or your basic old-fashioned, anti-government paranoids out in the woods."

"Right," John said. "It's pissed-off women blowing up buildings."

"These are dangerously subversive groups. They want to turn this country upside-down if they can."

"Why did you guys keep claiming it was gas leaks?" John said. "Either you didn't know what was going on or you had no idea how to put the right spin on it. Either way, it made you people look like idiots."

The agent looked uncomfortable. "We've wondered whether you're a feminist sympathizer," he said.

"Why should I be?"

"There's your—'association,' let's say—with a prominent feminist figure."

"You're interested in the priest, are you?"

"Let's say there might be some valuable work you could do for us."

"I'll save you time. She has nothing to do with violence. She's a harmless weirdo."

"She may know more than you realize."

"Is it true, Father?" he asked her later while he was fucking her. She tried to ignore him, tried to stay inside her own pleasure, but he kept on. "Are you that dangerous? To have the FBI gunning for you?"

"Harmless as serpents," she said.

~

Averil's office door was ajar. Peter hesitated at the threshold and watched her at the window opposite. A housefly buzzed madly, bumping against the glass while Averil fiddled with the latch. "I can understand your frustration," she said to the fly gently. "If you'll bear with me I'll lift the screen."

He was simply an administrator, a level-headed, practical man. What could he say to such monstrous innocence?

The fly looped around her and flew out the opening she had made at the bottom of the screen window.

"Averil."

"These things always stick," she said. "God forbid there's a fire."

"The archbishop called me in for a meeting."

"I know. You have that look about you."

"The Church doesn't issue official warnings," he said. "There's no cease-and-desist letter. If you don't drop this affair now, you'll be defrocked." The technical term was "laicization," a word no priest ever bothered using. "The order will come, and that will be it."

"The Church looks away when male priests have paramours," she said. "And when they raped little boys they got hush-hush therapy and were released back into their parishes. I have a . . . , a consensual—whatever it is, the point is it's with an adult, and you'd think the whole edifice of the Church was going to crumble."

"So you're going to be defiant."

He was surprised at his own anger. He didn't know why he should care. If the good Lord had wanted to create a person who was Peter's opposite in every way, Averil was it.

"What can you be besides a priest?" he said. "What have you ever wanted, other than to be a priest? Nothing. You know that. We're the same that way, if only that. Good lord, woman, if you want to have sex, have it. Just not with this one man. All you have to do is break it off with him and everything will be fine. You're not in love with the son of a bitch, are you?"

"Of course not."

"Then what's the problem?"

"There's no problem. I'll break it off with him. But don't expect me to ignore the hypocrisy. Don't expect me to be contrite."

~

She thought Honig would be indifferent to the news that she wasn't going to see him again. She expected an off-color joke, a shrug, a perfunctory goodbye.

She hadn't expected the anger.

"Defrock you for fucking?" John said. "They'd have to fire half the goddamned priests out there."

"They're making an example of me."

"They're bluffing. This is the Catholic Church. They'd rather sweep you under the rug than get any more negative publicity."

"They're not bluffing."

"Then fuck 'em," he said. "Get the hell out before the bastards kick you out. Don't give them the satisfaction."

Leave the priesthood. It would be easier to have her circulatory system removed. Yank out the veins, arteries, capillaries. Sew her back up and send her on her way.

~

In the church she sat before the long-burning candle on its stand of wrought iron, the flame flickering in glass that was the pink-tinged burgundy of a tumbled uncut ruby.

She knelt, forehead pressed against her clasped hands.

Help me help me help me.

There is the priest again, this time young, light brown hair and gray eyes, kneeling next to her, dangerously close.

"Look what you've done," Averil says coldly. "You're worth nothing and you're costing me everything."

He offers a Communion wafer, gently parting her lips with the host, sliding it back and forth on her tongue. "This is my Body," he breathes, and then she is on top of him, straddling him. Hands groping each other, pulling at clothing, but also wanting to slap, wanting to reach around throats and squeeze.

I'm damned, I'm damned, I'm damned.

~

She went to Peter Byrne's office.

"I've told him I'm going to stop seeing him."

Peter, wise in the ways of sinners and their intentions—in other words, human beings and their self-justifications—knew the difference between "I'm going to stop" and "I've stopped."

~

She did, in fact, stay away from John for several weeks. But somehow she found herself at the cottage again, being pulled-dragged to his couch, strong hands massaging her shoulders.

"You're so tense," he said. "You need to relax."

His hands radiated warmth that spread across her shoulders, down her arms, up her neck.

"You'd be tense too," she said, but then he kissed her neck, started telling her about his plan. Her eyes were closing, it was difficult to concentrate, but yes, she remembered the man he told her about, the one who bought a medieval chapel in Spain and had it dismantled and shipped to California. Now, John told her, he has bought this chapel. She wanted to ask him how he could afford it but before she could formulate the question his whispery voice near her ear reminded her that he was richer than God.

"I thought you were going to build your own," she said.

"Plans change, Father."

She wants to point out that he'll need a new thesis project for his architecture degree, but her attention is drawn back to his voice, and the two of them are at the top of a cliff, impossibly beautiful landscapes spread out beneath them: forests, farms, distant mountains.

"I'll transfer ownership to you, Father," the voice is saying. He is invisible now. Still she can feel his hands, feel his lips. "All yours," the voice says, "all of this. Isn't that what you want?"

"I can't own property. I'm a priest."

"You'll be *my* priest, Father. You can say the Mass just for me, in Latin."

All these things I will give thee.

~

She pushes through the main doors into the vestibule of the Refectory. To her left is a set of steps that she has never noticed before, cut right into the earth and leading down to a rough-cut wooden door at the bottom.

Slowly Averil climbs down, smells the damp earth, sweet and cool, all around her. The door is rough to the touch, the doorknob a rusty handle. She opens it.

An ocean shore. She feels sharp rocks beneath her feet, breathes in salty cold air. The waves, dark gray against a light gray sky, break roaring against gleaming black cliffs. At the top of the farthermost cliff stands a woman in a billowing black cloak. The hood slips down, revealing long hair the color of ashes.

Averil's heart jumps. How to reach her? There is no path up to the cliffs from the beach.

While she stands wondering, the far-off woman turns and walks away.

She hears a voice behind her, brisk and cheerful: "Don't worry. Come, let me read your cards."

A young woman, seated at a small table balanced somehow on the rocks, is dressed in flame colors that stand out vividly from the grayness all around her.

She smiles and hands Averil a Tarot deck.

Averil shuffles, cuts the deck three times with her left hand, draws the top card.

Death.

While the card reader watches calmly, Averil returns the card to the deck, shuffles again, and this time plucks a card at random from the middle of the deck.

Death.

No matter how many times she shuffles, or from where in the deck she pulls a card, it is always Death.

She turns over the deck and spreads the cards out in front of her.

All of them Death.

"It's not the end," the woman says. "It stands for transformation."

"I know."

The woman turns the cards over and shuffles. She offers the deck to Averil. "Try it one last time. Pick a card."

The Tower.

Monolith crumbling, bodies crushed beneath it.

As Averil looks at the card, she sees blue-ink lines tattooed into her own skin, coiling around her wrists and snaking up her arms. The woman gathers up her cards and disappears.

~

People called them the shadow armies, regardless of what they called themselves, and that is how they were referred to afterwards by historians.

The skirmishes seemed so random, so freakish, so far apart in tactics, in geography, in tone, that analysts at first saw no connections, no patterns. In a Nigerian town an armed group of women stormed a courthouse where a woman was being tried for adultery. The defendant was spirited away and the judge and prosecutor warned to "go and sin no more." In Paraguay a women's prison was invaded, the guards tied up and the inmates released. In Denmark a man who had grown rich off prostitution was taken hostage by gun-wielding masked women, released only when his entire fortune was handed over.

Questions were raised: Where did they get the weapons? Where did they train, and how? Then the incidents would fade from the news, with no realization that a new force had entered the global stage.

In hindsight, people realized that the standard surveillance techniques of any government should have been able to pick up these activities. Somehow this failed to happen.

As if the doings of women were beneath notice, as indeed they had long been.

~

A box of books arrived for Averil, bequeathed to her by old Father Saavedra from seminary. She hadn't even known he had lived this long, much less remembered her in his will.

It was late January. Two months had passed since the first rumblings from the archbishop. Averil hadn't seen John in a month, but now the winter break was over. His classes would start again. The cottage was waiting for her if she wanted it.

She wanted not to want it.

The simple act of unpacking the box, looking at each title and gently wiping it with a dustcloth, steadied her. She was greeting old acquaintances: Bonaventure, Anselm of Canterbury. And, more interesting: *The History of the Albigensians. The Cathar Heresy.* The skeletons in the Church's closet, the tortured skeletons, the flayed and burned-at-the-stake skeletons.

The next book was one she already had: *The Mirror of Simple Souls,* by Marguerite Porete. Another supposed heretic, burnt at the stake. Marguerite had no patience for the usual signs of piety: good works, self-denial, rituals of any kind. The soul needs to transcend all that. Nothing that Meister Eckhart hadn't said later, but the bonfire was lit only for Marguerite, a Beguine, a woman living independently of men, thinking independently of men. And daring to think that we humans are divine at our core.

She lifted out the last book in the box, one she hadn't read: *Schwester Katrei.*

Sister Catherine, in German. Averil smiled, thinking of her friend. She opened to a page at random: "Father, rejoice with me," she read out loud. "I have become God."

So much for any resemblance between the two Catherines.

111

She leafed forward a few pages. "There it happens that she forgets everything that had ever been named, and she is drawn so far out of herself and away from all created things that they have to carry her from the church. She lies until the third day and they think she is surely dead!"

She spent an afternoon reading the book, a work of unknown authorship presenting a dialogue between a woman spiritual seeker, Katrei, and her advisor, a scholarly priest.

Katrei wants "the quickest way to God" and is unsatisfied with the priest's advice—the usual things, praying, fasting. Her advisor is holding her back, she says. She wants more. She wants to know God. She wants union with God.

Katrei goes on a journey and comes back, transformed, and here, Averil reflected, was the story of Sun Bu-er, the woman who left her husband to make her own spiritual journey and became a master teacher, one of the Seven Immortals of Taoism. Moved from twelfth-century China to fourteenth-century Europe, but the basic plot remained. A woman spiritual seeker is held back by a man, breaks with him, returns to him after she's surpassed him.

~

"Is it done?" Peter said. "Have you ended it?"

"That's no one's business."

Peter resisted the urge to make a dramatic gesture: bury his face in his hands, tear out great tufts of his hair.

He tried not to think about the fact that he had yet another meeting with the archbishop scheduled, sure to take place in the imposing conference room with dead-and-gone bishops frowning down at him from oil paintings along the walls. Has she ended the relationship, the archbishop would want to know. Is she willing to cooperate? And Peter would have to scowl and bluster, grumble that he didn't read minds, he wasn't here to babysit.

Finally he said to Averil, "Are you going to apologize?"

"I'd be lying if I did," was her answer. "I'm not sorry for it."

"Of course, a principled stand. Wouldn't want you doing something unethical."

Peter Byrne's later doomed, heroic actions would never be known to Averil or to the scholars who eventually tried to piece together the history of the war years. He became one of the many who simply disappeared into the unforgiving chaos, his final resting place known only to a few others, who died soon after he did.

Right now he was merely an ordinary priest, an irritated administrator with the usual distractions of any pastor: parishioner committee meetings, repair bills. Averil was the extraordinary one, the gadfly, the visionary.

~

The snow was falling as she walked to John Honig's cottage without a coat. Had anyone been interested in investigating her actions, finding evidence that she was indeed breaking her vow of celibacy, the crisp tracks in the snow would have been proof, until they filled in and disappeared.

When he opened the door, standing there like a king's son with his brilliant predator smile, she saw how they were the same, she and he, so proud and arrogant, and justly so. The arrogance felt as good as a sweet, intoxicating wine.

"Jeez, your lips are blue," he said.

The next thing she knew she was in his bed and he was pulling off her clothes and then his own, pulling the down comforter on top of them both and rubbing his warm hands all over her body.

"Your chapel's waiting for you, Father," he said, as if it were the most normal thing to have a conversation at this point. "I won't put it in your name yet, though. Not until you leave the Church."

"I'll always be a priest."

It would be only a matter of time. The Church would throw her out and she would be *his* priest. On his altar.

Slowly her shivering stopped and her body relaxed. She was aware only of relief and gratitude.

For the first time, the sex was like lovemaking instead of the usual angry grappling, Jacob and the angel wrestling for they knew not what. He lay beneath her and she kissed him everywhere, amazed at how perfect his skin was, how beautiful he was. She forgot why she was supposed to feel guilty.

Afterward as they lay together she pressed her forehead against his.

"Close your eyes," she whispered.

He did. Silent, for once.

"Relax," she said. "Relax your toes, relax the arches of your feet, relax your ankles…"

He followed her voice as it slowly worked its way up his body, muscles relaxing, calves and thighs, abdomen and back and chest and all the way up to his mouth, his eyes, the crown of his head.

That evening was the one John remembered most clearly years later, during his long treks through the wilderness on foot, when hunger and exposure to the elements had whittled him down, when he was scarred and hollow-eyed and his other memories of Averil had been swallowed up in the fever-bright darkness and silence.

"Focus on your breathing," she said. "Empty your mind. When the thoughts come, let them melt away."

The skin on his forehead, where it touched hers, felt tight and stretched, as if something was inside, trying to open. His mind was moving, falling.

"Now lift off," she whispered, and they both did.

The air is silvery-gray and cold, and they are stone figures lying side by side on top of a sarcophagus in a chapel, a knight and his lady, perhaps, or two saints. They open their heavy-lidded stone eyes and the room spins around them.

Each feels a giant hand swoop down, clamp itself around one ankle and lift them up. They sway upside down from one foot, bend the other leg at the knee, and put their hands behind their backs so that each of them takes the form of the Hanged Man in the Tarot deck.

The people of the villages below see the stone saints dangling calmly, up in the sky, and wonder how to interpret it.

~

As Averil is falling asleep that night at the Rectory, her room begins to shimmer. She is in a forest of trees that grow tall and pillar-straight, translucent as if made of glass. Somewhere in the luminous forest is the voice of Schwester Katrei.

I am illuminated, says the voice. *I am perfected. No matter what manner of crime I commit, it is no sin, for I am firmly established in God.*

CHAPTER 11

TENEBRAE

When I ought to lament for what I have done,
I sigh rather for what I have had to forgo.

—Abbess Héloïse, 12th century

Catherine took the seat across from John Honig at the cafe. She signaled for the waiter.

"I'd like espresso." She looked over at John. "Anything for you? Top off what you have there?"

He shook his head no, but said nothing.

After the waiter left, Catherine settled into her chair, made a show of looking casually around at the other patrons before resting her glance on John. She was savoring the irony. She knew, from weeks of observation, that he went to cafés, bars, restaurants, sat down, and women flocked to him. He invariably left those places accompanied by a woman and took her back to his hotel room. Sometimes he would go through the whole process two or even three times a night.

So of course he would be thinking that she, Catherine, was his next conquest. Anyone looking at them would have thought them a perfect couple, two people of extreme and effortless beauty. Catherine had lived with this beauty all her life and felt no pride or satisfaction in it, nor was she fooled by its presence in others. It meant nothing. Averil of all people should have understood that.

"What's your name?" he said, relaxed and smiling. A man like that had probably never in his life felt nervous around a woman.

"Catherine."

"I'm John."

"I know."

That sparked a flicker of curiosity out of him, but nothing more. With an ego like his, he probably thought she'd been asking around.

"That's right," she said. "I know a lot about you."

"Such as?"

"Such as, you're a sound sleeper."

That got to him, but he barely showed it. She felt grudging admiration for a man who could hide his emotions so well.

"You're trying to think it through," she said. "How would *I* know about your sleeping habits? You hustle your various 'friends' out of that hotel room of yours before they can even think about falling asleep in your single bed. That's an interesting quirk, that bed. Are you trying to pretend you're a monk?"

"Would you like me to? If that's your fantasy, we can play that."

She could see he was stalling for time. She'd thrown too many things at him at once—how she knew about his bed, how she knew he didn't sleep with the women he had sex with, and of course the ultimate question of what living soul had ever been around him when he slept. Even her question about being a monk sparked something defensive. Her instincts never let her down in situations like this.

When they got to his hotel room Catherine sat on the desk, her feet propped on the chair in front of her. Honig took off his shirt and sat on his bed. She observed him calmly: the broad shoulders, the lean, muscular torso, the narrow hips. Men would kill to have that perfect V-shaped frame. The play on words made her smile, and it amused her even more to think how badly he was misinterpreting her smile. Not that he was in danger. Yet.

"I understand that Averil Parnell is a friend of yours," she said.

"The priest."

"Or maybe 'friend' isn't the right word."

"She can't stand me," he said, smiling, "but she can't get enough of me. I'll say this for her, she's the *strangest* woman I've ever fucked."

Catherine felt like she had when she first trained in martial arts and an opponent landed a blow. You're stunned but you can't pause to give in to the pain, nor can you strike out blindly in response. Do either of these things and the opponent gets an advantage you may never recover.

Killing him would be a pleasure.

She prided herself that she never killed for no reason, never killed out of passion or for a mere personal vendetta. With this man, for the first time, she was tempted to break her rule. But she could control herself. It was like sex. The more you did it, the more you learned to prolong the

116

anticipation, ride the feelings of arousal and put off the orgasms as long as possible, so that when they finally started, wave after wave, they were infinitely better.

"You want me," he said. "You proud bitch, if you want me to fuck you you'll have to suck me off first."

She would enjoy hand-to-hand combat with him. If he were trained properly he would be the perfect opponent. He was quick thinking, strategic, he had no scruples, was never hindered by guilt. You couldn't get him off-balance. Hit him and the pain would only make him laugh. And he had a sure and deadly instinct for what his opponent was feeling, what would cause the most pain. He had an instinct for everything, that is, except danger to himself. His ego got in the way there.

"You're not going to make it to old age," she said.

"Are death threats part of your sex play?"

"It's not a threat, it's a prediction." If she didn't get to him, someone else would. "I'll get to the death threats later."

"This should be good," he said. "Why don't I order us some drinks?"

"I'm going to tell you about myself," she said. "Then I'm going to tell you what I want from you. Then I'm going to leave. And then, because you won't believe what I've told you, I'll have to pay you one last visit, but after that, if all goes well, we'll never see each other again. If we do see each other, you can be sure that only one of us will walk away alive."

"This is fascinating," he said. He wasn't smiling anymore, but he had a confident, mocking look in his eyes. As far as he was concerned, he still had the upper hand. "What happened, I stood you up? I didn't ask you out on a second date?"

"Don't flatter yourself."

She shouldn't have answered him, she knew. It gave him control of the situation. She needed to stay with the point.

"Okay. So do you have a particular grudge against me, or do you pick your targets at random?"

"How does she stand you?"

"Who?"

"Averil." Enough, she told herself. Don't answer him.

"There's no way the priest is behind this. She might be ready for the psych ward, but she'd never hire someone to get rid of me."

"She has no idea this is happening. No one's going to tell her either. Now shut up and listen."

She told him about her work. Her most recent targets, some of the earlier ones. Strategies, details, results. She had never simply told the story

117

to someone else, a coherent narrative about her mission. If she were ever caught, her activities would come to an end, but no torture would ever induce her to give her captors the satisfaction of a confession.

She told him about the concerns of Averil's friends as they watched his effect on her. She told him about following him, watching him, visiting his room when he was dead asleep. She could have killed him many times, any number of ways. And now he had two choices: death or disappearance.

She didn't expect him to believe her, and at four o'clock the next morning she was there again, straddling his chest as she increased the pressure on the blade just enough for him to wake up and see the knife against his neck.

"Don't move or you'll kill yourself. And don't say anything or that'll be too much temptation for me."

His mocking, bantering expression was gone, finally. Replaced by hatred.

"I see you believe me now," she said. "I don't care where you go. Just leave. Now. If I see you again I'll kill you. I won't threaten, I won't warn. I'll kill you on sight."

~

He remembered, then, waking up and seeing Catherine. Some other night, maybe several nights. She had been so calm, not tense or startled the way an intruder would have been, that she seemed an image from his dream or a natural part of the nighttime room. He must have gotten used to her presence, ghostly visitations from a woman who contemplated killing him but didn't even disturb his rest.

In the years to come, in his rare moments of perfect clarity and honesty, John realized that he should be grateful to her. His hatred for Catherine Beck gave him a mission, the only clear purpose his life had ever had.

~

Averil knew he wasn't there when she stepped inside his cottage, but still felt a sense of his presence.

She had half expected to find merely coldness, a vacuum.

Lying on John's bed in the empty room, she sees him in the pale daylight of a northern midwinter, a monk in a scriptorium, his hands shivering with cold as he bends over a manuscript, his eyes troubled by the foreign language, the strange ideas.

The potential for good, buried unthinkably long ago.

As unsettling as looking at an old man and seeing for a moment the youth he must have been.

When she dialed the hotel she had no idea what she would say to him.

Mr. Honig checked out some weeks ago, they told her. He left no forwarding address.

~

Central America in the rainy season wasn't most northerners' idea of a vacation. Relentless sunshine in the morning, followed by hours of pouring rain in the afternoon, and at all times the air moist and hot like a physical substance that you had to struggle through to get from place to place.

It was only the end of April, but seemingly the season had started early this year. For John Honig, the discomfort was a relief. Took his mind off things.

He sat by the pier, sheltered by enormous canvas umbrellas that withstood everything short of hurricane-force winds, and watched the water in the bay get choppier and grayer by the minute.

He'd wanted to leave Connecticut. That blonde bitch might like to think she'd scared him off, but she was wrong. His degree was finished, the priest's novelty value was wearing off. It was time to move on before everything got stale.

He had breezed onto Long Island for the obligatory visit to Randolph Honig, their version of father-son bonding, more like protons held together in an atom's nucleus in spite of their repelling each other. Randolph Honig, between wives, prowled around the family's faux-European villa, irritable as an animal in heat. John dodged his father's verbal swipes, tried to ignore the tackiness of ubiquitous marble floors and pretentious crystal chandeliers, and pondered revenge against Catherine Beck.

Nothing extreme or crude. Nothing physical. It was pleasant to idle away the time thinking of subtle ways to strike back. He liked the idea of having someone break into her home while she was away, make it obvious that an intruder had been there. Maybe leave a knife. Better yet, a knife exactly like the one she'd held to his throat.

He wouldn't have known how to hire an investigator. No surprise, Randolph Honig had someone to recommend. John said something vague about doing a background check, and Randolph said briskly, "If there's anything to be found, this man will find it. She'll probably turn out to be your average gold-digger. It's wise to take precautions."

119

John had to grudgingly admire the old bastard. He could seamlessly weave an insult into any damn thing he said.

The investigator had looked more like an accountant than anything else, and nearing retirement at that. Clearly John would have to hire someone else for the breaking and entering, but in the meantime, he might as well get this joker to find out the basics.

Easier said than done.

The detective had an endless supply of complaints when he met with John again. Beck's driver's license didn't indicate the correct home address. He got nowhere with searches of credit card databases, voter registration records, property tax records. "Even the FBI didn't know exactly where she lived," he had said, proudly handing over a file the Bureau had compiled on her.

"This is fucking useless," John said. "Everything's blacked out."

The detective looked offended. "You don't know who I had to bribe to get it so fast. Do you know how long it takes if you do it through the Freedom of Information Act?"

He finally acted on John's original suggestion, which was to follow her from St. Anthony's and see where she went.

The little man was sitting outside Beck's apartment the next evening when she came out and stood smiling politely on the sidewalk. He rolled down his window—no point in pretending when the target catches you.

For years afterward, the scene was clear in the man's memory, how relaxed her body language was, leaning against the car door. Anyone nearby would have seen two acquaintances chatting, unaware of Beck's gun with its silencer pointing at the man's gut. She wanted to know who he was working for, her silver-gray eyes scanning him like lie detector equipment. He wouldn't have thought of lying. He told her everything.

"You're harmless enough," she'd said, glancing at the paperwork and dropping it back in his lap. "Might as well keep up the 'surveillance,' get as much money out of the fucker as you can.

"But tell Honig," she said over her shoulder as she walked away, "I'll be watching."

A week later she was gone. The detective had said something pompous about the "trail going cold," and John had to restrain the urge to shatter his jaw.

Now, with his dockside view of a raging storm in the bay, he remembered Catherine Beck kneeling lightly on his ribcage. He would have a good fuck tonight, but in the meantime he needed to move. He stood up, took off his shoes and shirt, ran down the pier and dove off the end. His diving form was perfect, his stroke strong and steady, though he'd never lasted on any swim team in high school or college. Clashes with the coaches were inevitable. Randolph Honig had taken a perverse pride in his son's expulsion from team after team: "No son of mine takes orders from a musclehead."

He swam through dark gray choppy water and thought about the priest. If she were with him he would have told her about the patron saint they have here, how on the feast day of the Lady of the Angels, everyone in Costa Rica goes on foot to her cathedral, no matter how many days the pilgrimage takes. He remembered his hands moving up Averil's body, feeling the knobs of her knees, her hip bones jutting out, her knife-edge ribs, the chiseled face of the starving martyr as she looked down on him, told him to kneel.

The trail wasn't cold. The government was keeping track of Beck, and thus of the priest. He smiled. Wouldn't it be a kick in the teeth for Randolph Honig if his promising only son went to work for the FBI?

He'd had John's life and stellar success already plotted out; he would give him capital to start his own firm, designing overpriced oceanfront houses for the overprivileged. Marble floors and crystal chandeliers for all.

He started swimming back. Untired, not at all rattled by the way the rain and the baywater mingled, the sound of the thunder and the sound of the waves indistinguishable. No other human was foolish enough to be out in weather like this, so only the dolphins and the sharks were able to observe his perfect form.

~

When the story broke, as Catherine knew it finally would, it was enormous. Bigger than the explosions carried out by still-anonymous groups of women.

Reporters were breathless with surprise: Years—no, decades—of reprisals had been carried out against men who had abused or assaulted women.

One had even sent a manifesto to the newspapers:

When a man raises a hand against a woman, we beat him bloody.
  When a man rapes his little daughter, we take him to a back alley and slit his throat, and while his blood pours out of his body, we tell him why he is dying.
  Where a cleric preaches against us, we set fire to his pulpit.
  When they deny us schooling, we bomb their ministry of education.

When they deny our right to vote, we bomb their polling places.

When they curtail all our rights, even our very movements, the clothing on our body, and throw acid in our faces if we resist, we use our warrior skills, turn their deadly violence against them.

We take their own anger, and unleash it against them.

Legislators demanded explanations, resignations.

Women felt strangely exhilarated even when they said they didn't support vigilante justice.

A storm of finger-pointing ensued as the FBI blamed the police and the police blamed the Department of Justice, and right-wing ideologues claimed that the tiny Republic of Erda was the epicenter of the reprisal campaign.

A sheepish FBI director admitted that the Bureau had known—all along, perhaps, though he was fuzzy on the timeline—but was trying to handle it covertly so as to undermine the "domestic terrorists" more effectively.

Falling asleep to these headlines, Catherine Beck dreamed she had blood on her hands.

Normally she was indifferent to dreams. Impervious to ghosts and visions, untroubled by things of the spirit and all their multiple illogics.

But this dream.

The feelings seeped into her waking consciousness. Confusion foremost: she didn't know whose blood it was. Also alarm at her own carelessness. Disgust at the raw, salty smell, the stickiness that she had failed to wash off.

She sat up in bed, examined her clean skin. Now all she could remember was that someone had called her to account for the blood, demanded an explanation. "I'm not the only one," was all she deigned to say in her own defense.

She tried to trace the dream logic.

Most likely, she thought, the dream sprouted from something she'd been discussing with a friend that day. A rural county in western Massachusetts, depopulated, economically depressed. That was one of the favorite excuses for woman-battering. Those poor, stressed, out-of-work men. This past month someone had been tracking down husbands of women in the battered women's shelter. The fuckers would get a surprise visit in the night, held down on the floor, both kneecaps pulverized with a hammer.

Blood for blood. Some deity may have said, *Vengeance is mine,* but women were tired of waiting. Women were taking vengeance back.

They were everywhere, these men who brushed up against the justice system and strutted away unscathed. Catherine never had to seek them out. They came to her every day, in newsprint, on the airwaves, too many to keep track of.

Asking for someone to wash the blood from their hands. Asking to be made right.

~

"I'm glad you've decided to join us after all." George B. Wilson took another look at John's file and set it on his leather-topped desk. "God knows men of your caliber aren't that easy to find."

John gave a slight nod, tried to look modest. God must have low standards. So did the FBI.

"Of course things have gotten worse," Wilson said, "since you spoke to our recruiter last year. Those quasi-military operations going on in godforsaken corners of the world. It can only galvanize the lunatic fringe here at home."

"I heard about that honor killing thing this morning," John said.

It had happened in Jordan. A teenage girl whose older male cousin had raped her. She had "dishonored" her family and was murdered soon after she reported the rape. Now all the male members of her extended family had been found with their throats slit. A "mercy killing," according to the notes left at each body.

John had to admire the balls it took to carry out something like that. Some women had sure as hell grown a pair.

He tried to look disapproving.

"I know you're interested in counterterrorism, doing undercover work," Wilson said. "Of course we couldn't use you with the feminist hate groups, but there are those militia groups out West that you could do some good work with."

"I guess I could pretend to be stupid and violent." One out of two.

"And as you've suggested," Wilson said, "it's a good idea to change your name. You're not exactly unknown, though you're not a regular on the society page either, like some other bad boys we know. The ones who play tennis all day and show up at Hyannis or Newport Beach with supermodels on their arm."

John did his best to look genial, look like a fellow member of the club who gave a damn about how "we" looked. "It's an empty life," he said.

Wilson nodded in approval.

There were two types of billionaire's sons. The stupid ones, like Wilson, were the ones who took salaried jobs and actually showed up for work. Of course, when you're the son of a Texas oil baron it's a lot easier to start out with a job close to the top. Like division chief at the FBI.

"There's another change we think you should make," Wilson said. "Don't get me wrong. I appreciate that you want to serve your country. But before we send a man out in the field for covert action, we need to be sure of him. We need to see that you're one of us, a serious family man."

"You're saying I should get married? That would prove I'm one of you?"

"Let's say it would create good will. It's important to be a team player."

Why, John wanted to say, do team members swap wives?

"You'd be proving your maturity," Wilson said. "Proving that you've grown out of your ... shall we call them youthful indiscretions?"

So that's what they called fucking a woman priest.

Everything he wanted to say was unacceptable. He had to censor each thought.

"But if you send me to infiltrate one of these groups," he said, "I would have to leave my wife to do that kind of work."

"She'll put up with it, John, for the good of her country."

~

When Catherine analyzed the incident later, she considered the possibility that she had become overconfident, that being in the flow during a mission made her take unnecessary risks. On the other hand, the flow helped her keep calm, think clearly when everything began to go wrong.

So many things she couldn't have anticipated. The twenty-minute power failure because of high winds. The man's surprisingly good reflexes and agility, thus the greater amount of effort and time to kill him. Worst of all, there was a witness.

No one else was supposed to be in the house, but here was this young man she'd never seen before and had no way to identify. A relative, neighbor, repairman—a burglar, for all she knew. No matter, he was in the house on whatever terms.

At times like this Catherine had a sort of double awareness. She was herself and yet also observing herself as another would, seeing her calmness as she stood over the body, the long moment in which she looked at the stranger while both of them knew she could kill him skillfully and quickly.

She had never killed a bystander.

It was almost abstract, the dilemma of whether to let him live or not. The matter seemed to be decided without much thought on her part.

One witness. One mistake. That was all it would take to allow at least an initial, tentative identification—if indeed anyone was investigating the killings in a systematic way.

What a triumph it would be for them if they managed to locate her, link her not only to that one killing but to others, maybe all of them.

It was a matter of time. If not this witness, then another. Not to know whether she was being tracked—or when or how she would get caught—added a pleasurable edge to her life. To be prey instead of predator was a novel challenge. To stay in New Falls, not clear out until the last possible minute, would be an interesting test of nerves.

~

John Honig's mother's family had a house in Iowa that she had inherited and passed on to him. He moved there, had it cleaned up, brought out of storage the furniture and even some of the curtains and rugs that had been there when she was growing up. A piece of property that Randolph Honig had never owned, had in fact never set foot in. When his wife wanted to visit her parents she went alone or with John. "A farmhouse on the outskirts of Bumpkinville," Randolph said when John told him about his plan to move there. "It'll be quaint. For a while."

Bumpkinville's real name was Gainestown, named after Gaines, his mother's family, which at one time owned almost everything of value there, the brick factory, the cannery, much of the farms, and of course the bank. Gaines money went into every civic project. The family name graced the main street, the park, the repertory theater, the town's minuscule museum.

That would be one way to impress a woman—tell her he was a Gaines. It would be slightly more respectable than the well-tried method of picking women up at bars and fucking them, which at least had the advantage of being easy and quick. But this had to be different. The perfect wife didn't go to bars looking for one-night stands.

The respectable way to meet women was to join a parish, or get involved with the PTA or the board of the public library. Get to know people, get invited to their homes, introduced to their friends. If he wanted to save time and simply introduce himself to a stranger it would have to be in a quasi-respectable place: the supermarket, a church fundraiser. But that still had the flavor of a pickup.

He drove into town on a mild spring afternoon, parked at the courthouse and walked around, looking at women. Waitresses at the family diner. Mothers dragging their brats to Little League at the Eugene Gaines Elementary School. High school girls acting bored outside a hair salon. There was a typical midwestern look: corn-fed, yellow-haired. Witless. He thought of George B. Wilson and the "threat" of feminist extremists. These women had probably never heard of feminism.

In the deli a woman waited at the counter to pay for cigarettes and a copy of *Women's World*. She was appealing in a trashy hick way, with too-tight blue jeans and long, peroxided hair that she tossed back every few seconds. The part in her hair revealed dark brown roots and a sunburn.

How do you do it, he wanted to ask her. How do you meet men, other than your fellow clerk at the Agway or the guy who lives in the trailer next to yours?

The problem with a wife was he would at some point have to have real conversations with her. That would rule out blondie here if he didn't want to be bored out of his wits. He needed a happy medium, something between a high school dropout and a Ph.D. He definitely didn't need a woman who had visions, a woman who would take a monumental vow and then break it. She was cheating on God. That would make God an angry husband, and John the adulterous lover. And Catherine Beck an incarnation of the Archangel Michael.

At a steakhouse, while he waited for his New York strip, he considered taking notes on the napkin. A list. Methods for meeting a woman.

There was a way that took less time than the respectable way but wasn't as sleazy as a one-night stand. Meet men. Join them in front of the TV in a bar during the playoffs. Buy them beer. Join a pickup basketball game at the Y. Make friends with sweaty, potbellied, prematurely balding men with no hopes, no lives. They would want to set him up on dates so he could join their married misery.

It was almost sunset, as good a time as any to start. He left the restaurant and started looking for a sports bar. On the next block was a movie theater where picketers out front held signs reading NO SMUT IN GAINESTOWN and SAVE OUR KIDS' MORALS.

A porn theater in the heart of Gainestown. This looked promising.

The movie titles on the marquee had mostly PG ratings. So much for porn. But there were a couple of R films—and one X. A reporter with a cameraman behind him was trying to argue with the protesters.

"Isn't this censorship?" the reporter said.

An older man, apparently the leader of the protest, looked around. "Valerie?" he called out. "Would you like to answer him?"

An earnest-looking young woman near him shook her head, panicked. She held a sign that said, YOUNG PEOPLE ARE IMPRESSIONABLE.

"Come on, Val, you can handle this."

The reporter held out the microphone.

"I'm not for censorship," she said in a tentative, high-pitched voice. At that point she seemed to lose her nerve. John watched her closely. She had light brown hair and eyes of some light color, he couldn't tell exactly in the twilight.

She cleared her throat and tried again. "That director had a right to make that movie, but the studio didn't have to buy it and distribute it. They could have chosen a project that wasn't so hateful and dirty. I'm... I'm a first-grade teacher, and I think of these kids growing up... I think those people out in Hollywood are cynical and greedy, and this is the only way we can make them listen."

"But this isn't pornography," the reporter said. "This is an art movie. Some high-quality films get rated X, like *Last Tango in Paris* in the 1970s, and *Only at Midnight*—that was, what, fifteen years ago? Now they're classics."

"*Last Tango in Paris*?" John said. "That *was* obscene."

He meant it, too. It was obscene to see someone as old and fat and ugly as Marlon Brando getting twenty-year-old pussy. Nobody should have to watch that shit.

The woman looked at him gratefully.

She was quite pretty, in a scared-rabbit kind of way. Not like Averil at all in face or coloring or voice or personality. Yet there was something about the way she kept her hair swept off her forehead, and her jacket collar, turned up against the cool evening air, reminded him of the priest's silhouette. He edged closer, looked down into her eyes and sensed it all, her need rising up off her like a scent: she wanted an engagement ring, wanted to take a man's name, give him kids. She believed in a fairy tale, wanted desperately to find a prince.

He hoped his smile didn't look too predatory.

"I'm John Harrison," he said, and she shook his hand.

He didn't even have to set foot in a bar and make his half-hearted attempts at male bonding. She was probably a virgin, too.

127

CHAPTER 12

TRANSFIGURATION

And on God's part I say to you
that you shall never be damned.

—Gertrude of Delft, 14th century

As much as Peter Byrne had been bracing himself for the letter from the Vatican, his heart sank when it actually came. A copy of the one sent to Averil.

He looked for her all over the monastery, finally found her in the church, sitting in a pew near the back. She stared straight ahead, her eyes large and teary and confused, as if her feelings had been deeply hurt. He sat down next to her.

"You know what's ironic?" she said. "He's gone. I haven't seen him in months. But still the Church in its wisdom—" she broke off. She wanted to be fierce. She didn't want to be part of an endless line of women weeping.

For the first time Peter took Averil's hand in his own. He could feel the tension in her body. She was high strung in the best of circumstances. Now she was like a drawn bow about to be released.

"When was the last time you ate?" he said.

"This is a bitter, bitter day," she said.

"Averil, come to the kitchen for some tea. You'll feel better."

"I need to be outside. To walk."

She walked the perimeter of the garden barefoot, then put on her shoes and walked all over the monastery grounds. As the sun set she climbed over the low stone wall, crossed a field and a stretch of woods, came upon the back of John's deserted cottage, followed roads leading now away, now back, until somehow she reached the monastery again.

The chill made the night seem like autumn rather than spring. She stood looking at the church, hugging herself to keep warm. The stained-glass windows gleamed faintly from the eternal flame and the few lamps that were kept on all the time.

The flame was in there, the only heat source for miles around. The holy water too.

That was the problem. She was out here with the earth and the air, and the fire and the water were trapped inside.

She wanted to grab the whole building and shake it till it fell down. Not one stone will be left standing in this temple. The grief hit her, finally, with its full force, the deep, inconsolable sorrow she had been feeling all day, as if at the death of one deeply loved.

Go in. Say goodbye.

She opened the outer doors and felt a sudden sense of urgency, pushed the inner doors with both hands so they flew open, and rushed down the aisle as if she were late and a crowd were waiting for her. No time for priestly dignity, stately ceremony.

In the middle of the nave she stopped. She whirled around. Where to begin?

Everything glittering and hard, brittle.

She ran to a pillar and grasped it at shoulder level as if she was going to choke it. The stones wanted to be freed. If she could find the right one and pry it loose, everything would tumble easily. She tried with all her strength to shake the pillar, but it refused to move. Useless.

She ran back to the entrance, where she pushed the holy water basin and sent it clattering to the floor.

The water is freed.

If she knocked some other things down, if she could start the vibrations, the rest would shudder and tremble and fall. She raced to the altar, knocked over the reader's lectern, tried her strength against the celebrant's podium, but it was too massive. She pulled at the altar cloth, swept her arms across the tables at the back. Candlesticks, books, the paten, the chalice went flying. The music stands, the organist's bench, anything not bolted to the floor was toppled, even the tall free-standing holder of the eternal flame. The glass holding the candle landed on the altar cloth, now puddled on the stone floor.

The fire is freed.

She smiled.

No time to rest, too much to do. The fire and the water were freed, but they needed to escape this place. Near the door she gripped a crowbar used by the restoration workers and climbed the scaffold, more nimbly than she would have thought possible, to the Rose Window, the stained-glass masterpiece that people from all over came to see.

She pulled herself onto the catwalk, level with the window, and swung the crowbar with all her strength. Glass shuddered, splintered, burst into the night sky, rained on her in radiant slivers. She could have sworn she heard a man give an agonized shout. Then she realized it was raining. The roof must have collapsed, though when she looked up into the darkness, it seemed there was a roof still there.

She slid down the scaffold and sprinted back to the altar.

The most important thing. The most important person to be freed. She pulled at the crucifix, and though she meant only to pull down the elaborately carved and painted wooden Jesus, the cross came crashing down with him too.

She cradled his bloodied head against her breasts, something she had always longed to do. She would bathe his wounds, restore him to life, poor broken son, poor tormented lover.

"Averil. Come with me."

The voice was unmistakable, but the only person Averil could see was a graceful girl at the foot of the altar steps. The girl held a gun in her right hand, barrel pointing up. She ran toward Averil with easy grace, lightly jumping over the obstacles now strewn between them.

"Come on."

"How strange," Averil said. "You remind me of—"

"It's me. Catherine Beck."

Her silky blonde hair had been cut short and spiky and dyed reddish-brown. She wore black leather pants, a tank top, quantities of the silvery chains favored that year by rebellious teenagers. And indeed, she looked no older than a college student.

"I don't understand—"

"You like the new look? It's about time for me to get out of town. And it seems you'll be coming with me."

She gently disengaged Jesus from Averil's arms and led her by the hand toward the side exit, still holding the gun aloft. When Peter Byrne burst in through a stairwell, Catherine aimed at him and said calmly, "I'll kill anyone who tries to stop us."

"Don't be ridiculous, woman. I'm not trying to stop you, I want to hurry you on your way. Our smoke detector system has an automatic notification to the fire station."

Peter's loud brusque voice gave Averil a moment of blessed normalcy. He seemed more inconvenienced than angry as he looked around him, not so much worried about the destroyed objects as annoyed at the bother of cleaning up.

"She needs to be on medication," he said to Catherine. "There's no shame in it. Take her to a doctor—when you get to wherever you're going." He turned to Averil and said sternly, "May God forgive you for this disrespect."

"May Goddess forgive us all," she said.

When they go outside, she pointed at the moon. "Our Mother is there."

"The car is this way."

Averil stopped. "The ancient beings." She was overwhelmed with love and respect. "They were here on this earth before us. They belong here more than we do."

"I don't see anyone... You mean the *trees*?"

Catherine gripped Averil's shoulders and looked her in the eye. "You need some rest. Hold still a second, there's a piece of glass stuck in your forehead. Now come on. We need to get out of here right away."

"I can't leave my things. My papers and books..."

"They're in the car. I packed them before I came for you."

~

A premonition, perhaps, had induced Peter Byrne to make his way to Averil's office and find Catherine Beck's phone number. "I don't think *I'm* the one she'll want to talk to tonight," he'd said. Back in his own room, he had almost managed to fall asleep when he sensed a commotion of some kind, though later he realized he couldn't possibly have heard the crashing and banging from all the way in the Chapter House.

Marc got to the church right behind him. They both spotted the flaming altar cloth.

"See to that," Peter said. "I'll get the fire extinguisher—oh good lord, the whole sprinkler system has kicked in." The water damage would be all over the church, much worse than the tiny fire that triggered it. "Marc, see about turning that damn thing off."

Marc was sputtering with shock and outrage. "This is sacrilege. This is desecration. We've got to stop her."

He saw Marc's eyes go wide with horror and turned around in time to see Averil shatter the Rose Window. The witless boy screamed as if he were in pain.

"Don't make me repeat myself," Peter said. He half-dragged Marc with him down to the basement. "The sprinkler system. Turn it off, now. And I'll find the circuit breaker."

Between that and herding Averil and her gunslinging friend out of there, he had no time to speak to Marc until he heard the sirens. Fire engine and police.

"I'll do all the talking," he said to Marc in a fierce whisper.

But Marc had already phoned the police, told them Averil had run wild in the church.

"Strictly an internal matter, officer. She's by no means dangerous, just overworked and distraught... a family tragedy.... No, officer, I was so flustered I can't remember what the other woman looked like. Maybe blonde hair, or light brown... No, I didn't get a good look at the car. I'm sure it's a sympathetic parishioner from town."

"We'll have to question her."

"Of course. I'm sure she'll be back in the morning."

~

They drove a few miles in silence before Catherine said, "You'll be less conspicuous if you take that collar off."

Silence. She glanced over at Averil, saw an expression she couldn't read. Stubbornness mixed with grief, edged with exhaustion.

"Averil," she said as gently as she could, "right now we need to be careful about drawing attention to ourselves. So do me a favor and give me the collar for now."

Averil undid the collar and handed it over. Catherine tossed it into one of the boxes in the back seat.

"If we lose that one," Catherine said, "we can always buy another."

"They don't sell clerical collars at the Catholic store."

"I promise you, if you want one I'll get it for you, no matter what I have to do."

She pictured Catherine with that gun she held so lightly, stopping priests at random and demanding their collars. She smiled briefly, then subsided into a wooden silence as she watched the road ahead of them.

After a few hours they stopped at a house off a country road. The people were friends of Catherine; they asked no questions, merely pointed the way to the bedrooms, bathroom, kitchen. She wept in Catherine's arms for hours before she fell asleep. When she awoke it was late morning. Catherine's friends fed her pancakes and scrambled eggs.

They left Catherine's car there and drove off in an old blue sedan.

"We have everything, right?" Averil said. "My things?"

"All your worldly possessions fit into two moderate-size crates," Catherine said. "I admire that. They're safe in the trunk, with all of my worldly possessions."

"Two boxes?"

Catherine flashed a brilliant smile. "One."

It was a cold spring day, but the sun warmed the car; sometimes they even had to open a window to let in fresh air. They stopped at a diner, where Catherine ordered a burger with all the toppings, and Averil had french fries and a chocolate milkshake. She wanted to start with simple things, salt and sweet, sunlight and air, things that would please a child just starting out in the world on shaky legs.

Part Two

Have women no country?

—Angelina Grimké, 1837

CHAPTER 13

ALL SOULS

And let people take you for a fool;
there is much truth in that.

—Hadewijch of Antwerp

Averil is at the Vatican, she is about to address the General Assembly. She stands at the podium and looks up at the rows and rows of seats that rise in front of her and curve around in the amphitheater hall. This is her great opportunity, her finest hour: she has an eloquent speech from the heart that is bound to impress everyone with its reasoned seriousness and deep feeling.

She opens her mouth. No words come out.

She makes a show of checking the microphone, as if the absence of words has nothing to do with the emptiness inside her, the lack of lungs and larynx and tongue, all the bodily paraphernalia for producing sound. She wonders how she's gotten so far in life, missing these basic and—one would think—necessary internal organs.

The audience members, all men of course, princes of the Church, listen solemnly as if she were indeed speaking. Perhaps they are listening to the voices swirling around Averil, female voices: "You let us down." "This was your job."

In some alternate dimension, she thinks, there exists some ideal Averil, focused, accomplished, untroubled by the desires of the body. That Averil would have changed history. She would have carried the memory of her dead companions lightly, instead of being crushed under it.

Averil walks out of the hall, joins a group of Flagellants passing through St. Peter's Square. They leave the city, trudge through forests, wade across rivers, lashing themselves with knotted cords and praying for forgiveness.

~

Their house was a small two-bedroom bungalow, rented fully furnished. Averil and Catherine weren't the only ones who arrived in Erda with almost nothing.

Sometimes people described Averil as a "renegade priest," but in fact she wasn't technically on the run, and as far as the Church was concerned, she was no longer a priest.

She spent those early days basking in the quiet she found inside that house. There were no Masses to say, no confessions to hear. No expectations to disappoint.

She watched the light play along the tree trunks in the park across the street, remembered the patch of woodland she walked through to get to John Honig's cottage. She played with her newfound appreciation of the forest. A place without sin.

Catherine came back from her morning run. Hollow-sounding, churchy music was playing on the shortwave radio she'd bought for Averil the day before.

"What is this stuff?" she said.

"Gregorian chant."

Catherine showered and dressed, the music seeping in through her closed bedroom door. The men's voices were affectless, as if they'd been brainwashed. Their music should have been merely repetitive and monotonous, but to Catherine, fearless warrior that she was, there was something oddly frightening about it, as if it could infect you, worm itself into your brain and make you placid and indifferent.

She knelt before Averil's chair, put her hands gently on Averil's arms to make sure she was paying attention.

"That which has been is now," Averil said, "and that which is to be has already been."

Catherine waited.

"It's what they're saying. The chant. From Ecclesiastes. It's in Latin."

"I have to go out," Catherine said, "talk to people about getting work. We'll need money for our expenses here."

"Don't worry," Averil said. "I often get invitations to give talks. What I'd make in speaker's fees could pay our rent."

"What would you talk about?"

Averil looked out the window.

"Trees."

"You need to rest," Catherine said. "The speaking engagements can wait."

~

Outside in the small, fenced-in backyard, the grass was silky and lush, a green miracle. Averil lay down and studied the enormous sky. Clouds scurried across and gave her the sensation that the earth was turning rapidly. She became acutely aware of the planet beneath her, felt the heft of the giant sphere, and suddenly it seemed to be behind her, not beneath her—she was pressed up against the side of an enormous ball hurtling through space, had to spread out her arms and flatten her body against it, to avoid slipping off the side.

~

Each shadow army burst onto the world scene full-grown, like Aphrodite from the forehead of Zeus, a process that must have given the divine father an unholy headache.

Take, for instance, the Daughters of Mother Africa, introduced in the West to those few people suffering from insomnia and paying attention to their shortwave radios in the small hours of the morning.

"Live from Riyadh. A car bomb has exploded minutes ago. According to police the victims are a prominent Islamic clergyman and his driver and bodyguards. The clergyman was reportedly one of the leaders of the renewed campaign to limit women's rights based on what critics claim is a spurious reading of the Koran. A group has already contacted the police claiming responsibility."

According to a pamphlet from the Daughters of Mother Africa, made available to the media at that time:

We are a group of Muslim, Animist, Christian, atheist, and other women. We insist on the right of women everywhere to enjoy the fullness of their chosen spiritual traditions without being suppressed by men who act out their hatred of us in the guise of enforcing religious orthodoxy. We act on behalf of enslaved women everywhere, and we will continue to target male self-proclaimed religious leaders until they cease their inexcusable crimes against women.

The radio reporter read the statement in its entirety. "It remains to be seen," he went on in a disapproving voice, "how widespread this group actually is, and whether they will continue to carry out these terrorist missions."

~

Averil stood at the kitchen sink washing lettuce, feeling the tender leaves brushing against her fingertips in the cool water. Her memories of her rampage at St. Anthony's were still fragmentary. She had no recollection of shattering the Rose Window but had a clear image of the glass splinters showering down on her in flashes of red and pink, how beautiful they had been.

Now, what she remembered instead was a sunny afternoon when she was in college, walking with Asher through a state park near their campus. Talking about their philosophies of life, as twenty-year-olds did.

He believed, he said, in what his senses could perceive, what he could measure.

She was comforted by his gentle agnosticism, had no wish to change his mind. Their leisurely disagreement was something more to enjoy about him.

Is love not real? she said. Is joy not real?

They stopped to sit on a sun-warmed rock. Averil lay back and looked at the dark blue sky edged by the tops of hemlocks and pines.

Asher lay back too, looked up, presumably saw the same as she did.

Emotions, he said, are merely physiological responses.

Averil had smiled and closed her eyes, pictured hormones rushing along blood vessels, electrical impulses leaping across synapses, felt the warmth of Asher's body next to hers, the rock below her, the sun above.

Reason was a path to God, the Bhagavad Gita said. Averil pictured a steep rocky path through a dry forest in relentless sunlight, the person on the path sweating, breathing hard, pushing onward despite sore muscles.

She was not startled to sense Catherine beside her.

"I've brought supper." She set down sandwiches on the counter. "Eggplant parmesan for you, roast beef for me."

Averil turned and saw people crowded silently around the kitchen table. Men. Looking dazed and aggrieved, sending accusing glances across the kitchen to Catherine as she pulled out plates and cutlery and found a salad spinner in a cabinet.

Averil knew who they were.

You have blood on your own hands, she told them.

They looked at her. All of them—Averil and the dead men—knew that that was no answer.

Averil spun the salad and put it on the plates. Looking at Catherine sitting waiting for her at the table with her perfect posture and unshakeable composure, it occurred to Averil that Catherine had no vices. Not only did she not slouch, she didn't smoke, needed no caffeine in the morning to start her day. She didn't sleep late, overeat, lounge around watching television. Her clothes were neat and clean. She worked out regularly.

She wasn't arrogant, had no pretentious ideas about her own intellectual superiority.

She had made no vows. And thus hadn't broken them.

"I had a lover," Averil said. "We take a vow of celibacy but I had a lover."

"I know."

"He disappeared."

Catherine was silent. The ghosts looked at her, at each other, at Averil.

~

Erda in those days, during the two years Catherine Beck and Averil Parnell found refuge there, was still in a state of equilibrium. Despite the growing unrest on the outside, no one had broached the country's borders, no one had challenged its sovereignty.

To a visitor, Erda may have seemed much the same as always: humming with tranquil activity, land of windmills and watermills, feminist hippie agricultural co-ops, artisans and artists, solar-powered daycare centers, health care provided free for everyone.

But a perceptive observer might have picked up a subtle unease, a heightened awareness that this state of affairs, idyllic as it was, couldn't last. Or perhaps this was merely what people claimed afterward, with the benefit of hindsight. How long, after all, have humans consoled themselves with the knowledge that nothing lasts forever?

Certainly some Erdans noticed a trend in the country's immigration patterns. Women were applying for entry visas as individuals, but upon arrival it became clear that they were members of groups that had already existed abroad, collectives that were reconstituting themselves here.

It was later assumed that Erda was the center of coordination of D.O.T. activities, but this is not only inaccurate but also simplistic, relying as it does on the old paradigm of a rigid hierarchy with one command-and-control center: the human and its brain, the army and its general. There are other patterns to be found in nature: spontaneous evolution of similar forms in different environments, for example. Subatomic bits or cosmic

141

debris, slowly coalescing, eventually drawn into the orbit of a nucleus, or a sun, depending on the scale of your metaphor.

~

They got back from their honeymoon late, so exhausted that John fell asleep immediately while Valerie was still removing her makeup. When he woke up the next morning he had the delicious sensation of being alone in the bed, and for a minute it seemed all he wanted in this life, to wake up alone with no living being looking at him until he was ready for it, hardened and shielded against all that ravenous looking.

But it was impossible to maintain the illusion of solitude. Some kind of fruity perfume lingered on the pillow next to him. In the kitchen Valerie had raised the shades, had even gone outside and picked a flower from the yard and put it in a water glass on the table. She was wide awake, smiling, dressed in a dark blue tank top and jeans, a white ribbon holding back her long brown hair. She stood at the stove making pancakes, smiling expectantly, and God help him he knew he was supposed to smile back instead of however it was he was looking at her, because it was making her smile go wavery.

"Hi," he said.

"What's the matter?" she said. "Did I make too much noise? Did I wake you up? I want everything to be perfect, especially today."

"Why today?"

"It's our first day."

He must have looked as blank as he felt, because she put down the spatula and put her arms around him. "The first day of our married life."

"We got married a week ago."

"The honeymoon doesn't count, silly. I mean our regular, day-to-day life as a married couple, in our home. Today's our first day."

Jesus fucking Christ. "I need some coffee." No, he needed a shot of whiskey, and then maybe another one after that. As he sat down at the kitchen table it took all his self-control not to put his face down on his arms and hope that when he looked up a few hours later she would be gone.

The first day.

He never kept track of things like that. Even when it was happening he never had the sense that this is the first day of whatever, I'll be looking back on it someday, I'll remember exactly how it was. First day of school at St. Bartholomew's, first day of high school at the Dominican Academy, first time he fucked a girl. First time he kissed a girl, that would have been later, he sure as hell didn't recall that.

He realized he did remember something about the first day of high school. He was having breakfast and his father seemed to take offense at something, maybe he expected John to seem nervous or act like he gave a damn. "The problem with you, boy," Randolph Honig said, "is no one's ever hit you. You wouldn't know what to do if you got into a fight." John couldn't believe what he was hearing. He and every boy he knew had done nothing but get into fights since first grade. Like everyone else he would come home with a ripped shirt, skinned elbows and knees, dust all over, a bleeding nose, and here was this man looking at him like he was some kind of sissy boy about to get his ass whipped. John had wondered idly how Randolph would react if he reached across the table and grabbed him by the collar and squeezed and squeezed until that blue-blooded face turned really blue.

That's what he remembered about his first day of high school.

~

Averil walked out into the blinding sunlight of an Erdan August afternoon, breathed in the scent of overheated sidewalks, and decided to buy herself a treat. Fried mozzarella sticks, perhaps, and iced tea. Who needed bread and wine?

Her search for a diner led her down random streets till she arrived at a community garden. Most gardeners were prudently waiting for the heat to subside a little. The few who were there were mostly clustered around the water pump, splashing their faces.

Averil stepped over a shin-high chicken-wire fence and squatted down in front of a thriving row of green beans. The weeds were almost half the height of the bean plants, but the soil was soft and well-watered. The weeds came out easily.

She was a third of the way down the row when something large blocked out the sunlight and a gravelly voice spoke from the dark mass.

"I don't know who you are, but I like you already."

Averil peered up at a woman who was the closest she'd ever seen to a live approximation of the Willendorf goddess figure: massive and bronze-colored, all breasts and bountiful belly.

"Mind if I take off my shoes?" Averil said.

She never did get to the diner that evening. Lucinda shared her cream-cheese-and-olive sandwich and they both had a long drink at the water pump.

143

As she left the community garden she started to put her shoes and socks back on but decided against it. She felt she was being daring somehow, stepping barefoot onto ordinary city sidewalks, the kind of thing grownups scolded her for when she was little: "You'll step on glass." "You'll cut yourself." Moving at a majestically slow pace, she set each foot down carefully, tested for the much-warned-of splinters of glass before putting down her full weight. Either the people of Erda were blessedly careful about undue bottle-shattering on public streets, or her feet had grown layers of tough gardener skin; she moved on without injury.

She started going for long walks around the town and then the flat straight country roads beyond.

The people of Reservoir figured out who she was. Her name had been familiar for years to feminists interested in spirituality, and now her jousting with the Catholic Church had given her a new level of notoriety.

At first they merely noted her presence, left her alone as she meandered by, stoop-shouldered, absent-minded. Gradually, if it were meal times, those who spotted her would gently herd her into a restaurant and set food down in front of her. Eventually they started speaking to her, and she to them, and sometimes her answers were coherent. Averil was aware that she was a slightly up-market version of the village idiot. The village idiot-savant, perhaps.

She would return to the small house by evening, tune the radio to something less irritating for Catherine than medieval church music. They turned on a few lamps and sat together, commenting occasionally on the music or the weather or the people walking by outside. Averil would pick a book from her collection and sit and look at it. Eventually she began to actually read. Eventually the words started to make sense.

CHAPTER 14

COMMIXTIO CORPORIS ET SANGUINIS

We are plotting revolution; we will overthrow
this bogus Republic and plant a government
of righteousness in its stead.

—Victoria Woodhull, 1871

B y the end of the year, the next shadow army surfaced on the world
scene, this time in southeastern Europe, where the on-again/off-
again Balkan wars had taken a new turn: Bosnian and other women had
declared an independent nation on a small patch of territory.

The leaders had a mission, they announced: to track down and bring
to justice any man, of any nationality, who had participated in rape camps.
"We're going to do what the international tribunal has been bumbling
over for decades," they said.

The name of the new nation: Nova Zemlja. In English: New Earth
or, perhaps, New Erda.

It was a slow news day in the United States, as luck would have it, and a
few television newscasts devoted half a minute or so to the fledgling country
and its mission. One journalist asked the opinion of a prominent Christian
fundamentalist who could be relied on for bombastic commentary.

"It's blasphemous," fumed the preacher, breathing heavily into the
reporter's microphone. "These women have taken a sacred biblical phrase,
'a new heaven and a new earth,' and twisted it to their own unholy
purposes."

The reporter asked whether he had any thoughts about the new country's mission to track down rape camp criminals.

"They should forgive," the preacher wheezed. "It's what Our Lord teaches."

Luckily for the citizens of Nova Zemlja, the preacher's offensive comments got more news coverage than they could ever have wished for, and donations from supportive women poured in from all over the world.

~

As the weather got colder, Averil's hold on reality seemed to get firmer. She found a job as an assistant to a bookbinder

She was easing into normalcy, she felt, getting up in the morning and walking carefully along snowy sidewalks to the bindery, sitting in the workroom with its old leather-topped oak tables and tall, mullioned windows, drawing a needle through a group of pages to stitch them together. So odd to take a sharp object to paper, without hurting it. The rules of paper, scissors, rock didn't apply here. Scissors weren't weapons but tools.

~

John Honig sometimes wondered what would happen if he said what he actually wanted to say, without having to think about the image he presented: New husband. Expectant father. Loyal FBI operative. Person who gave a damn.

This makes no fucking sense, was the first thing he would say.

They sent a handler—the word itself was ludicrous—to meet with John, instead of a quick conversation over the phone. Plus the guy looked like a mid-level computer geek: short-sleeved shirt plus tie, no jacket. John's cover was that he worked from home for one of the nationwide lending firms, thus explaining his home office and frequent absences on "business" trips, but there was no way this handler looked like anyone who had ever worked in banking.

Who the fuck is in charge of you idiots? might have been John's next uncensored statement.

He restrained himself. Shook the guy's hand—his name, he claimed, was Stan Brown (please)—offered him a seat across from his desk, poured him coffee, before getting down to the point of the meeting (which *could* have been handled in a phone call).

"I want to be stationed in Erda," John said. "I would be of more use there."

146

His whole reason for joining the FBI was to get access to information about Catherine Beck. Now he knew she was in Erda, living quietly as far as the FBI could tell. And like everyone else in Erda, probably unaware of the seething mass of race and gender resentment roiling in the guts of the Aryan Revivalists a few states over.

The same people John was busy arranging "business loans" for, in his guise as a loan officer.

He wasn't surprised that the FBI would keep tabs on a fringe extremist group. Nor did he question the legality or ethics of secretly funding them in their harassment campaign against another country. He didn't give a damn one way or the other. His job was to sit down with these ignorant rednecks and arrange "loans" for this tractor purchase or that landscaping business, with the full awareness that the money was being funneled into weapons purchases.

What irked him was the realization that these fucking yahoos had as much access to Beck as he did. Would maybe kill her before he got his chance.

"No can do," Stan Brown said cheerfully. "Those Erdans do a serious background check before they give you even a provisional entry visa."

"Like you can't create a fake ID? It's what you guys do."

"John, let's be honest—"

Yes, let's.

"You're not exactly the kind of guy who would—how do I put this?—fit in, in Erda."

"Why, because I'm not a pussy?"

That thought had failed to be censored. Stan Brown laughed awkwardly and acted as if he hadn't heard it.

"Besides," he said, "you've got a pretty young wife, baby on the way. Wouldn't want you doing anything dangerous."

John forced himself to smile.

~

Val tried to squirm away from his grasp, from his raging hard-on. She bleated about hurting "the baby," as she insisted on calling it, even though she was only three months gone. He had to wrestle her down.

The most payback he would get for this were reproachful looks over breakfast. She seemed to have convinced herself that Jesus said husbands should be the boss. Fine with him.

He had quickly found out there was no satisfaction in slamming her against walls or pushing her facedown on the bed with her arm twisted behind her, fucking her hard and deep. It made her gasp and cry like who knew how many other women before her, but her whimpers nauseated him instead of making him harder and angrier. She was as pitiful as an animal with no fangs or claws, who didn't even have enough backbone to get mad. There was no sport in it.

He'd always suspected that marital sex, by definition, would be boring. It was respectable. Approved by state and blessed by church. Where was the fun in that? But he hadn't predicted just how mind-numbing it would be.

It never got boring with the priest. They grappled and scratched, crashing against walls and down to the floor. He remembered her hands reaching into his hair, tugging at the roots, fistfuls of it. Her fingernails strafing his neck as if seeking out his carotid artery. Her eyes dark and intent as if she weren't a fully consenting sex partner but an assassin sent to kill him.

~

The sound of monk voices comes to Averil, not tiny and staticky as they have been on the radio, but clear and resonant as if her bed is located in the choir stall. But Averil is no monk, not for her the privilege of the brotherhood, safety of monastery walls, camaraderie of chanted-sung prayers. She is a ragged penitent, she is with the Flagellants, patiently flaying herself with a handful of stinging nettles. Their road has taken them to the sea, where the Ship of Fools awaits her.

And then there are two of her. She is Averil standing on the shore watching herself sail off in a luminous ship. And she is Averil standing on the deck, sea spray stinging her open wounds while the ship creaks and groans as it moves through purple-blue water.

Until now she and the other Flagellants, blood-flecked faces slick with sweat and sea foam, have been aware of nothing but their own sinfulness and impending doom. Now they look at each other and laugh.

I am a holy fool, says the Averil on the ship.

I am a priest of God, says the Averil on the shore.

~

Scholars dispute how precisely to date the start of the Revolution. Some historians point to the Erdan skirmishes with the Aryan Revivalists, while others place it earlier, during the first violent activities of the various shadow armies. Even the later, conventionally accepted milestone, the incursion of U.S. troops on Erdan territory, is difficult to pinpoint: did

148

it start when the first soldiers physically set foot there, or when they first fired on Erdans, or when war was officially declared?

People in Erda remembered the last summer before the war as a notably harmonious time, like a long hippie festival. Troubles in the rest of the world were only a distant rumbling: the Daughters of Mother Africa carried out bombings in Algeria, Sudan, and Kuwait. Somewhere a session of a legislature was taken hostage. Somewhere else a doctor was killed for carrying out genital mutilation on young girls.

But in Erda what people remembered were block parties, picnics, craft fairs and farmer's markets, bountiful gardens. What they remembered was the perfect weather. The days were hot, yes, but not plaster-you-to-the-deck-chair hot like the usual Erdan summer. The evenings brought just the right amount of coolness. The mosquitoes were few and easily discouraged.

~

John sat on the front porch, beer in hand, looking out across fields of soybean and corn to the setting sun. The place was flat as the desert, America's heartland, not so much as a hill or a lone tree to break the monotony.

Valerie came out on the porch, sat on the floor beside his adirondack chair. She looked around contentedly. A few weeks ago she had painted the porch floorboards and banisters pearl gray, and stripped and refinished the handrail with a golden oak stain and layers of varnish. She'd set up flower boxes all along the porch. A goddamned showcase of Americana.

John knew she was waiting for him to compliment her on her work.

He took a swig of beer.

"What are you thinking about?" she said.

"Some old science fiction story I read in grade school, I forget who wrote it, about a kid who develops these powers and in the blink of an eye their little town is in the middle of nowhere, like the kid made the whole world disappear. Then everyone has to be really careful not to upset the kid. When he gets mad at someone he makes the person explode or turn inside out and then the next instant they're buried out in the cornfields at the edge of town."

"That's creepy. You shouldn't have read stuff like that when you were at an impressionable age."

She seemed unaware that she had placed a protective hand over her hugely protruding abdomen. Can't let "the baby" hear anything inappropriate. He wondered whether she'd let him alone with the kid after it was born. "Honey," she was always whining, "you shouldn't say things like that. You shouldn't think that way." And he hadn't told her a fraction of the things that went on in his head.

And she had no idea, of course, about the work he did. Her plan was to stay home with the kid—she was sure it would be a boy—until he was old enough for preschool. Then she would go back to teaching, and come home every day the same time as the kid. John almost pitied the child. He wouldn't be let out of his mother's sight for a minute.

He planned to be long gone by then. He didn't care what the FBI idiots said, he would make his way to wherever the blonde bitch was.

Val picked a dead leaf from the potted hyacinth. She was looking out at the horizon with distaste, as if the mangled victims of the child-monster were over there in the neighbor's neatly planted rows of corn.

"In the story," he said, "the doctor who delivered the kid realized what a demon it was and tried to kill it as soon as it was born, but the mother stopped him."

"Honey, please, I don't think I want to hear any more."

~

A woman showed up at the house one day wanting to do a portrait of Averil, who felt it would be impolite to refuse. She helped her set up her easel in the living room.

Catherine wished she'd thought of it. But she would find a real artist, someone who would do it right, not like this woman applying swaths of dark colors to what looked like a piece of cardboard.

"Are those crayons?" Catherine said.

"Pastels."

Shannon, the "artist," sounded offended.

Averil caught Catherine's eye and smiled. The portrait would never do justice to that face.

Shannon did a double take when she saw Catherine take off her blazer.

"You've got—you—carry a gun around with you? In *Erda*?"

"Old habit."

"She never takes her gun off," Averil said.

"I take it off when I'm home."

"Not really."

Catherine was about to argue, but realized Averil wasn't speaking literally. Averil almost never spoke literally.

150

She sat down in an armchair near Averil, and the artist contemplated the contrast between them, Averil with her dark hair and black clothing and deep shining eyes, and Catherine with pale eyes and silver gun, hair the color of winter wheat.

"There's a new project I've been thinking about," Averil said. "I want to see about building a memorial."

When it seemed like she wasn't going to say anything more, Catherine asked her who the memorial was meant for.

"The Martyrs. Of the Cathedral Massacre."

There would be a stone, large and rough. Twenty-two names engraved on it. A stone basin filled with rainwater, set in the ground nearby, small and dark like a pool of blood.

Those were her thoughts as Shannon worked on the angles of Averil's lean face, the shadows playing across it. Despite Catherine's skepticism, the portrait did indeed capture Averil, though people said it was a shame she looked so sad.

~

Who gets to live and who dies is perhaps a question asked more by philosophers and poets than historians, who recorded the bare facts of the coalescing of white nationalist groups into the Aryan Revival that fall, their purchases of military-grade weapons, their first skirmishes across the border into Erda. Historians tell us the where and the when, tally the number of wounded and dead, note that this was the impetus for the Erdan government to hastily authorize the formation of a standing army.

Those who were there remembered other things. They remembered that after each raid, donations to Erda flooded in. They remembered the entry of trigger-happy "volunteers" who had showed up to help Erda's border patrol, and then rushed to join the army when it was finally mustered.

But as winter set in, with the long nights and dark, ice-bound days, raids by the Aryan Revivalists came to a temporary halt. People braced themselves for worse, but at the same time they insisted on going about their normal lives.

Catherine now spent most of her time in the barracks of the new Erdan army. But she was home on the weekends, and then she and Averil walked all over town. On snowy icy sidewalks they linked arms and pressed forward, Averil surprisingly steady on her feet, eyes shining in the crisp air. They visited the restored Art Deco theater for movies, the tiny museum, the community theater. They found an Italian bakery that reminded Averil of the ones she'd known in Connecticut.

Catherine got home one Friday night near midnight. Too keyed up to sleep, she stayed outside on the front step, tried to relax and think of something other than the belligerent noises coming from the United States, the woefully inadequate preparation of the average Erdan soldier.

Averil came out and sat down next to her.

"There's a full moon," she said. "No wonder I couldn't sleep."

Catherine smiled. She needed these non sequiturs now. They soothed her.

"D.O.T.," Averil said.

"Yes."

"I've never known what it stands for."

"You've never asked?"

"You know how it is in the confessional. Or no, I guess you don't. I felt it would have been unprofessional to pry."

Catherine had posed the same question years ago. She would have loved to know who originated it.

"Den of Thieves," she said.

Averil pictured the phrase written down, pondered it from different angles.

"Women are thieves?" she said.

"If you find yourself among thieves, no matter how honest a person you are, you're going to eventually turn to thievery yourself, to survive."

"And the parallel is, we find ourselves among violent men, so we turn to violence too."

"Like a contagion."

"Does it work the other way?" Averil said. "If you put a thief in a den of saints, does he turn saintly?"

"Hasn't happened yet," Catherine said.

CHAPTER 15

KYRIA ELIESON

Men go to war to kill one another, and you, sisters,
you go to repair the evils which they have done.

—Maria Teresa of Spain, 17th century

Anno Mirabilis 1

E rin Zhang didn't bother to look up from her desk when the next
draftee walked in.

"Assignment form?" she said, when the person said nothing.

A paper was placed gently in front of her.

Chaplain of the Erdan Military, read the assignment.

That made her look up.

The woman before her was thin to the point of emaciation. Staffing
for non-combat jobs didn't require any level at all of physical fitness. This
was no way to run an army, but no one was asking Erin's opinion.

"Yes?" Erin said.

"I'm respectfully declining."

"You're refusing to be drafted."

"I'll serve in the military. Just not that assignment."

"So you're refusing the position of chaplain."

"Respectfully."

The woman's deep-set eyes were so dark you couldn't see the pupils.
She leaned over slightly and looked expectantly at the form, as if hoping
Erin would make a note of it. *Refusal made with respect.*

Erin scanned the form. Name: Averil Parnell. Age: 47. Prewar
occupation: bookbinder's assistant. The form included brief notes about
education and previous experience, compiled from Immigration Division
records. The first item on the list: former Roman Catholic priest. The

name, the face, were vaguely familiar. She put it together with memories of a long-ago crime, a shooting rampage in a cathedral. The woman should never have been drafted.

Then again, no one should have been drafted. The United States should never have invaded, with its pretexts of "stabilizing" the situation after the Aryan raids, should never have shot at Erdan troops, then used the exchange of gunfire as a reason to declare war.

"A position like chaplain has to be voluntary," Erin said, "but for my records, would you mind telling me why you don't want it?"

Averil shrugged. Her gifts had abandoned her. She no longer had the gift of preaching or the power to forgive sins. So many gifts she had never had in the first place: prophecy, healing.

"Call it a power failure," she said.

Erin debated what to enter on the form. Burnout. Depression. Good old-fashioned sadness.

"Let's talk about other possibilities. You have a Ph.D. in history and an M.Div. degree. You were a pastor for years. I'd say you have useful skills in organizing, fund-raising, counseling work, public speaking. You would do well in our personnel division, or our communications department."

"I was never suited to those jobs."

Even before the visions.

She had had a respite, an idyllic time in the little rented house with Catherine, living as close as she could get to an ordinary life. Now it was over.

"There has to be some other job I can do," Averil said. "I can tend to a flock of hens, collect their eggs. Hens need to be kept calm, you know. I can relate to them. Or I could grow vegetables. I'm good at gardening."

"In wartime we have to plan on importing our food. Growing our own is too time-consuming and uncertain."

"There always have to be gardens."

Erin couldn't help smiling. "A garden isn't portable, it's on land. And territory changes hands."

The clear dark eyes became clouded. Erin couldn't tell whether Averil was formulating another argument or pondering the portability of gardens.

"My nerve endings have been scraped clean," Averil said, "and they've never regenerated themselves."

Erin Zhang was used to efficiency. Before she moved to Erda she'd worked in human resources in the private sector in the U.S.; before that she'd done the same in the U.S. Army Reserves.

She was trying to learn to let go of those old expectations: efficiency, common sense. She was learning to go with the absurdity.

~

Catherine was glad that at least Averil had accepted a remote, low-profile location.

"You're being assigned to a town called Glenburn," Catherine had told her. "Near the Canadian border. It's so remote there's no chance of an attack."

"We're going to be thrown around like dice in a giant's hand," Averil had said matter-of-factly. No fear, no regret. A simple observation.

"Didn't someone say God doesn't play dice with the universe?"

"Einstein. He wasn't a Catholic."

Averil would be somewhere safe. She could go on following her train of thought, an intricate, twisted thread. It should have been the plot of a fairy tale: generations of women working to undo an evil enchantment by reasoning it out, each one building on the previous one's work, taking up where she had left off. The villains closing in, determined to stop their work.

It is late at night. In a half-dreaming state between exhaustion and exhilaration, Catherine imagines the fairy tale peopled by the characters from Averil's Tarot card deck, those curiously detached-looking figures striking obscure poses with swords and sticks and enormous gold medallions, and it seems to her that she is beginning to understand them. The cards are like fairy tales in a way, they hold a hidden meaning, a truth no one speaks of or remembers consciously. We tell our stories in incomprehensible ways, wordless drawings in a deck of cards, mysterious songs, far-fetched tales. Captive daughters spinning straw into gold for ugly little men. The only way the stories can survive.

They are in battle outside the fortress, Catherine and the other Tarot card figures, fighting the enemy until the dark-haired witch in the castle learns how to dissolve the curse. They know in their hearts that if she succeeds, the world could very well cease to exist. Life might be unrecognizable when the evil enchantment is destroyed. Somehow they would know instantly the moment it happened.

Catherine would be caught mid-fight, sword poised above an opponent.

~

Averil went looking for the transport to her first assignment. People all around her moved with energy and purpose. They had orders to follow,

155

which they had received by some mysterious process Averil was never able to detect. War, in that sense, was like life. Everyone but her knew what was going on.

Behind the main building women were lining up next to a convoy of pickups and small flatbed trucks. She joined the line. As she moved toward the front, she looked anxiously for a sergeant with a clipboard, checking off a list of names, but saw no one orchestrating all that movement. This was no way to run an army. Not the way the popes had run their Church Militant over all these centuries.

Fortunately a woman leaning against the driver's side of a truck looked at Averil and said, "Noncombat?"

"Yes." So it was that obvious.

"Hop in."

Hours later the truck stopped. Averil got off because everyone else did. Here, finally, she was expected to give an accounting of herself, to a uniformed woman at a desk, clipboard in hand. Averil never could figure out military insignia. Something about her seemed like a sergeant. Maybe the clipboard.

"What's your name, soldier?" the woman said.

From priest to soldier.

The change would have been drastic enough if she'd switched from the clergy to the warrior class. From bishop to knight on the chess board, take off the miter and take up the sword. But Averil wasn't becoming a knight, she was joining the commoners, the cannon fodder and serfs, the peasant-pawns fated to be thrown about while the powerful jockeyed for position.

"Are we in Glenburn?" Averil asked the sergeant.

The woman looked surprised. "That's over a hundred miles away."

"I thought I was supposed to be stationed there."

The sergeant shrugged. "No offense, but you don't exactly have a crucial job to do. If you want to go there, I'll find some way to send you."

The first roll of the dice.

"I'll stay here," Averil said.

~

"Here" was an army outpost near a small town, where they were building a new hospital and training facilities. They put Averil on the early shift in the cafeteria, serving the civilians and military personnel working on the construction site. She made scrambled eggs by pouring pre-cracked, premixed eggs onto a griddle. She marveled at the efficiency it took, to make sure vats of liquid eggs, crates of dehydrated potato, were available when they were needed. Perfect for war.

It was a relief to work with fundamental elements. Food, water. She had to take them into herself in the right proportions at the proper times. She made a point of drinking water from a clear glass so that she could admire the glass's transparency, how it matched the water as if it had solidified.

Gradually she became aware of other fundamental elements. Calcium, for instance. She would put out a tub of yogurt next to the breakfast cereals every morning, and she could practically see how it was suffused with calcium. It would harden into bone if you let it. She couldn't believe there was also calcium in things like broccoli and acorn squash. Everything rich in calcium should have been white so you could see the correspondence with teeth and bones.

"Are you getting enough calcium?" she would say to the women filing past with their trays. "Your bones need to soak it up, as much as you can."

She wrote letters to Catherine, short updates on whatever she was thinking about at the moment. *Osteoporosis is unjust, don't you think?* she wrote. *Our bones* should *hollow out as we age, like birds, so we could fly.*

Salt was another element, crucial in a land as far from the ocean as it was possible to get. But she had to keep a balance, it was her responsibility. One morning the women complained that she'd forgotten the salt in the scrambled eggs.

"You don't need it today," she said firmly, annoyed at being challenged. "You've all gotten too salty."

The women looked at each other. One leaned over and said carefully, "Will we have salt tomorrow?"

"Yes, of course."

I'd like to start a compost pile out behind the kitchen, she wrote to Catherine.

But the sergeant won't let me. Says it'll attract mice. Of course, I told her, and cats and snakes and raccoons. That's the point. They eat the food, and what they don't eat goes back to the earth, reverts to fundamental elements. The sergeant looked at me as if I were speaking a different language. Imagine that.

She started feeding leftovers to a stray dog that came by in the autumn evenings when she sat outside, by the kitchen's back door. Averil had no idea how to relate to dogs. At first, this one wouldn't come near. She looked hungry, but when Averil would get up to go inside for some food, the dog would back away and scurry off. After a few days of this Averil spoke to the dog. "Look, I'm going to stand up now, there's no need to be startled. I can't leave food out for you because the sergeant will complain. If you want to eat you're going to have to wait here and let me bring you a plate." The dog backed up but didn't leave, and was still there when Averil came back and set down the plate a safe distance from the crate she was sitting on.

The dog was a yellowish, short-haired mutt who moved slowly, stiffly, as if she were old and ill. On the other hand, Averil reflected, she could have been a bad-tempered dog who got into a lot of fights and was recovering from her latest battle. Averil didn't know dogs well enough to tell. Unlike cats, graceful and free-roaming, dogs were territorial and loud and angry. Maybe they suspected that all humans were in on a scheme to keep them leashed. They were right to be angry. How else to react to injustice?

Eventually the dog began approaching Averil after she'd eaten her fill.

"I'll call you Sandy," Averil said. "For your color. I know it's not very original."

The dog didn't seem to mind. They sat together comfortably, watched the stars. Averil realized that night was another element necessary to her life. Night and cold. She was surprised how quickly she had gotten used to living without central heating. The heat of the cafeteria kitchen stifled her, where once she would have found it comforting.

Averil felt she should try to talk to the dog occasionally, out of politeness. Sitting so close to her, Averil could hear the odd, quiet breathing noises she made, almost snorts. She wondered whether the dog longed to howl at the moon and run in packs with her own kind. "I'm sorry we humans interfered with your evolution," she said. "You don't look like a wolf at all. I hope you're not offended by that." The dog turned her head to her briefly and then looked away.

~

News of the war came in constantly, on the radio, in the occasional newspaper: uneasy ceasefire, U.S. troops in disarray from internal dissension. Six months into the war, martial law was declared in the U.S., but some journalists reported that the laws were being enforced only against women: people arrested for curfew violations were almost all women; meetings broken up by police, even informal conversations, were rumored to always be gatherings of women or mostly women. The response from the White House: This is wartime. Seditious elements must be apprehended.

Fall turned to winter. The war news became even more perplexing as the United States allied itself with the Aryan Revival and other fringe militia groups. The new alliance called itself the Defenders of the American Way.

As if the world were dividing, Averil reflected, into two camps, two acronyms: D.A.W. and D.O.T. And none of the D's stood for Daughters.

The cold weather came as a relief. She hoped it would stop the war. How could you have battles in blizzard conditions? Maybe people would come to their senses.

~

A new letter from Averil. Catherine always made sure to read them when she was alone and relaxed, in the right condition to see these dispatches from the landscape of Averil's mind.

All that upheaval in the U.S., do you think it will break apart eventually? I hear the fundamentalists there are talking about End Times, but Christians have always talked about End Times. It's the end of their world that's coming, not the world, don't you think? Two letters, i and r, make all the difference.

There was a slight break after that paragraph, and then a different color ink. She must have come back to the letter after several days.

I'm reading that women there are being rounded up for anti-American activity. A witch hunt. My friends at the FBI would have put me on that list, don't you think? I could have wound up in prison if I'd stayed at St. Anthony's. From monastery cell to jail cell.

And beneath her signature a scrawled postscript: *I wonder how long Mother Earth will tolerate us before she shakes us off. We're like little mites on her skin. The trees her bristly hair.*

CHAPTER 16

GLORIA MATRI

Set aside all the melancholy to
which you have yielded,
and renounce the cowardice that is in you.

—Hadewijch of Antwerp

Anno Mirabilis 2

A year after the declaration of war there seemed no sign of an end. Chaotic as the United States was becoming, it had a limitless supply of military force to throw in Erda's direction. Averil, from the safety of the cafeteria, heard news of the war like an endless dirge that played in the back of her mind.

The hospital was built, new and shiny but as low-budget as anything else in Erda. With the construction work done, new faces were showing up at the cafeteria, medical personnel, the patients who were ambulatory, other soldiers coming in for training at things Averil had only the vaguest understanding of: signal corps, quartermaster, rapid-response.

And then one day, an old face.

Averil was walking toward the cafeteria to start her shift when she saw the woman and stopped short.

Elizabeth O'Hare.

Averil's sister-seminarian. Cut down in a hail of gunfire twenty years ago.

Standing right there, trim and elegant in the morning sunshine, her glossy brown hair threaded with silver and cut stylishly short.

Elizabeth, long dead. Smiling and holding out her arms.

Averil hugged her tight, hardly daring to breathe. Wanting to enjoy this gift before it evaporated.

Then slowly, understanding dawned. This was Lauren O'Hare, much younger than her sister and only now reaching the age Elizabeth had been when Averil knew her.

Averil wiped her eyes. "Don't mind me," she said. "It was just, for a minute there—"

"I know. Everyone tells me how much I look like her."

They stole a few moments to sit down and talk. Lauren was at the base to lead training sessions on disaster relief. She'd worked at FEMA before the war—"So I have loads of experience with underfunded bureaucracies."

Averil, still feeling dazed from the whole experience, finally registered that Lauren had started asking her about herself.

"You're the chaplain here, I'm guessing."

"I'm not sure I'm qualified. As you may have heard, the Holy Father has seen fit to relieve me of my duties."

"That trifling old man?"

Averil had to smile. It was exactly how Elizabeth would have put it.

"But seriously," Lauren said, "what have we been doing, what has this whole thing been about, if not rejecting the dictates of the fathers?"

Another quick hug, and Lauren was off to her next meeting.

Averil found the sergeant in charge of her shift at the cafeteria.

"Could I take a few hours off?"

The sergeant, convinced that Averil was about to faint, walked her back to her quarters. "Take as much time as you need. You really don't look good."

Averil slumped down onto her cot. She had never fainted in her life, but a brief loss of consciousness right then would have been a relief. Otherwise she would have to sit there and confront the question she had tried so long not to think about: what the sister-seminarians would be doing if they were still alive. Arranging disaster relief. Negotiating ceasefires. Comforting the afflicted.

And telling Averil some hard truths about herself. That since she'd arrived in Erda three years ago she'd acted like a jilted lover. That she was sitting on the sidelines of the most important event in her lifetime, because she was too busy licking her wounds.

She wept then, for the loss of those women, for the long years of hard truths unspoken by anyone else. For the person she could have been: valiant and unhesitating, dependable, strong. A leader. Instead of what she was: a failure, a dismal disappointment.

All right. Enough.

She didn't need a vision of their spirits to tell her to snap out of it, pull herself together. She could channel their brisk, loving voices as easily as if she had heard them only yesterday.

She opened her footlocker, rummaged down to the bottom.

When she stepped out of the barracks, she had exchanged her uniform shirt for a black cotton button-down, with clerical collar and a silver crucifix on a chain around her neck. She lingered a while outside the building, realizing she needed some time in the fresh air, the sunlight. She headed for a path behind the cafeteria, leading through a wooded area outside town.

Sandy the dog caught up with her and trotted alongside, displaying no surprise at Averil's new appearance.

"I smell the same, eh?" she said to the dog. "I guess that's what matters."

The path rose and reached an overlook, where she and the dog sat on a boulder, looking down on a wide stream bordered by trees.

She thought of the ancient path of mystics in all traditions, for whom the wilderness, the desert, the wasteland was a metaphor for the self, and the divine, and the meeting place of the two. *Wüste* and *wilde*, in the writings of the Rhineland mystics Averil had studied in her impossibly distant youth. Mechthild and Hadewijch and Marguerite. Emptiness, they had called it. Annihilation.

And then her mind *is* the morning air, the sunlight, the rocks amid switchgrass and bluestem, the leaves exhaling oxygen, the quick graceful movements of the ants.

And just as quickly her mind snaps back to its little space behind her eyes, and the wilderness is out there, the *stille wüste* in all its wordless wholeness.

Averil put her arm around the dog. "It would be nice to be a mystic in the desert," she said, "but I'm a priest, you know, with priestly duties."

~

The patient was in pain after the surgery, and all the staff in the post-op ward could do was monitor her for signs of infection.

Meredith Larsen, new to the chaplaincy, new to the ministry in fact, tried not to think about the types of infections that popped up in hospitals: funguses, viruses, drug-resistant bacteria. You survived the surgery and then some damn bug carried you off. Insult to injury.

The patient, grimacing and clenching her teeth to keep from groaning, was managing to gasp out a few words.

162

"Confession. I want..."

"Yes, it's all right. I'll pray with you for forgiveness. God hears us."

"No. I want a priest."

Meredith paused. "I'm sorry. I wish there were a priest on base. But I know that God forgives us if we come to him with sincere contrition."

The patient gave her a look as if she'd said the most ridiculous thing ever.

Meredith tried not to let her face betray her resentment of Catholics and their superstitions. Her exasperation that this poor woman refused to be comforted. She watched helplessly as the patient shifted around, trying to find a position that wasn't painful.

Suddenly a woman in a clerical collar was standing on the other side of the patient's bed, bending over her. Her unruly dark hair was starting to go gray, and her deep-set dark eyes were laser-focused on the patient, whose hands she clasped together in her own.

"*I'm* a priest."

"I want to make a—" the woman broke off, grimacing.

"Don't try to talk if it's painful."

Meredith recognized her face then. A celebrity of sorts, and then some kind of squalid sex scandal and she had disappeared.

Averil Parnell looked at the patient's chart, then turned back to her. "Eileen," she said gently, "I'm going to prepare our holy water first." She picked up a plastic cup from the bedside stand, poured water into from the carafe, and made the sign of the cross over it.

"In the name of the Creator, the Redeemer, and the Sanctifier."

Meredith had to keep herself from snorting. These Catholics couldn't deal in abstracts, they had to have their hocus pocus, their spells and charms and paraphernalia. Not to mention the whole thing about needing a priest to do it. That was pure arrogance, to think one human being could forgive another.

"Creator-Spirit," Averil began, "look kindly on your children, redeemed by the Savior, born to a new life by water and the Sanctifier. We ask that this water be blessed through Jesus our Beloved."

After dipping her fingers in the water she set the cup aside and made the sign of the cross on the patient's forehead. Her voice became clearer and more confident as she went on.

"God, the Creator of mercies, through the death and resurrection of the Redeemer has reconciled the world and sent the Sanctifier among us for the forgiveness of sins. Through the ministry of the Church may God give you pardon and peace—"

Meredith was forgetting her annoyance. She was wishing she knew the prayers by heart like this instead of always referring to her book. Wishing her voice carried this resonance.

"—And I absolve you from your sins in the name of the Creator, the Redeemer, and the Sanctifier."

The patient lay quietly, as if freed of the spasms that had been wracking her body just moments ago.

"May the Passion of Our Beloved Redeemer Jesus Christ, the merits of the Blessed Mother Mary and of all the saints, and also whatever good you do or evil you endure, be cause for the remission of your sins, the increase of grace and the reward of life everlasting."

Whatever good you do or evil you endure. The words sounded ancient, as if they had been said for millennia, but also as if the priest were saying them now for the first time.

"I ask that the Blessed Mother, the Archangel Michael, Saint Teresa, and all the saints and angels watch over you. In the name of the Creator, the Redeemer, and the Sanctifier. Amen."

"Amen," the patient said, and so did others around them. So did Meredith.

The priest was gone before the patient roused herself enough to say, "I wonder how she knew that Teresa is my patron saint."

Meredith couldn't take her eyes off the plastic cup with the holy water.

She knew she would be a good chaplain. She had been ministering for years before her ordination. She had helped people break opioid addictions, had organized protests when social service funding was cut, she knew her Bible inside and out, would sit and pray with anyone and never grill them about what and whether they believed.

And now she wanted that water. Wanted to touch it, feel it on her forehead.

~

Word of the impromptu service spread quickly, and people gathered at the hospital's nondescript, army-issue chapel one late afternoon, believers of various faiths, nonbelievers, the bored, the curious.

Averil stood in their midst, dressed in flowing black, with a length of purple cloth draped along the front of her blouse. The Catholics among them recognized it as reasonably resembling a stole.

Smiling, she lifted her arms in a graceful arc.

"In the name of the Creator, the Redeemer, and the Sanctifier, may the grace and peace of God be with you."

Those able to stand sat down, in folding chairs or directly on the floor in front of the wheelchairs.

"You'll have to forgive me my Catholic—and Trinitarian—leanings," she said. "When I use the word 'God,' please accept it in the spirit of ecumenism, with my love and respect, to represent whatever sense of the word is meaningful to you: a holy person or persons, a holy being, the ultimate source, goodness itself, the force of love, the ineffableness of existence."

There was a silent meditation, then Averil talked about prayer, about the force of our intentions in the world. "We bless each other," she said, "through our good will for each other. And we also bless God. The blessings go both ways, to and from God, to and from us."

Averil stood again, as did the congregants who could manage it.

"I leave you peace, my peace I give you," she said, and there was embracing and clasping of hands all round. People sang, and others managed to pick up the melody.

Averil produced a wooden bowl, filled with pieces of fruit and army-issue rice crackers, pronounced a blessing on them and handed them round.

"Lift up your hearts," she said.

"We lift them up" came the response, "to the Lord," said some, "to each other," said some.

"Take this, all of you, and eat it. This food is holy because we make it so."

There was more singing, another silent meditation, some more poetic prayers from Averil.

"Deliver us, Lord, from every evil," she said, "and grant us peace in our day. In your mercy keep us free from sin and protect us from all anxiety. For the kingdom, the power, and the glory are yours, now and forever."

And another blessing at the end, mirroring the one at the beginning:

"May the all-loving God bless you, the Creator, and the Redeemer, and the Sanctifier.

"Go in peace now, to love God and one another."

Later there would be hasty battlefield absolutions. There would be funeral masses. But for now there was only this joy, this truly holy communion.

People had trouble describing it to those who hadn't experienced it themselves. For many of them, the only clergy they'd known before had mumbled through their religious services, bored and distracted; even the sincere ones had often seemed self-conscious, half-embarrassed. But here for the first time, they recognized the power and beauty of ritual, of people gathering in the same place and saying the same lines in unison, making the same movements.

Others remembered the sense of being forgiven, or the surprising joy of hugging the strangers next to them.

~

The sergeant who managed the cafeteria was the one who insisted on making it official. "With all due respect for your flair with omelets and waffles," she told Averil, "you need to put in the paperwork and do that chaplain stuff full time."

~

"You're stepping onto the world stage," Catherine said.

"Hopefully I won't fall into the orchestra pit."

Catherine had mixed feelings about Averil being chaplain. She would be moving around more, and thus potentially in more danger. But Catherine would also have more chances to see her.

"If all the world's a stage," Averil said, "then what's the audience?"

Whenever Catherine tried to follow Averil's train of thought she felt an odd sense of disorientation, as if she were moving not downward but sideways. A horizontal vertigo.

~

Selene Marisela, Erda's civilian vice-president turned commander-in-chief, didn't want to permit any kind of worship service, no matter how ecumenical. "We don't have time for that foolishness. The whole chaplaincy should be dismantled."

Averil appealed the ruling to the Military High Command, which included Selene, Catherine, and several experienced D.O.T. division commanders, including Selene's brother Doug Marisela, and Gary Tramonte, the only other man on the MHC.

"Not to be clichéd," Averil said in her presentation to the committee, "but there's a reason for the saying 'There are no atheists in foxholes.' My recruitment as chaplain was an acknowledgment that my services are needed. Plenty of our people feel the need for some kind of spiritual expression and community. If it helps them carry on with their duties as soldiers, it's a win-win situation." The vote in Averil's favor was 5 to 2.

Now they had "spirituality gatherings," and Averil would on occasion "share her thoughts" in her capacity as chaplain. Often they did silent meditations. When Averil closed her eyes she felt alert rather than relaxed. She was vividly aware of the bodies around her, no longer distanced from her by long showers and perfumed soaps and lotions. Their sweat and adrenaline and menstrual blood and wound blood wafted to her nostrils and seeped into her pores, got caught in her hair and clothing.

This wasn't happiness. There was too much death and disaster to allow happiness. But she was electrically alive. They all were. Their country was invaded, surrounded, besieged, but they were radiating outward somehow, they were increasing, thriving. They were at war, but they were together and alive and that was all that mattered.

The new feeling of solidarity surfaced even in the simple act of reading the newspaper in the mess hall. No one had the luxury of reading it by themselves anymore; it seemed impossible to remember what that had been like. You learned to read each article while other bodies pressed against you, hips, shoulders, ribs. You read while you half listened to comments around you, and you mostly screened out the other clusters of readers and the women watching the TV news in the corner, when any broadcasts were available, and the ones listening to the radio news and shortwave radio, and the constant clatter of mess trays, chairs scraping back from tables, conversations, shouts, laughter. It heightened your concentration rather than distracted.

She and other women had stood pressed together like that when they read the electrifying news that D.O.T. troops had permanently occupied parts of Minnesota and Wisconsin. "We're all Erdans now," the field commander was quoted as saying.

They stood together when they read the news that a group of women in Serbia had established a "liberated zone." They called themselves Red Rain. *Our epics, our feast days, our legendary heroes,* said their manifesto, *are all in a tradition that tells us we must spill blood for the glory of our nation.*

We must always annihilate the enemy, we were told. We must never show mercy.

We have been instilled with hatred. Every leader, every writer, every poet—every man—has eagerly embraced the tradition. And we women are the main victims. Look at history. Look at the rape camps.

167

To all men on our territory, this is your first and only warning. Lay down your weapons. After today we will liquidate any armed man we encounter in our zone. We are tired of blood being spilled for the glory of a small piece of land, ruled by violent men. It is time to spill blood for justice.

For the first time in her life Averil knew what it meant to be in a group of people all thinking the same thing. Catherine had tried to describe the feeling. In an army, she'd said, you're part of something bigger than yourself, and at the time Averil thought she had the same experience as part of the Catholic Church. But this was different, more immediate. It was the opposite of losing yourself in the collectivity. You extended yourself. You became more. She knew that the women around her were thinking of the Serbian men's rape camps, wishing themselves there, with guns and knives, loving the beauty of the simple equation: if a man has a weapon, he must be killed.

~

Even as the war dragged on, historians started trying to piece together a coherent narrative of what happened after the initial invasion. Besides the original citizens of the Erdan Republic, people elsewhere started calling themselves Erdans, gathering on the fringes at first, the swamps of Florida, forests of the Pacific Northwest. Their numbers grew. There were advances, retrenchments, expansions. Erdan troops and Defender men swept back and forth across the continent like weather systems. Erda meant whatever folks wanted it to mean, wherever they were at the moment, a floating signifier, a tectonic plate like a raft atop roiling molten metal.

CHAPTER 17

LENT

Must I walk uncomforted for thy glory?

—Mechthild of Magdeburg

Anno Mirabilis 3

John Honig tried not to wince when he walked into the house and was confronted by Val with all her jangling emotions, all that nauseating, dog-like need.

"Is there any beer?" he said.

"My God, you've got a scar. You were injured." She reached out to touch his face but he shook her off.

She had a script in her head, some romance-novel version of how a homecoming was supposed to go. The lovers rush to each other, embrace. *Darling, it's been so long.* You'd think she would have figured out by now it was never going to be like that.

"I guess there's no chance of a steak," he said.

"Not with the rationing."

"Just cook me up something, okay, while I take a shower?"

"Of course."

He shut her out behind sturdy tile walls and merciful, plentiful hot water. Afterwards he shaved, then took the blade out of the razor and cut his hair, hacked off handfuls at a time.

The door opened just enough to show the boy's eyes looking round the edge. He carried a pile of neatly folded clothing.

"Mommy said give this to you."

John took the clothing and shut the door. He put on a pair of jeans but tossed the shirt and sweater aside. The house was stuffy. There wasn't much point to clothing if you weren't outdoors. He closed his eyes, ran his hands over his smooth face and short hair and clean body.

Val almost screamed when he got to the kitchen.

"For Christ sake, Val!"

"I'm sorry, I wasn't prepared. You look so ... harsh. Like a convict. Or, I don't know. Like a wolf."

"How can I look like a wolf when I've cut my hair and shaved my beard?"

He sat down to a plate of fried eggs and bacon and potatoes. She watched him, standing.

"What?" he said. "The scar? Am I ugly now?"

"Of course not."

~

One thing John had learned the last few years was patience. So it wasn't until his second night back that he got up, groped for his sidearm in the duffel bag, opened the bedroom window, and blew out the streetlight with one clean shot.

"The light shines right through the blinds," he said to Val when he got back in bed. "How are you supposed to sleep when it's bright as day?"

He could sense Val lying rigid next to him. She probably needed to get fucked, but he felt no desire for her. He wasn't used to such a soft woman—her voice, her skin, her body. The Erdan women were hard. Even the fat ones had firm muscles. None of them acted so trembly, so uncertain.

On the other hand, it had been at least a week since he'd gotten laid. He'd be horny for Val soon enough.

~

Two days later he headed for Jefferson City. Because of the roadblocks, checkpoints, and detours, it took John three hours to get there. The FBI counterintelligence branch office was in a cinderblock office complex. Sperber was in something called Haversham Services. But there were no signs, fake or otherwise, on the building when John pulled in to the empty parking lot. The doors were padlocked, and John didn't want to draw attention to himself by going up to the doors and trying them. He swung around and drove out, as if he had made a wrong turn.

Damn Sperber! If they'd moved their offices he could have let him know somehow—relayed something to his wife, or be watching when John came to the meeting they'd arranged. He'd had all the dates and times memorized. The meetings were his only contact with Sperber. He pulled off into a diner down the road from the office building. If Sperber was looking out for him he could follow him there.

He ordered chicken potpie, which arrived covered in a waxen gravy. In the booth across from him a woman and man sat talking. Or rather, the man talked and the woman watched him closely, nodding in agreement, focused on every word. The man said something about the weather being bad for fishing, and the woman's face clouded over with concern. He bragged about the fish he'd caught last week and she beamed. It had been a while since John had seen a woman act so girly.

For dessert he ordered the only thing they had, lemon meringue pie, and cup after cup of black coffee. He waited an hour for Sperber while the hick food sat in his stomach like a lump. No wonder they were so slow and stupid, they ate food like this all the time.

At the edge of Jefferson City he pulled into a service station. The lone mechanic looked to be about eighty years old.

"What's happened to Jefferson City?" he said to the old man. "It's almost deserted, half the businesses closed, no one out on the streets."

"There's a war going on, mister."

"I know that. But it's not as if there was a battle in Jefferson City."

The old man looked at him blankly. He must have forgotten the question. Nothing could have happened in Jefferson City. Val would have told him.

"Who's in charge around here?" John said.

"I own this place—"

"No, in Jefferson City."

"You mean, who's the mayor?"

"Who's in control, man, what side? The Defenders, the Americans? Or have the Erdans taken over?"

The old man looked confused. "I've wondered that myself."

John slammed his hands against the steering wheel and drove off. It took him less time getting back, as if the detours and checkpoints had shifted in the meantime, which was impossible.

He turned on the radio. When he was close enough to Erdan territory he could get their transmissions, which at least were more entertaining than the DAW hate-talk. Occasionally they would broadcast something from the priest; she would harangue DAW troops, tell them to lay down their arms, turn against their officers. "I have come with a sword," he heard her say one time. No doubt the dumbfucks around here pictured her brandishing an actual sword like some kind of pirate. Too ignorant to realize she was quoting Jesus.

171

This time there was nothing but static all along the dial.

When he got to the house the boy was sitting on the front steps, expressionless. He watched John step out of the car, then stood up and went inside without a word. John could hear him in the kitchen, saying to Val, "When is he going to leave?" and Val's response, "Your Mommy loves you so much," which made no sense. When he got to the kitchen Val was still hugging the kid tight. She looked at John, then said to the boy, "Okay, honey, run over to Greg's house now, and I'll pick you up on the way back from my prayer meeting. Make sure you listen to Greg's mom and do whatever she says." The boy hurried out.

"Where's the aspirin?" John said. "My back's killing me."

"We don't have any. It's heavily rationed."

"Aspirin's cheap as dirt. There's no reason they can't make as many as people need."

"We'll do a healing prayer for you at our prayer meeting."

"Well that's goddamned fucking wonderful."

"John." Her face turned pale, her lower lip started jutting out.

She was going to make a scene. Another thing he never had to put up with when he was in Erdan territory, along with all the other things that assaulted his senses here. The constant buzz of electricity—he couldn't believe he'd never noticed it before. The humming of the refrigerator. Her perfumed soaps. Stifling blankets and central heating that kicked in at night as soon as the temperature outside got slightly bearable. Lights on all over the place at night, never let your eyes get adjusted to the dark.

When have you known a moment's hardship, boy? Randolph Honig would have said.

He was already starting to forget what the old bastard looked like. Give him enough time, and he'd forget the voice too.

"John," she said softly, "you're going out on another mission again, aren't you?"

"I can't talk about that."

"I don't understand—"

Her voice started to rise and choked off.

There were two different species of women now. The ones here were still so goddamned needy. He felt like an anthropologist, taking notes on their strange behavior. He'd forgotten how they make their voices rise in pitch and tremble, while a tear forms slowly and spills out of each eye.

"At least if you were in the regular armed forces I'd have some way of contacting you, or at least keeping track, knowing you were all right. And those men have much shorter terms of duty before they get a break."

"I said I can't talk about it."

"I know, I know." Then came the tears. "It's just that, people keep asking me, Mrs. Harrison, when's your husband coming back?" Her voice was reduced to little more than a gasp. "And I never know how to answer them."

According to the script, this was when he was supposed to put his arms around her and hold her while she sobbed against his chest.

"I'm going out," he said. He needed a drink and a fuck. Not necessarily in that order.

At the tavern he ordered a whiskey, straight.

"All's we got is wine and beer," the bartender said loudly. "We've joined the Temperance movement these days. Swore off the hard stuff."

"Beer, then." For fuck's sake.

The man served him and in a quieter voice said, "It's actually a lack of supplies. Liquor distribution's all shot to hell. But we say it's Temperance. Keeps the church ladies happy."

The evening went downhill from there. Women seemed to be as unavailable as single-malt. By the time he got home, exasperated and horny, Val was home from the prayer meeting.

"How's your back?" she said. "Does it still hurt?"

"No, actually."

"See? We prayed for you."

More likely it was the beer. He wondered if the priest ever prayed for him. He fucked Val for almost an hour. The sex wasn't bad, but nothing memorable. Jesus didn't get off his cross or Mary step lightly from her pedestal.

~

Val noticed when he stopped shaving. "You're leaving again," she said. He didn't bother to deny it, and thus began a new round of tears and accusations. "You can't just pick up and leave like this. You have a wife and a child." Her voice rose to a pitch that made him want to slap her, except it would have only prolonged her wailing.

"I don't understand what motivates you," she said, "what rules you operate by, that allow you to think that what you do is okay."

What rules? That wasn't in the marriage contract. Miserable document that it was, at least it didn't require that you lay out your psyche in a neat little chart: hangups, ulterior motives, least of all rules by which you operated.

It was easier for Val with her simplistic beliefs. For her the rules were listed on two stone tablets, carved out by some voice from a burning bush while John had been down the mountain with the revelers and the gold and the good cheer saying, What do you mean don't covet my neighbor's wife? What the fuck kind of rule is that?

~

Most days he sat on the porch, avoiding the overheated house and waiting for his hair to grow. Val bundled up the boy in a coat and hat and mittens and nagged him to go out there too. "Spend some time with your father." She practically had to push the kid out the front door.

"Don't tell him scary stories," she warned John. "He's sensitive."

About as sensitive as a sociopath. He watched the kid walk along the porch railing, agile as a cat. He was self-contained, indifferent to the world. He'd probably grow up to be a serial killer.

John read whatever newspaper he could find, usually weeks old. He especially studied the photographs of Beck. The press speculated on her strategy, her plans. They routinely referred to her as a renegade. It made her seem rash, impetuous, not the cool, methodical blonde who knelt over him with a knife at his throat as he slept. He was going to return the favor, he would find a chance, make the chance, to come face to face with her when her defenses were down, when she thought she was among friends. And he wouldn't give a thought to a wife far away who spent her time on curtains and malls and prayer meetings, who lived as if there were no war.

"I'm going to be famous one day," he said to the boy.

The boy sat on the railing and leaned backward, reminding John of the priest on her swing, looking up at the clouds.

~

He'd gotten plenty of sex when he was around Erdan women. They were aggressive, asked for it matter-of-factly, as if looking for someone to play darts with.

One of them explained it to him. "We were raised to think we didn't want it. You men were raised to think you wanted it all the time. So you had this economy of shortage, and all this hostility. Women didn't trust men, men resented women. We had to deal with men making lewd remarks to us on the street, bosses bullying, threatening, boyfriends treating us like shit."

174

"Who thought this up?" John said.

"Exactly. Withhold it and men call you a cocktease, give it and they call you a whore. The only solution, of course, is to make sure that what men think doesn't matter."

~

If John had any paternal instincts at all, he would sit down with the boy and explain to him about life. Or at least sex. Or tell him about Val's Ten Commandments. They could go down the list together.

Honor your father and mother. Forget that one, boy, but he didn't need to tell him that. It was obvious the child had no feelings for them. Val was just someone who gave him food and protected him. John was an intrusive stranger.

What was next: Do not steal. It's every man for himself, kid. That's how people get rich and if you like being rich you have to have no qualms.

Do not kill. That rule's out too, kid. There's a war going on.

Tell you what, the only rule you can count on is this: If there's an afterlife, you'll pay for what you've done.

Before he left he heard a rumor that women with no husbands were going to be rounded up. "Good luck," he said to Val silently while she was still asleep. She'd probably have to leave to avoid the roundup. She wouldn't have access to his money anyway. At least he didn't tell her their marriage had been a sham. His one act of mercy.

He set out before dawn.

He would miss the cooked meals, the indoor plumbing.

Don't look back, that was the most important rule. It should have been added to the Ten Commandments. Too late to tell the kid.

He probably knew it already.

~

Anno Mirabilis 4

Captain Ochoa looked up from his paperwork and saw a woman standing in front of his desk. Goddamn Corporal Nordlund had let someone walk in unannounced, probably unscreened. He could hear Nordlund and the others making their usual racket in the outer office.

"Can I help you?" he said coldly.

"I've come to minister to the prisoners," the woman said.

He put on his glasses and she made an instinctive move to touch her own, a universal gesture of nearsighted people. When Averil Parnell's face

175

came into focus he felt like cussing out loud. At her, at that idiot Nordlund, at all the nitwits who let an enemy combatant in unchallenged, at Colonel DiFrancesco for refusing to move the prison to more secure territory, at all the goddamned five-star generals who were too busy squabbling with each other to assign even the bare minimum of troops they needed for a town in the demilitarized zone.

Ochoa prided himself on being a professional.

"You may be seated," he said, and then realized he sounded like a priest saying Mass. "You have to realize I can't give you access to the prisoners. You shouldn't even have been allowed inside the prison gates."

"No one questioned me," she said.

He could well believe it, and not only because all his men seemed to have turned into mental incompetents today. How many men ever paid attention to a stooped-shouldered, middle-aged woman in shabby clothing? Parnell was working hard at being overlooked. But she was taking a risk. A shambling, dusty stranger could be as easily shot as ignored, no consequences one way or the other. She was either mentally unstable or outstandingly brave. Or suicidal. From the news reports about her, it was hard to tell.

"If there's a problem with regulations," she said, "you could take me prisoner. Then I'd be here legitimately, right?"

"That's absurd. These are soldiers captured in combat. It's not my job to arrest anyone else."

If she was trying to infiltrate the prison, she wasn't doing a good job of it.

"I'm a chaplain in the Erdan army," she said in a helpful tone. "I have some kind of rank."

"I know who you are, and your rank doesn't matter," he said, but she touched her lapel and then her shoulder, as if feeling for insignia. He watched as her forehead wrinkled into deep lines of concentration.

"You're a lieutenant," he said. "That has no bearing on—"

"Do I outrank you?" she said hopefully.

"You're in a different *army*."

"Yes. Well. I was hoping it would count for something."

"Why?" he said. He was irritated and amused at the same time. "So you could *order* me to let you serve as chaplain here?"

She smiled like a nervous kid on a first date. "It was worth a try. I've never understood hierarchy very well."

She looked directly at him for the first time. Her eyes were deep-set, black, alive with intelligence.

176

"You don't *look* demented," he said.

"Thank you. That's reassuring."

~

Ochoa lost track of how many times Averil came back, never deterred by his refusals.

"The Geneva Conventions require you to let me in," she told him on her second visit.

"Find the section and paragraph and show it to me."

He had too much on his mind already, trying to run a prison in a building that wasn't meant for that purpose, with never enough supplies or competent personnel.

He had never wanted to be a warden, but he'd been ordered to do it and he was a good officer and a professional. Even if he didn't want the post, he could at least instill military discipline in the place.

When he first got there, professionalism meant dealing with guards who raped prisoners. He had one of them shot in the courtyard, with all guards and prisoners looking on, and that took care of that.

Averil showed up with a badly creased microfiche copy of part 2, section D, paragraph 3.

"It's ambiguous," Ochoa said, handing it back to her with distaste. "Our lawyers could see it one way, yours could see it another. Who's going to judge?"

He had visits from Colonel Hevesy, jumpy from rumors about General Stoneroad. "He's gone crazy," Hevesy told Ochoa. "He suspects everyone. He's had a lieutenant colonel and an adjutant general shot for treason. He thinks General Kobayashi wants to take over his division. There's going to be mutiny any minute, and how are we supposed to hold off the enemy with all this going on?"

Ochoa tried to calm him down, told him rumors were always overblown. Ochoa had seen once what paranoia had done to a small unit. He hated to think of it spreading through a whole army.

Hevesy sent him cables written in code but incomprehensible even when decoded. The latest one said, *Clash of the Titans beginning.* Ochoa read it on a hot, clammy day when the few remaining electric fans in the office seemed to make no difference. He went outside and sat on a bench on the shady side of the courtyard, but outside was no relief. He seemed to sense the frustration of the imprisoned soldiers like a force pressing against him, their restlessness and watchfulness. He was a soldier, not a jailer. He wouldn't even have this miserable job if he hadn't been such a straight arrow, rejecting this bribe, refusing that favor. All around him his corrupt comrades rose through the ranks and stepped on him for not playing along.

The priest walked quietly through the courtyard and sat next to him. She handled him another grimy piece of paper. "A petition," she said. "The prisoners want me to be their chaplain."

He took the paper, said nothing. He remembered the day the rapist guard was shot, the shock waves that radiated out from the dead body crumpling to the ground. Memory and imagination. Two potent, dangerous forces.

"Are you Catholic?" Averil said.

"I'm Mexican."

She seemed to accept his answer as reasonable.

In some alternative life, a life where he wasn't an atheist, she could have been his spiritual advisor. He would have been challenged by her ridiculous statements and comforted by them at the same time.

"I could earn my keep," she said. "I can cook for large groups."

He had to laugh. The sound of it made him wince, a dull, coughing sound from somewhere tight in his chest, and there was the priest leaning into him eagerly, nodding and saying, "The absurd is the closest we come to understanding God," and for a moment he seemed to understand her perfectly.

"All right," he said, "you're the chaplain." She nodded, not surprised at all. "Don't try to act as a go-between or smuggle anything in here. You'll be executed if you're caught."

"Understood."

There was no change of expression on her face, no defiance or hostility. Certainly no fear.

He tried to recall that expression later, after the escape. A delivery truck had entered the compound with a cache of weapons that made their way to the prisoners. The first he'd known of it was the feel of a gun barrel against his temple, a calm order to surrender his sidearm. He and the guards had been herded at gunpoint to a room and locked up while the prisoners made their escape, admirably efficient.

You have to make cool calculations when you're a soldier, like whether to report back to a delusional, power-mad general after allowing a massive escape of POWs, or whether to turn and run in the opposite direction, even if it's onto enemy territory.

He was captured by an Erdan recon unit, then released with no explanation. It happened again: capture and release. As if the name Cauhtemoc Ochoa were a secret password. Finally he was caught outside a major Erdan stronghold, and this time the icy General Catherine Beck herself met with him and offered him safe passage across the lines. He said either make him a prisoner or let him fight on their side, he wasn't going back to be executed after a five-minute trial. Beck smiled and said, "They're devouring their own."

He no longer knew what the rules were, what it meant to play fair. He knew the priest had promised nothing. She was being loyal to the side she believed in, how could he blame her? A fellow soldier, after all.

Long afterward, when they drew up plans for the Wall of Righteous Men, Ochoa's name came up. Women remembered him from the prison.

A man of honor, they said. A man who refused to be a pawn to tyrants.

CHAPTER 18

LAMENTATION

Death is before me today,
like the coming of health to a sick man.

—"Dialogue of a Man with His Soul"
(Egypt, c. 2200 BCE)

Anno Mirabilis 5

Tobias, drawing doodles on the prescription pads, suddenly sensed he wasn't alone. A man had come in and stood by the clinic door, waiting.

"When you're not busy," the man said, "I'm supposed to get a medical exam."

A smart-aleck. Tobias wanted to make an equally sarcastic retort but couldn't think of any. He took refuge in professionalism. Pointing to a cot, he said coldly, "Have a seat."

The man threw a file on Tobias's desk and lay down on the cot, as if he was exhausted. The performance was obviously exaggerated.

Tobias got out a Medical Exam form, copied the man's serial number and name from the file. John Gaines. Escaped from an Erdan prison, debriefed already by Lieutenant Vargas. He looked at the Med-Ex form. *Does the patient have any injuries? If yes, describe (gunshot, knife wound, bone fracture, etc.).*

"Are you injured?"

"You're not a doctor, are you?"

Tobias wasn't sure whether the man was making fun of him. "I got trained as a medic. Back at the beginning of the war, when things were a lot more organized."

More organized. What an understatement. He could hardly believe how things had deteriorated. Mexico had been seizing territory—

"reclaiming" it, the Mexicans called it, but since Tobias had never studied the Mexican-American War in the first place, he knew nothing about the original land grab made by the United States.

Then there were the rumors about Indians taking over patches of land adjoining their reservations, and even other areas. Tobias knew dimly that there had been a few people, perhaps, on the land before the settlers got here from England, but again his knowledge of history was rudimentary. He was left with a sense of resentment and confusion. His country was falling apart. No map was current anymore.

He returned to the Med-Ex form.

"Are you in pain?"

"No, just fatigued."

Tobias scanned the list of questions. Nothing about fatigue.

Check for signs of fever.

"I'll need to take your temperature." Tobias searched through the drawers for a thermometer.

"I'm not putting that fucking thing in my mouth."

"I'm cleaning it with alcohol. It's sterile. No germs."

"I *know* what 'sterile' means. You don't have to define it, for Christ's sake."

"Are you running a fever?"

"No."

Temperature: normal, Tobias wrote. Just as well. If he had an infection there wasn't a thing that could be done about it.

"So what happens if I pass this exam?" Gaines said.

"If there's nothing wrong with you, I guess Sergeant Bradford will find something for you to do. He's kind of putting together a unit from the people he winds up with."

"And what about you, when you don't have any patients?"

"He finds something. Guard duty. Kitchen duty."

"Garbage duty. Latrine duty."

"Basically."

"And if it turns out there's something wrong with me?"

"I'd have to stay with the patient, of course."

Tobias studied the Med-Ex form so he wouldn't be tempted to smile. Gaines closed his eyes.

Does the patient seem disoriented or mentally impaired?

Ha. Crazy like a fox.

"I might feel sort of dizzy," Gaines said after a minute.

"Mm. Could be hunger. Or lack of sleep. Not serious."

"I think my throat's starting to bother me. You wouldn't want the whole camp to come down with strep."

"In that case, it's my duty as medical officer to order you to stay in the infirmary."

"If you insist, Doctor," Gaines said, and in seconds he was snoring quietly.

A few hours later Tobias brought him a tray of food from the mess hall. The noise or the smell of the food woke him. He sat up and took the tray.

"Nothing wrong with your appetite," Tobias said.

"The strep thing, it comes and goes."

"Could be something else."

"Like what?"

"Malaria. Typhus. Yellow fever. Now if you had spots showing up, it could be smallpox."

"No shit?"

"Or bubonic plague."

"Yeah, right. Did you forget to take notes during your medic training?"

"It's not as weird as it sounds. I've heard stuff about some troops in the Central Command district." He stopped. He didn't want to spread rumors, especially about an infectious disease. But Gaines was looking at him like Tobias was some sort of stupid hick. "It's showing up other places too. Symptoms are odd, no one's figured out what it is."

"Are you talking about an epidemic?"

"Too soon to tell."

At least the man looked impressed now, but Tobias felt guilty. "It's probably nothing," he said. "Like most rumors."

"Yeah," Gaines said. He handed Tobias the tray and fell asleep again.

~

The next day Gaines convinced Tobias to push him around in a wheelchair. After circling the perimeter of the camp, they stopped at the makeshift bleachers where Vargas had tried to set up a parade ground.

"I got better food at the POW camp," Gaines said.

"Shouldn't have left, then."

"I got tired of raising my consciousness and getting in touch with my feelings."

"In prison?"

"It was one long fucking encounter session. You know how women are."

Tobias didn't know how women were, not really. The war had broken out when he was about to start college. The contact he'd had with Erdan troops was mostly with the Traitor Men.

"They interrogated you?"

"It wasn't like that. They make a bunch of us sit in a circle and take turns talking about our childhood and how we were raised to think about women, why we were fighting against them."

"What'd you tell them?"

Gaines stood up from the wheelchair and stretched out on a bleacher. "I'm tired, Doc," he said, and closed his eyes, but he didn't start snoring. After a few minutes he said, "Those women, they try to convince you that men are into war for its own sake, you know, like we love the male bonding of it, and the excitement."

"That's crap," Tobias said. "We're fighting 'cause it's our duty to our country. We want to have a normal, decent life, with families and all, like nature intended."

"Defending the American way, in other words."

Once again, Tobias couldn't tell whether the tone was sarcastic or not. He thought back to the way that guy on the radio put it. It had made so much sense.

"These women are trying to tell us what to do," he said to Gaines, "and we're standing up to them, fighting for our rights. Like the Rebels in the Civil War."

"Like *Confederates*?" Gaines smiled for the first time. It transformed his face. "OK, so if we're the Confederates, what are women, the slaves?"

"No! Women are, like, the federal government, trying to interfere with states' rights. I don't hate women, that's not what this is about, just like a lot of guys in the Civil War, they got nothing against blacks, most of them didn't own the shirt on their backs, let alone slaves."

"Rebels for a cause."

"Well, yeah, we want things to go back the way they were, 'cause that was working fine for most folks."

"I don't know what the fuck those women were complaining about," Gaines said. "I liked the way my life was going."

The snoring started again.

It occurred to Tobias that Gaines's need for food and sleep was excessive. Like his body was recovering from something, or fighting something off.

He wondered whether Gaines was one of those men who had killed civilians at random. Or maybe Gaines thought Tobias was. You couldn't exactly start a conversation with, "So, have *you* committed any atrocities?"

And if you believed the rumors, the men were starting in on each other. He'd heard wild, vague talk, no one knew any details, about executions, reprisals among D.A.W. forces. His own battalion had been dissolved for no reason, though he'd heard that it had something to do with in-fighting between General Haradon and General Theriot.

He was glad for the distraction when Gaines woke up and had to be taken back to the infirmary tent. But then a corporal from Vargas's office came in, talking so fast Tobias could hardly understand him. They had to evacuate that night, he said. Two Erdan regiments were bearing down on them from the east, they'd be there in a day or less.

Gaines sat up. He looked so excited Tobias wondered if he was feverish.

"Beck's troops?" Gaines said to the corporal.

"No, she's sitting on her ass, well behind Erdan lines."

"Where?"

"North of here, fifty miles or so. We'd have to cross some Indian territory, I think, but General Theriot isn't looking to engage her division."

The corporal left and Tobias started packing up what few medical supplies they had. Gaines got up, looking cheerful and relaxed.

"You've been great, Doc," he said. "You've healed me! I'm going to go see who I can help out."

"Okay, I'll see you when we're unpacking again."

But he never did, and he never found out how Gaines had managed to get left behind in the move.

~

After walking north all day, John Honig hitched a ride with a ragged Erdan convoy of slow-moving pickup trucks and jeeps. The Erdans asked no questions when they found him at the side of the road. In his gauntness, his exhaustion, he looked like them, and unlike D.A.W.s, he showed no fear of them. They were partly right, of course. John had no interest in the Defender Men or their cause, but nor was he any more interested in the Erdans. Whatever side they were on, they may as well have been giant chess pieces in an enormous game, serving only as obstacles to him or, rarely, facilitators.

He sat in one of the flatbed trucks, accepted a piece of the salted meat being passed around, along with some rock-hard crackers.

Exhaustion hit him and he closed his eyes. It occurred to him as he dozed that sometime in his wanderings over the years he must have come close to where the priest was. He pushed the thought away, as he always did. Only one destination mattered on his map.

The convoy pulled over by an abandoned house. Someone produced a metal container that served as a kettle and proceeded to make a soup from a few potatoes, gallons of water, and a touch of salt. While it was cooking John went around a corner of the building and sat down.

Averil sits next to him and he feels only mild surprise.

"You've mutated," she says.

"Interesting word, Father. Why not 'changed'? Or 'evolved'?"

"Because you've mutated."

He felt a stabbing pain in his side but managed to keep from groaning. Someone was grabbing his shoulders, shaking him out of his fever vision.

"Soup's on. You okay, buddy? Seemed like you were mumbling something."

"I must have been asleep."

"You don't look so good."

He ate the watery soup and fell asleep. Occasionally he coughed between snores, and the ones still awake looked at each other uneasily. Some of them had heard rumors of the plague. But they were too battle-weary to care or too hardened to think of themselves as vulnerable, and when the stranger jumped off the convoy the next day when they started veering west, they thought no more of it, even when their own symptoms started up.

~

John kept going north. He had no food or water, but he was used to going without for long stretches of time. It was easy not to think about food when he was concentrating on his goal. And *she* was near.

It was late afternoon when he stopped to rest by a crumbling stone wall separating overgrown fields. The ground was hard, but he fell asleep almost instantly, as if his body had never known the luxury of a good mattress, down pillows and silk sheets.

When he woke up it was dark, the stone wall casting a shadow in the moonlight. He lay on his back, admiring the beautiful indifference of the clear night sky, and for some reason he thought of his wife, or "wife," his courtship of her, his proposal. He remembered how nauseated he had been by her foolish joy when she'd seen the engagement ring. A bauble that meant he "loved" her. A piece of super-hard carbon that happened to be shiny—like a hundred other things: glass, stars, tin foil. The only thing distinct about it was its hardness. In the world he lived in now, a diamond would only have been good for raking open someone's face, or bartering for a carton of cigarettes and a liter of grain alcohol.

He told himself he had to plan. He hadn't worked out what he was going to do after he shot Catherine Beck. With the exhaustion, the lack of food, the constant travel, it seemed to him he had no energy left beyond squeezing the trigger that one time. He leaned against the stone wall and closed his eyes.

He could imagine Averil in her office, in the church, in his bed in the rented cottage. He could imagine her looking at him with irritation when he showed up to talk to her after Mass, could imagine her straddling him, her face suffused with pleasure and resentment. But he couldn't picture her bivouacked in this ravaged landscape, couldn't picture her exhausted, scarred, holding a gun. If she were here right now, if she were sitting propped up against the other side of this stone wall and closing her eyes, he would get up, slowly, painfully, limp over to her, lean against the wall and smile down at her.

"Hello, Father. Did you miss me?"

She opens her eyes, closes them again. "So you're not dead," she says drily. "Why did you disappear?"

"Things to do, places to see. You know how it is."

He kneels down in front of her, grasps the sides of her legs and runs his hands up and down her thighs, squeezing them together as he makes his way from hip to knee. Her legs are as hard and bony as ever.

"I got married," he says.

"And I suppose you want absolution."

"Only after I fuck you. Because that would be adultery. Will you give me a Hail Mary for every woman I fucked after my wedding night? Or one for every fuck?"

Her eyes are so dark, so intent on boring into his skull.

"Do I disgust you, Father?"

"Of course," she says, and he can tell she's getting aroused, her breathing is shallower, she's giving him that old look of desire and contempt at the same time, in equal measure.

Her hair has become more gray, he has seen that on the news coverage, usually glimpsed from a distance. She hardly speaks to reporters anymore. She must have people seeing to that; even her allies probably have no idea what she'll say next. But in the few times he's seen her close up in the last

186

few years he's seen the light in her eyes: she's burning up, soon she'll be nothing but flaking black cinder.

His hands rest on her hips as he kneels on the ground in front of her, and she pulls him forward to kiss him. Her hips, her whole body has become hot to the touch, like metal left out in the sun, and her lips burn his, but he likes the pain. She's right that he needs her forgiveness for getting married, he needs her forgiveness for everything his life has been, when all he ever should have done was kneel in the dirt and embrace a mad, burning woman and feel the pain shooting from her body to his.

~

Despite running battles not fifty miles away, the Erdans had held the Northern Missouri Watershed territory for so long and so securely that they finally decided to make the change from a mobile HQ to something that had a prospect of staying in one place for the foreseeable future.

Foreseeable future—what a luxury it was, Catherine Beck knew, to think in those terms, to busy oneself with such mundane logistics as finding a regular building without giving first priority to figuring out how it could be defended.

She and Major Perales drove along quiet country roads on a sunny afternoon and stopped at a squat, one-story structure that used to be a township administration building, set in a field at the end of a winding dirt lane. They were walking toward it when Perales spoke her name. From the tension in her voice and the movement of her body Catherine knew someone was aiming a weapon at them, and Perales wasn't armed.

Catherine remembered later a deep confusion: they weren't on enemy territory, they hadn't just taken a town, but while her mind was groping for reasons, she had already drawn her sidearm and turned around, sweeping her glance in the direction Perales was diving away from.

She felt a pain above her ear. The impact spun her around and her knees buckled.

A man was standing not twenty feet away.

The fact that she was still conscious meant either that the bullet had only grazed her, or she was going to pass out any second.

Then she recognized him.

It may have been a cliché that time slows down in life-or-death situations, but Catherine experienced the truth of it. She was able to register the rush of adrenaline she felt, and then, oddly, to fast-forward in time, see herself as an old woman looking back on this moment, this last moment when she and John Honig were alive on this planet together, their perfect bodies, their beauty already marred by dirt and fatigue and time.

Her instinct was to shoot immediately, but she knew she had to take time, seconds that felt too long, to steady her arm and aim true. Honig seemed to sway, as if he were drunk or feverish. His next shot went wide. Her only shot hit him in the chest.

Perales was chasing her, shouting, "General, you're injured," as Catherine ran to where Honig lay motionless, curled up on his side as if taking a nap. She pushed him on to his back, grabbed his dogtag chain and was about to rip it off his neck when she noticed the name: John Gaines.

She let the metal tags slip from her hand. Perales was staring at her.

"Get me a shovel," Catherine said. "And then find something to do with yourself for the next few hours. I'll radio you when I'm ready. And Perales. Forget you've seen this. Not a word to anyone. Ever."

~

Honig was still alive.

There was a faint pulse. He drew a loud, gasping breath.

She sat back on her heels.

"You didn't get me, you son of a bitch." She wanted to make sure he knew that before he died.

The next breath sounded weaker. More like a wheeze, or a sigh.

She hadn't expected this. She thought she'd shot him through the heart, or near enough.

There was no point calling Perales back. The wound was mortal; he was sure to die en route to the nearest field hospital. Other people would be involved. Word would get out.

When he was ruining Averil's life as surely as if he were a drug addiction, Catherine had wanted him to disappear completely. She wanted Averil never to see his face, never hear his name. Never think about him again.

And she didn't want her to think about him now.

She noticed another chain around his neck. A second set of dogtags. This one Erdan.

"Played both sides, eh? Most likely neither."

She looked at the shovel Perales had left before driving away. It would be too cold-blooded to dig the bastard's grave while he was still alive.

She should have been glad. Should have gloated. But her anger was fading. She was alive, and he was dying.

"So what are the ethics here, Catholic boy?" she said out loud. "If I shoot you again, is it cold-blooded murder or an act of mercy?"

She sat down on the ground, pulled out a bandana and wiped the blood from her face.

She remembered the last time she'd seen Honig, how the key had engaged silently, the door clicked shut behind her, its sound absorbed into the choking, muffling mist of her invisible self as she moved into his dark hotel room. She remembered the sound of his breathing then, slow and regular, part of the cobalt shadows.

She looked down and realized his breathing had stopped. Just like that.

Why the hell was he smiling?

~

What came to John Honig in those last moments was a long-ago conversation with Averil at St. Anthony's. She was transplanting flowers, was irritated with him as usual. Something about insects. That he should have more regard for them, they were shiny and they could fly. "Can you say the same about yourself?"

I'm shiny, Father, and I can fly.

~

In the following days Catherine tried to piece together what happened. Her worst fear was that the incident meant there were other well-entrenched infiltrators who were going to assassinate officers, create havoc. But the soldiers from the Montanist Division said he'd shown up at the barracks the day before, claiming to have come from Sioux Falls, and no one saw any reason to doubt it. Catherine asked around, as discreetly as possible. One woman knew him from some skirmishes early in the war in Iowa. Another remembered him from the Salt Lake campaign.

"Why are you asking, General? Is there a problem?"

"Nothing important. Anyway, he's gone now."

The tiredness crept up on her gradually. Then came the headache. It was late at night and she was sitting on her cot reviewing supply line maps. At first it felt like a twinge where the bullet had grazed her. The only wound she'd received in all this time. Not many soldiers got shot in the head and survived, or knew the name of the person who did it.

She closed her eyes and massaged her temples. The twinge was turning into a headache.

She had heard about the unnamed plague. More than rumors. Whole D.A.W. units in the Plains states were succumbing, and D.A.W. leadership was desperately trying to keep it quiet.

Tiredness and headache, the first symptoms.

She lay down on the cot. If it kept on like this, she'd have to see the medic. They'd need to set up some kind of quarantine. If it wasn't already too late.

She hears a familiar voice.

"You know what I miss?" Averil says. "The smell of sidewalks when it's pouring rain. It's a city smell, though, when you think of it. Nothing like that in nature."

Catherine reflects that she hadn't heard the door hinge creak, hadn't felt the night air when it opened, hadn't noticed the lamp flame flicker.

"My senses must be getting dulled," she says.

"I've always loved the term 'dark-adapted eye,'" Averil says. "It's like a minor miracle, isn't it? You turn off the light and fall asleep in darkness, then you wake up briefly in the night and the room is soft gray, as if now the dream world is real and the supposedly solid world has been muted and dimmed, waiting its turn."

Hallucinations. The next symptom, they said, of the new, mysterious plague. She should go to the medic, now. But she's so tired. She'll rest a little more.

They say hearing is the last thing to go when you die, even after your own thoughts cease. Catherine wonders what Honig would have heard, whether something was lingering there after he stopped breathing. He would have sensed her looking at his face, heard the shovel digging into the soil.

She'd had no intention of giving him burial rites. He wasn't an honorable enemy, she felt no after-the-fact, hypocritical guilt or superstition. Nevertheless, words went through her mind to the rhythm of her digging. Bend, fill, straighten, empty. Man of earth, return to earth.

It had been a remarkably beautiful day. She paused sometimes as she worked to admire the late-afternoon sunlight, and then the sunset with its streaking flame-colored ribbons. By the time the grave was ready, Honig's skin seemed blue in the dusk. The circles under his eyes were purple, his fingernails the color of blueberries before they reach their sweetness, when they're still small and hard and bitter.

The transfer, the infection, must have happened sometime during those hours, his dying breaths rising to her when she bent down, her scalp wound dripping on him and his gunshot wound oozing onto her when

190

she wrapped her arms around his torso to drag him to the edge of the grave. The mingling of their blood, their essence.

Except his blood was diseased. And he knew it.

No wonder the motherfucker was smiling.

Catherine imagines herself empty of everything, even her own consciousness, only Averil's voice sounding in her mind during her last moments of life. That would be a comfort. A good death.

"Why are you thinking of death, Catherine Beck? It isn't your time."

~

During her convalescence, Catherine received a letter from Averil every few days. It was only years later that she wished she had kept some of them. But war was no time for self-indulgence.

Averil's letters were extended musings—on the Oversoul ("we should rename it 'Mothersoul'"); on old European linear scripts, never decoded; on why the Romance languages had evolved from Latin in such different directions.

Catherine rarely wrote back. She could hardly confide battle details to paper. And what else was there to say? She wondered how Averil interpreted her silence.

I killed your lover.

Averil's next letter returned to a favorite theme: the Church.

Obedience—that was the problem with Catholicism. All those rules, a hierarchy of pope-bishop-priest-layperson, knight-rook-pawn. We've been put on a chess board and set in motion, each one acting in the only way it's allowed, killing and being killed. If everyone were equal and unranked, there would be no game. We could just walk away.

The world is better off without him.

~

Selene Marisela's brain felt wobbly. The most annoying part of the illness wasn't the headaches, the bone-deep tiredness, the cough that sounded like a death rattle. The worst part was the way your train of thought whirled and dipped and then picked itself up and started chugging along again and then rammed into one memory, one particular thought, and got stuck there. A rattling cough and you're swung back and forward in time.

"We have to think fast," the doctor had told her. "We have to act fast."

A week ago, it had been. Or more?

"You're the commander-in-chief. You're the only one who can authorize this."

The whole expanse of the empty room between Selene and Dr. Brodber, a severe-looking Black woman with a multitude of long braids, wearing a green surgical filter over her mouth. To protect Selene? To protect herself? Think fast. Act fast.

"Is Catherine dying?" Selene had said.

"No. And that's what's interesting."

Though Selene knows she is lying on a cot in a small empty room, she feels presences all around her, heavy and warm in the darkness, bumping her softly the way she imagines it would feel if she were swimming with manatees in a starlit lagoon.

They are women. She knows without seeing. The Foremothers.

"Do you remember learning about the discovery of the smallpox vaccine?" Dr. Brodber had said.

Cowpox. Fifth-grade science class. A story about a doctor and some milkmaids. You get one, you're immune to the other. George Washington's in the story somehow. Valley Forge.

Selene realizes she can ask the Foremothers whether she's made the right decision. If she had ever imagined this encounter, she would have pictured it like the typical committee meeting back in Erda. Women seated at a table like a panel of judges. Selene would stand before them and they would offer advice, interrupt each other, argue. *Here's what you need to do, child.*

Instead, this wordless, physical contact, gentle and random, in the dark. She is able to forget, for whole seconds at a time, the stress of the war, the ever-present ache of her brother Doug's death. She feels smooth skin, senses the warmth of their breath. She feels wisps of hair, springy, straight, kinky, braided. There is a dark black woman, elegant and sad-eyed, and a tiny woman with skin the color of milky spiced tea. There are white Foremothers too. A woman with long glossy brown hair has a smoker's raspy laugh and arms well muscled from chopping firewood.

Selene and Dr. Brodber had looked down at Catherine, semi-conscious in her bed. "The worst is over," the doctor said.

"Any idea who she caught it from?"

"She said she doesn't know. From what I can tell it's not as infectious as the stronger variant. It requires fairly intimate proximity."

Catherine had shifted around in her bed but her eyes were still shut. They studied her wry half-smile.

Selene is buoyed up by the women, up toward the surface, where she breaks through and thinks about all the ways the doctor could be wrong. Catherine could have a natural immunity, could be passing on the deadly variant of the plague. Or maybe this mild version is enough to kill them off, exhausted and undernourished as they are.

The Foremothers are pulling her back. It would be so easy to rest in their arms, submerged again.

"Some things to remember," Dr. Brodber had said, needle at the ready, "after we do the inoculation. You'll feel ill, that's for sure. You'll run a fever. And right before it breaks, there'll be a brief time when you'll feel disoriented, maybe delusional." Punctuated by moments of clarity? Selene wonders as she sinks down to the Foremothers and the calming darkness. Any milkmaids around here? she says, and there is a ripple of laughter. She pictures Catherine's ancestors, white women with slender hips and long legs, wearing leather bodices and short chain-mail skirts, gold bands around their wrists and upper arms like comic book superheroines.

"My throat's dry," she said.

She sensed someone waiting at her bedside, felt a pair of strong hands hauling her into a sitting position and holding a glass to her lips.

"Don't you have any water colder than this?"

"Water's water," Catherine Beck said. "Your body doesn't know the difference."

"General, your bedside manner needs work."

"Get some sleep," Catherine said.

CHAPTER 19

NIGHT PRAYER

God guides his chosen children along strange paths.

—Mechthild of Magdeburg

Anno Mirabilis 8

In years past, all Peter Byrne had known about the Southwest was that people said it was beautiful. Never mind the temperature, they said, it's dry heat. He'd experienced it for himself now and all he could say was, heat is heat, it makes you pour sweat and if it's dry heat, then so much the quicker to dehydrate.

He could also do without the supposedly stunning landscape. Not a blade of grass to be found. He'd had no idea you could have loose dirt all over the place, barely a green living thing to keep it from being eroded down to rock or whatever it was beneath soil. He'd never taken much notice of grass back East. You don't notice something when it's everywhere.

If he got through all this, he'd have to have a word with the locals. Plant some grass, folks. Holds down the dirt. I can't believe I'm the first one to suggest it.

If he got through it.

He moved through the ward, adjusting a pillow here, filling a water glass there. A calm day, no crises so far. He spoke heartily to everyone, never let them see how tired he felt.

"It's not a death sentence, men. Look at Dominguez over there." They knew the odds, but there were a few tired smiles anyway. "He pulled through it, and as you can see he's enjoying an illustrious career mopping our floors."

"Death is starting to look good, Father."

"Don't worry, Ingold, you're too ornery to die."

In the back office Quiñones shouted into a radio headset, then tore it off and threw it onto the console. They had to communicate this way, like a leper colony contacting the outside world.

"The Platte Regiment keeps giving me the runaround," he said to Peter. "Cold Springs isn't even answering. The supplies sergeant at the Ramirez Division wanted to talk barter. What the hell do we have to trade in return?"

The moral authority of dying men.

"Tell them we'll go over there and breathe on them."

"They probably won't think that's funny."

Their needs were simple. They had no delusions of getting their hands on antibiotics, sterile dressings. They would settle for soap flakes, for any cheap and simple thing that could kill germs: vinegar, lemons, boric acid.

"Oh, and Peter, General Kozlovich wants to see you."

"He was next on my rounds."

Kozlovich had arrived two nights ago, complete with chauffeur and jeep convoy. Insisted on a private room. They would have had to rig something together, use curtains on a frame to seal off a corner of the ward, and the man would have suffocated in the heat. They ended up setting up his bed outside under an enormous live oak.

Kozlovich watched with hard suspicious eyes as Peter sat down by his cot.

"I've just found out about you, Byrne. What's a goddamned civilian doing in charge of this setup?"

"I haven't noticed any military men clamoring to run a plague hospital."

"Eh? Well, you've got something military about you, anyway. Probably have most of these patients fooled."

Typical bully. Backing down when confronted. But he had a point. Peter had found that if he bellowed loudly enough people tended to do what he told them, figured he was somewhere higher up on the food chain. Most likely it was for that same reason that the Erdan women never seemed to trust him. He'd heard some of them refer to him as an "old-school man." As if he had willed his large body, his deep, gruff voice into existence just to offend them.

"Kozlovich, you might find it hard to understand," he said, "but there are some people who don't want to take sides. They want peace."

Peter didn't address him as "General" or even "Sir." He had no intention of legitimating this thug or others like him. They were nothing but strongmen, gang leaders, with their warring factions and power struggles, purges within the ranks, executions. When an occasional

195

general seemed even remotely willing to attend peace negotiations, the other vultures made sure to engineer a coup and he would disappear, no doubt into some unmarked grave.

More and more it was beginning to look like they would have peace by default. This disease was so fast and so deadly. At first there had been vague rumors about the Erdans stumbling across a milder strain, inoculating themselves with it, nursing each other through. By the time the rumors were confirmed, the D.A.W. forces were already too depleted. It would have been the time to sue for peace. Peter had been in St. Louis at that point, with the remnants of Oxfam and Pax Cristi and other groups. There had been scientists there, desperately working on a vaccine—he wondered how many of them were still alive. And there were the D.A.W. generals strutting around, saying they'd have nothing to do with any disgraceful surrender. The prospect of 40 percent of their forces dropping dead was evidently not a strong enough incentive.

Now, all the Erdans had to do was wait them out.

It was ironic—those women were so anarchic, they hardly had any leaders you could identify, yet they'd stuck together, hadn't turned against each other. They'd even discussed it in terms of survival of the fittest. That Erdan commander, Selene Marisela, called it "stark evidence" of the evolutionary advantage of cooperation over competition. One group meant to survive, the other one to fade away. She clearly meant to include women in the former category, men in the latter. But there was no way they could do without men altogether. Not if they were interested in human survival.

Kozlovich flinched away when Peter reached over to touch his forehead.

"I have to check your temperature, man."

"Nursing is women's work."

"Yes, well, in their absence you'll have to pretend that I'm the next best thing."

"Don't worry, Byrne, I'm not saying you're a fag. I can tell you're a man even though you *are* a priest. Bet you've had some fun with your lady parishioners."

"Something on your conscience, Kozlovich?"

"Not at all. I've enjoyed every pussy I've nailed, not a shred of guilt. Breaking the rules makes it that much sweeter. I remember McCallum— you know McCallum, don't you, head of the Rove Division, always competing with me, the bastard, he almost had me set up for treason— anyway, you should have seen the son of a bitch gloat when he found out I was coming down with this damn flu."

Plague, Peter almost said, but stopped himself.

"'Think of me on your deathbed, Kozlovich,' he said, and I said, 'McCallum, I'll be too busy thinking about that ivy tattoo your wife has, under her right tit, and those red lace garters your sister wears.'" Kozlovich laughed so hard he started wheezing. "The look on his face, I tell you—"

"Those women have probably been tortured and executed by now."

"Eh?" Kozlovich seemed to suffer hearing loss at strategic moments. "You're a dry stick, you know that, Byrne? You've got no zest for life."

Peter left before he said something he'd regret. He went to his combination office and sleeping quarters, a lean-to next to Quiñones's radio room. You couldn't call a dying man disgusting, no matter what a slimy lizard he was.

He felt the pain before he figured out where it was coming from: a pressure on his temples, something invisible trying to crush his skull. He fell to the floor. He wanted to scream but the pain was too intense, he could only hold his head in his hands and open his mouth in a silent roar.

He didn't know how long it was before the pain subsided into something heavy and dull. A headache. One of the first symptoms; some people described it as the worst they'd had in their whole lives.

"My God," he said out loud. He wasn't resentful. But he did feel a bit surprised. It had seemed, after all this time, that he was one of those with a natural immunity. He had almost dared to hope.

Remember, man, that you must die.

Well, that was pretty damn comforting.

You are dust, and to dust you shall return.

His memory had decided to serve up his religion's least appropriate lines. You say those things to healthy people so they don't get frivolous and superficial. You refrain from such observations after the prognosis has come back.

He was still lying on the floor, face up. It seemed easier to think, or something, from that position. He noted the passing of time from the fading daylight.

The pain eased. He sat up, contemplated the cardboard cartons that held the hospital's files. He needed to focus, get everything in order. He would have to make sure Quiñones and some of the others understood the procedures.

A common stage, right before the end—or before the fever broke, for the lucky ones—was delusional thinking. He had heard that the Erdans would ask each other, after pulling through, What was it like? What kind of hallucinations did you have? Averil probably hadn't even noticed the difference. For Peter it would be the first time in his life.

197

Whatever the delusion was, he hoped it would feature water. Mist, drizzle, the sound of a foghorn, boats at their moorings bumping against the pier. There was probably some man right now in a New England seaside town, dying of plague, listening to these sounds. The poor bastard was probably wishing for Arizona sunshine and dry heat.

A line of poetry entered his head. *I will arise and go now.* William Butler Yeats. Peter's father had loved that sort of thing. He smiled to think of old Sean Byrne, his nationalist pride in a country he'd never seen.

He rested his head in his arms, thought longingly of his office at St. Anthony's, the rows of file cabinets, the neatly printed color-coded labels. He even felt nostalgic for parish council meetings, for the boring details, choir rehearsal schedules, repair of a leaky roof.

And I shall have some peace there.

Focus, old man. Here and now. Procedures.

The basic principles were simple. When you had no supplies and no trained medical personnel, principles were all you had. Sick people need a bed to lie on, a roof over their heads. Food for those who can eat. Water. Basic hygiene and the most minimal recordkeeping. Welcome to the Peter Byrne Clinic for Those Who Have No Alternative.

He'd come to the area because he knew it had been the hardest hit, but he hadn't expected to find no infrastructure at all. At the fringes of military outposts men were lying on the ground, practically in piles, shunned by the healthy. He had found an abandoned elementary school, bribed someone for the use of a flatbed truck. He remembered how his muscles ached from dragging delirious men by their armpits, heaving them into the truck.

He managed to get some healthy men to agree to help, whether influenced by his exhausted face or the desperation in his voice: "For God's sake, man." If not for anyone else's sake, then for the sake of an abstract ideal of goodness that no one had ever satisfactorily explained, much less proved to exist. Tend to these hopelessly ill strangers at the risk of your own life. For the sake of that.

The files could wait till the morning. Peter stood up, stiffly, and moved to his cot. There would be no priest to hear his last confession. He pulled out a rosary, kissed the silver crucifix dangling from it. He liked to picture Jesus in his rough robes, doing carpentry work, or standing on the shore watching that other Peter haul his nets onto the fishing boat. He looked down at the small, tortured figure.

"I'll tell you when I see you," he said.

Part Three

Now the Soul is fallen from love into nothingness, and
without this nothingness it cannot be all.

—Marguerite Porete, 14th century

CHAPTER 20

SURSUM CORDA

If you bring forth what is within you, what you bring forth
will save you. If you do not bring forth what is within you,
what you do not bring forth will destroy you.

—Jesus, in Gospel of Thomas

Anno Mirabilis 10

Historians later had trouble pinpointing the end of the war. It would be
most accurate to say that the anti-Erdan forces simply disintegrated,
due to disease and infighting and general malaise. The Erdans, having a
feel for political theater, arranged for a few leaders of scattered remnants
to give up their arms at a formal signing of a peace treaty, no doubt
counting on an Appomattox-like moment in which General Catherine
Beck accepted a warlord's surrender amid a pile of forfeited guns, a fine
subject for portrait painters and myth makers, though Beck did not care
for the comparison to Ulysses S. Grant, nor could the men's forces claim
a leader as complex and interesting as Robert E. Lee.

Later artists deliberately altered aspects of the scene—most notably
effacing Beck's sardonic expression and the scruffiness of the half-starved
former combatants on all sides.

"Time made us beautiful," Beck was said to have remarked, decades
later, at the unveiling of one particularly prettified version of the scene.

In any event, the war was over, D.A.W. soldiers safely consigned to
processing centers while the Erdans figured out what to do with them.
Slowly people returned to their prewar homes, or made new lives for
themselves in other places, always mindful of an irretrievable past. They
were shocked at the soft, wasteful lives they used to live, with hot running
water, central heating, electric cookstoves, phones and televisions,
mattresses.

Chaplain Averil Parnell, long accustomed to her location being determined by others—the Catholic Church, the Erdan high command—found herself in a demobilization center in Maryland, staring up at a wall covered with road maps—rare commodities, at one point made almost obsolete by the Internet, then banned from the possession of anyone but high-level military, for reasons of security.

Her formal honorable discharge papers had arrived the day before. Since she was now in the Reserves, as was mandatory for all former Erdan military, she thought of herself as a quasi-civilian and once again felt grudging admiration for the way the military did things. There were no such things as discharge papers in the Church. She wondered whether she was in the Catholic Reserves, how she would react if called on someday to perform priestly duties.

It was time to leave, and Averil had to decide on a destination. Perhaps northeast, to Connecticut, to the ruins of St. Margaret's and St. Anthony's. Or northwest, to the former Erda/North Dakota, where she had experienced the one respite she had known, the pause between the Church and the War.

She contemplated flipping a coin, or to make things more interesting, looking for omens. Finally she decided to go in a general northward direction, and veer off wherever she saw an interesting road. She filled a canteen with water, put some army-issue rations in her knapsack, and set off one fine spring morning, joining scores of others walking along the mostly empty expanse of the former Interstate 81. She made her way north, occasionally picking up supplies at de-mob centers, other times bartering chores for food and a night's shelter. Often people recognized her and took her in without payment.

Sometimes she posted a letter to Catherine at army high command. Since Averil had no fixed address, of course, Catherine couldn't write back, but Averil knew what she would have said. What she'd said before, written before, as the war was winding down: come to IxChel, the new capital.

Maybe, Averil had responded.

Maybe it would be the end point of these wanderings.

Over days and weeks she walked, spring into summer. She had to move slowly, step carefully. The soles of her shoes were worn thin, and her calf muscles were jolted when she set her feet down hard at her usual brisk pace. But it was all right, it was good. She moved slowly and saw everything around her. She had time to notice with satisfaction that her fingernails needed trimming. If they grew, that meant she was still alive, new cells forming, old ones dropping off.

Don't carry money, Jesus had told the apostles. Don't bring an extra coat or pair of shoes. Averil had stumbled into the apostolic life, with no coat at all, let alone an extra one, though she did have a small collapsible tin cup and a canteen. She pictured a world in which everyone decided to lead that wandering Jesus-like life, everyone on the road, carrying nothing. The ones who tended gardens and henhouses, who baked bread and cooked soup, would carefully close their picket gates behind them, take off, leaving vegetables unpicked, cows unmilked. Drifts of people moving along roads and sleeping in abandoned barns, getting hungrier and shabbier, no one to feed them.

Clearly, Jesus hadn't thought it through.

In her imagination, the itinerants eventually had meetings, agreed to take turns being householders. Things sorted themselves out.

Over the weeks and months she walked, she started to think about walking away from the apostolic path, living the rest of her life in a new way, not as priest or chaplain. She had done her duty for eight years and it had drained her completely. She was a spent battery now. She wanted only to find simple, honest work, settle in to tasks that had nothing to do with calling down blessings and curses, nothing to do with fasting and meditating and yearning for a glimpse of a deity—god, goddess, cosmic source—who had no interest in her.

News of the outside world drifted her way now and then. At de-mob centers, or in kitchens where people offered her coffee and bread, she heard that the High Military Tribunal declared Selene Marisela Erda's first peacetime president, with full-scale elections scheduled in four years. She heard once that some warlord had broken out of a military prison, but then people said no, it hadn't happened, and others said he'd been recaptured. She heard rumors about a possible new outbreak of plague. Men, it was said, were once again especially vulnerable, and were ordered to report to Public Health centers for observation.

But half the time she spent nights in abandoned houses, usually sheds or barns since she felt self-conscious walking into people's homes without permission. And while she played with the idea of an ordinary life, she continued her solitary trek. The kitchen-table conversations were few and brief, the rumors merely background whispers in her walking meditation.

She crossed the border into Pennsylvania, passed through farm country in the central region, now known as the Susquehanna Watershed and luckily mostly untouched by combat. By late summer she made her way into what geologists called the Ridge and Valley Province, an area of long, low mountain ranges running close together. From the air it looked as if a giant hand had crumpled the surface of the planet and then tried, unsuccessfully, to smooth it out again, leaving long crinkles running diagonally across the landscape. The roads in this part of the state followed the contours of the land, running parallel along the foot of a mountain ridge for miles before encountering a gap that took it to the other side, and then more sideways wandering along the next ridge, and so on. No straight north-south road existed to take a traveler through the area in a direct line.

The zigzagging suited Averil: long miles in the shadow of this or that ridge, then a steep climb over it, into another lovely vista of farmland in the narrow valleys between.

Of course she had no map of her own and had failed to notice the names on the large wall maps in the de-mob centers and travelers' waystations. Road signs, even on the interstate, had been scavenged long ago for scrap metal, so she had to rely on local residents to tell her the names of towns, rivers, hills. This time, however, on a steep curving climb up another pass, she saw a rundown building whose name was painted on its side, still visible in fading wind-bleached letters: SHADE MOUNTAIN INN.

So she was on Shade Mountain. The name conjured images of sheltered front porches on summer days. Or shades in the sense of lingering ghosts, an old bootlegger or hunter, someone the people told stories about on those front porches at night. The forest was too thick for her to get a view of anything at the top. She knew she was at the crest of the mountain only because the road before her started a gentle descent, and in a few hours she was in a town, at a crossroads. Time for another decision.

She looked left. Shade Mountain stretched along that way. This town was at one end of the ridge. Someone at the tavern said it was eleven miles long. Tomorrow morning she would take the road that ran parallel to it. She would go west.

Since it was getting late she found a de-mob center and slept soundly on a good mattress. For breakfast the next morning she had a slice of bread from a not-too-old loaf, with a fair amount of butter and large quantities of milky, sweet tea.

Six miles to the next town, according to the green and white sign Averil found in the weeds by the road. The sign was faded, its edges corroded, no trace of the pole it had once been fastened to—either rusted away or someone took it, desperate for a weapon of any kind, or maybe a gardener needed it to stake her tomato plants. Averil preferred to think of it that way.

She was well fortified for her six-mile walk. She didn't miss cars. Driving the high-speed freeways in the old days had been nerve wracking. On country roads at night she used to cringe each time a dry leaf skittered across the asphalt. She would brake hard, straining to make sure it wasn't a mouse or some other night creature. Now she could walk down the middle of the road as if it had been made for foot traffic all along, enjoying the blue sky and hilly farm fields and low forested mountains to the south and the north.

She noticed another lopped-off square of metal in a ditch, this one advising her that she was not to move any faster than fifty miles an hour. "It's a sign," she said out loud, and laughed at her own joke.

Near an abandoned farmhouse was a tree heavy with some kind of fruit, perhaps small pears, but when she got closer she saw they were plums on the verge of ripening. Gently she touched a few. They weren't green, but they seemed too firm to be fully ripe. Then one of them, fragrant and yielding to the pressure of her touch, dropped into her hand.

The plum had a dusty light purple skin, like a concord grape. Averil bit into the sweet flesh. Maybe Eve hadn't been interested in the knowledge of good and evil. She just wanted a bite of fruit. And fruit trees multiplied everywhere the poor outcast humans went, offering pears, plums, apples in defiance of the vengeful god, announcing, "It was worth it."

She came to yet another sign, this one still standing. A silhouette of a busy walker against a bright yellow background, and beneath it the words, PEDESTRIAN CROSSING, NEXT 1/2 MILE. She kept looking around her as she passed that half mile. To the right was a cornfield, then a weathered building with a sign reading CHRIST LUTHERAN CHURCH, then a cemetery, then another cornfield. To the left were hilly plowed fields, their boundaries marked by lines of trees stretching away to Shade Mountain, dark blue-green in the sunlight.

She felt a growing respect for whoever had stolen the signposts. The person carefully left the signs, for the sake of maintaining order (we must know how fast to travel, and for how many miles), and yet the only sign left intact was the most absurd, warning drivers of people crossing the road at any time, from field to church, from graveyard to field, masses of them.

It was a morning to give thanks. For signs and wonders. Blue sky, open road. Legs grown muscular with so many miles of walking.

People had argued with her about the question of gratitude. It was a servile position to take, some said, to feel dumbly grateful for a sunny morning as if it had been dispensed by a personal deity up there in the clouds, giving and withholding. Even if you did believe in a personal god, he had assured everyone that his rain falls on the just and unjust alike. There was no reason to think the sunny morning was meant for you.

Can't I just feel grateful? Averil had argued. Can't I feel a moment of attunement with the universe and express it with the word "thanks"?

She thought of lines from a hymn once popular among Episcopalians and flower children. "Praise for the sweetness. Praise every morning." That was it exactly. Address the compliments directly to the thing itself. Praise the pedestrian crossing sign. Praise the plum.

At the outskirts of the next town she passed a farmhouse with a low sprawling building behind it, its faded sign still visible: C & G Pig Farm. The pigs obviously were long gone. Townspeople would have had little reason to spare them, unlike hens and cows who could give eggs and milk. She preferred to think the pigs had escaped and led fulfilling lives out in the wild. She hoped no one told her otherwise.

Soon she was in the town itself. People were out running errands, avoiding sidewalks that heaved up into shards that sloped in different directions. A woman approached Averil and said they'd heard she was coming. "Can I offer you something to eat?"

The woman, who introduced herself as Margaret, lived in a large two-story house with a crumbling stucco façade. She invited her into the kitchen and set a kettle on a woodburning stove.

Averil wondered whether Margaret's name was an omen, whether it meant she was supposed to go to St. Margaret's.

"This is how the house was in my great-great-grandmother's time," Margaret said. "They didn't squander anything. This table top is from the back of an old piano. The grape arbors in the side yard were made with metal piping from the old brick factory."

Averil found it difficult to concentrate after Margaret served her the coffee. The mug had a reproduction of the painting *Starry Night* on it, vivid shiny colors on the white ceramic. She could hardly breathe for how beautiful it was. People used to criticize reproductions of artwork on mugs and t-shirts and refrigerator magnets, as if everyone was supposed to get on airplanes and fly to every art museum to look at the originals personally. She wondered whether the original still existed.

"You probably don't know what it's like," Margaret was saying, "to be the sixth generation in the same house. When you were a priest, didn't you have to work wherever they told you?"

"I got used to it," Averil said.

"There've never been any of that kind in this town," Margaret said. "We didn't think much of Catholics."

"What churches do you have here? Left standing, I mean."

"There's the Dutch Reformed near the cemetery. And St. Paul's Methodist across from that. The Lutheran Evangelical's been demolished."

"Do you have any... beads I could borrow?"

Margaret looked at her with calm curiosity, or maybe pity. She left the kitchen, returned in a few minutes with a necklace made of slender red glass beads. "I'd give these to you to keep," she said, "but I hear you give away anything you own."

"Sooner or later."

"I'll lend you these, then."

~

The church was musty, the windows so dirty they barely let in sunlight. Averil sat down on a dust-covered pew and took out the necklace, counted the beads through her fingers. Twenty-eight, no spacers between. The beads shone in the dim light. The Sisters of the Precious Blood of Jesus should have had rosaries like this. Praise the red glass beads. Praise the precious blood of everyone.

She thought of St. Francis's Canticle, where he thanked God for Brother Sun, Sister Moon, Brother Wind, Sister Water, Brother Fire, Mother Earth. And the last one, Sister Death.

That was Francis's stroke of genius, Sister Death. A librarian, perhaps, or an elderly church helper, keeping things orderly, thinning out the ranks.

Averil closed her eyes, squared her shoulders back against the high wooden pew. Her fingers slid from bead to bead, the simplest of chants resounding in her mind: *om, peace, peace, peace*. It took on its own momentum. The repeated words lost meaning and were merely sounds, or the awareness of something resounding through her body, and she could feel herself lifting off, leaving thought behind.

She had had no visions for a long time, and their absence was a relief. These days her meditations were blissful escapes into a huge, silent peacefulness. When she returned she didn't know how long she'd been away, but she felt as if she'd had a long midwinter sleep. She opened her eyes and felt her contentment seeping out and filling the dusty church.

She would stay here, she resolved, stay in this town and live here like an ordinary person. Forget the vows, the prayers, the priestly energy that used to flow through her.

~

For several months it seemed as if Averil Parnell would settle into a life in Swift Run. She helped Margaret pick concord grapes and make grape jelly, pick Bartlett pears and can them in glass quart jars. They picked the last of the chard and put the garden to sleep under a winter cover crop of ryegrass.

A house in town had radio equipment that served as a community station. Volunteers took turns being on the air, reading announcements, reading messages people needed to send to others who had no phone service, playing music when they ran out of announcements and messages.

Averil went every day to fill in for the other volunteers during their lunch breaks. She read from an old book she'd found at Margaret's house, *The Self-Sufficient Life*. People in Swift Run got used to Averil's lunchtime lessons, read slowly and patiently: how to make bricks, how to unravel thread from old clothing. How to shear sheep. There were no sheep around anymore, but you never knew when you'd need it.

When there was less gardening work, Averil borrowed rags and a bucket and mop, and with a few precious drops left in someone's bottle of Murphy's Oil Soap, she started the long process of cleaning the Dutch Reformed Church. Why bother? someone asked, and she had no good answer. Only a generation or so ago the people of the town had been deeply religious. Even now, they appreciated hard work, and some of them joined her. They talked about making it a meditation space.

Eventually an assignment letter from the Reserves arrived. Averil hitched a ride on a mail truck as far as Glen Iron, walked the remaining seven miles west, and presented herself at the White Mountain Army Camp for her three-day stint.

It was her first experience at a processing center. Of course she had known they existed. She hadn't quite pictured the fences looped with razor wire and the armed sentries in watchtowers.

They didn't know what to do with her. Most reservists were placed on some form of guard duty, but Averil was known to be useless with a gun; presumably at least some of the men would have heard of it too.

"You don't want to—'hold services,' is that the phrase? That religious stuff?"

"I'm not a chaplain anymore," Averil said. "I can do cafeteria work."

"That's handled by the inmates. Trust me, you don't want to be around them for any length of time."

Averil pondered the use of the term "inmates," while Corporal Willasdottir pondered the advanced academic degrees listed in Averil's file.

"There's the beginnings of a library here. Not that these apes would be interested."

"I could catalog it," Averil said eagerly. "I can teach people to read, too."

The corporal looked skeptical but showed her to a corrugated metal shed with a few dented steel bookcases and a long wooden table.

"Let a guard know if there's trouble." Willasdottir pointed to a young woman at the doorway, rifle slung across her body.

There was only one person in the library, an old wreck of a man with sagging jowls and a horrible pallor, his wool cap pulled so low on his forehead it almost touched his oversized glasses. Averil said hello and asked what he was reading. He looked nervously at the guard and silently held up the book so she could read the spine. Dostoevsky's *Crime and Punishment*.

She got to work, typing up each title and author on index cards. After half an hour the old man put his book down and shambled out. No one else came in during the several more hours she worked that day, or the next. She reorganized the books by category, and alphabetically by author within each category, arranged the author, title, and subject heading cards for each book, placed them neatly in a cardboard box, and typed up a sign-up sheet for loans. There was nothing more to do.

The grounds looked like a typical army arrangement: sleeping quarters, latrines, offices. What would have been training fields were sectioned off with chain-link fence for basketball, soccer, weights. The building nearest the library was labeled the infirmary, but as she went toward it she noticed a smaller sign, obviously added later: Public Health Center.

To add to her confusion, the place was empty of patients. Hadn't there been some kind of order for all men to report?

"No plague around here," the medic said. She was reading a week-old newspaper. "We're lucky."

"So, the civilians, you tested them and released them."

"They're still here. We need to keep them under observation."

"For how long?"

The medic shrugged. "Long as it takes."

"Do you need me to do anything? Disinfect some instruments?"

"They'll get dirty again before we need them."

"I can dust. Mop the floor."

"You're making me tired. Sit down."

Averil sat down by the medic's desk.

"I could donate blood."

"For *these* guys?" The medic smirked, but she looked Averil up and down, then leaned over and put the back of her hand on Averil's forehead.

"You're running a slight temperature. And anyone can see from looking at you, you're underweight and borderline anemic. If I took your blood you'd pass out."

"All of that's normal for me. I've given blood lots of times. O-positive, universal donor."

"Tell you what. I'm going back to my barracks for a nap. You can come get me if you need me."

Averil settled in to read the newspaper. A small item on the fourth page mentioned the continued health of the first AP baby, AP standing not just for her own initials, but for assisted parthenogenesis, the in vitro fertilization of two ova.

She remembered hearing about the research during the war. Nothing about a baby, but this article made it seem old news.

The baby's name was Star.

The things she'd been oblivious of.

She closed her eyes, listened for the gentle thrum of pulse inside her head, sensed her overheated, low-iron blood flowing around, contained in her skin, some of it circulating inside other bodies now.

A sound in the doorway made her open her eyes. The old man from the library yesterday shuffled in, sat down heavily in a chair across from the desk. Averil wondered if anyone had checked for underlying causes of that shuffling gait.

"I'm the mayor of Weikert," he said, in a surprisingly deep and resonant voice. "Or used to be, when there were still elections."

Averil remembered passing through Weikert on her way here. In its heyday it couldn't have had more than five hundred residents. The mayor's job was probably part-time, even unpaid.

A genuine, old-style male, born and raised and grown old before any of this had started. In the world he grew up in, a woman would defer to him, agree with him, look impressed when he presented his credentials.

She felt she should speak slowly and clearly, as if encountering a being from another galaxy: Do … you … have … a message … for me?

"I'm also a historian," the cello voice continued. "Not like the ones with the fancy university degrees. I'm unfashionable enough to care about the truth, and to hope that someone writes it down, and gets it right."

Again a pause, for audience reaction. Averil tried not to look annoyed. The man cleared his throat.

"In any event," he said, "welcome to the First Circle of Hell."

His eyes flickered to the door, then to her.

"You've heard of Dante, young lady?"

She decided not to comment on the "young lady" part of his question, though she was in her fifties and her hair was mostly gray. Nor would she mention that she had studied *The Divine Comedy* in scholarly editions that presented the original Italian and the English translation side by side.

"If this is the first circle," she said, "what's the ninth?"

The man harrumphed and snuffled, counting silently on his fingers.

"I admit the parallel with Dante is imperfect."

There were five circles, it turned out. Among the men "rounded up," in the Mayor's words, by the latest Public Health campaign, were pro-Erda men, even veterans, as well as men who had taken no sides ("which means everyone here despises us"). So the pro-Erdan men were the first circle, the neutrals the second. In the third circle were decommissioned D.A.W. soldiers. The fourth circle were those who had still been in prisoner of war camps at the time of the peace treaty. And the fifth circle (or the ninth, if you skipped a few for greater effect) were the war criminals, housed in formal military prisons.

Finally he had Averil's attention.

"Where do they keep the Erdans?" she said.

"Where they keep everyone else."

"Mixed in? Everyone together?"

"That's right, young lady. Except for the military prisons. It's Prison Lite for the rest of us."

He seemed unaware that he had demolished the Dante analogy even further.

"What's more," he said, "we're not getting out. None of us are."

"That's paranoid."

"Mark my words."

A guard came in, gun drawn, and gestured with it at the old man as if shooing him away.

211

"Get along, you old gasbag. The Reverend doesn't need to waste her time with you."

"Did you have to do it like that?" Averil said to her after the Mayor left. "An old man?"

"What? The safety was on."

~

She was an ordinary citizen, Averil reminded herself. A civilian. There were mint leaves growing riot at the edge of her neighbor's garden, and she was going to help her dry them this evening. Tomorrow there was the work at the radio station, and she'd promised to help other neighbors repair a shed so they could turn it into a henhouse. The church cleanup still wasn't finished.

They were at peace. They were rebuilding their lives.

She reminded herself how good it felt to do ordinary work, work with visible results, not like saying Mass and hearing confession and doing amorphous research into a long-ago time that no one wanted to know about anyway.

She was at peace. And some things were easier not to think about.

Like the White Mountain Army Camp/Processing Center.

"It will get worse," the Mayor said, the next time Averil was at the facility.

"You don't know that," she said.

"Larger forces of history are at work, young lady. Don't think you can do anything to change that."

"What was this whole war about, if not women changing the world?"

The three-day stints passed slowly. She catalogued new books, folded sheets and towels in the infirmary, listened to the Mayor's gloomy pronouncement without challenging his flawed logic. She went for walks in her off hours. Corporal Willasdottir wouldn't let her go alone, even when she went off the base, so Averil often ended up escorted by the corporal herself, listening to variations on Willasdottir's favorite theme: the psychology of the prisoners.

"There are other camps," the corporal said, "where guards shoot troublemakers pointblank, no questions asked. Our commander won't allow that." She noticed Averil's horrified expression. "It's the only way to control them," she said defensively. "Otherwise it becomes like prisons used to be, factions fighting for no reason, the strong dominating the weak. They revert to their nature."

212

One bright November afternoon, she and the corporal took a hike to the top of White Mountain.

"You'd like this place in July, Chaplain," the corporal said. "Mountain laurel's in bloom. Flowers everywhere. This whole area up here, it's like you're swimming in them."

"Are they white?"

"Pinkish. They look white from a distance."

"That must be why they call it White Mountain." She liked that. Mountains named for flowers. Massive things with ephemeral names. Tulip Mountain. Mount Sunflower.

At cliff's edge they looked down at Penn's Creek below, with the facility directly across. Beyond it Averil saw something else.

"Who's doing that construction?"

"That's ours, the army's."

"But—it's obviously for something much larger. Something permanent."

"You didn't expect us to keep the men in those ramshackle buildings indefinitely, did you?"

"You could let them go."

Corporal Willasdottir laughed long and hard. "You always have to buck the tide, don't you, Chaplain?"

~

A funny thing happened in the months following the re-quarantining of men by the Public Health Service.

Women relaxed.

Even the ones who hadn't shaken off their patriarchal conditioning.

Even fervent matrilineal Erdans who missed the good men in their lives, brothers and lovers, comrades in arms.

They all had to acknowledge that the quality of their day-to-day lives had changed drastically.

They weren't used to being relaxed.

They were used to feeling self-conscious. Used to knowing that whenever they ventured out in public there were bound to be male eyes passing judgment on their faces, their hair, their bodies.

They were used to feeling defensive at work, wound-up in expectation of subtle condescension or outright harassment.

They were used to feeling afraid. Refraining from long solitary walks in nature preserves or on late-night city streets. Being uneasy at the mere sight of a male stranger in a deserted place.

All of that was over.

They discovered they *liked* not having men around.

Averil reflected that it gave added meaning to the name of Shade Mountain. Shades in the sense of ghosts, and Swift Run a town of absences, of ghosts, except the ghosts were still alive. And ghost towns were usually desolate. This place was not desolate.

In fact, the happiness was what lulled her into complacency.

So much talk, in those days, about moving forward, creating something new. Something unprecedented.

No one remembered exactly when the term "sequestering" entered the discussion.

Their absence made it even more starkly clear: men raised under patriarchy were dysfunctional. Perhaps irredeemably so.

It was not only a question of reeducating. They had to be resocialized. Reshaped. This was going to take a long time.

President Selene Marisela traveled throughout the republic on the functioning rail lines, giving speeches. "We can't rush into anything," she said. "An early release policy could derail the progress we're making."

The points she made were so reasonable, they seeped into people's minds until they felt like their own original thoughts—and perhaps they were.

When the confinement of the men continued, the women nodded understandingly at the new reasons floated about: the danger of plague was over, but now the confinement was for the men's own protection against possible reprisals. The implication was that traumatized survivors of patriarchy had turned to random violence against men as a whole. Just because no one had heard of any actual instances, it didn't hurt to be safe. You never knew. Besides, military tribunals were still sorting everything out. Wouldn't it be better to wait so the men who were released could hold their head up in public, free from taint of suspicion that they had collaborated with the anti-Erdan forces?

Sequestering, in fact, was a fait accompli. The men were already confined. And the women were too busy feeling relaxed to think much about it.

CHAPTER 21

DICO VOBIS

Those things which God has ordained in me
are beyond understanding.

—Christina Mirabilis, 13th century

During her next stint at the processing center, Averil searched fruitlessly for productive tasks to do, but ended up back at the library. She was sorting through a box of book donations she had collected at Swift Run when the Mayor walked in.

He looked around, even under the table, then went to the doorway and looked out before closing the door. Averil, struggling to keep a straight face, concentrated on dusting off the books and sorting them.

The Mayor, standing close to her now, was obviously making an effort to speak quietly, but his voice still boomed out.

"Young lady. Do you remember what I told you about the circles of hell?"

"We're in the first," she said. "Or is it the second?"

He frowned at her lightheartedness. "I was mistaken about the levels," he said. "I thought the war criminals' prison was the ninth circle. But there's a deeper level."

Gradually she got the whole story out of him. A prisoner had arrived, in transit to someplace else but kept isolated. Rumor had it that he was in a special category, had never been charged, had no access to attorneys, no access to the outside world. The officers in charge had a hard time deciding where to put him, finally settling on a windowless storage room down the corridor from the medical office.

"You've got it wrong," Averil said. "It was your lot who specialized in secret prisons."

The door banged open and the Mayor cringed as though expecting a bullet. A young guard looked in. "This stays open," she said sternly, but she was barely finished before the Mayor had scuttled out, mumbling apologies.

"I'm the one who closed it," Averil said. "What difference does it make?" She hated this kind of bullying tactic.

"Regulations."

"And god forbid we question—"

But the guard was already gone.

~

That night, in one of the tiny barrack rooms allotted to reservists, Averil lay awake.

What kind of test is this? To see if I can be kind to torturers and rapists and war criminals?

Then I've failed.

She thought of other prisoners. St. Paul as the walls of the prison crumbled before him.

My stint is over tomorrow.

Marguerite Porete, refusing to recant, refusing even to speak to the inquisitors.

This is none of my business.

It was one of the few unambiguous directives from the mysterious wandering holy man who had started it all. Feed the hungry. Comfort the sick. Visit the prisoner.

A voice resounds in the small dark room.

Are you a priest of God?

The room dissolves around her. Walls, ceiling, bed beneath her, all gone.

She doesn't know how to answer. She and Jesus are estranged. Mary has never drawn close no matter how much Averil prays to her.

"How about this?" she says. "You promise no more visions, and I'll go and see him."

The thunderclap is so sudden and loud that it makes her seize up, her teeth rattling in her skull. Then she is outside herself, watching as her foolish little body is struck by lightning and disintegrates into flaking black ashes.

~

She didn't overthink her strategy the next morning. She saw a guard with a food tray heading toward a particular corridor, caught up with her, talked her into giving her the tray and the key. Later the guard claimed Averil had said the colonel in charge had authorized it. Averil's exact words, however, were "I've been asked to speak to the prisoner," which was true and had the advantage of being heard however the listener wanted to hear it.

She unlocked the door and stopped short. She hadn't expected to recognize the man.

He in turn, slumped on a box of medical supplies, looked up only because he hadn't heard the expected sounds—a tray being slammed down, an insult flung his way.

Gary Tramonte had been a celebrity from the moment he defected from the U.S. army and joined the Erdan side during the earliest days of the war. He was a handsome, square-jawed white man who photographed well and was relaxed and charming in endless interviews with journalists. "I can't say I understand all the theoretical stuff about patriarchy and all that," he would offer, modestly looking down while the camera caught the play of his long eyelashes against perfect cheekbones. "But I know what's right. And what my country is doing isn't right."

He had proved an astonishingly successful battlefield commander, had risen through the ranks on his own merits, was even appointed to the Military High Command.

He and Averil were comrades—not on the battlefield, of course, but they had formed a bond that people do in wartime, had spent time together, moments of high tension and moments of deep emotion, the last one being the funeral of Doug Marisela, the beloved brother of Erda's commander-in-chief.

And here he was, undernourished and exhausted and scarred—like the rest of them, except for being buried alive in the postwar Erdan penal system.

Averil was gripped by conflicting emotions. Horror that this man of all men might have committed some atrocity that she didn't want to think about. Horror that he was innocent and suffering an unjust sentence. Guilt that she hadn't known about this before, hadn't been there to support him.

The look on his face, the sheer relief, made her swirling ambivalence resolve itself into pity. She opened her arms and they embraced for a long time.

~

By the time the transport truck dropped her off a mile or so outside town, it was late evening. Averil reached Margaret's house just before the cold air on her face turned painful. Margaret called out a greeting through the thick curtain they had tacked up across the entrance to the living room.

The fireplace there was the only source of heat in the house, besides the wood-burning stove in the kitchen. Once the nighttime temperatures dipped into the single digits, Margaret slept in the living room.

"I have another sleeping bag," she told Averil. "I think it's time for you to abandon the upstairs."

"I'll be okay."

Sensation was returning to her chilled face and hands, and the fire seemed almost too hot. Using the tongs, she pulled out the brick Margaret had placed there, and wrapped it in some dishtowels. A centuries-old technique: a hot brick tucked under the covers at the foot of your bed.

On the small desk in her room Averil found a circular candle holder, with four candles set in it and pine branches interwoven around them.

An Advent wreath.

Tomorrow would be the last Sunday of November. One of the luxuries of peacetime: to enjoy the ordinariness of consulting a calendar, thinking about what the date meant. To even have a calendar to look at.

She smiled. Margaret must have noticed it somewhere and bartered for it, a jar of her canned peaches or sour-cherry preserves. She could imagine Margaret's rueful expression at the idea of wreaths and candles—superstition, paganism, and Catholicism inextricably mixed in her mind, all equally suspect.

She lit one of the candles. Advent. The coming. There was no reason, of course, to think that Jesus had been born at the Winter Solstice. And He didn't want to hear from her anyway.

She reached for the red glass beads, closed her eyes, tried to clear her mind.

Gary had convinced her not to make an outcry about his situation. The whole thing was a glitch in the system, he said, it would be resolved at preliminary hearings. Most of all, he didn't want word to reach Selene Marisela. "She's always hated me. Blamed me for Doug's death, as if I was the one who'd sent him into harm's way."

"I need to do something," Averil had said, and she flinched at the surprise she read on his face. He had assumed that she of all people would have been involved all along in opposing sequestering. Protests, petitions—something.

Simple, honest labor was what she'd wanted. Tend gardens, preserve vegetables, feed chickens. She'd been enjoying her quiet, ordinary new life, while men had been rounded up indiscriminately.

The beads, usually slippery-cool in her hands, feel oddly warm, then hot. The beads are angry, she realizes, their anger is searing outward in every direction. Flames, yellow-hot, leap toward Averil like current along a wire.

218

The bed itself is hot beneath her. Averil is sure that if she opens her eyes she'll see waves of heat shimmering in the room, as if flames are raging right outside the door. It's getting difficult to breathe.

The sequestering was a careful plan, she realizes. The circles of hell, the conveniently timed quarantine for men who had remained at large. And now the whole system is in place, entrenched, irrevocable.

Now the beads in her hands turn into flames, joined in a loop. A single flame hovers above her head.

Pentecost.

Jesus is gone, but she and the other apostles have been given the gift of eloquent speech. They're supposed to wander the earth, spread the word.

She has no gifts, she argues. She wants no gifts.

The tongue of flame above her only flares higher, and the flames in her hands turn to bright, flowing blood, the sacred blood of her dead sister-seminarians. Their blood had been all over her, ingested by her, become one with her, is still flowing inside her. She's grasping their flowing red-glass blood in her hands and they're giving her their priestly blessings.

To do what? Averil says. *Argue? Debate?* A hopeless task.

She hears singing. Men's voices, plainchant, soft and low. Perhaps downstairs, where surely Margaret slumbers before the fireplace. She can make out differences in the voices, some tired, some out of tune, some quivering with age and others vibrant with youthful devotion. The monks of St. Anthony's. Together their voices are sweet as love. She hasn't heard them in years.

If she could get the women to hear this beauty. If the beauty could outweigh the anger.

And suddenly there is Abraham, in that fractured story of ill-fated Sodom. He's standing with God (when had He appeared? The narrator of Genesis is silent about that), and God is musing about the possible misbehavior of the people. *I've heard things,* God says. *I'm going to go over and find out whether it's true* (wouldn't He know, being omniscient and all?). And Abraham is reasoning with God, Averil standing next to him:

"Will you destroy the righteous with the wicked?" Abraham says, and Averil is struck with admiration. Challenging God like that. Especially back then, when God was so bad-tempered. "What if there are fifty good men?"

"If I find fifty good men," God says grudgingly, "I will spare them all."

"What if there are only forty-five? Will you destroy the righteous with the wicked for the lack of five?"

"If I find forty-five good men I will spare them all."

"What if there are only thirty good men?"

"You're wasting your time," Averil tells him. "I know how this ends."

"What about twenty?" Abraham persists. "What about ten?"

God walks away without answering. Next thing they see are the tiny faraway figures scurrying from the city, Lot and his anonymous wife and daughters (no names, it's all about the men anyway), and then that town and the next and the next, the whole valley engulfed in flames and billowing black smoke.

She opened her eyes to the cold, dark bedroom. The Advent candle had gone out.

~

There needs to be public debate, Averil told people. About everything. Sequestering. Parthenogenesis.

For the sake of fairness. For the sake of the principles of this new society we're building.

"It's a prison sentence," she said of sequestering, and was met with a host of arguments.

"It's not prison. They have comfortable sleeping quarters, meals provided, useful work that they're compensated for, state-of-the-art exercise equipment."

"Better conditions than what *we* had in the Erdan army."

"Hell, better than what we have right now."

Results were similar when she tried to talk about parthenogenesis:

"We can't let things drift on in the direction they're going," Averil said. "If we have parthenogenesis, and if the remaining men are confined, there won't be any men, ever. We're changing the whole direction of our evolution."

"Don't be melodramatic," people told her. "There are lots of sperm banks. We can go back to having boy babies later, when things stabilize. And they won't grow up with pigs as role models."

Inevitably the conversation would turn toward its source, toward the anger. Look what they've done to this world, the women would say. The women would point to the constant wars, the bottomless greed, the casual, everyday violence. The ceaseless need for domination. They almost destroyed the planet, they said. We're not going to let that happen.

The High Military Tribunal called for the formation of a civilian Council of Elders. People weren't surprised when Averil Parnell stood for election as a delegate to the Constituent Assembly to decide on the membership of the Council. She won easily, and got on the train to IxChel. Taking the slow route. She got off at every stop, talked to anyone she could find. People started expecting her, they showed her the way to the town hall or some other meeting space, or when the weather was mild they were waiting for her at the train station.

"Think back," she would tell them, "to times in your life when a man showed you kindness.

"When you were small, do you remember a man's loving arms wrapped around you? A big hand holding your own small one when you crossed the street?

"Think about the time when a man made you laugh," she said. "Or explained something you had been confused about, taught you something you were glad to know.

"Think about a male comrade who saved your life in battle.

"Have you ever seen a painting that took your breath away? Or heard a song that gave you joy? Were any of them by male artists?

Selene Marisela was making whistle-stop speeches too. She got the feeling that wherever she went, she was just behind the irritating priest.

"Chaplain Parnell sounds convincing," she said, "until we start to analyze what she's saying. She's appealing to our sentimentality. She's asking us to leave logic behind.

"She says think about the man who was kind to you as a child. I say think about the man who rapes little girls, rapes his own daughters and gets away with it.

"She says think about the man who was a helpful neighbor. I say think about the man who kills his wife rather than let her leave. The man who rapes his date, his wife, a passing stranger. Think about the man who happily participated in and helped defend all the woman-hating practices of his time and place, instead of challenging them.

"Chaplain Parnell points to the painters, the poets, the musicians. They moved our hearts, she says. She tells us, listen to them sing. I say listen to the silence. Think of all the masterpieces unpainted, unwritten, unsculpted. All those voices we never heard from. Those were our foremothers. Those were our sisters. They would be us, if men were still in power.

"She quotes from that quaint piece of tribal myth, the Judeo-Christian Bible. Well, I can quote from it too. 'There is no virtuous man on earth who is without sin.'"

Averil was listened to respectfully but silently. Selene got the roars of approval, the boisterous applause.

CHAPTER 22

PASSION

How will we know the difference between the power
we promote and the power we oppose?

—Judith Butler, 1993

Anno Mirabilis 11

The war dead lingered over Erda, disoriented, as is often the case
when large numbers meet a violent demise all at the same time.
They weren't used to being dead, weren't used to the curious feeling of
detachment from the drama in which they had been passionately involved
in life.

Soon they would move on, become a whole new cohort of heroic
ancestral spirits, invoked on holidays by politicians in photo opportunities
and stirring speeches at battle memorials. But for now they drifted on
breezes or clustered like wisps of fog under the eaves of abandoned
buildings. When they revisited the scenes of their deaths, they argued
lazily over battle tactics (friend or foe in life, it hardly mattered now),
looked ruefully at bullet holes in fences and walls.

Like bored guests, attending out of politeness, they sat in on the
deliberations of the Constituent Assembly as it voted on a Council of
Elders. They observed the debates over parthenogenesis, heard the
Council's carefully worded decision to ensure that the procedure did not
become the sole method of reproduction, for reasons pragmatic rather
than ideological: the method was high-tech, and if the means of carrying
it out were to be lost one day due to some future disruption, the human
race would die out.

Some of the war dead fluttered around Selene Marisela, moths to the
clear, true flame of her anger. That anger was their own so recently, the
energy that gave purpose to their actions. They knew its source, and its

goal: a controlled burn. Purifying flames to clear the way for lush new growth. *Deadwood, yes*, they murmured in sympathy. *So much of it still here. Something to be said for getting rid of it.*

The war dead were the only observers at the trial of the Erdan war hero Gary Tramonte.

There had been no announcement that the trial was scheduled. There was no jury. The judge assigned the defendant an attorney the morning of the trial. No research was done, no depositions taken, no witness lists drawn up. Whoever was on hand, and wanted to testify, was sworn in and questioned.

Is it more slapstick or Kafka-esque? the war dead murmured to each other, connoisseurs of the absurd. *Perhaps a splash of Shirley Jackson and Leonora Carrington, an undertone of Eugene Ionesco? A nod of acknowledgment to Dante?*

Averil Parnell showed up, looking disheveled and harried, adding a note of piquancy much appreciated by the spirit-spectators. That morning she had been tipped off by a friend in the IxChel Bureau of Prisons. Gary had been transferred to a small military outpost in the countryside outside IxChel. The mess tent was being used as a courtroom.

Averil intercepted the judge before the trial was called to order, and the war dead hushed each other so they could listen.

"Your Honor, the defendant only found out this morning what the charges against him are. We can't mount an adequate defense unless you grant an adjournment."

"Justice delayed is justice denied," the judge intoned.

Oh, brav-o!

Did she really say that?

Delicious. Could we do an instant replay?

The prosecution had two witnesses, a sergeant and a corporal in the Erdan army.

From their rambling and inconsistent testimonies, Averil gathered that Gary had supposedly ordered the wholesale destruction of a town even though civilian residents were still inside the houses.

Inexplicably, Gary's defense attorney asked them no questions at all.

Averil took the stand, spoke of Gary's courage, his integrity, all the people he had inspired.

"Regardless of his admirable traits, Reverend, the fact remains that you weren't there on the day in question."

"I'm here as a character witness."

"What do you think of the testimony you've heard about the actual crime for which Major Tramonte is being tried?"

"Each witness is internally inconsistent, and the two of them contradict each other. If there had been time to conduct a real defense, his attorney would have been able to verify whether the incident even took place at all, find out whether these witnesses were even there, and whether Gary was even there, and if so, what exactly he did. There's nothing at all here to corroborate what they're saying."

"Are you accusing the witnesses of lying?"

"I'm answering your question."

At that moment, President Selene Marisela walked into the mess tent.

The prosecuting attorney stumbled over her words before losing her train of thought completely. It was hard to tell who looked more nervous, the two lawyers or the judge.

Selene took a seat, flanked by bodyguards. She seemed unaware of the stir she caused, or else had come to expect it.

They didn't even take the handcuffs off Gary when he was called to the witness stand. Averil winced when she realized his feet were shackled too.

"Your Honor," he said calmly, "I didn't know the charges against me beforehand. I should have had a jury trial. I should have had an attorney with time to prepare my defense. All I can do now is state unequivocally, the charges against me are false. I swear it on my life. I fought for a just society. I put my life on the line. Judge, all I'm asking is for you to postpone this so I can get a truly fair trial."

The closing remarks were brief and unimpressive. Instead of granting a postponement, the judge banged the gavel and said in a monotone, "Gary Tramonte, I find you guilty of war crimes and sentence you to death by firing squad."

Averil had a moment to wonder about an appeals process—how to go about it, whether there *was* an appeals process—before she heard the judge continue:

"The sentence will be carried out immediately."

It took three guards to drag Gary out of the mess tent.

"This is cruel and unusual punishment," Averil shouted at the judge.

Even as she spoke, a firing squad was being set up. Soldiers put a blindfold on Gary and slammed him against a fence. Other soldiers stood in formation, guns ready. Selene, behind them, watched poker faced, as if this had nothing to do with her, as if all were going according to standard procedure.

"I demand an appeal," Averil said.

"This is a military court," the judge said as she walked away. "Different rules."

Kafka, the war dead murmured. *Definitely Kafka.*

They were inured to pity, to horror at random cruelty, having lived it so recently and passed through it to the other side, but even they drew in their collective breath when Averil pushed past the soldiers and threw her arms around Gary.

"I won't let this happen!"

"Shoot her if she doesn't move," Selene said calmly.

Two soldiers dragged Averil off, holding her back long enough for the shots to be fired, for Gary Tramonte's shuddering, bleeding body to jerk back against the fence and slide to the ground.

Now the soldiers had to hold Averil back from lunging at the president. The bodyguards drew their handguns and aimed them at Averil, but the soldiers pressed against her protectively.

She pointed in fury at Selene.

"You—"

She was going to pronounce anathema on her, she felt the priestly energy surge through her, the righteous anger that would smite the sinner.

And then she couldn't speak, couldn't move. She was paralyzed by the futility of words, a futility she now saw with terrible clarity. The uselessness of words, and the weight of her own inadequacy. She was turned to stone, ancient stone that was about to crumble into dust.

~

Medical personnel flowed through Averil's room in a constant stream, changing course just enough to avoid the immovable obstacle that was Catherine Beck, sitting with head bowed by the bedside of the silent, staring patient.

Although Selene Marisela had had Averil court-martialed for attempted assault, a military judge had ordered her hospitalized, and now there seemed no end of white coats swooping down with stethoscopes, blood pressure cuffs, penlights to peer into eyes and down mouth. Throat swabs were taken, reflexes were tested, lymph nodes were prodded.

"You were just here," Catherine said irritably when yet another latex-gloved hand reached out to take a blood sample. "She'll have no more blood left."

"That must have been someone this morning" came the unruffled reply.

"Can't keep you straight, there's a swarm of you in here all the time."

"I guess *healing* isn't your thing, is it?"

Everybody stopped.

No one, ever, had thought to even hint at criticism of the warrior spirit embodied most perfectly by General Beck.

Catherine looked around, curious rather than angry, but everyone backed off and she wasn't sure who had made the remark. One of the doctors present said later that the look in Catherine's eyes had reminded her of an arctic wolf, calculating and deadly calm; while another saw something even more impersonal in the gray eyes: the surface of a glacier, perhaps, an endless cold surface on which people could wander off and be lost forever.

The days seemed to merge together, the only difference being that Averil was now sitting up in bed, but no more responsive than earlier.

An eager young neurologist read and re-read Averil's chart. "Too bad we don't have access to high-resolution brain imaging anymore," she said. "I would love to get a look at what's going on in there."

"Maybe she'll donate her brain to science," Catherine said. "You can slice it up and put it under a microscope."

"Don't tease me," the neurologist said wistfully.

Catherine sat up straight. She thought she'd seen a hint of a smirk on Averil's face.

"You like that, do you?" She leaned forward, took Averil's hands. "Is it that you can't think of the words? The words won't come? *Ghoulish*, is that the word you're looking for? *Morbidly funny?*"

Averil gazed straight into Catherine's eyes for a moment, then lapsed back into that inward-focused expression, watching or listening for something that no one else perceived.

Catherine wondered if she was thinking about Gary.

She'd done all she could, she told herself. She had demanded he get a hearing as soon as possible. She had assumed he would go free.

The truth was, she could have done more. She had dragged her feet. And now Gary was dead.

Catherine was not used to feeling guilt.

She had no one to blame but herself for the shoddiness of the proceedings. She had been in charge of the Erdan military almost from the beginning. Years ago she delegated the setup of the military court system to people who seemed to have legal expertise. She hadn't overseen their work or even read the damn regulations they'd concocted.

Now she didn't even know who to demote. Other than herself.

226

"There's no evidence of stroke or other seizure," the chief neurologist told her. "No heart arrhythmia, no neurological damage. We don't know what's wrong with her physiologically. I would say the aphasia is a combination of shock, emotional fatigue, and depression. Post-traumatic stress disorder. Looking at her file, I'd say she's suffered it most of her adult life."

~

Averil's room at the peace officer's house was small and blessedly simple: a bed, a small window, a framed poster of Van Gogh sunflowers. There was no crucifix on the wall, which puzzled Averil but did not upset her.

She sat on the bed and closed her eyes.

A sunny afternoon. She's walking along a country road. Soon she comes upon an estate enclosed by a brick wall. The red bricks are weathered to pink, festooned with ivy.

Averil has walked past this walled estate for years, admired the work of the masons who built it, but never questioned the smooth, solid face it presents to the world. Whatever is on the other side, she is not meant to see.

She has had her share of mysteries in her life. There are too many decades and deaths behind her now for her to feel a spark of curiosity about anything made by human hands.

But today, something is different. Today there is a door in the wall, a wide, stout wooden door, arched on top, painted dark green, and its hinges and knob and paint all look weathered, as if the door has been there forever, though Averil has never seen it before. She feels no surprise at this. Maybe this is death: a door opens that was there all along, and you don't see it until you're meant to. It isn't exactly a pearly gate, but she likes this door better.

She pushes it open and goes inside, and immediately the weather changes. She has left behind bright sunshine; inside the gate it's gray from an overcast, threatening sky. Up ahead is a dilapidated mansion, like the ones in ghost stories and scary movies. Unhesitatingly she walks up the path, picking her way along the broken, upturned flagstones choked with weeds.

She approaches the front door and it opens soundlessly before she touches it. She steps inside boldly.

She knows who lives here.

He's waiting for her to question Him, to ask Why? Why everything? She could start, for example, with, Why did you allow nuclear weapons?

227

Or bullets, for that matter? Gunpowder, arrows, the forging of steel for spear points and swords? He is waiting to thunder in response, as He had to Job, *Where were you when I created the earth and the heavens*, and all the rest of that magnificent, poetic, but completely illogical answer.

She won't give Him the satisfaction. She isn't going to ask. Not even God Himself is going to make her speak.

Suddenly she's outside the house, but this time it's sunny and warm. The perfectly laid flagstone path meanders through a garden where the trees bear fruit and flowers at the same time. Jesus walks next to her as if they had never feuded. *I don't understand why people fret about weeds,* he says. *They're lovely. They should be welcomed.*

She hears footsteps in the hall, light and sure and fast.

Catherine looked in, her face full of love and pity. She knelt by the bed, reached for Averil's hands.

"Remember when you and your doctors went before a judge the other day?" Catherine said. "She's made her decision. She says you're unfit to stand trial."

Averil remembered why there was no crucifix on the wall.

"You can leave here right now. I'll get your things."

A C-84 missile had struck St. Anthony of Padua Church and obliterated it, finishing the work Averil had started. She smiled at Catherine because that was the most beautiful thing she, Averil, had ever done, send rose-colored stained glass raining into the night, and Catherine had been there to see it, all those years ago.

~

They moved Averil back to Catherine's house but she seemed lost in it, bewildered by the excess of space, perhaps, or confused about notions of ownership and property. Catherine could read all this in her face as plainly as if Averil still spoke. Where is everyone, she seemed to be wondering, and where is the church?

She moved her to a communal house, where Averil happily occupied one small room. She presented herself every third day at the kitchen, as if she were on a rotation with two other people, but the things she tried to make never seemed to coalesce into a coherent meal, and since she wouldn't write anything down on the shopping list, she simply made do with whatever was in the refrigerator. No one needed more than a taste of her lettuce soup, or some sort of flour-and-broccoli fritter that disintegrated on contact with oil, before they steered her away from cooking duties. Averil contented herself with the menial work. She would fill the sink with water, dump in the salad greens, spend long stretches of time gently washing them, tearing off the overripe or stringy parts, putting them in the salad spinner.

~

The Council of Elders continued, now sans Averil, with its deliberations over arrangements for the men.

The meeting space was not particularly large; there was seating for perhaps a few hundred in tiered rows like a theater in the round, looking down at the stage. The Elders themselves sat in a group of seats ringside, as it were, at the same level as the stage. They invited five or six individuals at a time, representing various views and interests, to come down to the stage and engage in a freewheeling debate, then after a while those individuals would be dismissed and another group would come on and hash it all out again, with plenty of enthusiastic yelling from the Council members and the audience.

Catherine, watching from the farthest row, contemplated the range of positions being taken on the issue. When she was young there was left, center, and right, or progressive, moderate, and conservative, but there was no way of aligning the parties to this debate on that antiquated spectrum. A whole new continuum was operative now. From strict to permissive, perhaps. Or from angry to forgiving.

There was the group named for the decisive Battle of Shenandoah. The Shenandoahists thought the "current crop," as they were known— meaning the entire contingent of men alive now—were hopelessly tainted by patriarchy and would never be able to overcome the conditioning of their male privilege, even if they could overcome their hostility to women. They would communicate it all to future generations: sons to expect to dominate, daughters to expect to be dominated, marginalized, objectified.

In this view, the men should be treated humanely, but kept in a tightly supervised living situation. And not allowed out. Ever. When all those men, and for that matter all the women living now, have died off, the thinking went, those women who wished to conceive could go back to doing it naturally rather than using either parthenogenesis or artificial insemination (selected for female children) from sperm banks.

Further to the left—or the right?—of this general consensus view were the Irridentists, who insisted that men were innately depraved.

229

Even a "new crop" of men, they said, will re-create patriarchy if given the liberty to do so.

In opposition to those two schools of thought were the Unitarians (called "Bleeding Hearts" by their detractors), who insisted that even the "current crop" of men could be reeducated.

Then there were the Constitutionalists, who fell at different points of the spectrum about male nature and its capacity for redemption, but who were united in the insistence that sequestering could not be squared with the rule of law, even under the emergency exception advocated by Selene Marisela.

At the moment, a few women from each camp were onstage, politely taking turns presenting their evidence, but mostly talking past each other rather than engaging the points the others were making.

With a moment of nostalgia for her younger days, when she had her knife-edge focus on her own mission and gave little thought to politics, Catherine requested permission from the moderator to join the debate that was under way. She stepped onto the stage to thunderous applause. She looked up at the rows of cheering onlookers, feeling like a gladiator in a ring. Everyone, it seemed, expected that Catherine agreed with them and was about to soundly trounce the other side.

She made a gesture toward the evolutionary biologist who had been speaking, indicating for her to continue.

"Male violence is not only useless from an evolutionary perspective, it's counterproductive," the biologist said. "We have to think about the good of the planet and the good of human civilization."

Catherine knew how involved Averil had been in the preparations for this debate. It was all Averil thought about, in the weeks before Gary was executed.

The biologist held up a sheaf of papers. "Even after women broke men's stranglehold on science," she said, "male scientists still vastly outnumbered women. When I was growing up, you couldn't turn around without a new article purporting to prove that men are 'naturally' aggressive and competitive. The whole point was to claim that there was no use trying to change them. They were *meant* to be in charge."

Snorts and hoots from the audience.

"So I say, fine, let's take them at their word. They're naturally violent. They naturally dominate. They naturally despoil the earth and establish vicious, inflexible hierarchies. They naturally oppress women. Let's take it as a given. Now what should we do about this fact?"

"Lock them up!" came the shouts from the audience. There were even cries of "Eliminate them! For the good of the planet!"

"But why should we accept that claim as fact?" Catherine said. "How do we know their domineering behavior isn't socially conditioned?"

"Whose side are you on?" someone called out.

"Truth," she said. "Logic."

She almost said Justice, but that was too close to her heart. It was bad enough that she was channeling Averil now. She'd be damned if she'd look like one of those bleeding hearts.

"We know there have been human societies that were more egalitarian," Catherine said. "How would that have been possible, if men were incapable of it?"

An Elder spoke up from the sidelines. "Those societies were less complex. Structurally there was less chance for domination. You haven't proved your point."

"Isn't the burden of proof on you?" Catherine said. "The Council is considering keeping those men locked up for the rest of their lives."

"That is not a foregone conclusion. The debate is about the timing and circumstances of the release, not whether to hold them forever."

"Really? Because I've seen all that new construction. Big, sturdy facilities, beautifully designed, all the comforts and amenities you would want to keep the occupants pacified. What an investment, for a temporary situation. Then we'll have all those abandoned buildings on our hands after the sequestering is over."

The final decision was, in effect, no decision. By a close vote, the Council opted to revisit the issue after an unspecified period of "evaluation and reeducation."

CHAPTER 23

ORDINARY
TIME

Thus I have lived quietly as a human being, so that I have
taken repose neither in saints nor in men on earth.

—Hadewijch of Antwerp

Averil's room in the communal house had a window by the bed
and another facing west. Each consisted of two panes of glass that
opened outward. It was important to Averil to be able to thrust them
open like tiny doors and let in the sunlight and the air, because that was
all she needed, light and air. The single bed had a thin, firm mattress on
a dark wooden frame, a white sheet, a tightly woven bedspread of a color
somewhere between gray and beige. The desk was made of the same dark
wood as the bed frame, and also the wardrobe. It had taken Averil a while
to get used to the wardrobe, but now she had made her peace with it and
no longer worried whether it would topple over and crush her.

Now that she no longer read or wrote or spoke to people—or, indeed,
listened to them—time opened out for her in whole new ways. When she
dusted the furniture in the communal living room, for example, she was
no longer rushing through a mindless chore for the sake of getting it done
quickly and moving on to the things she really wanted to do. Drawing
her dustcloth across the top of the upright piano, the bookcases, the card
table, was in fact the task that she really wanted to do.

When she noticed the dust on the blades of the ceiling fan, the logistics
of getting up there absorbed all her attention: how to locate a stepladder,
whether a dry rag would be enough for the accumulated grime. She
pictured herself accidentally knocking over the stepladder and hanging

on to the fan like a character in a slapstick silent film, and had a good, soundless laugh.

She beat the braided rugs. She folded laundry. She learned to knit and sew, and mended everyone's detached buttons and torn sleeves. Her sole effort at communication was a certain sharp, impatient gesture that called attention to her empty hands: she wanted something to do.

Outdoors she raked leaves, shoveled snow, transplanted herbs from indoor pots as soon as it was warm enough. Often with the help of Catherine on her days off, Averil staked up tomatoes and pea plants, planted corn, string beans, potatoes, carrots. She refused to pull weeds. She pitchforked the compost pile so it was evenly turned. She fed the chickens but would not collect any eggs. In fact she unlocked the henhouse and their fenced-in area, but the chickens never wandered far. Same story with a housemate's pet bunny, which lazed around the yard and scurried back into its hutch when it sensed predators, although it made its peace with the recently arrived cat, an enormous gray Mehitabel lookalike who wove around Averil's legs and eyed the hens and bunny, but reserved her predator skills for the occasional fieldmouse.

Averil, freed of language, had the luxury to wonder for the first time in her life why the plural of mouse was mice but the plural of house wasn't hice. She felt pleasantly disengaged from the problem, like seeing someone else work a jigsaw puzzle.

Sandy the dog reappeared, or at least one identical to the yellowish mutt she had encountered outside the cafeteria in the old Erda. The dog settled into life at the communal house, kept Averil company, sat next to her while she knitted on winter evenings in the living room, each one looking equally inscrutable.

When Averil had no tasks in the house she wandered around the neighborhood and pitched in wherever anyone was hard at work. She helped fix flowerbed borders, lay paving stones for paths, scrape paint off windowsills and old wallpaper off walls.

People tried to pay her for her help but she refused, so they followed her home and found someone else to handle it—"A donation," they would say. "Put it in the house's general fund."

Before long, the membership of the house shifted. As individuals moved away, the openings were filled by people who were applying specifically because of Averil's presence there. For them the house wasn't just a convenient arrangement, a temporary waystation on the way to something more permanent with sisters and friends, daughters and nieces.

As the years passed, they expanded into the houses around them and transformed into a contemplative community known as Via Dolce. The Sweet Way.

They had no common creed, made no efforts to attract others to join. Each of them had found something about the silent priest that made her want to stay. It was as simple as that.

Averil taught herself to play the recorder, although no one, including Catherine, had seen any indication before that she knew how to read music. Members of Via Dolce tried to interpret the meaning of the tunes she played, since this was the only sound she had produced in years. Some said the preponderance of dirges and forlorn odes merely reflected the contents of the old music books Averil had somehow scrounged up. Others were unconvinced.

"She's communicating," they whispered in awe, until Catherine wanted to knock the silly worshipful looks right off their faces.

The living room in the main house had been turned into a contemplation room, for those members who liked silent meditation in groups. They explained to Averil what the room was for, hoping she heard, hoping she understood. Sometimes she wandered in and sat down, but she didn't close her eyes or take up any position that people recognized as conducive to meditation. She seemed like someone in a doctor's waiting room, well behaved but slightly bored.

She joined them about once a week, usually when she had run out of chores or had spent a few hours doing yard work. They could tell by the way she stood up slowly from her gardening that her knees and lower back were bothering her, but she ignored offers of heat packs and doctor's appointments.

One day when she came in and sat down, she did close her eyes. Sitting perfectly still, she seemed to the others to be breathing slowly and evenly—perhaps, indeed, meditating.

The others, smiling, settled in again. Although each one had different practices and techniques, on that day each individual experienced an effortless silencing of her thoughts, a profound peace more relaxing and refreshing than anything she had felt before. Each one, of course, thought her experience was unique.

Over weeks and months, they realized that not only were they having particularly vivid visualizations while Averil was in their midst, they were all actually experiencing the same visualization.

With Averil sitting among them, silent as always, they wandered through fragrant apple orchards, hopped from stone to stone across mountain streams, clung to the tops of tall pines in a stiff wind. One day they even rode through the night air on brooms.

~

"This might be a sensitive subject," the woman said, "but it's important for us to plan ahead."

Her name was Amaryllis, which had to be the frilliest, girly-girliest name Catherine had ever heard, but the woman was as somber as a funeral director, had that same air of quiet but tasteful unctuousness that made Catherine feel like she needed to run outside and get some fresh air, even though they were already outdoors.

She had to force herself not to laugh out loud when Amaryllis proceeded to talk about funeral arrangements.

"The members of our community all write wills—not that we own much property, but to give some idea of how we would like our personal effects disposed of, and also what we'd like for the final ritual."

"I guess you've tried asking her."

"Oh yes. We even tried naming all the options we could think of, hoping she would nod her head at something. She made no response to any of them—at least, not that we could tell."

"It's probably because she doesn't care."

"That may be. In which case it's up to her loved ones to decide. And it's always better to think it through sooner rather than later." Amaryllis handed her a book. "This is a collection of some of her sermons and her later talks when she led meditations. There's a passage here that might help you make your decision."

~

"So," Catherine said when she found Averil in her room, "you want your corpse exposed to the elements when you die. I have to admit, it's creative."

She opened to the page bookmarked by Amaryllis and read aloud: "*Some commentators made it sound like a horrible practice, but I think its original meaning is lovely. What is a dead body, anyway, but a discarded shell?*"

Catherine felt embarrassed. As far as she knew she had never willingly said the word "lovely" in her life. Or terms like "discarded shell."

"*No need for gravestones, or even graves,*" she read, looking up at Averil to see a faint half-smile forming, which made her even more self-conscious.

"*Let the birds take what they can, and the animals, and the insects; let the wind disperse it. Let our Mother the Earth slowly, gently, take it into Herself*—Christ almighty, Averil, you think this is funny."

Averil was giggling. She made no sound, but her body was shuddering with laughter, a delighted smile on her face. For a pained moment Catherine wondered whether Averil's larynx was paralyzed somehow and the doctors hadn't caught it, and that had been the problem all along. Not that she didn't want to make a sound, but that she couldn't.

Averil hugged her, and Catherine had to laugh. *Her* speaking Averil's words. Like a goddamned bear trying to play a piano.

The thing about Averil was, she sincerely believed all this Mother Earth claptrap, yet could laugh about it at the same time.

And this hug. Such a rare thing.

"Damned if I know," she told Amaryllis later. "Can we say cremation and leave it at that?"

The community members held a meeting and decided on a funeral pyre as a compromise solution: it combined exposure to the elements without, as Amaryllis put it, the more complicated questions of sanitation and eventual disposal.

~

Averil Parnell wasn't what you'd expect—or, indeed, want—in a saint. There were no benevolent smiles and gestures of blessing. When her face wasn't entirely blank, her most typical expressions were mild irritation and confusion. Also, saints were true believers, radiating the conviction that they were carrying out the will of the deity, whereas Averil seemed sure of nothing. Afterward, scholars debated whether she even believed in a deity in those later years.

Yet people were drawn to her. Each visitor seemed to take what she needed from her encounters with Averil. The Via Dolce community grew larger. The administrative posts, once assigned by rotation to every communard, became more specialized and were chosen by election. People started squabbling over the chance to meditate with Averil, since the contemplation room was too small to accommodate everyone.

Granted, they didn't always understand her. One day Averil was contemplating the lemurs, tiny primates who floated away from Africa sixty million years ago on rafts of woven vegetation and reached Madagascar, where there were no predators and no animals competing for the same food sources. They evolved into hundreds of distinct varieties, including, famously, some varieties exhibiting what surprised patriarchal scientists described as "female social dominance" ("male social dominance" eliciting no special comment). They were our best hope, Averil reflected. She wanted to be reincarnated as a lemur. A small complication was that she got lemurs confused with lemmings. As a result, some of the communards experienced visions that day in which small furry things—a cross between rodent and monkey—lived idyllic forest lives but then ran off a cliff together.

Some communards felt bemused affection rather than reverence. The children especially were disinclined to awe. One of them, Maria de Lourdes Pereira, came to Via Dolce with her mother when she was eight and proceeded to treat Averil like a severely impaired sibling. Averil would feel a tap on her hand to get her attention as if she were hard of hearing, and there would be Maria de Lourdes standing before her, tiny and severe: "It's lunchtime. Come."

Now Maria de Lourdes was in college. As a math major, she took it upon herself to study Via Dolce's account books and begin to make sense of them. One evening she was in the kitchen inspecting the most recent inventory of kitchen supplies and food, comparing it to receipts paid. Her mother, Luisa, was kneading bread while Averil was doing dishes. Catherine, at the scarred oak kitchen table with Maria de Lourdes, was sharpening knives.

"Child," Luisa said, "go help Dona Averil with the dishes."

"I'm busy. These books are a mess."

Averil looked admiringly at the girl, with her gleaming black braids beaded with lapis lazuli and clear quartz. Our Lady of Lourdes, munificent healer of the countryside of France, come to life with severe glasses and frightening efficiency.

Luisa was affronted. "So it's all right that Dona Averil does the dishes while you sit there at your leisure."

"We can't afford for all of us to be silent mystics," said Maria de Lourdes. "Someone has to pay attention to the bills."

Averil gently lobbed a wet dishcloth at her, which hit her arm with a soft *thwap* and made her giggle. The others noted Averil's expression, so typical when she was amused: a private, inward half-smile.

She loved that kind of humor, Catherine knew. Not a single one of these acolytes surrounding Averil knew how sharp-tongued she had been, what a ball buster. Not one of them had ever had the chance to hear her irreverence, her gallows humor. She told unpleasant truths when no one wanted to hear them.

And the enormity of Averil's transformation hit her afresh.

Averil's thoughts, in the meantime, had moved on. Would there be no more pilgrimages to Our Lady?

Scholars, poring over the journals and correspondence of the communards decades later, would declare that the dishcloth episode was one of the few times Averil was known to have communicated, albeit nonverbally, in the presence of more than one witness.

And, in fact, despite the spectacular downfall of the Catholic Church and all male-monotheist ideologies, devotion to Mary did survive among the followers of the Afro-Caribbean traditions, which had always included female sacred figures, as had the Meso-American, Indigenous North American, African, Siberian, and other Asian traditions.

Marian and other European goddess symbolism was also retained, not only reproductions of Neolithic-era figurines, but medieval Christian abstract representations. Rose windows appeared everywhere in Erda, including in the new spiritual center built in those early years in IxChel.

The center's design was based on drawings discovered in the ruins of a university, signed by an otherwise unknown architecture student named John Honig. Although no one knew the intentions or the spiritual orientation of the designer, it was clear that he had aimed at re-creating a sense of a forest. Light streamed through stained glass whose colors were carefully modulated: green like springtime leaves here, blue like winter sky there. Lining the central aisle were rough-textured, branched pillars forming a colonnade like an avenue of trees.

People brought Averil to the spiritual center when it opened, but she tried to walk through a wall of rose-colored stained glass and had to be restrained by friends.

~

Averil closed her eyes.

The others sitting with her closed their eyes, breathed deeply.

She had been thinking about the planet, its four and a half billion years of turbulent existence, studied briefly in college, back when the ages of the earth had seemed to her mere backdrop to the infinitely more interesting topic of humans and gods.

The communards floated peacefully in cosmic darkness.

The planet pulled itself together, as planets do. There was roiling molten rock. Eventually there was water. Continents floated about, converged in a clump at the southern end, and then—something about

238

warm ocean currents being blocked—the whole planet was covered in mile-deep ice, killing most of the single-celled life forms that had managed to show up. The snowball effect.

The communards shivered, on this sweaty August day.

More cataclysms. The massive volcano eruptions that lasted a million years—who could ever conceive—and once again almost all the long-suffering amoebas were wiped out.

Did we used to be bacteria?

Then, much later, single-celled to multi-celled, plants and fish and creeping crawling shuffling things on dry land—only to look up and see that asteroid coming right at them.

Did we used to be dinosaurs?

What would come next?

War and plague. Plague and war.

But in the meantime, blue sky, blood pumping through veins, how sweet to be alive, to be together.

The communards happily settled in to a vision of bliss. Averil opened her eyes and went out to the garden.

So many questions. How could a thoroughly benign deity create a world in which people had to kill to survive and suffer to love?

She mowed no grass, pulled no weeds, pruned no branches. No sharp instrument in her hands. As if the whole world were Samson's hair—nothing cut. Nothing locked in.

It wasn't enough.

She sat down in the grass next to the compost pile, hugged her knees, looked up at the sweltering blue sky. Flies were buzzing loudly on a banana peel, reveling in decay, drowsy with sugar and heat. Souls in transition, was what some cultures said about flies. One life form to another. This dimension to that.

You had to love the Trickster on her own terms.

CHAPTER 24

RESURRECTION

The more she understands, the less she speaks.

—Mechthild of Magdeburg

Anno Mirabilis 27

Wesley never could get used to the new calendar system. It was twenty-seven years after the Revolution, but that did no good when he was trying to figure out ages and birthdates to put on the gravestones. He had to use paper and pen to calculate the age of the newly deceased, and then translate the old system into the new one so he could carve out the dates.

Behind him, Reg squinted through a haze of marijuana smoke. "So how old was he?"

"See what that stuff does to your brain? Just because you grow it doesn't mean you have to smoke it all the time."

"Shit, I never was good at math. At least now it doesn't bother me."

"He was 84."

"Lucky fuck. Lived most of his life free. The war didn't get him, the plague didn't get him."

"On the other hand," Wesley said, "most likely he's one of the ones who pissed off the women." He moved on to the epitaph the guy had requested: *Under the wide and starry sky.*

He read it out loud to Reg. Neither of them knew what it meant.

He found a good angle, a good rhythm with the hammer and chisel. He forgot about a wide and starry sky and instead thought about the curves of the capital *U* and the small *n*, the interesting differences between them.

When Wesley paused, Reg said, "Did you hear from the sperm bank? It's been two weeks since you turned forty."

He didn't want to talk about it, but on the other hand, his silence would make it obvious that it bothered him.

"They don't want me."

"You have high blood pressure, man? Cholesterol? You look pretty healthy to me."

Wesley threw the tools down on the wooden bench, rousing puffs of granite dust. "The bitches wouldn't give me a reason."

"You asked?"

"Of course I asked. I go for checkups. I'd know if I had high blood pressure or some shit like that."

He had a full head of hair, he was tall and strong. Women still liked to fuck him. He was chosen all the time when he went down to the guesthouse by the west gate. There was no reason he should be turned down for sperm donation.

"Took some balls to ask," Reg said.

"They owed me an explanation."

"See, that right there is male privilege. You think you're perfect, and you think they have to explain themselves if they don't agree."

"What the fuck, Reg? Did you drink the Kool-Aid?"

"If you don't drink the Kool-Aid, you're never getting out."

"We're never getting out anyway."

Male privilege. Something no self-respecting man ever talked about before the damn war. Now they had to read all those books, sit through the classes—Ethics, Integrity, Creation of Knowledge, History of Inequality. I'm the son of an auto mechanic and a waitress, Wesley had said once to one of those so-called reeducation specialists. I don't remember anyone telling me I was master of the universe. Then he had to write a ten-page paper about "intersectionalities between privileges and oppressions."

Still, even back then, he knew he'd be pissed off if the situation were reversed. If he had to sit through classes where the wisest philosophers said men were inferior beings and women were the only ones worth learning about. If he lived in a world where only women did important things and only women were in charge of the government and business and religion and the military.

Back when he was growing up, a guy could be an average Joe and still get a woman to make him the center of her universe, because she was under so much societal pressure to be part of a couple. A man didn't have to give a thought to keeping himself fit or attractive or even minimally presentable for her. He didn't have to waste a moment's energy thinking about his appearance or the way he treated her and the ramifications of it.

241

It was a standard complaint men made, groaning to each other over beers: She always wants to talk about the *relationship*.

Not having to talk about it. Or even think about it. That was privilege.

And then there was the violence. From husbands, from boyfriends, from random strangers. It kept getting worse, right up until the war.

He had to admit it: men were always fucking things up.

That evening, to cheer himself up, he took a stroll down to the guesthouse, tucked away near a remote exit to the compound. None of his regulars were there, but he was quickly chosen.

"You into kissing?" he said hopefully when they got into the room.

The woman's laugh sounded more like a grunt. "Not going to happen."

Maybe somewhere along the line someone had decided to get pregnant by him. Just because the sperm bank didn't want him didn't mean anything. He just wished he knew for sure.

Some of the men said no one should donate sperm, as a form of protest. But at least with the sperm banks, they knew there would eventually be men again, not only the parthenogenic women. And those men would be free.

The woman dressed hurriedly after the sex was over. Wesley sat on the bed. He wasn't sure where to look, whether looking at her would make her uncomfortable or whether not looking at her would seem insulting.

She put on a jacket made of burgundy cotton and a hat that looked kind of like a fedora, with a burgundy silk flower attached to the ribbon.

He was always trying to understand women, trying to piece them together. Whenever he was with one, he tried to find out more.

"Why silk flowers?" he said.

"What?" She looked annoyed.

"I mean, just in the abstract, why use silk, or cloth or whatever, to imitate flowers?"

"Because you're an idiot."

He was pretty sure that not all women would answer him like that, but then who knew? They were a hard lot, hard enough to lock away every man for the rest of his natural days.

~

In those years after the war, the spirits of the Erdan foremothers came into their own. They were honored at public events, invoked with candles and chants in private homes. They weren't as boisterous as the newly minted war dead, who entered the afterlife in thunderous herds during the long years of combat and plague. What the foremothers lacked in piquancy and refreshing irreverence, however, they made up for in gravitas.

They fulfilled their role well, strong and protective ancestral spirits. Call them, they were there, advising, warning, supporting. If you were unused to dealing with spirits but you wanted to try, the foremothers sounded like murmuring voices heard from another room when you're half asleep. If you were a staunch atheist and had no time for such foolishness, still you had inklings of their presence—a sudden sense of well-being, a feeling that things were exactly as they should be.

If you already understood the complex interplay of the living and the dead (perhaps you were a practitioner of traditional pre-monotheistic Native American or African spirituality, perhaps a Wiccan, or a Catholic), the foremothers were as much a part of reality as the visual world. This is not to say you walked around hearing voices all the time, in a constant flow of communication. But you knew that someone had your back. And sometimes you did hear voices.

The foremothers were generous with their blessings on their daughters' achievements. They gathered at every civic celebration and seasonal fest; hovered supportively over meetings to improve energy efficiency; nodded approvingly at the vegetable gardens everywhere, the compost piles and solar panels. They admired the construction of the Wall of Righteous Men. They applauded the audience-participation dance performances.

The more hippie-inclined of the foremothers—the ones who in life had worn diaphanous skirts and wispy scarves and hand-made jewelry with stones carefully picked out for just the right vibrational energy— were the ones who took note of the new Erdan Tarot deck.

The Queen of each of the four suits, needless to say, had now become the highest-value suit card, as she did in ordinary decks too, where Queen trumped King instead of the other way around. Instead of the sequence King, Queen, Knight, and Page, the new Tarot featured the Queen, the Counselor, the Sage, and the Novice.

The foremothers felt a tinge of sadness at this. They knew that even in the heyday of patriarchy there were true Kings, not abusers of power but men of strength and wisdom, natural leaders. While they never should have been valued more highly than the Queens, there would now be a whole generation of women who would have no experience of a worthy man.

Other drastic changes occurred in the Tarot's Major Arcana, where the Magician became the Sorceress-Crone, for example, and the Priest disappeared. The Tower still existed, but its depiction of a collapsing building no longer was an augur of doom. It stood for—it had always stood for, some insisted—the overthrow of patriarchy, and it was only the early, male interpreters of the Tarot who saw this as something to be dreaded. No longer did it stand for disaster. Now it meant the end of oppression, or more generally, in this post-patriarchal age, the end of a negative situation.

Another new card was the Warrior. No matter which artist was designing it, this card always ended up looking like Catherine Beck. Just as the Priestess card always ended up looking like Averil Parnell, despite her own earlier identification with the Fool and the Hanged Man. Averil-type women showed up in other cards too: the Hermit, with her asceticism, her hint of madness. The Four of Swords, a dark-haired white woman who has thrust four swords into the ground in a protective square around her as she retreats from the world.

In the city of IxChel the real-life models for these cards often went for long walks together, neither of them aware of their status. Averil no longer read anything, and Catherine had never been remotely interested in spiritual matters.

It was on one of these long walks that they saw the man, or rather, Averil saw him first. Catherine, walking with her, sensed Averil go stiff and followed her gaze.

A work detail from the IxChel East compound was repairing a stone wall. The man, one among many, dressed in the same drab work pants as the others, was standing up after mortaring the base. Catherine could tell, even from this distance, that his knees and back were stiff and he was standing to stretch them, staring straight ahead without noticing anything.

If they hadn't passed by that minute, or if he hadn't felt the need to stretch, or if he were facing in another direction, they never would have seen him. They both would have lived and died without seeing that face again.

"It's not him," Catherine said quickly, but she couldn't tell Averil how she knew, couldn't say that she'd shot and killed him all those years ago and he was safely dead in an anonymous grave where he belonged.

"I know it's not him," she said again, more calmly this time, because Averil had frozen and was staring at the man, as expressionless as he was.

"Averil, it's nothing. It's a coincidence." Still no reaction. "We'll get closer. You'll see."

Averil crossed the street and went up to him before Catherine could stop her.

The resemblance was disturbing. The man, stripped to the waist in the hot weather, had the same lean, muscular chest, broad shoulders. Same hair, dark brown that was almost black, the same finely curved black eyebrows, the hazel eyes. The shape of the face was identical. In another world he would have been arrogant from his handsomeness, a white man rewarded for his outstanding beauty by being treated as something better than the rest, coming to expect that treatment.

Even here, no doubt women had noticed him. The ones in charge of the men's compound would have nominated him for sperm bank donor.

There were differences. His hair was cut short and jagged. He was stoop-shouldered. Probably barely articulate, as men of his generation were.

But the sharpest difference was his expression. This man was dull-eyed, betraying no interest in the world around him. He looked as if he had never smiled in his life.

John Honig, without the spark.

Catherine wondered whether this shock would move Averil to speak. But when she saw the raw grief on Averil's face she knew she couldn't bear to hear what she would say.

"He would be almost sixty by now," Catherine said, but she could tell that now Averil had the same thought she did: this was John's son.

"That's not possible, either," she said to Averil. "I'll prove it to you." She turned to the man. "You. What was—what's your father's name?"

"Harrison," he said. He showed no curiosity about the question.

She pulled Averil away. "You see, it's just a coincidence."

~

How strange, to hold a pen in her hand. To sit looking at a notepad, blank paper waiting for her words.

Since words were useless, how fitting to address them to the dead.

Why seek ye the living among the dead?

He was such an optimist, that Yeshua son of a carpenter, wandering holy man among so many holy wanderers.

Just after the war, when words weren't futile, when Gary Tramonte was not yet a bullet-riddled corpse, Averil had walked into the Erdan Central Registry Office in search of information, like so many others trying to track down loved ones. Or enemies.

A separate form for each one. Blanks to fill for full name, possible aliases, date of birth, place of birth, date and place last seen.

There was only one form she could fill out completely. She knew Asher Rothenburg's date of birth precisely, along with his hometown, height, hair and eye color.

Date last seen: the day before the Cathedral Massacre.

Relation to querent: she had paused over this. *Lover* seemed too personal to write down on an official form. *Friend*, not personal enough. Man who cut me out of his life. Person I loved more than my own self. Finally she wrote: *Brother*.

The other request forms ended up with little more than the names. Peter Byrne, colleague. Marc Cvetko, colleague.

She filled out a form for John Honig. Hair, black. Eyes, hazel. Height, 5'11". She had no idea of his age, birthday, place of birth.

Other distinguishing characteristics: Inability to look people in the eye, she wanted to write. Smile evil and beautiful.

Relationship to querent: Lover. Ex-lover. My worst self.

Finally she wrote: *Brother*.

She gave no thought to the confusion of future biographers, who found no evidence that either of these "brothers" of the famous Averil Parnell had even existed.

She had filed the forms, had never received a response.

She had done her share of seeking the dead among the living. Now she would seek the dead among the dead.

She uncapped the pen. She formed each letter laboriously. They had become hieroglyphs.

Dear John.

She put the pen down.

~

He was still there in the late afternoon, looking more blank-eyed than before. Catherine got his attention and gestured for him to go over to her.

"You said your father's name was Harrison." Past tense again. She didn't bother to correct herself. Averil wasn't there to hear.

The man nodded. He seemed to be looking at the sidewalk between them.

"What was his first name?"

"John."

She couldn't stop looking at him. It was impossible to believe that such an exact physical replica wouldn't have Honig's personality, his deviousness and charm and coldness, his unshakeable self-regard.

This man would have been a child when Honig disappeared. Not that he would have been better off raised by a father like that. More likely he would have grown up neglected and unloved.

I did you a favor, she wanted to tell him.

There was nothing more to say. She couldn't tell him she'd known his father, that years before, she had threatened to kill him, had been on top of him in his bed, a knife at his throat, the power of life and death in her hands. Impossible for two people to be more intimate than that.

She'd carried out her threat. A climax too long postponed.

And this man in front of her, the image of that other. She didn't want to hate him. He didn't deserve her hatred. She was reacting to him based on his appearance, and also based on anxiousness and guilt—what patriarchal men had always felt for women.

"What's your name?" she finally said. "Your first name."

He showed a flash of surprise, meeting her gaze for a second before his eyes dropped to the pavement.

"Parnell," he said.

~

It was days before Averil opened the notebook again.

Dear John,
I know, now, that you're dead.
    That sounded awkward, I suppose. You'll have to bear with me. I can't get over the strangeness. The feel of the pen, the shape of the individual letters, all alien to me. I have to stop and think how to draw each one, it's not instinctual anymore.
    So of course in a situation like this, style flies out the window.

A metaphor.

She stopped, struggled to regain her train of thought.

I never would have imagined that I would forget how to write, after doing it for so long. I've been out of the habit of using language for years now. Decades. I stopped speaking soon after the Revolution. If you were dead by then you wouldn't know that. But then again maybe you do.
    It's fitting to write to the dead, it makes the futility clear, and that's what people don't understand well enough, John, futility.

She put the notebook away. It took another week before she looked at it again.

~

Some things survived the war, lasted intact into the post-revolutionary period. One of those was therapy-speak, the smug, neat compartments in which to shelve the bewildering variety of human behavior. Had the post-revolutionary generation of therapists known of Averil's affair with John Honig, they would have slung around terms like enabling, co-dependency. The stimulation of pleasure centers. Sex addiction.

They may have thought they could have predicted Averil Parnell's reaction to this seeming appearance of a long-absent lover. After all, what does a recovering alcoholic do when she comes across a bottle of contraband scotch, sees the amber-gold liquid poured out, feels the glass in her hand, smells the sharp enticing aroma?

Averil Parnell would have asked them where the pleasure center was located, whether they took walk-ins or insisted on reservations. And whether it was near the hostility center. The competitiveness center. The resentment center. Or were they all parts of the same building?

~

Catherine couldn't stop thinking about that damned man. Parnell Valson. She had even checked his dogtags to be sure.

Hell of a joke Honig had played, naming his son after Averil. Most likely he'd bestowed first and last name on the child. Of course he would have had a patriarchal marriage, though it was hard to imagine Honig getting married for anything other than a bet or a drunken dare.

And the resemblance was damned eerie. Not many people get to look on the living face of a man they've killed.

She didn't want Averil even thinking about the motherfucker. God knew what the sight of the son had done to her already. Catherine had come back to the topic over the next few days. "They say everyone has a double," she'd said one time, and another: "He wasn't unique-looking. We probably can't remember what he really looked like after all these years."

Now she realized Averil would wonder how Catherine knew who Honig was, what he looked like. God damn it.

She would have to rely on Averil's fractured memory, hope she would assume they'd come across each other sometime during the St. Anthony years.

As indeed they had.

~

Parnell Valson listened to the belltower in the west quadrant chime the hour. He was thinking of his father, after all these years. A man he had never liked. A man who had ignored him when he wasn't ridiculing him. It had always been a relief when his father went away on his "missions."

He remembered John Honig coming home one time with a fresh scar and the smell of forest on his skin. He was like a feral animal, restless and suspicious. His first week home he had taken a gun and shot out the streetlight next to the bedroom window.

Parnell remembered going out in pajamas and slippers to stand under the shattering streetlight. The shower of glass seemed to go on forever. The memory was one of the clearest he had, yet of course it would have been impossible. A four-year-old out in the middle of the night, underneath the lamp just at the moment of the bullet's impact.

~

From the look of the starlight coming in through the window, Averil decides that it's almost time for the mother superior to wake them up for Vigils. Puzzled by the sound of chanting outside, she parts the curtain and sees the monks processing slowly, in single file, through a dusting of snow in the courtyard. She leans against the stone windowsill, watching.

They are the chosen of God. The sons. Tranquil in the knowledge that they are the true followers of Jesus and heirs to His priesthood.

What place for women among the deep voices and the tall, strapping bodies?

Do you find peace, brothers?

She sat down at her desk, turned on the desklamp. By that hour the summer heat had eased. There was even a whisper of air from the open window.

She took out the letter.

So where are you now?, she wrote. *How did it happen and what was it like? Were you in one of the refugee camps when the plague got you? Are you in a mass grave by some battlefield?*

Did they pull the nails out of your hands and feet when they took you down from the cross?

She drew in her breath, crossed out the last sentence. She needed to focus.

You were beautiful. I guess I never told you that. No matter how you tried to veil it, tried to veil yourself. Some of your countless lovers must have thought that if they looked in your eyes at the moment of climax they would see your true self, you would let down your guard and let your eyes express what was going on in your heart. I don't know, John, I never bothered to look, and now for the first time I wonder whether you looked at me to see the same thing.

Did it linger, your last moment, or did it pass quickly? I thought I would have known the very second your life ended. I would have felt it in every cell.

After all these years you're nowhere to be found, like Jesus, and sometimes I wonder if I have turned both of you into a pretty myth.

But last week I saw your son, John, and as soon as I saw him I knew you were long dead. Catherine said he wasn't your son, but she was lying to keep me from getting upset. The resemblance is too close to be coincidence. He doesn't smile, John. Did he smile when he was a child? Did you even know he existed, and if so, did you care?

I'll have to have a funeral service for you, John. In the fall, I think. A sheaf of wheat will be your body, golden and beautiful. Perhaps I'll ask your son to the funeral; maybe they'll let him out of the men's compound for me. He and I will look at your body in the light of the setting sun. Maybe he'll understand you after he's seen that. Maybe I will too. And we'll bury you, John, and on the third day I'll visit your tomb to see if the stone's been rolled away.

CHAPTER 25

BEATI
MISERICORDES

One night, with the help of God, her chains and fetters
fell off and she escaped and fled into remote desert forests
and there lived in trees as though she were a bird.

—*The Life of Christina Mirabilis*, 13th century

P arnell Valson woke up confused. Then he felt confused about *why*
he was confused. He was aware of an antiseptic smell and, vaguely,
movements and sounds. And through a haze of headache and tiredness, an
insistent aching in his groin.

He heard a man's voice, low and cheerful, and opened his eyes enough
to see a nametag—Kyle.

"You're okay, man, everything's cool. You're in the hospital, but
you're doing fine."

"Are you a doctor?" Parnell said.

"You must be having a flashback. Or do I sound like a woman to you?"

"Huh?"

"Best a man can do around here these days is orderly. Listen, you've had
general anesthesia. You're going to feel like shit for a while. Days, maybe."

He must have fallen asleep, because the next time he opened his eyes
it was nighttime. The pain in his groin was getting worse.

He remembered, finally, something about a tumor. They had to
remove it, they said.

And then it was daylight again, and Kyle was leaning over him taking
his pulse.

"The tumor," Parnell said. "Did they get all of it?"

"No tumor, buddy. You're still confused. Chart says you had a vasectomy."

Kyle breezed out of the room, leaving Parnell alone with the pain and the confusion.

Over the next few hours he pieced together some more memories.

The woman who had spoken to him on the street, who'd asked his father's name, then came back later to ask his own name. She'd shown up the next evening, at the compound.

"Here's the thing," she had said as soon as the guard led him to her. No preliminaries. No introductions—though of course he knew who she was.

"Here's the thing. I want you to disappear. There are two ways of making that happen."

He didn't have to be told what the first way was. Quick and painless would be the best he could hope for. But he couldn't rule out slow and painful.

Up close he could see that her pale hair was more silver than blonde. Her eyes were silvery too. He had never imagined it possible to have such cold eyes.

"What's the other way?" he had said.

Now she was sitting by his hospital bed. It was nighttime again.

"Have you recovered?" she said briskly.

"Why'd they do that to me?"

"Don't start whining."

"A *vasectomy*? I've never raped anyone."

"I'd've had your damn cock sliced off if you were a rapist."

"It hurts like hell."

"Consider it the price of freedom."

She pointed to a stack of books on his nightstand.

"You don't have much time," she said. "You can't keep these. You need to read them, quick. And remember."

Then casually, while she was halfway out the door: "I'll give you a knife and other supplies when you leave."

Parnell looked at the titles after she left. Books on survival. How to fish, trap, hunt. Build fires, make shelters.

There were a few more brief days of recovery. Reading frantically. Skills other people accumulated over years, lifetimes. Then he was in a car, General Beck driving him out to the countryside. She parked at a bend in a road, near what looked like a foot trail that led uphill into a forested ridge.

"Get out."

The sound of his car door opening and shutting. Then her door opening.

He could hardly focus on what was happening.

"They say there are clusters of escaped men here and there," Beck said, scanning the top of the ridge, almost as if she were musing to herself. "Be interesting to see if they survive without cutting each other's throats."

She handed him a backpack. "I suppose I should say good luck." She started to get back in the car.

"Wait," he said. "What'll I do when the weather gets cold?"

Her face transformed when she smiled, just as his father's had, though he had long forgotten that.

"Head south," she said.

He tried one more time.

"Do I get an explanation for any of this?"

How fitting it would be, Catherine thought, to close the circle. Tell him she would kill him if she ever set eyes on him again. But that was foolishness.

"It's not personal," she said. "Something that happened long before you were born."

"Before I was born," he repeated. Still not believing, not understanding.

She almost pitied him.

"It's how history works," she said. "Hell, it's how we all get fucked over."

~

The guard at the north entrance of the IxChel men's compound was so awed by the world-historical figure standing there that she opened the gate right away. There was no need, of course, to ask Averil Parnell for identification. And no point in posing questions.

The women in the hastily assembled security detail didn't know what to make of her. The men of the compound were baffled as well. She seemed to be in search of something, yet she didn't look directly at them, gave no sign she was even aware of them.

"Diogenes seeking an honest man," one inmate quipped as Averil passed by, but the others didn't know what he meant, formed no mental image of a cantankerous old philosopher roaming around with a lantern in broad daylight.

Monk-spirits followed her in solemn procession, chanting.

She passed neatly tended gardens, evidence of thrift and ingenuity: scrap-metal scaffolding set up for climbing tomato plants, salvaged barrels repurposed into chairs, the back of an old piano turned into a table top. Small but sturdy buildings made of logs or stone.

Adoremus in aeternum sanctissimum Sacramentum, the monks sang. *Laudate Dominum omnes gentes: laudate eum omnes populi.*

She walked through a hops field, among men carefully tending the plants and discussing upgrades they wanted to make to their brewery equipment.

The rule regarding mind-altering substances was that the men could use what they could produce themselves. Among those who tried to forage for hallucinogenic mushrooms, the efforts resulted in numerous trips to the emergency room and a subsequent prohibition of the project, but there were all kinds of other things that could be fermented and distilled: wine from grapes, cider from apples, ale from hops, a range of homemade rotgut from corn, potatoes, wheat.

Vidi aquam egredientem de templo, sang the monks. *A latere dextro, alleluia.*

I saw water coming forth from the temple, on the right side, alleluia.

At the edge of a garden plot planted in marijuana, Averil watched the gardener relax in the shade of a maple. He daydreamed about poppy fields, coca leaves, thought wistfully of the warm temperatures and long months of sunlight they would have required.

Averil breathed in the fragrance of apple trees, while the orchard tender thought ruefully of the cider-brewers who would soon put the ripening fruit through the fermenting process. So many other things that could be made: apple crisps, apple pancakes, baked apples, apple strudel, alchemy of flour, butter, eggs, sugar. Men would get drunk on his apples instead.

If Catherine Beck had been there, she would have worried that the visit would excite Averil's pity.

Remember what things were like, she would have said. Remember the world they created when they were left to their own devices. Nothing but suffering. Nothing but injustice.

Catherine need not have been concerned. Averil didn't particularly like men as a group any more now than she ever had. She knew what men were capable of, had never been deferential or intimidated back when they had run roughshod over the world. And the good ones were dead, the Peter Byrnes, the Asher Rothenburgs, the Gary Tramontes and Doug Mariselas.

Nevertheless, she loved their voices.

Et omnes, ad quos pervenit aqua ista,
salvi facti sunt, et dicent, alleluia, alleluia.

And all those to whom this water came were saved, and shall say, alleluia, alleluia.

Nevertheless, there were things shaken loose by grief.

This confinement of men was no monastery. The comforts they gathered around themselves were threadbare blankets pulled across shivering bodies.

Once again she had allowed herself not to think about what was going on around her.

It was time to do penance.

~

People later wondered how Averil Parnell would have reacted if she had sensed the catastrophes looming, for her personally and for the people around her who were going to be caught up in a historic tragedy.

This was her dilemma all her life: Take action, you're a failure. Refrain from acting, you're a failure.

Some biographers argued that one could see her life as a series of situations that always ended disastrously:

One foolish tangle after another with the hierarchy of the Catholic Church, making her an outsider.

Her ill-considered affair with the man whose name was lost to historians.

Her intervention in the case of Gary Tramonte.

Her final sermon and the subsequent bloody turmoil triggered by her death.

But one could say the historians were ignoring the counterarguments. She had avoided the Cathedral Massacre precisely because of an earlier ill-considered liaison with yet another unsuitable man.

And as for John Honig, we might say he fit the definition of a saint, which is: performing miracles in life and after death. Certainly it was not much of a feat to wreck the career of an eccentric priest. But to mutate the plague virus within one's body? To transmit it, posthumously, in a less-deadly form? And then, also posthumously, to rouse the said priest out of her decades-long somnolence?

255

~

The second-to-last day of her life, Averil Parnell woke up smiling. She was lying on her side, shifting in the gray early light from half-awake to half-asleep to asleep. Asher, cuddled up behind her, had taken a lock of her hair and was tickling her ear with it.

"You're cruel," she said, grinning. The tickling stopped, then resumed. She resorted to an old joke between them, in which she compared his behavior and stature (since she was the taller of the two) with Thomas Hobbes' famous description of human life:

"You're nasty, brutish, and short," she told him, swatting at his hand. He laughed, and she fell asleep.

And woke, completely, a few minutes later. To an empty bed, an empty room.

She put on a clean short-sleeved shirt and trousers, socks and shoes, tucked in stray wisps of her unruly hair with barrettes and hairpins.

She needed to get a grip on things. She needed to focus.

She needed to think about the living men behind those razor-wire walls.

A simple matter, to do penance. Find a priest. *Bless me, Father, for I have sinned.* The women priests were so few, Averil had hardly met any, had never confessed her sins to anyone but a man, God help her, Goddess help her, ineffable Godhead and all the saints, and all the sinners, for that matter. Bless me, fellow sinners. Bless me, for I have sinned. Blessings on us all, sinners on this remote clump of whirling rock.

She went out, walked till she found people doing hard physical work, a volunteer group repairing a burned-out building. No one objected when the undernourished-looking old woman joined in. People were used to Averil Parnell and her capacity for work, her willingness to help. She swabbed sooty windows, stirred paint, trundled wheelbarrows, sanded floors. Later there was a supper of sorts handed out to everyone, fresh sourdough bread and farmer cheese, vegetable soup in mugs. There was no lavish meal on Averil Parnell's last full day of life. Then again, there had hardly ever been lavish meals, and no doubt she would have made no such request, had she known.

She went home and slept soundly through the early evening.

After midnight she woke up again. There was something she needed to find.

In the silence of the sleeping house she went down to the basement.

It was as far from crypt-like as possible. No catacomb of saints' relics here, thanks to well-placed ceiling lights, storage boxes carefully organized on metal shelving units, and Averil's frequent visits with bucket and mop and dustrag. Nevertheless, she had the feeling she was going to find something here long dead.

In a remote corner, one of the sagging cardboard boxes bore her own name on its faded label. She carried it unopened back to her room, where a lit candle sputtered in the hammered-tin holder on her nightstand. She didn't remember having lit it, but she was used to finding candles lit, or extinguished, while her back was turned. Instead of feeling grateful for these small, sweet messages from elsewhere, she felt annoyed. Her night vision had been disrupted.

Nor was Averil lulled by the sound of monks' voices singing nearby as she started to open the box. Why are the voices always male, she thought irritably, once again demonstrating her unsaintliness, if we define a saint as a serene being, blissfully attuned to other dimensions.

The box, tucked away during the war and then unearthed somewhere and shipped to Via Dolce, contained two clerical collars, some candle ends, a rosary, some worn paperback books on theology, and a small metal crucifix. She lifted one of the collars to her neck and there it was, the energy, jolting through her body now and pouring out the top of her head. What she felt when the boundaries between things started trembling and fading. The keys to the kingdom. The power to damn and forgive, to speak words that flowed through her and out of her mouth without her consciously thinking them beforehand.

A lifelong pattern, this surging of energy: find it, lose it, regain it, lose it again. The second she stopped feeling it, she doubted its reality.

She was a fraud and she was damned, but she would pretend she understood this surging jolting force, pretend she controlled it. She would try to act the part.

She picks up the crucifix and closes her eyes, feels the small metal figure, John's beautiful body, his poor tortured body twisted and scarred. And here is Jesus, her long dead and vanished lover, wanting to know where she's been, why she's failed him. She wants to cradle the thorn-scraped head, touch the rough-knuckled carpenter's hands of the wandering holy man.

"I'm coming," she whispers.

~

On the last day of Averil Parnell's life, a man stepped out the back door of the house of President-Emerita Selene Marisela. He headed for the tool shed, followed by a plump orange cat and two little girls, aged three and four.

There had never been an official explanation for why Anthony Sojourner Marisela was the one male in Erda allowed his freedom. A war hero like his long-dead older brother. A lean Black man of impeccable beauty who often stood next to Selene at ceremonial occasions, sorrowful and silent while she made eloquent speeches about the irredeemability of patriarchal men—and she didn't always use the modifier before the noun. Her brother being, presumably, the exception that proved the rule.

Outside the tool shed he adjusted the flow rate on the seed spreader and checked to make sure the hopper wasn't clogged. His grandnieces clamoring to "help," he handed each one a small handful of ryegrass seeds that they could disperse themselves. He stooped to re-button the cardigan of the smaller girl. "Don't make me trip over you, now," he murmured to the cat threading herself around his legs.

"We're putting the garden to sleep," the older one told the younger one. "This is a crop cover."

He debated whether to correct the child, decided her term made sense too.

He was about to push the spreader onto the plot nearest the back lane when he saw the woman. Stagger-marching toward him, with the alert eyes and lurching movements of someone beyond physical exhaustion.

Anthony was momentarily disoriented. During the war or just after, you saw people like that, you offered them a sip of water, a bite of whatever food you still had, tried to talk them into relaxing enough to fall asleep.

He had to remind himself the war was over.

Then he recognized her.

Averil Parnell cleared her throat, tried to form words.

Nothing came out.

He waited. She tried again.

"I remember you," she said hoarsely. "You're a good man."

She seemed confused then, perhaps surprised at the sound of her own voice or the difficulty expressing herself, someone who all her life had used words to make things happen: I baptize you. You are forgiven.

Anthony understood. He knew silence. He knew confusion.

Historians now argue over whether the encounter with Selene Marisela was incidental, whether Averil Parnell's intention all along had been to address her first words in decades to a man. But in the immediate aftermath of that day, what people were most anxious to know was what precisely Averil had said. They wanted to gather up the rare precious words, ponder and savor.

Anthony felt that in those short moments when he and Averil Parnell had faced each other, there was perfect understanding between them. He didn't know what she said to his sister, who had come out of the house and shooed him away before she turned to the priest. Later he guessed at the short, awkwardly phrased sentences the priest must have eked out before she turned and stumbled away.

"We have to stop this. We have to make it right."

Or it may have been more confrontational than he imagined:

"You started this. You need to undo it."

CHAPTER 26

PACEM RELINQUO

> In the last year of her life, solitude and the desert
> place were frequently her home.
>
> —*The Life of Christina Mirabilis*

Normally at gatherings in the IxChel Spiritual Center, people put their chairs in a circle and if someone wanted to address the group, she simply stood up and spoke informally, unamplified.

That evening, however, the place was so crowded—with both the living and the dead—that speakers had to use the podium at the front. Many of the living, and some of the dead, had originally planned to be there for the Center's Fall Equinox festivities. Many, many more had come because they'd heard the rumor that Averil Parnell had broken her silence and had asked to address what she called the "parishioners," in that quaint, old-fashioned Catholic terminology she had always been known for using.

All the folding chairs were in use, and women crowded the aisles on every side, pressed in by the spirits of the Erdan foremothers as well as the war dead, the monks of St. Anthony of Padua's, Averil's sister-seminarians from the Cathedral Massacre, even a few Flagellants from medieval Europe.

They jostled to get a better look at her as she took the podium. The famous priest—notorious, maybe, for those who hadn't loved her. But everyone loved her now.

She looked tired and fragile, they noted with concern. But, they consoled themselves, her dark eyes were as bright and piercing as ever. And after all, even as a young woman she had often gone without food, without sleep, in quest of—whatever spiritual experiences she had been seeking all those years, a quest they assumed she would talk about now. Where *had* she been wandering, they wanted to know, during those silent decades?

"Sisters, daughters," she said, "I greet you at this time of perfect equilibrium, this time of balance between night and day. Perhaps it's fitting that I come to you with my request, on this day of all days."

Catherine Beck had only heard the rumors like everyone else. No one at the commune had thought to send for her; no one had told her that Averil had been cured, had started speaking. She would blame them, among others, later, but now she was too happily dazed to feel slighted.

Her bodyguard instincts didn't immediately surface. This was a different world. Still she began to look around, scanning the crowd (for what, in a safe space like this?), and gradually moved forward, picking her way closer to Averil.

"I would never claim," Averil said, "that Christianity originated the Golden Rule. Treat others the way you want to be treated—that's something humans have always understood. You treat others the way you want to be treated, not to get some reward in the afterlife, or to avoid some punishment, but because it's right.

"Notice it doesn't say to act this way only to those who deserve it. Notice it doesn't say that those who have wronged us have forfeited their claim."

She pauses. Brother Jesus's voice resounds in her mind: *Who among you is without sin?*

That was your finest hour, she says to him silently now.

Instead of concentrating on the speech she is giving, she sees herself standing in front of an enormous, forbidding door. To her timid knock she hears *Who goes there?* and answers, *A sinner.* Now the door seems familiar, not sinister at all. She is about to join a festive banquet, she has only to let go and she'll be there.

"We have to ask ourselves," she said, "would we want to be confined the rest of our lives, for enjoying privileges we were born into, for using power that was put into our hands unasked?

"Yes, men should be stopped from acting unjustly, stopped from latching onto that power and oppressing others. They should not be allowed to continue in their privileged ways."

She was aware of how unimpressive she must seem. This was nothing that hadn't been said before—and more eloquently, at that. She must

261

have imagined that surge of inspiration the night before. The only thing propelling her was the momentum of a delusion.

No one was going to listen.

Still a failure.

"But it doesn't mean they should be locked up," she said, "deprived of freedom for the rest of their natural days. I know we're angry. I know it's hard to forgive. I know."

She doesn't hear it when it hits her. No massacre this time around, just a single gunshot. A man from the compound, trained as a D.A.W. sniper in the war. A bullet to the chest and she falls.

Just let them out, she was going to say. Even if they don't deserve it. They're not going to take over. They can't.

Her first, wry thought—typical Averil!—was that the speech must have really deteriorated if she's on the floor and the place is in pandemonium. But the pain, the blood, the look on Catherine's face when she props her up—she won't be finishing the speech, won't be finishing what she tried to start, weak and belated as the effort was.

"Get down," she managed to whisper to Catherine. "Sniper."

"I'm all right. Let's put some pressure on this till the ambulance comes."

She is conscious. And she is aware that she is conscious, and thinks back to her childhood when the nuns told her that if she prayed to the Sacred Heart of Jesus during the Vigil for the Blessed Sacrament, that would be her reward—time to repent before death. And here it is, as promised. She is mildly surprised, as if trying out a dubious magic trick and seeing that it works.

I was hoping to die of old age, she says to Brother Jesus, who is wiping the perspiration from her face. *Not this time around, I guess.*

Catherine is saying something, but it's harder to concentrate now. Averil wants to comment on the irony, the whole "He who lives by the sword, dies by the sword" thing, because here she is, dying, and Catherine the warrior, hale and perfect, will die of natural causes, and it's right, it's beautiful.

Catherine, pressing against the wound, feeling the pulse weaken, thought she heard Averil say, "beautiful." Or maybe "beauty." And then, perhaps, "blessing."

For a moment Averil was alert. "Don't kill him," she said clearly. "The shooter."

She has heard the distant cries: "Kill him," "Rip him to shreds." She doesn't want his tortured soul, whoever he is, linked to hers, passing at the same moment into eternity, back into other lives together, working out some kind of revenge, some kind of détente. She would rather not know. She would rather leave him behind.

Catherine hesitated but finally shouted to the crowd, "Averil says not to kill him." The women paused, let the man's broken, motionless body fall to the floor.

It is time. The voices around Averil trail off, mercifully. The anguish, the pain, all fading. Faintly she hears the monks. *May angels lead you into paradise*, they are singing, and Averil is sitting in the armchair in her room at St. Anthony's. It is time for Night Prayer.

Then she is standing on a rugged ocean shore, and at a great distance she sees Sister Death on the cliffs above her. An old woman dressed in black, her long hair the color of ash. The color of Averil's long hair now, in old age.

Sister Death becomes translucent. Even her hair begins to gleam. Beyond her Averil sees her beloved parents, gleaming also, and others pressing around, too many for her to take in at one glance. Averil is illuminated. She is rushing toward them.

Welcome, beloved daughter, says Sister Death. *The blood in my chalice is sweet and holy.*

Glory be to everyone, always. So be it. Alleluia.

~

Q. *I'm sure many interviewers over the years have asked you this, General Beck, but what made you decide to intervene the way you did during the turmoil after the assassination?*

A. It was a crisis. People don't always act from clear, reasoned-out motives.

Q. *Are you saying you acted instinctively?*

A. I wouldn't put it like that.

Q. *Surely you see the irony in the situation. Reverend Parnell was killed by a man, during a sermon in which she advocated that we forgive men and release them. She was an old and dear friend, and yet you led the defense of the men's compounds.*

A. In the heat of the moment, irony wasn't on my mind.

Q. *Well, General, we think you acted with integrity and great valor.*

263

~

It wasn't what people said at the time.

And after the fact, what was the point of rehashing it? Catherine had never been in the habit of making self-serving statements like *It was the right thing to do.*

Moreover, she couldn't truly answer the question of *why* she had acted to stem the tide of the riots. She didn't know what spurred her decision. Nor was she at all sure that her actions had indeed been effective. Rage and grief burn themselves out eventually, whether anyone's there to put out the fire or not.

There had been other questions at the time, much more pointed and not nearly so deferential, at the hearing before the Council of Elders.

Catherine was amused to hear President Rhiannon, Selene's successor, testify about the brave resistance she had made to Catherine's demand that she denounce the rioting. In reality Rhiannon had sputtered incoherently about precedent, about due process, about respecting the chain of command.

"General, according to the Honorable Rhiannon, you made threats about what would happen if she failed to cooperate with your demands. She says your exact words were, 'Don't worry about precedent. It's a time-honored tradition in Erda to declare martial law.'"

There was scattered laughter among the participants at the hearing. The chief councilor gaveled for order.

"The president misunderstood me."

"The director of the government radio station testifies that you pushed her aside and took control of the microphone."

"I have no recollection of that incident."

"Are you perhaps blaming stress, General? An adrenaline surge that affected your judgment?"

"Or at least my memory, Councilor."

More laughter.

She remembered precisely the words she'd sent out that night over the airwaves: *Anyone found joining in the reprisals against men will be arrested. Anyone convicted of leading these reprisals will be shot by firing squad.*

The hearing would resolve nothing. Catherine knew they would never find evidence of who had arranged to extract the assassin from the men's compound, get him to the spirituality center, give him a weapon. People didn't stop to ask themselves that question, then or later.

For Erdans it was a simple matter: the assassin was proof of the damage men were capable of, the irreparable harm that men inflicted on the peaceful and the good.

The Erdans needed to justify to themselves those days of grief-maddened riots. They needed to slap Catherine on the wrist for not going along with it.

Perhaps it was true, after all, the quip she had made to the councilor about her memory of the riots. There were moments Catherine recollected with perfect clarity, but they were isolated, like scenes from a film, spliced together with nothing in between.

She remembered being inside the men's compound, pressuring a guard to help her find the storage unit with the riot gear—equipment originally acquired to respond to uprisings by the men.

She had no memory at all of the injuries she sustained, she who had gone unscathed through the whole Revolution. She wound up with a mild concussion, a strained shoulder, a nasty jagged cut on her face, all kinds of bruises. No doubt she herself had trained many of the women who'd given her such a pummeling.

There had been no need for demagogues to whip the crowds into a frenzy. They were already there.

Luckily weapons weren't so easy to find in peacetime Erda.

The rioters dug out twenty-year-unused firearms, not cleaned or maintained, impossible or even dangerous to shoot.

But the rioters had the bayonets on those faulty rifles. They had knives, bows and arrows, they had clubs improvised out of chair legs and fence posts. They had bottles stuffed with rags soaked in oil. They had fighting skills, and fists. They had anger.

The compound's defenders, few as they were, had body armor and bullet-proof visors. They had night vision equipment. They had tranquilizer spray, tear gas, stun guns. They had unacknowledged and unresolved ambivalence about their actions.

Ancient warriors they were, on the castle ramparts, Catherine thought while in the midst of hand-to-hand combat, women against women. Except you couldn't actually stand atop the angled, razor-wire fences of the men's compound. The momentary image brought with it a lingering sense of unreality, or rather, hyper-reality.

She had felt it a few hours earlier too, holding Averil in her arms. Those last moments of Averil's life had plunged Catherine into a feeling of boundarylessness, nothing between her and Averil, not even bodies, they were swirling, intertwined like serpents, like the double helix. Then

Averil was dead and Catherine was alive, holding her, and knowing that there was something else. Not nothing.

And now, as she fended off a blow from a baseball bat, she suddenly knew that riots were occurring all over the world, a collective howl of pain for the killing of the madwoman saint, the eccentric visionary. She felt herself expanding, she was here and all those other places too, in her expanded consciousness she understood that this was no true battle, there had merely been some kind of choosing-up of sides, not that the besiegers especially hated the men or the defenders especially cared about them. People were playing their roles, skilled performers, and she admired the dance-like, ritual-like inevitability of it all.

~

The funeral took place on a brilliantly sunny day, as if the earth celebrated rather than grieved, as if one of the most famous women of her time had not died, as if the bloody riots had never happened. Though the communards of Via Dolce tended to the logistics of the pyre, there were no leaders of the ritual itself. Instead of carefully prepared eulogies there was call-and-response improvised on the spot:

> *Our sister has left us.*
> We say amen.
> *Our sister is here.*
> We say amen.

Instead of a choreographed event, there were spontaneous expressions of grief and joy, here a dance, here a chant, here people sharing memories, here others sitting on the ground, doing a group meditation.

Catherine was going on her fourth day with almost no sleep. Her earlier feelings of ineffable wonder—perhaps fueled by adrenaline, she reflected later—had faded as her exhaustion grew, and at this point she was so tired she could no longer see any kind of larger perspective. Thus she failed to hear the chanting of the monks of St. Anthony's. She was oblivious to the place of honor given to Averil among the newly dead. She took no comfort from the temporary confluence of the dead and the living, the flow of love they created, or universe-energy or whatever you wanted to call it.

~

At home after the funeral Catherine went straight to her bedroom. She didn't bother to check the windows. She wasn't sure she had closed her front door, let alone locked it. It had been long years since she worried about such things.

She lay down, stared at the ceiling.

There was no soft thing in Catherine Beck's house, nothing to muffle sound, to soften the brightness of the moon shining in. The place was all high-gloss hard surfaces and sharp edges, glass and marble, rock maple, river stone. She felt she could hear the moonlight bouncing off the walls and floors.

I should sleep, she thought.

In a purely abstract way, she had to admire the tactical skill of whoever was behind this. They had silenced a critic and in doing so had set up another wave of anger against men, thus assuring that what Averil had hoped for would never come to pass.

She who lives by the sword.

Averil had thought blades unlucky. Catherine remembered how she made sure to put away scissors, letter openers, nail clippers before she sat down to write, or meditate.

Ironic, then, to learn from one of the communards that Averil was portrayed in the Erdan Tarot deck as the Four of Swords.

But the number four was solid, Averil had liked to say, it created a stable structure: chair, table, walls of a house.

Catherine slept, the sound of chanting in her ears. Sets of four words each.

North south east west.

Earth air fire water.

~

Most evenings, Catherine heated up a can of soup and stood eating it by the stove, listening to the resounding silence of the house, its spotless cleanliness serving only to accentuate its emptiness.

She would light a fire in the stone fireplace and sit in a recliner chair, books piled next to it. Among them was one titled *Famous Last Words*, a worn paperback she had found recently.

Her favorite entry concerned the final conversation of a writer, apparently well known for her eccentric style. Catherine had never heard of her. "What is the answer?" the woman was heard to say, although no one was nearby. She was silent for a moment, as if listening, then said, "In that case, what's the question?"

Catherine kept mulling over the last thing Averil said to her. She may have been saying that to be beautiful was a blessing. Or maybe she was pronouncing a blessing on Catherine. God damn it, did even her final words have to be so ambiguous?

Among the other books in the pile were volumes on meditation techniques, instructions on breath control, the proper posture. Catherine tried to steer clear of books with fuzzy words like "mindfulness" in their titles. She simply wanted to learn how to do it, without the soft-headed babbling about energy and chakras. Even worse were the people who called death "the other side" or spoke of those who have "transitioned." They died, she wanted to argue when she heard such nonsense.

And they were still here.

That was the thing she couldn't get around. The evidence of her own experience. Those moments of Averil's death, that perception of—something else, was the closest she could get to describing it. Something else. Not nothing.

She had been an atheist all her life. Had never been interested in anything remotely connected to religion or, worse, spirituality. You were born, you died, and that was the end. Nothing had been able to shake this calm conviction. She could have spent a lifetime of exposure to the most stunning works of art, the sublimest music, could have lived surrounded by breathtaking natural beauty, could have read the world's sacred literature and heard the voices of holy ones, and none of that, none, would have done for her what Averil did for her in her dying.

It amazed her, how people could change their minds, their understanding.

She didn't believe in God, of course. Or heaven, hell. Holy water, incense. Prayers and blessings. But no longer could she say that there was nothing more to this life than this life. Averil had showed her there was something more. Call it the soul. Call it another dimension. Something.

Not nothing.

CHAPTER 27

PENTECOST

All shall be well, and all shall be well and all manner of thing shall be well.

—Dame Julian of Norwich, 14th century

Anno Mirabilis 38

The Wall of Righteous Men stood in a tree-shaded park, a long slab of black marble highly polished to set off the chiseled names.

A young woman, notebook in hand, meticulously wrote down everything she observed about the wall and its surroundings. The quality of the sunlight, the freshness of the air, the sound of a nearby stream.

She was a graduate student in the history of religions, studying public monuments as expressions of spirituality, with a particular focus on battlefield commemorations and other war-related installations. But right now her thoughts turned to the philosopher Averil Parnell and what she had written about the holiness of running water. Later commentators had come up with the phrase "secular sacredness" to describe Parnell's tendency to ascribe holiness to things without reference to a deity or any articulated system of religious belief. Parnell, of course, was not the only person to do this; in fact it was a staple of what had been called the New Age movement during the patriarchal era. But Parnell's work resonated with post-revolutionary thinkers to a greater degree than other writers.

Catherine Beck had come to see the monument that morning also, walking slowly along the wall, reading. Many of the men she had known personally. Near the end she saw Gary Tramonte's name, posthumously exonerated after Selene Marisela's death.

She touched the cool marble and wondered if she would have felt comforted by a grave marker bearing Averil's name. A place to visit, lay flowers. Averil's ashes had been scattered in the air—as different as possible as burial in the earth, commemoration by stone.

Catherine saw the young woman and was reminded momentarily of her younger self. Something about her hair, the set of her shoulders.

It was possible, she knew, that the woman could be her daughter. Catherine had donated eggs for parthenogenesis at the request of a friend, and she heard later that all the eggs she donated were snapped up. She supposed that made her the father; she couldn't help wondering if someday she would be confronted by a daughter resentful of her absentee dad. Catherine had to laugh at herself. She still thought in the old ways. She and the men on this wall had been produced by the same society, were more similar than she cared to acknowledge.

Instead she pondered the futility of symbolic acts like this. Why carve their names, why visit? The men couldn't know, didn't care.

She wanted to approach the reverent-looking young woman, pose these questions, argue with her.

But she herself was here.

And, as she had discovered after the funeral, there were certain things—the sound of running water, the smell of fallen leaves, the feel of fresh air in her lungs and soil against her feet—certain things, damn it, that made her sense Averil's presence, made her feel some kind of ongoing connection with her.

No one knew of this. Catherine would have had to give up too much if she had spoken the thought aloud, admitted the possibility. She would become unrecognizable to those who knew her.

And as if all of this weren't messy enough, now Catherine had heard about the miracles.

Not that she believed they were genuine. But many people did. As far as they were concerned, Averil was responsible for all manner of miraculous cures and other unexplainable events.

This kind of talk had been circulating for years without Catherine's knowledge. She was not, after all, the type for casual gossip, not the type to want to hear any discussion of religion. And reputable news sources were resolutely silent about it. But somehow the rumors eventually filtered down even to her.

A woman had been healed of fibromyalgia, from one day to the next, after going through a guided meditation in which she visualized Averil as the Afro-Caribbean orisha Babalu-Ayé, traditional healer of the sick. Other such sudden reversals had happened—disappearance of tumors overnight, sudden cessation of chronic pain. Others claimed that whenever they thought of Averil, they suddenly smelled wonderful fragrances—baking bread, fresh flowers. It was widely claimed that her famous portrait—the one that supposedly had wept during the war—had mysteriously disappeared.

That last rumor bothered Catherine. She had been there when the portrait had been made, remembered thinking that the artist with her pastels and broad strokes would never do justice to that face. But now she wasn't sure. Odd things were happening to her memory. She remembered the small house she'd lived in with Averil, for that brief time before the fighting broke out, more clearly than any place she'd lived before or since.

But out the window of their small living room, Catherine clearly remembered a view of a deserted beach, water hardly breaking into waves, tossing up a hint of sea foam that would catch the afternoon light.

This memory was impossible. The house was in North Dakota (as she got older she called things by their old names), a landlocked state for God's sake. There was no ocean out the window. There were neat little yards, sidewalks and trees, a placid life going on outside—and was that a contrast or a complement to her life inside the house, because she remembered it now as long, serene hours of easy conversation and silent companionship between conversations, but that couldn't be possible, could it, because back then everything had been in turmoil, she was in love with Averil, and Averil was so fragile and confused, and everyone knew there would be war any minute.

All those decades of handling weapons and being around munitions deposits, who knew what-all solvents and fumes she had inhaled, and instead of giving her cancer they had gotten into her brain and rearranged a few neural pathways here and there.

Or maybe, Catherine reflected, it was one of Averil's miracles. In that case, even as a dead, wonder-working saint, she still had her sense of humor.

~

The house Catherine lived in now was so beautiful she sometimes felt a sense of pleasant confusion when she woke up in the morning. This was no barracks room with the smell of dust and sweat and a tang of disinfectant floating in on moist air. This was no battlefield tent or hastily assembled campsite. No anonymous apartment like the ones she had rented in endless succession before. Before everything, before Averil and Erda and the war.

In this bedroom she would wake up to the bright morning sky seen through enormous, southern-facing windows. She would sit up in her bed with its carved oak headboard, step barefoot across the oak-plank floor and choose her clothing from a bureau of rosewood inlaid with mahogany. In the kitchen she would eat an orange and a muffin, maybe some cereal. It was the last quiet time she had before the evening. During the daytime people were always in her house—friends, neighbors, admirers. They cleaned everything before she had a chance to get it dirty. There were never any dishes in the sink, the floors smelled like Murphy's Oil Soap and the bathrooms like lemon juice, the windows were so clean the glare almost hurt her eyes.

By the time the house got crowded, around midmorning, Catherine would go out and spend the rest of the day in the garden, coming in only to take meals, and that was only when they went out to her and insisted.

Sometimes historians came to interview her, or biographers of Averil would show up, lugging old photos they hoped Catherine could help them identify.

So many pieces of the puzzle she held, pieces that Erdans were desperate for, not only historians but also ordinary people.

There was the unspoken question, the one that her own biographers didn't dare pose: *You've killed a lot of people. Do you regret what you've done?*

"I've searched my conscience," Catherine would have answered, had anyone the courage to ask, "and I don't regret a single one. But here's what's interesting: I'm beginning to believe there'll be consequences for what I've done. I'll suffer for the suffering I caused, no matter how evil my targets were, no matter how much they deserved to die. I understand that, and I accept it."

Then there were questions that people didn't even know to pose:

John Honig's name, for one thing.

During the affair with Averil his identity had been an open secret, but the extant news sources about her conflict with the Vatican referred only to an inappropriate relationship with a parishioner.

Honig's role in the plague, for another. Whatever strain he'd caught, however it mutated—and Catherine had to acknowledge that maybe the mutation occurred in his own body—and then there were the impossible odds of him transmitting it to her before disappearing from the scene.

Honig's role in Averil's life.

Catherine had thought more and more about this. Averil had been drawn to him, Catherine couldn't deny it. There had been something between them, something that hadn't existed between John and the endless parade of other women he'd had. Something that wasn't there between Averil and Catherine.

Not just sexual—though the sexual pull was obviously part of it, from the evidence of Averil's distracted, almost starved-looking expression toward the end, before John disappeared the first time. Catherine had had the impression that Averil disliked Honig, that they argued constantly. And yet somehow that was part of the attraction.

Averil explained to her once that the biblical patriarchs had forgotten that their male deity had had a female counterpart. You couldn't truly understand Yahweh, Averil had said, without considering Asherah.

And over the years Catherine had had to come to grips with the possibility that John Honig was Averil's male counterpart, that you couldn't understand her in isolation from him.

So there he was, an integral piece of the puzzle.

She would not tell the historians. Let the story be simpler. It was easier that way.

~

When Catherine was seventy-seven, her doctor diagnosed an abdominal aneurysm.

"We need to operate, General, it's a time bomb waiting to go off."

"Let it," she said.

The doctor, exasperated, tried to talk some sense into her. She remembered later Catherine's odd response:

"You know, I never felt more alive than during combat. It was the high point of my life."

"I don't understand how that's relevant—"

"There's something wrong with a society like that, wouldn't you say?"

~

At the height of the growing season, the ragged, wild-eyed young woman appeared at the edge of the garden while Catherine picked tomatoes.

"You're the last link," she breathed reverently.

"I know you," Catherine said cheerfully. "Or of you, anyway."

They were called the Flagellants, a group of religious extremists who had sprung up around their common devotion to Averil. Somehow they had worked Catherine into their complicated theology. She was the last living link, they said, to the sainted figure, though of course the older communards of Via Dolce vociferously disputed that. Quite reasonably, Catherine acknowledged. They had spent as much time with Averil as she had.

The young woman was thin and gaunt, with unruly dark hair and fever-bright eyes. She could have been Averil's daughter. Granddaughter, Catherine corrected herself.

Another belief they held was that Averil had stopped speaking because of her deep disappointment in the human race, just as the goddess had withdrawn from people after patriarchy had set in. Catherine presumed this meant they saw Averil as a goddess, but she didn't want to know the details.

"A scrap of memory," the young woman said in a pleading voice. "It's all we ask of you. Something you remember of our Holy Mother, something you may have forgotten before now."

"It sounds urgent," Catherine said. "Like I won't be around much longer. Should I be worried?"

When she was younger she had figured she'd die somewhere her body wouldn't be found: in a battlefield under heavy fire, or in a plane crashing into the North Atlantic. None of these scenarios were likely to happen now. She imagined being called back to battle at her age, like a hero of an epic poem. There she'd be, between the rows of limas, the call to arms would sound across the land and she'd have to fling down her gardening gloves, her trowel, haul herself up creakily from where she'd been pulling weeds.

But then something did occur to her, and she was glad. She didn't want to disappoint the young woman.

"She told me something, once, from some religious writing or other, I don't remember what. It was about love."

The Flagellant-devotee waited expectantly. She remembered the image later, when people asked her, the last person to see Catherine Beck alive. Catherine squatting in the rich garden soil, holding a deep-red tomato in her hand like Mother Goddess Eve in the Garden of Eden.

"Love, she told me, could carry you over your sins," Catherine said, "like a raft across the ocean."

It was sometime later, maybe hours, that the pain came and knocked her flat. She had a few moments of perfect clarity at the end, just as Averil had had.

How many people, Catherine thought, could close their eyes on this world and know that they had fulfilled their task?

"Beautiful warrior spirit," Averil chanted at the funeral, unheard by the mourners except perhaps as a warm breeze brushing against their hair. "Silver wolf. Truth teller. Devotee of Justice." They gazed at the simple gray-marble headstone Catherine had chosen years ago, the epitaph carved beneath her name:

> *In one hand a sword.*
> *In the other hand a sword.*

~

Anno Mirabilis 57

They called them Witnesses. The people who had known Averil Parnell, worked with her, spoken to her. As the decades passed, they became fewer and fewer.

Ciara Neal was one of the last.

The night after the interviewer contacted her, she dreamed they were still at war.

It was the night before a major battle and Ciara was sleeping on a blanket on the cold hard ground. She was her real age, eighty-seven, in the dream, but sleeping on the ground was no hardship. At dawn she was well-rested and alert.

She didn't recognize the women around her preparing for battle.

The rest are dead, she thought to herself, long dead. Then she woke up.

She said nothing about the dream at breakfast. She sat at the large kitchen table and allowed the usual morning commotion to comfort her— her daughter, Plum, her friend Sigrid and her daughter and granddaughters, moving around between refrigerator, stove, and sink, bantering, getting in each other's way.

Ciara picked up her coffee mug and her journal and went out to the screened-in porch.

They're afraid I'll die off before I write something down.

Knowing that these were Ciara's last hours, the spirits started to gather. Not just the usual complement of ancestral spirits, but others too, Erdan foremothers and war dead, friend and foe, to keep vigil, give comfort.

Ciara wondered what Averil had dreamed of the night before she died. Those who didn't think she was clinically insane thought she was prophetic, so perhaps, Ciara reflected, her last dream featured bullets and blood and statues and books and songs and memorial services every year. People had to reenact somebody's death, and Jesus wasn't an option anymore.

She opened her journal to a new page.

She hardly remembered the angry young woman she had been, those long-ago conversations with Averil, those desperate questions about revenge. She would never have guessed that she, Ciara, would become a soldier, or that the befuddled priest she consulted would someday have a cult following all across the planet.

Averil had counseled her against violence.

But then came the war. They brought their violence to us.

And after that came all these decades of peace. True peace, not merely a pause between wars.

The women alive today, most of them, had been born afterwards. They didn't know what it was like to be belittled, silenced, harassed. Careers stymied. Doors slammed in their faces.

They didn't know what it was to fear walking down a dark street alone, hiking through a forest alone. Didn't know what it was like when women had been prey, and the predators had been in charge.

But Ciara didn't want to remember.

The opposite of revisiting, that was what they should do. They should forget the past, forget patriarchy. Let it fade into a murky legend. Let future scholars debate whether it had ever even existed.

And Averil.

Ciara imagined a fairy tale. At the beginning is an angry young woman with a question. She goes on a quest, to find a wisewoman. An extraordinary woman, a saint, whose coming was foretold in prophecies. But the wisewoman's answers make no sense.

Ciara closed her eyes, rested her head against the wing chair. In the moments before her heart fluttered to a stop, the spirits caressed her forehead, held her hand.

And then in a later version of the tale, the wisewoman is sane, has the answers.

And in a still later version, the wisewoman doesn't even appear. She is the ever-receding goal, the pretext for the young warrior-novice's adventures. The holy grail.

Let no man be so audacious as to add anything to this writing, or to take anything away from it, lest he be blotted out from the book of life, and from all happiness under the sun, for these things were brought forth by the inspiration of the Holy Spirit.

—Hildegard of Bingen

ABOUT
THE AUTHOR

R osalie Morales Kearns, a writer of Puerto Rican and Pennsylvania
Dutch descent, is the founder of the feminist publishing house Shade
Mountain Press and the creative prose editor at *Women's Studies Quarterly*.
She's the author of the story collection *Virgins and Tricksters* and editor of
the short story anthology *The Female Complaint: Tales of Unruly Women*. A
product of Catholic schooling from kindergarten through college, Kearns
has a B.A. in theology and an M.F.A. in creative writing.

CPSIA information can be obtained
at www.ICGtesting.com
Printed in the USA
BVHW031948040119
536779BV00042B/132/P